VASILY MAHANENKO

SURVIVAL QUEST

*Books are the lives
we don't have
time to live,

Vasily Mahanenko*

THE WAY OF THE SHAMAN
BOOK 1

MAGIC DOME BOOKS

THIS BOOK IS ENTIRELY A WORK OF FICTION.
ANY CORRELATION WITH REAL PEOPLE OR EVENTS IS
COINCIDENTAL.

Survival Quest
The Way of the Shaman, Book # 1
Second Edition
Published by Magic Dome Books, 2017
Copyright © V. Mahanenko 2015
Cover Art © V. Manyukhin 2015
Translator © Natalia Nikitin 2015
All Rights Reserved
ISBN: 978-80-88231-12-7

TABLE OF CONTENTS:

CHAPTER ONE
INTRODUCTION

"...To FIND THE DEFENDANT DANIEL MAHAN *guilty of hacking the control program of the city sewage network, resulting in total system shut-down, and sentence him to confinement in a correctional capsule and resource-gathering labor for the term of eight years, under Article 637, section 13 of the Penal Code. The place of confinement will be automatically appointed for the defendant by the system. Should the prisoner meet the conditions stipulated in Article 78 Section 24 of the Penal Code, he will be given the opportunity to transfer to the main gameworld. The Court appoints the defendant the following specifications: race — Human, class — Shaman, main profession — Jeweler. The sensory filters are to be turned off for the entire term spent in the capsule. Parole is possible if the defendant pays an amount totaling one hundred million gold in gaming coins. The sentence is final and cannot be appealed."*

T HEY SAY THAT GOD IS TRUTH. I don't know, really. Maybe that's how it is — it's not something I ever checked, so I'm not going to argue. But all arguments are evil and a great evil at that. And that's a Truth against which there's no argument. A play on words, if you like.

Let me introduce myself — I am Daniel Mahan, as it has already been mentioned. I am a thirty year-old specialist in IT security and everything that involves. I am a freelancer, periodically hired by corporations for finding exploits in the virtual game of Barliona. This game had filled the whole world with itself and had become the entire world for some. I can't say that I am the best security specialist, but I'm in no way the worst either. Something between a genius and totally useless. Fair to middling.

Each year all the specialists officially involved in looking for exploits in the Game must go through retraining. What it was we had to be retrained in remained a mystery to us, because for many the search for exploits was the only source of income. But the Corporation had strict demands: if you want to look for weaknesses without breaking the law, you had to go through retraining. Moreover, the additional training mainly meant the study of new laws that increased the punishment for hacking and we were never shown any tools or methods for finding exploits. The Corporation kept a stringent control over preventing any internal know-how from being leaked to outsiders, especially to the likes of us. Today we might be honest and rule-abiding and tomorrow any one of us could turn into a malicious attacker and try to break into Barliona.

At one such retraining session I ended up sharing a table with a fairly attractive girl and striking up a conversation with her. Unfortunately she was, of course, also a freelance artist, as all those engaged in finding exploits in the game called themselves, whether they actually worked anywhere or not. I was all set to start throwing around clever and obscure terminology, expecting the girl, stunned by the brilliance of my mind, to fall into my arms. Far from it. Marina turned out to be clever and sufficiently professionally experienced: her main job was providing information security for the city sewage system, while the search for game exploits was just a hobby.

Well, well. Never tell a girl, especially a smart girl, that her place of employment is not worthy of having a freelance artist working there. We started to argue. And then, struggling to come up with anything better, I threw in my killer argument of why you shouldn't work in a sewage system, which seemed a sure win to me: "It stinks there!"

It would seem that she had been irritated with this kind of comment once too often. So irritated, in fact, that she left my table and put an end to our developing acquaintance. What a pity. I had already started to make certain plans. Well, never mind. I immersed myself fully into yet another report on how the new law was increasing the punishment for the hacking and destruction of programs. Heigh-ho! Now they give eight years for hacking. This is serious. In the break between the seminars Marina sat next to me again.

"So you say that a job like mine is only fit for

amateurs?" she said in an irritated tone, and I noticed how a crowd of onlookers started to gather around us.

"Listen, I never said anything of the sort. I didn't say that you were an amateur: I said that this kind of work can't be worthy of a professional of your caliber."

"It's the same thing. If I am working there it means that I'm not good enough to work somewhere else, which means that I'm a talentless idiot!" It's no use arguing with a girl in a state of rage. You won't prove anything to her and you'll end up looking like a fool to everyone else.

"Let's talk about something else. It's my fault. I'm sorry for my poor choice of words. I invite you for a truce over a cup of tea, coffee or whatever you prefer. I don't want to quarrel with such a beautiful and enchanting lady," I made an attempt to pull the carpet form under Marina's feet. Better for her to be indignant because of my compliments than on account of her work.

"Tell me, do you have a wife or a girlfriend?" I involuntarily shuddered at this question and automatically shook my head. It seems Marina was going on the offensive, pulling the carpet from under my feet instead. My thoughts were confirmed when her next question virtually floored me:

"Would you like to go out with me? Do you like me?" Damn, what is it with women these days? Now they are the ones throwing themselves at men; although I admit that such 'attacks' made me more than happy. Marina really was an attractive girl, pretty, with a slightly upturned nose, so I thoughtlessly nodded to her.

"Listen up, everyone!" Marina suddenly shouted. "If in a week's time Daniel manages to break through the security system I installed on the city sewage system Imitator, I solemnly promise to be his girl for at least a month! Without showing in any way that I find any of it unpleasant. But if he fails, then he'll spend a month working as one of the waste collector cleaners. So — ready to make this bet? A test server would be set up for you with a full copy of the working system, and your hacking attempt would be officially recorded as a test of our security. By tomorrow you'll receive all the necessary papers, ensuring that you remain clean in the eyes of the law," said Marina and gave me her hand to shake on it.

Who forced me to take this bet? I could have dismissed the whole thing as a joke and brushed the entire conversation under the carpet. We would have gone for a pint of beer together and parted our ways in peace. But no, Marina's eyes drilled me with such force that I involuntarily shook the hand in front of me.

"Great! Tomorrow you will get the scan of the request to check the security of our system and its virtual address. In exactly a week's time I'll be here again — either with a job offer for you or fully prepared for a date. The time is ticking, hero!"

A murmur of approval went through the crowd around us and made me go into a total stupor. Marina left and people I knew, as well as strangers, started to come up to me and slap me on the back, shake my hand and offer their services in hacking. Of course, if such a girl risks herself for a whole month, everyone should lend a hand. And if I failed, it would mean a good laugh at my expense when I'd be working the sewage waste collectors.

They are right when they say that the rarest friendship in the world is a person's friendship with his own common sense. Who stopped me from heeding it? But once I committed myself there was no retreat. I spent two days gathering information about the I.I. of the city sewage system and about Marina, and then started to work.

Of course it would be a bit much to call intellect imitation programs 'I.I.': everyone will immediately starts thinking that this is real artificial intelligence and beating themselves in the chest and screaming that in our world this cannot be done and, even if it can, humanity can do without such a 'boon', because then the machines will replace humans and we will all die out. One must not mix up completely different concepts, or it would be like trying to compare 'soft' and 'green'. Imitation programs have no personality matrices. Naturally, if you program them right, they will show emotion, character and the rest. You could even get them to do it so well that when interacting with them you would struggle to tell right away whether you're even dealing with a program; but they lack the key component, which is self-awareness. Thus a program would not ask questions like "Who am I? Why am I here? How much will I get paid? When is my holiday?" It just wouldn't — unless, of course, such a parameter had been included in it from the start. And this means that it would not get anxious on account of its place in the world and would carry out all of its functions to the letter. With time, imitators, as such programs came to be called, started to be used in all spheres of human life, fully replacing human beings. And not just human beings — even pets, or rather robots that looked like pets, became a permanent feature of our world, having replaced their real animal counterparts. Of course, some, staunchly clinging to the old ways, still keep these balls of fur in their homes, but each year the number of such people grows smaller. Do you want your beloved pet to work as an alarm clock, a vacuum cleaner, an iron, a security guard and so on and so forth, while not shedding fur, making a mess on your carpet or ruining your furniture? Would you have something which, on top of all that, in no way differed either in looks, behavior or touch to a familiar house cat? Then give us a call... Damn, I think I'm getting side-tracked here.

They say that with the creation of intellect imitators humanity was only one step away from creating artificial intelligence, a full-fledged robotic mind, but this is little more than speculation. After all, there are rumors that artificial intelligence had been created some time ago somewhere deep in military laboratories, that it is currently in operation and is making itself very useful. In general, with the appearance of the imitators life became happy and carefree. But the resulting unemployment brought little joy to anyone, so the tension in society following the emergence of the imitators constantly increased...

Right, I'm getting carried away again. Backtracking.

I won the bet. In two days I gathered all the information available on the net on Marina's education background and on the seminars and training sessions she attended. If she did anything, it must have been based on something she had already studied, rather than inventing the wheel from scratch. Having bought myself new hardware in order to keep my beloved notebook safe from the defense systems that vigorously attack computers of hapless hackers, I started on the break-in. I didn't even try to hide behind a chain of servers, as is usually done by the break-in gurus. Why would I? I was working strictly as ordered and only one person could track my activities on the test server, namely Marina. I was convinced that she would spend the whole week stuck at work, waiting for my attack. So there was little reason for me to encode anything. The actual break-in only took me a few hours. I was right: a very rare but effective defense system was used. Naive girl. The author of this defense system was one of my acquaintances and when I contacted him and described the situation, I was soon told how to circumvent it. Not even to circumvent it, but where to start digging.

"The defense is solid, but it depends on access settings," said my friend. "In large cities this is an issue, especially if there is a bunch of idiotic superiors with different demands. Everything might be fine during the initial installation, but once it starts to operate there might be leaks – 'dead souls' with rights of access to the setup. Here a simple administrator would be of little help — leaks with access rights of such an organization are beyond his level!"

In the end things turned out exactly as he said. After just a couple of hours' work the analyzing program produced several potential leaks that I could work with. Now I regretted getting the new hardware, having erroneously thought that everything was going to be very complicated and dangerous. I spent two days preparing the password attack, so I had little doubt of my success.

A wise person once said that the devil is in the detail. It turned out that several numbers were confused in the extremely long test server number (346.549.879.100011.011101.011011.110011.) Who made the mistake — I, when I entered it, or Marina when she wrote me the letter, still remains unclear. What in fact happened was that I wasn't working with the test system, but none other than the real and functioning system, which controlled the sewage system of the whole city.

This is why I am currently in court listening to my sentence being read out.

I broke into the server, in the process completely crashing the I.I. of the city sewage works. And it turned out that after the imitator went down, the large lake in the centre of the city, just opposite the City Hall, was turned into a very foul-smelling entity. The unforeseen had taken place — the I.I. administrative perimeter was turned off, leading to a jump in pressure and the collector pipe under the city bursting in several places. And if the underground breaches remained unnoticed by the majority, the breach at the centre of the lake resulted in the crowds of demonstrators, which usually gathered in front of the City Hall demanding the ban of the imitators, suddenly remembering that they had urgent business elsewhere. The same went for the people in the City

Hall. And in general, the whole city centre was suddenly gripped by a strong desire to visit their relatives in the countryside, where the air was so clean and fresh.

This case gathered a lot of publicity and everyone decided that this was a terrorist attack. There was a protest demanding that a stop should be put to the imitator-powered services and the investigators started digging around to find the party responsible.

I worked without trying to cover my tracks, so finding me did not present much of a challenge. I really did not try to hide: as soon as I became aware of the consequences and of the fact that the police were looking for the culprit, I confessed and gave myself up. I did not believe that my punishment would be very severe — I might get reprimanded or fined. No more than that.

How wrong I was! The police had gathered so much material that I could only shake my head in astonishment as I read it. Someone became ill from the smell and filed a suit against the city. Someone didn't like the appearance of the lake that I 'updated', and decided to sue the city. Some others simply sued the city not to seem out of touch with the general sentiment. On the whole, the losses that the city suffered amounted to no less than 100 million, which was laid at my feet in its entirety. I tried to defend myself with the piece of paper that said that I was hired to do this, but the sewage works lawyers dashed all my hopes, asserting that the paper was signed by someone who lacked sufficient authority to hire external specialists and was thus invalid. This meant that, in effect, I carried out a hacking attack with all that it entailed. And it really entailed quite a lot. In general, all the damages were hung on me. And they threw in hacking charges on top of it too. During the investigation I, as someone who gave himself up, stayed at home with a signed undertaking not to abscond. I kept myself busy by taking an in-depth look into how I could help myself in Barliona. But the more I read, the more I understood that there was nothing I could do that would help me. Nothing at all.

It so happened that the upkeep of prisons became extremely expensive for the Government. Yes, that's just the one Government I'm talking about, since at a certain point the territorial fragmentation on our world had come to an end. I didn't witness these events myself. The unification happened before I was born and the history lessons stated that this was the common will of all the fellow citizens of the world. Yeah right, the will of the fellow citizens. More likely the heads of governments came to an arrangement between themselves and presented the people with the fact. But, never mind. This is not important. So, as soon as the imitators became an established feature of our world, increasing the number of the unemployed, prisons began to get filled up at a catastrophic rate. The Government faced a global question: how to solve the problems with public disorder and the increase in the number of criminals? There was a need for a 'carrot'.

And then, Peter Johnson went before the Government with his proposal. He was the owner of the factory that made capsules for virtual reality games, including the game named Barliona. It was an ordinary game, designed in the 'Sword & Sorcery' style, with a medieval setting, no firearms or combustion engines, featuring magic, orcs, dwarves, elves, dragons and many other things that did not exist on the real world. Like all similar games, the gameplay in Barliona involved full immersion, which was ensured by the virtual reality capsule. And these were the capsules that the Johnson factory made. Inside the capsule the player became inseparable from his character and felt everything that the character in the game would feel, including taste, shape of the objects, pleasure, tiredness and pain. Although the regulating authorities demanded that all the senses that the player could feel in Barliona were blocked by default. In order to turn on the sense perception it was necessary to go through psychological evaluation of mental capacity and get tested for the degree of sensitivity. This would determine the extent to which the senses could be turned on in the capsule. The corporation looked after its players. The capsules were calibrated individually for each person and supplied him or her with every necessity for a long time: from food to physical training through stimulation of muscles with electrical impulses. People could spend months and even years inside a capsule without feeling any physical discomfort on leaving it.

What was Mr. Johnson's proposal? For a modest fee he proposed to put all the prisoners inside his capsules and send them to special locations within Barliona, where they would spend their time in useful activities, like resource gathering. The Government liked the idea and a year-long experiment involving such a virtual prison led to them buying all the rights to Barliona and appointing Johnson General Director of a new state corporation. All the necessary laws were passed for securing the status of a state-run game for Barliona and the Government itself acted as a guarantor of the game currency, facilitating its free exchange for real money. This was followed by an advertising campaign and funds started to flow into the game. Virtually anyone who was dissatisfied with his life ran to Barliona in order to cheat the government and earn money on quests, resource gathering and killing mobs, and so live without a care. Such naive little children. The completed quests produced game money, which could be easily exchanged for real money — that was clear enough. However, any action within the game also demanded some sort of payment, however little. If you wanted to stop in an inn, you paid, if you wanted to get something, you paid, and so on. One of the most important inventions for draining money out of the players were the Banks.

One of the core rules in Barliona states that when a character dies the player loses fifty percent of all the cash he had on him. At the next death he lost another fifty, and so on. Of course, if a character was killed by a mob, after reviving in a couple of hours he could always go to his place of death and pick up the lost money, which would be lying on the ground. Unless it was picked up by another player first. But usually players did not die from mobs, but at the hands of other players, who made it their goal to make money on such kills. Such players had many penalties imposed on them: it was permitted to kill them for eight hours after they themselves had attempted to make a kill; killing a PK (player killer) came with a reward, which could be collected from any representative of the authorities; a PK gained no experience for eight hours after the killing and so on; but nevertheless there existed players who liked killing others, even if only inside a virtual world. This is why the Banks emerged. If a player gained some money, he could put it in a Bank for storage. A one-off payment gave you a card to be used with an account that no-one else was able to access. Keeping such an account cost 0.1% of the total money deposited, which was paid to the Bank on a monthly basis. It might not seem like much, but even one thousandth of Barliona's total turnover is an enormous amount of money, which is why the Corporation would never close down the PvP (Player versus Player) mode of play.

The Corporation's next step for making profit was selling off the results of the prisoner's work to the main game world. Arbitrary generation of resources by the Corporation was prosecuted under the law and special committees kept a close watch to ensure it didn't happen. However the sale of resources obtained by people serving a sentence was a totally different story: such resources were validated by real work. In general everyone has been happy and satisfied with this arrangement for the past fifteen years, ever since Barliona was officially given the status of a state game. The gamers enjoyed a high quality game, the Corporation received unthinkable amounts of money while continuously improving their creation, and the prisoners stayed in special locations and gathered resources. At the present time about 25% of total Earth's population over 14 years of age plays Barliona and this number increases every year. The only limitation imposed on the characters was that until a player turned 18 he or she had no way of using the PvP mode — either as a victim or as a hunter. The Game was very strict in enforcing this.

One more fact about the prisoners serving time in Barliona should be brought to light. It is a fact of some importance. Around seven years after the launch of Barliona a gang of delinquents beat up and raped a girl by the name of Elena. Her surname was Johnson and her father's name Peter. She was the daughter of the Corporation's director. She and her friends had the poor judgment to go for a ride in one of the rough areas of the city, which still housed those who disagreed with the introduction of imitators and who had no intention of logging into Barliona. As it always happens in such cases, they suddenly ran out of gas.

Naturally, the perpetrators were found almost immediately and Johnson himself intervened in the trial. No, he did not even bother to arrange a capsule accident. He did something else. Following the trial a law was passed that regulated the turning on of the prisoners' sensory stimulators. The capsules initially came with special filters that regulated the level of sensations, but these were completely removed for those who attacked Johnson's daughter. I don't know what the observed results of this were, but in about a year's time the law was extended and now all prisoners served their sentences with their sensory filters disabled. The rate of crime fell sharply and there were hardly any repeat offenders. The prospect of having to gather resources with disabled sensory filters was a very effective crime deterrent.

So there you have it. I will now tell you a little about what I was given.

Character race: Human. It was the first race created in the game and the only race that has no additional bonuses except faster reputation gain with the NPCs (Non-Player-Characters). They don't have the ability to generate a stone skin, like the dwarves, nor do they have sharp vision and extra proficiencies with bows, like the elves. Only reputation. The Shaman class was also one of the weakest classes in Barliona. It is universal, allowing you both to do damage and to heal, but in one-on-one combat it lost out to virtually all other classes. The summoning of the Spirits just took too long. My skill specialization of Jeweler also had little going for it: in Barliona only the richest people could afford to spend time on perfecting this skill. All the things made by Jewelers — adornments, rings, necklaces, decorative objects — could be easily bought from NPC traders. The Jeweler's main useful skill, the cutting of precious stones, was not worth the effort that had to be spent on it. Precious stones are worth a lot, but in order to obtain the materials to make them, you had to spend months mining and processing ores. And even if some were obtained, the chance that the stone would spoil during the cutting process was very high. Of course it was possible to train in other skills, which were virtually endless in number, but it came with a serious restriction: none of the additional professions could exceed the primary one by more than ten points. It was a stupid limitation, but nothing could be done about it.

Another downside was that my Hunter, whom I had spent several years building, and in whom I invested quite a lot of money, was to be deleted, because only one character at a time was permitted in Barliona. After you were set free you could keep the character played during imprisonment and to continue playing it, but many could not find the strength to do this. It was psychologically difficult. As far as the Hunter was concerned, all the items and money that he earned would either be handed over to me after eight years of swinging the pick, or, should some miracle happen, after I am permitted to leave the mines for the main gameworld. Sometimes criminals are released, most probably by mistake, from resource gathering to spend the rest of their sentence in the main game, after they hand over 30% of the money that they earned to the Government. Otherwise there are no limitations – you can develop, level up and get to know people as you like. The only sign that a player is a prisoner is a red headband, which various quest-giving NPCs tend to dislike and which could only be removed if you pay one million gold to the Treasury. In other words – it cannot be removed.

And the worst thing of all was that Marina never appeared. She didn't turn up at the trial or at my home, while I waited for the conclusion of the investigation. It was as if she vanished. Was the eight years of my sentence worth such a frivolous girl? I think not.

"Well, in you jump!" laughed the technician as

he put me into the capsule. Everyone's a comedian. With one voice all the newspapers in the city called me 'Sewage System Killer', probably the mildest nickname I was given during this time. The main thing was for this name not to stick with me while in prison. Lightning flashed before my eyes and for a while I was unconscious.

"Attention! Barliona entry through prison capsule TK3.687PZ-13008/LT12 in progress." The cold metallic voice, whose message was repeated with a running line of unpleasant white text, sent a chill down my spine and I immediately came to myself. The voice, devoid of any emotion, made you feel uncomfortable. This was done on purpose: I knew that a voice could be soft and have a calming effect. "The initial parameters have been set and cannot be changed. Gender: Male. Race: Human. Class: Shaman. Appearance: identical to the subject. The scanning of the subject has been completed. The synchronization of the physical data with the features of the chosen race has been implemented. Physical data has been set. Starting location has been chosen. Place of confinement – the Pryke Copper Mine. Purpose of confinement: the harvesting of Copper Ore. Character generation has commenced."

In the initial loading window I was looking at myself wearing a striped robe with number 193 753 482. It would appear that quite a few prisoners have gone through Barliona in the last 15 years. The robe was supplemented with prisoner's trousers and boots, whose total value could be seen in their striped pattern. Even the boots were stripy, at which I couldn't help smiling. I looked like some sort of a zebra. One could say that I was dressed at the height of fashion. The pick in my hand completed the bleak picture of 'Myself', making it clear what I would be doing in the coming years. Only the pick wasn't stripy, something to be thankful for, at least.

"Enter a name. Attention: a prisoner's name cannot be composite."

Well, the technician did cheer me up after all. He did that by giving me, for some unknown reason, the opportunity to choose my own name. The gaming name in Barliona was provisionally unique: in the same gaming environment you could meet three hundred 'Bunnys', a hundred 'Kitties' and endless numbers of 'Pwners', but the uniqueness was guaranteed by a composite word. For example you could easily see Pwner the Great and Pwner the Charming next to each other, but there were no two Pwner the Great's in Barliona. However, prisoners were not allowed to pick a composite name for themselves, because usually these were generated automatically. But if they deleted my Hunter...

"Mahan," I said, setting all my hopes on the fact that the name of my Hunter, who was taken from me, was already deleted from the system but not yet picked by anyone else. So what if I liked to play with this name? That's what I've become use to, despite the fact that it was just a surname. Moreover, my hunter's name had only one component, and I bought it from another player for almost ten thousand gold and had no wish to see all that money go to waste.

"Choice accepted. Welcome to the world of Barliona, Mahan. Users connecting from prison capsules have no access to the introductory training area. You will be transferred directly to the Pryke Copper Mine. We wish you a pleasant game."

There was a flash of lightning and the world around me filled with colors. Though for some reason among these colors grey predominated.

CHAPTER TWO
THE PRYKE MINE. THE BEGINNING

T HE PRYKE MINE LAY BEFORE ME in all its beauty. Great rocky cliffs, about 100 meters high, rose along the whole boundary of the mine. Their tops hung over it, forming a cap around the perimeter. Like the roof of a stadium, an association flashed in my head. No amount of effort would allow you to scale such a wall, although the scattered ledges seemed to dare you to try. 'Interesting,' I thought, 'I wonder if the mine is surrounded by mountains or goes deep inside the earth?' I should ask someone, in case the idea of digging a hole out of here catches on. Another thought was just as interesting: is this mine even connected to the main world or is it in a separate location within the server memory? I could dig a hole and end up nowhere. At first glance the mine itself comprised quite a pleasant-looking valley approximately several kilometers in length and about a kilometer wide, with a somewhat uneven surface. The valley was divided up in two parts: the first, about 300 meters long, contained wooden buildings, one of which I immediately recognized as the smithy. For now the other structures remained a mystery, but were most probably barracks for the prisoners. The second part of the valley was separated by an unimposing wooden fence, which had grown lop-sided and rickety in places. The shouts of prisoners and sounds of mining picks were ringing from that side of the mine. So, this is where I'll be working. The place where I stood allowed only limited visibility because the view was obscured by an enormous cloud of grey dust. It was strange: I could see the dust, but could not feel it at all. It was probably just a graphic effect imposed on this location to give it a more authentic look.

Not far from where I appeared and at some distance from the other buildings stood a house that sported the sign 'Welcome to the Pryke Copper Mine." Right, so this is the local administration office, housing some intimidating official who had the power to grant me access to the main gameworld.

Yes, access to the main gameworld. Just before I was placed in the capsule I looked up the contents of Article 78 Section 24, cited by the judge when speaking about the possibility of entering the gameworld. I somehow missed this part before, while I was preparing myself. Reading this even lifted my spirits somewhat. The text stated: "If the prisoner earns Respect with the guards at the place of confinement, he or she may be given the opportunity of being transferred to the main gameworld." It contained a lot of other text that stated that for the first six months you would have to live in a special colony, even if you earned Respect on the second day of your imprisonment and that 30% of all the earned money would have to be paid to the Corporation upon leaving the mine. There was something else, which I didn't recall, but the main thing was that I had a chance of getting transferred to the main gameworld.

So my chief aim in the near future was to earn Respect and to get the person in charge of the mine to like me. Or the other way round: get liked and gain Respect. It didn't really matter as long as it resulted in me leaving the mine. Great, I've spent just a few minutes here and I'm already making plans on how to leave.

Now I just need to figure out what I have to work, play and, in general, live with in the next eight years. I had to have a good look at my character, his stats (statistics) and description. When I was getting ready for prison I would never have imagined that they'd give me a Shaman, because all the forums said that prisoners usually get assigned either Warriors or Rogues. So these were the classes I read up on, pretty much becoming an expert in them. Not a single bastard wrote on any of the forums that a prisoner could be given a spell-casting class. Blast! I don't even know how to cast spells and figuring this out by myself will be very difficult.

I brought the window with the character description before my eyes:

Statistics for player Mahan					
Experience	1	of	100	**Additional stats**	
Race	Human			Physical damage	11
Class	Shaman			Magical damage	3
Main Profession	Jeweler				
Character level	1				
Hit points	40			Physical resistance	6
Mana	10			Magical resistance	0
Energy	100			Fire resistance	0
Stats	Scale	Base	+ Items	Cold resistance	0
Stamina	0%	4	4	Poison resistance	0
Agility	0%	1	1		
Strength	0%	1	1	Dodge chance	0.6%
Intellect	0%	1	1	Critical hit chance	0.4%
Not selected					
Not selected					
Not selected					
Not selected					
Free stat points		0			
Professions					
Jewelcraft	0%	0	0		

Racial bonus: reputation gain with all factions is increased by 10%

What 'fantastic' stats. My virtual heart began to ache when I compared this Shaman with my level 87 Hunter. He looked so wretched next to my former character. Sigh...

Energy. The biggest headache for all the

prisoners. In the main gameworld even if Energy fell all the way to zero, the character simply suddenly stopped and rested for several minutes, waiting for it to recover, and then continued to carry out the player's commands. But they say that here things are not so simple. As Energy is lost, you get tired for real and your Hit Points slowly diminish. A sudden fall in Energy could even lead to character death. I would have to test this parameter in more detail, since I paid little attention to it with my Hunter.

Stamina. It determines the number of Hit Points in the ratio of 1:10; the higher the Stamina, the slower the rate of Energy loss. What the ratio was in this case I didn't really remember, but was aware it existed. I must level up my Stamina as much as I can, as this is important for survival.

Strength. This is the main stat necessary for mining ore. I didn't know what influence it might have on the ore itself, I found nothing about it in the manuals. This parameter also influences the strength of my physical attack. Because I'm not a melee fighter, the calculation is quite simple: Physical Damage = Strength + Weapon Damage. No modifiers. I'll have to do without, I guess.

Agility. Ehh... Something I knew so well when I was playing my Hunter, but now I don't even know what to do with it. In my case Agility did little else than determine the dodge chance and the critical strike chance. So if I don't engage in melee combat, this stat will remain useless for me.

Intellect. This is what Hunters, Warriors, Rogues and several other classes lack. In place of this statistic they use Rage. Intellect determines the amount of mana in the ratio of 1:10 and the rate of its regeneration, although the exact formula slipped my memory. Intellect also determines the strength of my magical attacks. Here we have a modifier: Magic Damage = 3 x Intellect. I had no idea how it all worked, despite having seen Shamans in action, as they banged their Tambourines, danced and chanted some sort of songs. There must be a reason they do that.

Not selected. So here is that stumbling block, which makes virtually all the players rant about Barliona. They rant, but continue playing. Yeah, they keep burning their fingers, grumble, but still go for the cookies. In Barliona with the four main stats, which were fairly standard for all games, each player was allowed to pick additional four. What is more, they were not chosen from a set list, but you had to perform certain actions that would lead to the system allowing you to pick a particular stat. For instance, when I played the Hunter, I needed Marksmanship, in order to be sure of hitting the opponent and having a chance of dealing him triple damage. But then I knew beforehand that I would need this stat and spent some time hitting the training dummy until the system allowed me to select Marksmanship. Only four additional stats could be chosen, so picking them needed serious thinking. Of course it was possible to remove an undesirable stat, despite the system saying it could not be removed. But this could only be done personally by the Emperor and gaining an audience with him was often out of question for an ordinary player. Even if you managed to obtain an audience, the privilege of removing a stat cost around 20 thousand gold, so players wrote angry messages on the forums and threatened to leave the game. But after some time they usually simply deleted the old poorly calibrated character and rolled a new one. The game called and beckoned.

And then there was Jewelcraft. A zero level in a profession meant that, although it was included by default, it had to be activated via a trainer. Probably this wasn't that important — where would you find a Jewelcraft trainer in a mine?

I'll give you a brief view of how these statistics could be increased. With each level a player gains 5 points that could be invested in any one of the stats, thus increasing its importance. But that's not all. Certain activities level up the stat that ends up being used the most. For example, if I shoot a mob with my bow — not only do I gain Experience for the kill, but also gain a certain percentage in my Agility progress bar. As soon as the progress bar is filled to 100, Agility value is increased by one, the bar itself is reset in order to go through the same process again. Thus the more I hit mobs with a bow, the higher is my Agility. Here in the mine the main stat is Strength and it will level up before anything else.

I was suddenly torn away from my daydreams.

"Don't just stand there! Get a move on!" the rough yell of the overseer returned me to 'reality'. Judging by the manuals, all the overseers in the places of confinement were NPCs, but their programmed behavior model was completely in the hands of the designers building the locations. Since no-one likes prisoners, the guards were developed with appropriate temperaments. All this quickly flashed through my head, leaving my 'castle-in-the-air' thoughts of freedom, which I had began to put together, somewhat shaken.

"Move, move! The boss doesn't like to be kept waiting," the guard repeated, roughly pushing me in the direction of the local administration office.

The interior of the building turned out to be surprisingly pleasant and quiet. I had the feeling that I had ended up in a completely different world — there were exquisite statues, paintings on the walls, a large crystal chandelier, carpets, carved wood and a quiet cool breeze brushing past me. All of this made such a harmonious whole that put you more in mind of an out-of-town residence of some rich aristocrat than an administration office of a mine full of prisoners. The governor of the mine sat behind a luxuriously crafted table in a separate office. He was a huge orc, about two meters in height, green and menacing, like all the representatives of that race.

"Shaman Mahan," the governor's low and calm bass travelled across the room as he was reading some document — probably my case file. The orc's appearance reminded me of someone, but I just couldn't remember who exactly. The governor was calm and dignified, like the Snow Queen, though in looks there was little resemblance. But who did he resemble then? "Sentenced to eight years for the crime of hacking into the city sewage network control program which led to system shut-down. "Was it your idea or did someone put you up to it?" the orc asked the question showing virtually no emotion. Such a play of intonations, or rather their total absence, did not exactly inspire you to 'burst into song'. Songs.

'And now I will be singing my last song...' Akela!

That's who the image of the orc reminded me of! Akela from Kipling's 'Jungle Book', the Lone Wolf, Mowgli's mentor. A picture of the majestic wolf sitting on a rock from the ancient animated film rose before my eyes. That's right, if the wolf could be colored green, punched in the face to squash it and have his fangs pulled outside, you'd have the spitting image of the Pryke Copper Mine governor. Although no, for a complete resemblance you'd have to color the old wolf's eyes red.

"So, you're playing the silent game. Well, well. That's your choice," said the governor, while I enthusiastically dressed him up in the wolf's hide. Suddenly I was hit by extreme heaviness, my legs gave way and I fell on the floor, without taking my gaze off the orc. A message immediately flashed before my eyes:

Your reputation with the Pryke Mine Guards has fallen by 10 points. You are 990 points away from the status of Mistrust.

Attention! Racial bonuses do not apply on the territory of the Pryke Copper Mine.

"I repeat the question!" it was immediately clear that he knew how to raise his voice. He was good at it too: it made shivers run down my spine and I was ready to tell him anything. That's what I call 'influence'. He probably had his Charisma value bumped up sky-high. "Did you decide to destroy the Imitator yourself or did someone put you up to it?"

My body felt heavy and leaden, but something

clicked inside my head and the ability to think rationally returned to me. Incidentally, lying down on the floor turned out to be ideal for having a good think. I should add this method to my arsenal in the future. So, I have two possible lines of action — to stay silent or give him the whole story. In the first case I will most probably gain a negative reputation before I am sent to work in the mine. The second option meant that I would tell one imitator how I destroyed another imitator. And would thus also gain a negative reputation — who knows how this orc had been programmed. One should expect the worst. So, I lose out either way... Darn, nothing else for it, I have to respond.

"I did not destroy the imitator. I had an assignment for running a security check and I carried it out," I tried to speak in a calm voice, but under the orc's heavy gaze only a whisper came out. "And I'm hardly to blame that the imitator was so poorly protected. I was simply carrying out an assignment," I repeated once again. I hardened my resolve and focused all my strength on picking myself up, at least to my knees, but my arms refused to cooperate and I hit the floor I once again.

"An assignment..." the orc said thoughtfully. No, if you really tried, you could discern emotions in his voice. They were just very deeply hidden. "All right, let it be an assignment, as you say. So listen, performer of assignments on the murder of imitators. You will now go to Rine, where you will be given the Mining profession and the starter bag for collecting ore. After this you will be shown to your place of work. We have the same rules for all prisoners — you have to fulfill a daily quota: 10 units (pieces) per each level in the Mining profession. Anything above that you can sell to Rine. Meals are twice per day, in the morning and in the evening. Water can be found in the mine. Questions? No questions! You're free to go!"

The heaviness fell off me and I was again the master of my own body. As I got up, I looked at the orc, who already forgot that I was there as he studied another document. Damn, you can't end a conversation on such a note. I have to ask him about something, but what? About the mine? He'll immediately send me to Rine. About getting out of here? He'll say that it's possible once I paid 100 million gold. What can I ask? Right, hang on a moment! I'm a Jeweler!

"If I find a Precious Stone, who do I give it to? Am I able to work it by myself?" I asked the governor, as the overseer started to push me out of the room. I only knew enough of mining to ask a stupid question of this kind. Barliona's developers played the following joke on Jewelers: the Uncut Precious Stones could not be simply bought from NPCs, who only resold stones that had already been worked. Jewels have very low drop rate when killing mobs and can otherwise only be obtained from ore veins or from ore processing. There were no other places to get hold of Precious Stones. With my Hunter I was lucky enough to glimpse, a couple of times, how people picked up pieces of Topaz or Ruby from loot dropped by high level mobs. There were no such mobs around here and I had little idea of what sifting through the ore involved; it probably required certain tools. However, obtaining a Precious Stone from a vein seemed quite possible. At least in my view.

A silence descended on the room. Even my escort stopped breathing and looked his boss.

"We have many stones, as you well noted," he replied, and I wondered if the governor could be brought to a state of rage. He seemed as calm as a python. Suddenly, as if hearing my thoughts, the orc smiled: "But if you find a Precious Stone among them, for each one I would personally record a day's quota of ore next to your name. One stone — one quota. As for processing them... You're a Jeweler, so if you find a precious stone, you'll be given a recipe for its cutting. Or you could go to Rine, who won't cheat you with the price. So, Ore Miner Mahan, the Conqueror of Imitators and Hunter for Precious Stones, go for it. It's all in your hands and in your pick," the orc leant back in his armchair, which had a strong resemblance to a throne, and continued to smile.

A message appeared before my eyes:

Your reputation with the Pryke Mine Guards has increased by 10 points. Current level: Neutral.

Whew! I had been all but crestfallen when stripped of those ten reputation points. Incurring such a loss on the first day was very stupid, considering my plans to leave the mine. I had to be more careful with Rine: the last thing I wanted was to run up any losses with him. I turned around and was taken by the overseer to see Rine.

I discovered that he was a dwarf, working some piece of metal with a hammer in the smithy nearby. He was about a meter-twenty, stocky and compact, with powerful arms and thick eyebrows, which hung over keen sparkly eyes and a potato of a nose. A pretty typical dwarf, whose like I'd met many times across Barliona. As I approached Rine, I laughed to myself: what else would a dwarf do other than work in a smithy or mine ore?

"I see that reinforcements have arrived," said Rine in a businesslike manner, looking me over head to toe. "Very good, we were getting short-handed. So, you want to learn to swing the pick and not take your legs off by accident?"

Taught by the harsh experience with the mine governor I replied straight away.

"That's right, honorable master Rine, I'm going to be a mine worker for the next eight years, so I would be grateful to receive a grain of your wisdom and experience in mining ore," I said with all the charm I could muster.

"I have enough experience, as you well noted," mumbled the dwarf, looking pleased, "teaching you to mine ore isn't hard — just remember not to hit your legs with the pick and the rest is simple. Look — here is a vein of Copper Ore, which you will have to mine." Suddenly a rock pile with some kind of nodules appeared next to the dwarf.

"You take the pick and start to hit this," the dwarf continued. "Don't just stand there! Grab your pick and start hitting the pile of rocks."

"What happens to those who refuse to work? Or to those who fail to meet the daily quota and simply sit and rest?" I asked as I slowly approached the rock pile.

"Those are dealt with simply: no daily quota —

no food. You spend a day without food and your body begins to eat itself. Few could stand the pain of their own stomach beginning to self-digest. Then comes death and a respawn back here in the mines. And this will repeat until the prisoner starts to work like everyone else. In my memory, the toughest prisoner could endure four such respawns. Then he broke. They say that the sensations from your own death are no laughing matter. You want to try starving? No? Then, like I said, grab the pick and start mining the ore," said the dwarf matter-of-factly.

I came up to the meter-high pile of stones, which the dwarf for some reason called a Copper Vein, took a swing and hit it, putting all of my pent-up anger behind it, trying to get it over and done with in one blow. The hit generated a flurry of sparks and the pick, rebounding from the rocks, hit me quite painfully on the leg. This didn't seem to lay a scratch on the Copper Vein, which stood there as a hostile witness to my total ineptitude as a miner.

"Copper-banging bastard," I whispered in pain, "that bites!" Somewhere on the edge of my vision flashed a message:

Damage taken. Hit Points reduced by 5: 11 (weapon damage + strength) — 6 (armor). Total: 35 of 40.

"Er-hem..." coughed the dwarf. "I see it's not exactly working for you, is it? Your pick really showed you. Don't get too carried away with hitting the pile. This isn't Mithril ore, all you need is a little force. Easy does it — go at it bit by bit and aim better. You have to hit between the rocks. What's the point of hitting the stone itself?"

So, being a miner is not all that easy. In my past life, as I now call the days when I was playing my Hunter, I spent most of my time shooting mobs rather than gathering resources. After all, few people actually bother with the latter, since there are prisoners like myself doing the job for them. Some of us mine ore, some gather herbs, some do something else: there are many prisoners who have plenty of work to get through. Virtually 90 percent of all resources in Barliona is gathered by prisoners.

So, I had to hit between the stones, instead of going at them directly and do it with a moderate force, which, at the same time, should not be too weak. All right, let's try it. I lifted the pick once again, found a place where two stones touched each other and went for it. This time my blow went home — the pick did not bounce off, but got firmly lodged between the stones.

"That's it," said the dwarf, looking satisfied. "Now you understand what I mean. Well done lad. Now you must loosen the stone and continue as you started."

I took out the pick with some difficulty and started to level a blow after blow. The first thirty blows came easily. I'm an ore digger, a real miner! I will get through the daily ore quota right now and the rest will be just for me. I will mine money, will gain Respect and will soon be free and wealthy too! The next thirty strokes were more difficult, but I still continued to see myself as a successful ore miner. But my plans for enrichment were waving a white flag in farewell, and a funeral march began to play somewhere inside my head.

In about two hundred blows I only managed to break off a few stones and understood that I wouldn't be earning enough money from the ore. The pile continued to stand there just as before. And if the dwarf was right, I had to make just four hundred more blows to get to the finish line. Just! My hands were shaking and barely able to hold the pick, sweat covered my eyes, my legs were bending beneath me, but there was still a lot of work to do. Insistent flashing of some message at the edge of my view was beginning to annoy me, so I moved it in front of my eyes to read it properly. It made me somewhat thoughtful:

You are tired. Current level of Energy: 35 of 100.
You hit points have been reduced by 4. Total: 31 of 40.

"You're not getting tired, are you?" the dwarf suddenly asked me. "That's normal. Look at how much you've got through. Here, have a drink," and he gave me a large cup with water. The cup looked like it had seen better days: it was dirty and covered in some kind of stains, but, reluctant to disappoint Rine, I took it and carefully tried its contents. As I took the first draught I felt as if I was struck by electricity — the water invigorated and cooled me and renewed my desire to keep going. I drank the whole cup almost immediately, noting to myself in surprise that ordinary water could be a source of such great pleasure. Before I had to use special extortionately priced elixirs for the same purpose. But here you had simple water... As a bonus a message appeared:

You restored your Hit Points. Total: 40 of 40.
You restored the level of Energy. Total: 100 of 100.

And so I kept working, swinging the pick and drinking the water in turn. After three hours of such work the pile was in pieces, leaving several modestly-sized reddish rocks in its place. So, here it is — Copper Ore.

"At last," mumbled the dwarf. "I nearly fell asleep here. This here is your ore. As you see, you've got five pieces, which is half of your daily quota. The more ore you mine, the quicker you will level up your skill and the less time you'll have to spend on each vein. So, from now on you are an official ore miner, and now you can see how much durability the vein retains. Useful to know as you work. Here is a sack for your diggings. It might be small, but it will do for a start.

Straight away I saw a message:

You gained the "Mining" profession. Current level 1
You received an object: Small mining sack (8 slots. Total free: 8)
Attention! No Achievements can be gained in the "Pryke Copper Mine".

I put the sack over my shoulder and we went down into mine, where Rine showed me the site where I would be working from tomorrow. At last I could get a view of the place without the cloud of dust. The fence separating the barracks from the mine had several entrances, which the workers used to get to their designated sections. The territory was divided into squares about twenty meters across, with an entrance on one of the sides. All the other sides of the square were made up of piles of rock about a meter and a half in height and entering a section through them wasn't exactly effortless. Small paths ran between the sections and overseers walked up and down them at a leisurely pace. I later discovered that the sections could only be accessed by their owners and by those to whom they granted permission. Anyone else was simply unable to enter. As we walked across my section we passed prisoners at work, who gave me appraising looks, and I noticed with surprise that there was neither disdain nor aggression in their eyes. Strange; prisoners do not usually behave like this. Something wasn't right here. I made a note to myself that I would look into this. My section was located all the way at the end of the mine, but it contained as many as twenty Copper Veins. Was this many or few, I wondered.

"This is where you'll be working," said the dwarf. "Twenty veins will last you a good while. The veins are renewed every day, so you should have enough work for the next year. Water is over there." Rine pointed somewhere towards the middle of the mine. "Your neighbors won't bother you, everyone here is well-behaved. I think I told you what you need to get started. But ask if you have any questions, I could have left something out."

I had no desire to ask about ore mining (I'd figure it out as I worked), but I had to ask something. I decided to ask him about my profession. Jewelcraft skills were locked for me for the time being — I needed a trainer in order to unlock them and to tell me what I should do with them and how. But where would I find one in a mine? Perhaps the dwarf could tell me.

"Honorable Master Rine," I began, trying to fill my voice with as much esteem and respect as possible, "I was designated the profession of a Jeweler, so I would like to know if you have someone in the mine who could teach me this profession, so it isn't wasted."

"A Jeweler, you say?" the dwarf smiled. "We only have industrial artisans working here: an Artist, a Sculptor and a Glass-blower; we even have a Woodcarver. But we've not had a Jeweler yet. You've seen our boss's den, right? It was decorated by the local prisoners. As far as you're concerned, I could be the one to teach you the basic Jewelcraft skill, but for the time being you should forget about it. I won't do it for free and you have no money on you yet. Once you start making regular earnings from selling ore, then we can talk. By the way, I buy the ore at 10 copper coins per unit and in order for you to learn the cheapest Jewelcraft recipe you need 10 silver coins. You can do the maths. And don't forget: In order to learn Jewelcraft, you first need to unlock it, for which you will need another 20 silver coins. And at 1 gold Jeweler's tools aren't cheap either. Now you have an idea of how long it would take you to become a Jeweler. I'll be going now: I've spent enough time on you as it is. There is no need for you to eat today, so I advise you to get a good rest. In the next eight years you won't be getting much of it. And don't be late getting up in the morning: the food is only served for two hours after the wake-up call."

Wake-up call?

CHAPTER THREE
THE PRYKE MINE. DAY ONE

"TOO-OO-OO! BAM!

I sprang from the bed, looking around in a panic: what, who, where, how? A fire! I have to run! My ears were ringing from the horn that came out of nowhere and my feet were giving way under me. All I knew was that I had to do something to save myself and so started to dart around the bed. Strange, my brain seemed to be working fine, but my body was moving all of its own accord. So that's what Panic is like! Even my eyes were failing me. The other prisoners continued to dress themselves calmly, seemingly oblivious to this terrible ringing.

"Sit down, close your eyes and try to relax. It will pass," I heard a voice next to me say. "They probably forgot to warn you about our alarm clock. It only affects the newcomers. Once you learn to wake up at the right time, you'll stop hearing it. For now try to calm down — the more agitated you are the worse you'll feel."

'So here they are — the undocumented details of my imprisonment! No need to mention them; leave a surprise for the prisoners instead,' I thought angrily, then sat on the bed, closed my eyes and tried to relax. I didn't make a good job of it — I was still very tense, my head was splitting and the ringing in my ears could rival a bell tower in volume.

'I need to distract myself in order to relax,' I thought. This means I have to force my brain to work. What was the first thing I needed to do? I had to create a plan of action for the next day, week and year. So then, if any planning is to be done, it should be serious and long-term.

Let's think. Today I will need:

1.   To get acquainted with the local customs and people.

2.   To determine my capabilities as a Shaman.

3.   To be certain to achieve the daily quota.

4.   Optional: try to exceed the daily quota even a little and assess money-earning possibilities.

I think that's enough for today. Next comes the plan for the week:

1.   Evaluate the prospects of improving my capabilities and understand how quickly these will develop.

2.   Find a change for my striped clothing.

3.   Earn 20 silver coins in order to unlock the Jewelcraft trade.

Then there is the plan for the year. This is simple:

1.   Survive and don't go crazy.

2.   Find a Precious Stone.

3.   Optional: leave the mine for the main gameworld.

Having made a plan of action for the near future and put my thoughts in order, I opened my eyes and saw another prisoner sitting on the bed next to mine and looking at me intently. The human — and it was definitely a human or I understood nothing of races — had a remarkable resemblance to a dwarf: he wasn't tall, was of a stocky build and had bright, penetrating eyes. And, as I noted to myself again, there was no aggression in these eyes. There was an interest, some sympathy — anything but aggression.

'Something is wrong with the prisoners here,' I thought to myself, 'Maybe they're digging up the wrong sort of ore.'

"Have you recovered?" he asked and from his voice I understood that he was the one that helped me deal with the local alarm clock. "Get dressed, we should go and get the food." You won't be much of a worker if you don't eat. And take your pick and bag too, you'll not be back here until the evening."

"Th-thank you, Kartalonius," I said with some effort as I read the man's name, which was glowing faintly above the player. I quickly dressed in a clean robe (it seems imprisonment had at least some advantages — the clothes cleaned themselves; nice!), grabbed the pick and followed after Kartalonius.

"Just call me Kart," he laughed, looking back and slowing to my pace. "A bit of a chore to say this tongue-twister every time, so Kart will do. I've gotten used to it now — after all, it's my eleventh year here... And I still have four more to go..." he added sadly, after a brief pause. "Well then, let's not dwell on the negatives... We'll have to live side by side, so let's get off on the right foot from the start. You're not too excitable, I hope? You were racing around the bed so much first thing this morning you'd think you've been hitting your feet repeatedly with your pick. You were screaming too: 'Fire! Save yourselves!'"

I felt my face begin to color involuntarily. Had I actually been screaming too? From outside, my darting around must have looked stupid. With a heartfelt curse at the smart asses who thought up such a wake-up call, I had a look at Kart. So the "little guy" was far from simple. You don't get fifteen years for nothing — you would have had to try really hard to be given that.

"You shouldn't worry so much," smiled Kart, seeing my reaction. "This is a unique mine, where they don't send just anyone. Here we mostly have fraudsters and embezzlers, we even have one kidnapper. But we have no violent sorts here. At least — so far. Did the governor tell you what happens when you break the rules?"

I shook my head, ticking 'the NPCs in the mine are real bastards' box in my mind.

"The rule is quite simple." As soon as you cause anyone intentional damage, irrespective of what you use — a hand, a pick or a stone, your Energy quickly falls to zero and you hit the floor, totally drained. At zero Energy you lose 1 Hit Point every 5 seconds, all this while no Energy regeneration takes place. So if you are not immediately given some water to drink, in a couple of minutes — you're dead. And I can tell you right away — death is a very unpleasant experience, especially since on death you lose all the skill levels that you managed to acquire. So this is what's special about our mine. For many residents this is worse than death, because crafting at a low level of skill is a tedious undertaking. Also levelling up costs quite a lot."

Crafting? What's he on about?

"It's just as well this is the case. I myself stick to the rule that if no-one bothers me, I don't bother anyone. But tell me, why I haven't met a single hostile gaze at the mine so far?" I asked, pointing to a gnome who walked past us and cheerfully winked at Kart. "You get the feeling that the people here are not criminals, but ordinary workers, who have been hired to do a job and soon would be going home to sit in a comfy sofa, take out some cold beer and... Blast! Daydreaming aloud here. But in any case, things don't normally work this way! This might be virtual reality, but the people here are real and every last one of them a criminal, and they look at you like dancers at a ball — with interest, almost enthusiasm. I've not seen such looks in real life, while this is prison, whichever way you look at it. So, what's the secret?"

"Well done, got to the heart of things right away!" noted Kart, standing at the end of a queue, lining up for the food.

"Look here, this is Altarionus, or simply Alt," he slapped the man in front of us on the shoulder. "Hi, Alt, have you managed to buy some green paint for the canvas?"

Despite such an unceremonious greeting, Alt turned around and instead of starting an argument smiled in greeting.

"Oh, hi Kart! No, I haven't bought it yet. The

darn thing costs almost five gold, but I have just over three. Here, you can work as hard as you like, but you won't earn more than ten silver coins in a day. So the governor will only get his new painting in a couple of weeks. Hells, my hands are already itching to complete it. I'll be climbing the walls if I don't finish the work soon! And I tried to approach Rine this way and that — tried to get him to gift it to me or give me a discount, to appeal to his softer side by saying that I only have ten percent to go to level five Artist, but the dwarf is stubborn. It's true when they say: it's easier to bargain with a wall than a dwarf. And you, young man, what is your profession?"

And then it finally hit me. The luxurious interiors of the administration office, the absence of hostile looks from other prisoners (creative people cannot look at others like that) and Kart's words that "this is a unique mine, where they don't send just anyone": I had ended up in a mine for master craftsmen: those who were given a profession when their sentence was passed. This is why it's so quiet here and why Kart is quite friendly with me and why Alt is readily talkative. If you've spent the past ten years in creative crafting work, you'll lose your negative attitude sooner or later. So you get some sort of a zone for prisoner rehabilitation and re-education instead of a mine. What a place to land in!

"I'm a Jeweler," I muttered, somewhat at a loss, now seeing other prisoners in a different light. The mine contained about a couple of hundred living souls — humans, gnomes, dwarves and even one orc. As Rine said, there were Sculptors, Glaziers and even a Woodcutter here. The Woodcutter was most probably the orc that stood not far down in the queue and was turning around some piece of wood in his hands.

"Oh! You have quite a rare profession!" Kart exclaimed enthusiastically. "We've not had any Jewelers in my time here! A piece of advice for you, lad (and don't look at me so suspiciously, I won't give you any bad advice): pull yourself up by your bootstraps, forget tiredness and exceed your quota. Your aim is to earn money and unlock your main profession. And when you level up in that profession then... But no, I'll not tell you – you'll see for yourself. By the way, the more you make of something, the more money you get, and more money means an easier life here. Ain't that true, Alt?"

Alt nodded in agreement.

"And what are you? What's your specialization?" I asked Kart, already figuring him for a Sculptor.

To my surprise Kart remained silent and grew gloomy, then turned away altogether and started to examine some distant mountain top in the distance.

"Did he spot a dragon there suddenly? Or did I ask an unpleasant question?"

"Our law-enforcers played a cruel trick on Kart. His profession is even more rare than yours; he's an Informant," Alt replied for him. "Kart didn't tell you, but I will. You see, the higher the level of the main profession, the more we get — how shall I put it? — pleasure, if you like. Satisfaction. This is why everyone at the mine tries to level up. Everyone except for Kart. In order to level up he has to inform on us to the camp governor. If you take into account that in ten years of imprisonment Kart's level of Informer is still zero, you can see how often he engages in that activity. When you increase your Jewelcraft at least to level 1, you'll understand what he's been deprived of."

"I'm sorry Kart, I didn't know," I mumbled, somewhat lost.

"That's all right, I'm used to it now. But then I'm level eighteen in Chattiness: there is such a stat, would you believe it. That's what keeps me going. By the way, from our talking today, I increased it by 0.5 percent, and we didn't even talk properly yet. So in the near future, you'll find it hard to get rid of me."

Now I got the reason for Kart's interest in me. And I had been so naive and thought that it was all pure goodness and mutual help. Far from it — it's all totally mercenary, give and take relations.

As we talked we didn't notice how the queue arrived at the place where food was handed out. I failed to see it yesterday, located as it was right behind the smithy, by one of the entries to the mine. And the food place could hardly be called a place; all it contained was a meter-high vat standing on the ground, from which one of the guards was ladling food out to the prisoners. That's all there was to the "place". No fires, tents, shelters or anything else. Clean plates were lying in a large pile right on the ground in front of the cauldron and the prisoners took one and came up for their portion. Spoons were attached to each plate by a string. Like a child's rattle of some sort. And where did the dirty dishes go? There was no collection point in sight. All right, I'll see what Kart would do with his and copy him.

When I was given my plate of food, my first

thought upon seeing it was 'No way will I be eating THIS. Not going to happen.' You just could not call what the overseer handed me 'food' under any circumstances. It was a muddy homogeneous mass of pale-green color, with bubbles slowly floating to the surface. Although the food looked liquid, it did not flow, but froze in an ugly mass on the plate. It was a good thing that it completely lacked any smell, or I would have thrown up there and then.

"Take it and shove off," said the overseer with a smirk, seeing my long face. "It's no resort here: you eat the porridge or starve to death. Well?" he thrust the plate at me once again.

I took it, walked away and glanced back. To my surprise the prisoners were all calmly eating it, taking no notice of the appearance of the food. 'Either they've gotten used to this out of hopelessness or I simply don't get it,' I thought, perplexed. So that's what choice is like — to lock your sense of revulsion into some distant corner and eat THIS, or enjoy the unforgettable pleasure of your own stomach eating itself. Those developers were some bastards!

The strange thing was: when I played as a Hunter I never noticed that the character started to feel bad without food. If you didn't eat for a long time, you gradually became sluggish, less mobile, you gain experience more slowly, but there were no catastrophic consequences. And not even in my worst nightmare could I imagine the stomach digesting itself. Another undocumented feature of imprisonment? Or do normal players play under simplified settings, while here you end up with extreme version of hardcore? Or perhaps everything

I've been told was a bluff and nothing will happen to me? My head started to ache from this avalanche of thoughts. Now I had the chance to regret not checking out this detail when I was preparing for imprisonment.

Whether I wanted to or not, I had to make a decision. Was I prepared to take a risk and verify the information that one can die without food? Though I was ashamed to admit it, but I was not. Even if this was a game, I wasn't psychologically ready to die, even in a virtual sense. In all my 87 levels as a Hunter I only died a couple of times, before I gained the ability to control my opponent at level 30. From that time on I'd been playing like Koschei the Deathless. I even smiled at the thought: on account of Marya the Wise (Marina) my Koschei (my Hunter) was destroyed. Moreover, when I was free the sensory filters were turned off and death simply meant disconnection from Barliona for a couple of hours. 'Well, well... So I have to eat', I thought, and gave my plate a look of hatred, as the porridge continued to bubble. I overcame my aversion and slowly started to eat, carefully watching those around me. At first I felt light tingling in my mouth, as if I was eating a fizzy sweet. Then to my surprise I discovered that the porridge had a taste and that this taste was a pleasant one. When the tingling in my mouth gave way to euphoria in my whole body, I quickly finished the entire portion before I knew it. The pleasure was so great that I wasn't even surprised when I saw the message about receiving a buff:

Buff gained: Strength +1, Energy loss

reduced by 50%. Duration — 12 hours.

As soon as I read the message, the plate disappeared from my hands. Great: only if such things happened in reality — you eat and dirty plates vanish forever! Putting my pick over the shoulder I joined the flow of people moving towards the mine. My first day of work awaited me.

The site greeted me with graphic dust effect, lack of wind and the burning sun.

I had only 1 level in Mining. This meant that, irrespective of how much I increased it today, I had to gather 10 pieces of ore. The quota was calculated on entering the mine and not on exit, or at least that's how I understood Rine. Keeping in mind that I should beat my quota, I had to gather 20 pieces today. So, let's go! With this thought I threw the bag on the ground got a good grip on the pick and started to hit the stone pile.

'Not too strongly or too weakly, aiming between the stones rather than at them' — thoughts flew through my head as I worked. 'I must watch my breathing and Energy level....Strike right between the rocks... "Isn't it funny How a bear likes honey? I wonder why...?"' Striking between the stones... I wonder, did Rabbit really put everything he had on the table for him, or did he leave something for himself for a rainy day? Must watch the Energy level... Damn it, swinging this blasted pick is so hard... '

In approximately an hour I decided to take a break. The durability bar on the Copper Vein had stopped at 60%; so I had to hit it for another 2 hours at least. At this rate I'll be able to get through 3 veins at the most today. Not a flippin' lot! I must speed up!

The Energy level showed 43 units, Hit Points fell to 35, so I decided to get some water to restore them. I would also find out how things work at the local watering hole.

The water supply was right at the centre of the mine and consisted of a twenty-meter square site, similar to those in which the prisoners worked, with one difference: there were no piles of rocks on its borders. It contained six small wells, about half a meter wide and deep. They had no lids: just a simple hole in the ground with stones set around it. At the same time there was only one cup for drawing water. It was carelessly lying on the ground. How unsanitary! It's just as well that microbes don't exist in a virtual world. That's harsh. One little bowl for six small wells — for two hundred prisoners. It seemed inhuman. There were no prisoners at the watering hole, so I took the cup and leant over a well, dipping it in the water. What smart ass came up with the idea of putting only one watering hole in such a large mine? And so inconveniently placed too. Having drank the water, which didn't taste anything like the one that Rine offered me, I restored the lost Energy and Hit Points and saw a strange debuff text in front of me:

Water used. Duration expires in: 6 hours.

I had no access to the properties and description of the debuff, so I decided to forget about it and return to my section.

In the next hour I single-mindedly worked on

destroying the vein. Only 40% of durability remained now, and soon it was 20%. A little more, just a bit! I bit my lip and inflicted a frenzy of blows with my pike. I wondered whether I would have been able to work at such a pace in the real world or would have already dropped from tiredness. Now only 10% left... Suddenly the pick dropped from my hands and I fell to the ground.

You are tired. Current level of Energy: 10 of 100.
Your Hit Points have been reduced by 30. Total: 10 of 40.

Well bang my copper! How could I forget about Energy? I went to the settings and set up a message that would flash as a warning if my Energy fell below 30. Now, the main thing was to crawl to the water and not kick the bucket on the way! The strange debuff did not disappear, but the timer in it changed:

Water used. Duration expires in: 4.5 hours.

As soon as I got to the water, I took the cup and drank a couple gulps. Feeling the tiredness recede from me, I stared blankly at the text that appeared before my eyes:

You used water for the second time in 6 hours.
Penalty incurred: the number of skill points reduced by 10%. The next degree of reduction: 20%. Attention: You have not yet earned any skill

points, total penalty: 0
You restored your Hit Points. Total: 40 of 40.
You restored your Energy. Total: 100 of 100.

Despite regaining my Energy, I was too dispirited to curse or express my emotions in any way. I got up and, downcast, headed off in the direction of my site: the daily quota had to be met one way or another and I had to wait another 4.5 hours before I could drink again. Now it finally began to dawn on me that the place where I ended up really was a prison and not a recreational work and leisure resort.

The vein only had 5% of Durability left. I automatically took the pick and methodically started to make blow after blow, completely switching off to everything around me.

A few minutes later the Durability bar of the vein flickered one last time and the pile of rocks disappeared, leaving six pieces of ore on the ground behind it. I quickly glanced at the message that appeared before me and waved it away, gathering the ore into the bag and starting on the second vein.

Experience gained: +1 Experience, points remaining until next level: 99
Skill increase:
+ 50% to Mining. Total: 50%
+ 10% to Strength. Total: 10%
+ 5% to Stamina. Total: 5%

They give just 1 experience point for a vein...

Blow.... I need to break 99 more veins to gain a level.... Blow.... 3-4 veins a day... Blow... At least a month until I can gain a level... Blow... I'll die here... Blow... What's left of my spirit will, for sure...

In the hour that I spent on the second vein, its Durability went down to 65% and my Energy level to 30. The water debuff showed me that I could not drink for two more hours, so I lay down in the shade cast by the vein to get out of the burning sun. I closed my eyes and imagined myself swimming in cool water, it running down my face, slowly drinking the sweet, cool, invigorating moisture...

A quiet squeak sounded next to me like a thunderclap on a clear day, drowning out the piercing ringing of the picks, making me jump up and glance around wildly.

A huge Rat, coming up to my knee in height, stood on one of the veins of my section and looked at me. I stared at the Rat, stupefied, and for a while we engaged in this 'staring contest'. What was a Rat doing here? There were only rocks in this place. What's there to eat for them here, after all? Were the prisoners themselves on the menu? These questions remained unanswered, but one thing was clear: the Rat was there and it was looking at me. Appearing to come to some kind of a decision, the Rat snorted and, jumping off the Copper Vein, disappeared from sight.

For some minutes I stared at the space that was just occupied by the Rat.

A Rat in a stony mine! This is impossible! This is... This is free Experience! A source of Experience that did not depend on ore gathering! And if I gained a second level, I will put all my points into... Right, I must definitely go on a rat safari inside my section. After taking the decision to hunt down the Rat, I remembered Kart's words that dealing damage to someone leads to Energy falling to zero and then I bite the dust. Blast! Does this rule also apply to Rats? I must find this out so I don't end up in a pickle.

To my surprise in the time that I rested and daydreamed of a rat safari, my Energy rose to 80, my Hit Points were completely restored and the water debuff indicated less than an hour until expiry. I grabbed the pick and decided to bring my Energy down to 30, then wait until the debuff wore off and go to the watering hole, where I would ask (from the overseers if it came to it) what the punishment was for killing Rats.

Either the inspiration from the coming hunt increased my physical strength or I got the hang of the work process, but by the time I was down to 30 Energy, the Durability of the vein was only 15%. The water debuff had completely expired and, aching all over, I ran for the water.

The watering hole was quite crowded — it seems that the debuff had expired for many people. Having refreshed myself, I started to look for Kart, but to my disappointment he was nowhere to be seen and the same went for Alt; so, having weighed up all the 'pros' and 'cons' I went to an overseer.

'I wonder,' I thought as I came up to the guard, 'where did the developers find the template for such a despising stare? After all, it's not something that can be contrived — you'd have to be born with a stare like that. You feel as though the guard is looking at you like a piece of something small and indecent. Well I'll be... this really is quite unsettling...'

"What is it?" barked the overseer and it seemed to echo around the whole mine.

"Is there a penalty for killing Rats?" I quickly asked my question, thinking that politeness would be wasted on a guard.

"Rats? Ha-ha! So, you've decided to become a Rat hunter, have you?" laughed the guard. "Aside from the fact that it will make a nice snack of you, there are no penalties. In any case, you'll never catch it with those stubby legs! It can only be hit from afar, but what will you hit it with? A stone? So quit drooling over Rats and get your ass back to work!"

Right. Aside from the stare they also gave this law enforcer an angelic temperament. But at least I got all I needed out of him — a Rat can be hunted without fear of punishment. And if there's no punishment, I should make use of this opportunity.

"Halt!" The guard shouted after me as I began to head off. "If you do somehow manage to kill a Rat, you could claim a reward for it from Rine. They get on his nerves even more than you get on mine. Don't forget to bring a Rat tail as proof."

Message for the player!
If you kill a Rat, bring the Rat tail to Rine and claim your reward: 10 Copper coins and
+2 Reputation with the Pryke Mine Guards for each Rat tail.

After I returned to my site, I decided to finish off the second vein quickly, make a start on the third and then, once Energy had again fallen to 30%, go on a hunt for the Rat. After all, this gave me an additional opportunity to earn money and raise my reputation! I must make use of it. In my mind I was already at the hunt, so I did not notice the moment when the Durability bar flickered and the vein vanished.

Experience gained: +1 Experience, points remaining until next level: 98
Skill increase:
+50% to Mining. Total: 100%. Mining increased by 1. Total: 2
+10% to Strength. Total: 20%
+5% to Stamina. Total: 10%

I quickly glanced at the message that appeared and waved it away so I could gather up the ore and start on the third vein, and then...

A light, virtually weightless, pleasure, like a glass of cool fresh beer that you drink after a hot sauna, engulfed me from head to toe. This was so unexpected and at the same time so pleasant that I wanted to jump, sing and hug someone. Where are you, Rat? I love you!

The euphoria did not last long, but left a deep mark in my soul. Yes, this makes slaving away for 12 hours a day well worth it. I could not even imagine what I'd be feeling when I levelled up one of my stats or my main profession. So there are some advantages to having the sense perception in the capsule turned on. And Alt was right, it is an unforgettable feeling.

I had another 6 pieces of Cooper ore from the second vein, which allowed me to forget about the daily quota and opened my road to money-earning. So, what did we have: Energy: 95, vein Durability: 100%, Mining: 2. There are about 5 hours left until the end of the day. Here goes!

The message that I added to the settings for monitoring Energy popped up after about an hour of work. I sat on the ground and was pleased to note that with the second level in Mining working became more enjoyable and after approximately the same hour of work, only 45% of the vein Durability remained. And I wasn't even trying that hard!

Now I just have to decide what to do about the hunt. I can't run after the Rat, since I don't have enough Energy and Stamina. Agility would be of little use: with a score of 1 in this stat I will only hit my own legs instead of the Rat. Should I perhaps put down some traps? Looks like I have my work cut out for me...

The Rat population in my lot turned out to be quite healthy — I counted around five of them. Like all animals in starting locations, the Rats were not aggressive and had 30 Hit Points. These nimble beasts constantly darted to and fro between the stones and only rarely entered open space for a few seconds, which made all my grand plans crumble before my eyes. Having selected one of the Rats, I examined its properties.

Pryke Mine Rat. Description: this darting animal appeared at the Pryke Mine right from the time it opened and has been a troublemaking headache for its administration ever since. There is a reward allocated for killing Rats. Hit Points:

30. Attack: 10. Armor: 2. Magic resistance: 2.

As no clear solution was forthcoming, I automatically began to go through my stats and skills, continuing my intense search for possibilities.

Race: Human. The first race in Barliona. The Capital: Anhurs... Looking further... Mining — character profession, enables the gathering of ore. As the level of the profession increases the rate of Energy loss slows down... Next... Class: Shaman. A spiritual mentor, who is able to communicate with Spirits and call them to his aid. The summoned Spirits help the Shaman to defend himself or to heal wounded comrades, and strong shamans can... Next.... Stop! Backtracking!

Shamans can work with Spirits! Why am I so slow? Didn't I make a special note to myself this morning to get to grips with the Shaman class?

It took me a bit of time to understand how to open the spell book, which I then selected and began to study. I only had two spells in the book, but these spells were really something!

Summoning of the Lesser Healing Spirit: You appeal to the world of Spirits, summoning the Lesser Healing Spirit, which gives part of its essence (life force) to the injured person. The strength of the summoned Spirit and the amount of the essence given is determined by Intellect. Kamlanie (casting) time: 2 seconds. Cost of summoning (before initiation as a Shaman): (Character level) of the summoner's Hit Points, Cost of healing: (Character level)*4 mana. Restores

(Intellect*3) Hit Points.

Lesser Lightning Spirit Strike: You appeal to the world of Spirits, summoning the Lesser Lightning Spirit on your opponent to take away part of his Spirit (life force). The strength of the summoned Spirit and the amount of life force taken from the opponent is determined by Intellect. Kamlanie (casting) time: 5 seconds. Cost of summoning (before initiation as a Shaman): (Character level) Hit Points of the summoner. Cost of attack: (Character level)*4 mana. Damage: (Intellect*3) Points. Range: 20 meters.

Phew! I had to read this text several times to make something of it. They didn't exactly make it simple. And they were clever about it too. It is possible to summon Spirits before becoming an initiated Shaman, but you pay for it with your own Hit Points. At the same time the higher your level, the greater the cost. A bit cruel, really. But I still have to figure out how to use all this, especially as the very word 'kamlanie' remained a mystery to me, as I heard it for the first time. What is it and why did I have to spend 2 seconds doing it? All right, let's test it out. I looked at the area of my plot where the Rats were darting around and saw one of the rodents sitting on a pile of rocks and looking at me. Did I remind it of cheese or something? Well, you just keep sitting there and I'll...

"Spirit Strike!" I shouted and aimed my hands at the Rat.

My shout made the Rat's whiskers twitch, it turned its nose this way and that, but continued to sit as if nothing happened. What a flop!

"I call upon the Lesser Lightning Spirit to smite this Rat! Attack!" I pointed my hands in the direction of the Rat.

"Spirit! Summon! Drop dead!" I kept trying, but it began to dawn on me: something wasn't right here. Usually things like the use of spells, and especially summoning of Spirits, were explained during the initial training, which prisoners did not have! And the only magic that a Hunter, which I played before, could use were the spell scrolls. Blast, if only I could read the Game manual, but who'd give me access to that now?!

Maybe the problem was with the spell book itself? I carefully touched the pictogram drawing of the Lesser Healing Spirit, thinking that nothing bad would happen if the spell actually worked. Suddenly my hands contained a glowing projection of a cross. It was small, weightless and seemed to be stuck to my hand: when I opened up my fingers, the cross remained in my palm. I even shook it a little and the spell did not detach. Well, that's something. But how do I activate it now? I clenched my fist and tried to crush the cross and immediately saw a message:

Do you want to add the spell of Lesser Healing Spirit Summoning to the active section?

Yes, I do, now what?

The spell of Lesser Healing Spirit Summoning has been added to the active spells section. To activate the spell pick a target for

healing, activate the Summoning with your thought and perform the shamanistic ritual (kamlanie) in the course of two seconds. Until you are initiated as a Shaman, you can use any object instead of a tambourine for the ritual. Attention! Due to the limitations imposed on this location, summoning Spirits to heal yourself is FORBIDDEN.

Available slots in the active spell section: 7 of 8.

Kamlanie has to be done with a tambourine? Does this mean that in order to heal or inflict damage I have to make a dance with a tambourine or even some 'tambourine stand-in' until I become a real Shaman? Now I get why this class is so unpopular: few people want to look like some dancing, muttering idiot. When I played as a Hunter, I saw mages, quietly standing there, stretching their hands towards the enemy, and firing lightning, fireballs and ice darts. No tambourine-accompanied dances in sight. That was real magic. And here... I was crestfallen. I remembered the Shamans I've seen before: it was true, dancing and muttering idiots was exactly what they looked like. And I can't even heal myself, they even stitched me up in this. Hit Points were lost as Energy fell, so a nice bonus like self-healing would have been very welcome. Dreams, dreams... Oh well, I still had the Spirit of Lightning!

Touching the icon of the Lesser Lightning Spirit Strike, I was ready to see its projection in my hand, but a message suddenly popped up:

Due to the imposed restrictions, using the Lesser Lightning Spirit Strike spell on the territory of the Pryke Copper Mine is only possible if your reputation with the Pryke Mine Guards is Friendly or higher. Current reputation: Neutral.

I slumped to the ground, entirely disheartened. How could this be — the bonus is there, but using it is 'out of bounds'? Why did they even leave it in then? 'Well, Mr. Rat, now you can celebrate! Your life will be long and peaceful,' I thought bitterly. Goodbye reputation and goodbye money. And happiness had seemed so close...

With a deep sigh I got up, put my pick over the shoulder and went to the shade to have a rest and restore my Energy. From disappointment and dashed hopes, as well as the annoying gaze of the Rat, which continued to stare at me, I mentally selected the Rat and grabbed my pick, pressed the icon of the Lesser Healing Spirit in my mind and imagined dancing around myself, banging on the pick like a tambourine and muttering the first song that came into my mind:

- *The Shaman has three hands, o-o-o....*

Take that, you grey-furred beast, drop dead and quit laughing at me.

The Rat gave a strange squeak and ran off making some weird sounds, but I took little notice of all that. My attention was held by the message appearing before my eyes:

Skill increase:
+10% to Intellect. Total: 10%
Your Hit Points have been reduced by 1.

Total: 29 of 40.

The happiness that engulfed me (I found another method for levelling up!) was so great that I did not notice how something grey and incredibly fast jumped at me from behind the pile of rocks.

Damage taken. Hit Points reduced by 4: 10 (Rat bite) — 6 (armor). Total Hit Points: 25 of 40.
Attention! It is recommended that you turn off the detailed description of damage during fighting.

My leg was pierced by a terrible pain. Damn Rat, have you gone completely nuts? I give you healing and life and then you attack me for it? 4 Hit Points for a bite... Blast! It could bite me to death at this rate! Forgetting my pick, I kicked the Rat with full force. Its Hit Points did not fall by much, but the Rat bounded away from me, giving me the chance to catch my breath. I grabbed the pick with both hands and prepared for the next attack. So you want war? I'll give you war!

As a Hunter I levelled up mainly by killing mobs, so I didn't panic now and I had a clear idea of what to do with the Rat. I may not have a bow, but I do have experience, which is not so easily lost! The Rat quickly recovered from my kick and instead of biting my leg again, jumped, aiming straight for the throat. This is more or less what I expected of it. I swung the pick, caught it in mid-jump and made it fly off again. Critical hit! The Rat's body flickered and it was already a weightless rodent-shaped cloud that I sent flying; it quickly dissipated. Only my loot hit the ground in place of the Rat.

Experience gained: +4 Experience, points remaining until next level: 94
Skill increase:
+20% to Strength. Total: 40%
+5% to Agility. Total: 5%
+10% to Stamina. Total: 20%

That's some bonus! So many things levelling up at once and, more importantly, you get 4 Experience for one Rat. This way, if I kill at least 5 Rats and get through 5-6 Copper Veins a day, I will get around 25 Experience every day, which would mean that it would take me under a week to gain a level! The new level would bring new stat points and new stat points equals a new level. My life has a goal! But I must figure out why the Rat actually attacked me. Why did it dislike my healing so much? Does it generate aggro with mobs? I have to get someone to explain this to me.

Picking up the items left behind by the Rat (the Rat pelt, meat and tail) I went to have a rest. Around three hours remained until the end of the working day, in which I had to finish off the third vein and, as soon as my Health recovered, 'heal' another Rat.

In the remaining time, I managed to finish off the third vein (+5 pieces of ore, +1 Experience, +10% Strength, +5% Stamina, +50% Mining) and also complete a fourth one (+5 pieces of ore, +1 Experience, +10% Strength, +5% Stamina, +1 Mining Skill), thus increasing my Mining Profession skill to 3.

Having once again felt the same euphoria upon levelling up, I made a firm decision to increase at least one stat as fast as possible, to see what kind of pleasure such an increase would bring.

As for Rats, I only managed to kill one more. I sung the song twice, thus 'healing' the next Rat, and dispatched it fairly quickly, letting it get close to me only once (+4 Experience, +20% Intellect, +20% Strength, +5% Agility, +10% Stamina). Although, truth be told, the Rat used that one chance to the full, biting me for 10 Hit Points. I did not see any more Rats — perhaps they had all gone into hiding. That was fine; for my first day I'd done more than enough.

The horn sounded, announcing the end of work for the day. Grabbing the heavy bag, I headed towards the exit. I joined the queue to Rine, so I could hand in my quota and sell the surplus, of which I gathered a fair amount. I also had to figure out what to do with the Rat tails. I waited my turn and poured out everything I had gathered during the day onto the table, noting Rine's surprise with pleasure.

"Not bad work, for the first day," mumbled Rine, still surprised. "Right, 10 pieces of ore taken off as the quota. Don't forget that it will be 30 pieces tomorrow. Now, let's have a look at the rest. As I said before, I am prepared to buy the surplus ore at 10 coppers a piece; you have 12 pieces, which comes to: 2 silver and 20 copper coins. Here you go," Rine put the money on the table.

Ah, yes. I forgot to explain about the ratio between the Copper, Silver and Gold coins. In Barliona it was 1:50, that is, 50 Copper coins made up 1 Silver, and 50 Silver made up 1 Gold (which could also be made up from some large amount of Copper, but who would change Copper for Gold?).

"As far as your Rat loot is concerned, I would give 1 copper coin for the meat and 3 for the skins, agreed?"

"That's not much," I said, surprising myself, because I never bargained before, not even at the market: I always paid the price that was asked.

"Well, only because you're new around here, and because I see you also have Rat tails — we'll get around to them soon enough — I am ready to take both Rat pelts off you for 5 coins each and give you 2 for the meat. Does that suit you?"

Suddenly I saw a message:

A new profession has been unlocked: Trade. The higher the level in Trade, the better the price offered when selling and buying. There is some probability that traders will offer you non-standard goods.

Your reputation with the Pryke Mine Guards increased by 1 point. Current level: Neutral. You are 999 points away from the status of Friendly.

Skill increase:

+10% to Trade. Total: 10%

Of course I agree! So, levelling up in the Trade profession depends on how often I bargain. That's good to know. I'm no expert in bargaining, but I can learn if need be. I was also glad to find out that the sale of gathered resources increased reputation, even if just a little.

I agreed and handed over the meat and was

about to hand over the pelts when I was stopped by a shout:

"Mahan, hold on!"

I turned around in surprise. The approaching man had a striking resemblance to Salvador Dalí, with his prominent moustache, mad gaze and upturned chin...

"Mahan, I heard that you intend to sell Rat skins to this honorable dwarf," he said, bowing in Rine's direction. But everyone in the mine knows that Batiranikaus (or simply Bat), would be exceedingly pleased to buy them off you for 15 copper coins a piece. Do we have a deal?"

"15 coins? But this honorable dwarf," I said, mimicking his tone, "was offering to buy all my pelts for 20 copper a piece. So, since we've already come to an agreement, I am not prepared to risk damaging my relations with him for less than 25 coins," I winked at the dwarf, who was listening to our bargaining with a pleased smile.

"25 coins! Oh gods! Weeell... all right, I'll give you 25 coins per skin: here you go," Bat agreed surprisingly quickly and handed me a silver coin. "Now hand over my skins."

Skill increase:
+10% to Trade. Total: 20%

"Take them," I pointed to the Rat skins that lay on the table and turned around to Rine to move on to Rat tails, only to be interrupted by a terrible scream:

"Guards!" Bat screamed at the top of his voice. "Guards, Mahan swindled money out of me! He's a cheat! I demand protection!"

Immediately a crowd of prisoners formed around us, through which the overseers were trying to make their way.

"What happened here?" one of them asked in a low bass.

"Dear law enforcement officer! This unworthy man," Bat pointed at me, "took advantage of my foolish naivety and swindled me out of 2 silver coins."

"Is this true?" the guard turned to me.

"Of course not, I..."

"He threatened Bat, I saw it myself!" a shout from the crowd interrupted me. "He said that he would kill Bat if he would not give him the money!" "Don't give him any food!" "Let him croak!" came shouts from the crowd, which put me in a state of shock, as I looked around, not getting what was going on. All the people had amiable expressions, even Bat, who stood next to me and with a totally genial and friendly gaze, shouted that I was a piece of scum that cheated him. I started to think I was going mad. What was going on here???

· "Quiet," a stern growl from the overseer silenced the crowd. "Now we'll get to the truth!"

The guard mumbled something and a hologram appeared next to him, where you could see how Bat handed over the money to me. He gave me the money and then I waved my hand in the direction of the table where the pelts were lying, but this gesture could be read as 'Get out of here", I then turned away from Bat as if saying that the conversation was over. Blast it! It really didn't look too great from outside; as if I was some dodgy racketeer. The projection disappeared and I stared at the guard in silence.

"Here's my decision," the overseer growled once again. "Mahan immediately gives Batiranikaus back one, I repeat, ONE silver, and, because it's his first time and he's new here, the incident will be overlooked. If he is caught doing anything like this once again he will be punished by being stripped of all his skill points. I'm done here! Now everyone back to their barracks!"

I silently gave the money back to Bat, and reached out to pick up the Rat skins, but it was no use. My hands simply passed through the skins as if they were no longer mine. That's right! I had already handed them over to Bat!

"Thank you!" Bat said with a smile, shoving the skins into his sack. "Come to me if you get any more."

Bat smiled once again and left, leaving me to stand next to Rine in a state of total incomprehension: how could people with such open and nice expressions, always smiling and greeting you, be so cruel and backstabbing? After all, aren't they creative people? Why do they have so much hatred for everyone? Those shouts: "Let him rot... I saw how he threatened...". Why?

"Why are you holding up the queue?" Rine's voice pulled me out of my thoughts. "Let's deal with your Rat tails, can't abide these grey critters."

"Yes, of course," I mumbled, feeling lost as I turned back to Rine. I need to get a grip. So what if I lost the skins: I'll be wiser next time and will hand them over personally.

"Right, for each Rat tail I usually pay 10 copper coins. Here's your money and be on your way, the queue behind you isn't getting any shorter!

Your reputation with the Pryke Mine Guards has increased by 4 points. Current level: Neutral. You are 995 points away from the status of Friendly.

After getting my food, I headed for the barracks. I had no desire to talk with other prisoners today and for a long time I could not fall asleep. I turned this way and that, but the oppressive feeling of injustice I experienced just would not let go.

"Quit spinning around or you'll drill a hole through your bed. You're keeping the rest of us up! Did something happen?" I heard Kart's voice next to me.

I described what happened today, even getting up in the process, but Kart suddenly laughed. What now? I'm telling him of the terrible injustice of this world, but he's laughing at me! Seeing that I was about to get all indignant, Kart waved me down and, clearing his throat began to explain:

"Well, my friend, you sure gave me a good laugh! Best I've had in a while. What can I say... ? Congratulations: you've encountered the second peculiarity of our mine, usually newcomers don't get it from the start. If I understand correctly, you still haven't grasped what's really going on here, right?" Seeing that I shook my head, Kart continued: "I will give you a couple of clues. First: today you probably levelled up in the Mining profession and got to feel what happens when you do that. Right? Right. Think about that. Second: there are myriads of stats that a character can have. Of these a fair number are non-standard, but you can pick only 4. As you know, I have the little-known stat of Chattiness — I get experience from telling everyone about everything. Get it now?"

I felt that either I was stupid or Kart and I were speaking a different language: I simply failed to see where he was going with it. What did Chattiness, free stats, and pleasure from levelling up in a profession have to do with anything?

"All right, I'll put you out of your misery, and it'll give me more chance to level up in any case. First of all, think about what you noticed in the morning. Though no — I'll start with the main thing. You already felt the pleasure involved from levelling up in a profession and I am sure that it was a sensation very much to your liking. This is nothing compared to levelling up in one of your stats. The pleasure from levelling up in a stat is so intense that you want more and more. And the higher the stat level, the harder it is to level up again — that's the axiom. This is why players who reach level twelve, which is the maximum level for the main stats in Pryke, disappear. I have no idea where they are sent, so no point asking me. This pleasure is the main difference between a mine for prisoners from the rest of the gameworld. The main world doesn't have this feature; after all, they play using filters, which are virtually impossible to remove. Now, about what you saw in the morning. Almost everyone in the mine walks around smiling at each other and everyone seems so nice for one simple reason — the Amiability stat. At the starter levels it gets levelled by you simply walking around and smiling at everyone, but from level 6 you actually have to believe that you like the person in front of you, that you like talking to him and smiling and so on; you shouldn't feel any falseness. That's the only way to continue gaining experience. I remember one guy who got his Amiability as far as level 32. After all, this is not one of the main stats and you can get it up as high as one hundred."

Kart was silent for a moment, catching his breath, and then went on:

"As far as what happened this evening is concerned... A person finds it easiest to level up in what he practiced in real world. So what comes out on top here is... It's the skill of Meanness. In our mine most are levelling up in Amiability and Meanness at the same time. So that's why everyone tries to play some low and dirty trick on someone else: you can't strike directly, but arranging something that could lead to injury is quite doable. This is why people get very inventive in thinking up newer and more effective methods for doing this. You're new here, so people will be using the simplest stuff against you, like the trick that was played on you in the evening. Gradually these will get more complex, for which fact you have my condolences. Everyone has gone through this. As one good man, who, by the way, left for the main gameworld on parole, said, you can give our mine the following motto: 'The Hypocritical Mine' or 'The Mine of Hypocrites'. So that's the way things are around here."

Only swear words came to my mind for commenting on what Kart just said. God, what a place to end up in!

CHAPTER FOUR
THE PRYKE MINE. THE FIRST WEEK

"TOO-OO-OO! BAM!

So here we are. The second day has begun. I was having quite a dream before that interruption... There was me and there was the ore; I was mining it, but it was having none of that. It was running from me on little legs all around my section and throwing Rats at me. The Rats were dropping tails which were crawling after me. What nonsense!

As nice as it was to lie in bed, it was time to get up — the work was calling me. I glanced at Kart, who was dressing next to me, and in the end couldn't help asking:

"Kart, can you tell me something? You've already spent ten years here and I'm sure had all kinds of dirty tricks played on you by other prisoners. What else can I expect? I really don't want to be a 'training dummy' for those after experience gain. At the least I could snap back at them."

"The favorite occupation of everyone levelling

up in Meanness is to force someone to inflict an injury intentionally. The dirty bastard gets injured, falls down and suffers, but the person who inflicted the damage drops to the ground drained of Energy and dies in a couple of minutes. The higher the level of the person you downed like that, the more experience you get in Meanness. So many people here form groups in order to have at least some security. Bat, who you met yesterday, is the leader of the largest of these groups: his gang is made up of almost eighty people. He has the highest level in Meanness in the whole of the mine. You're new, so there's little sense in killing you straight away, but playing dirty tricks on you is easy enough."

"Are you part of any group?"

"Me? No, I'm not. Not interested. My goal is to serve my time and leave the Game forever; and those who level up in Meanness are the ones that plan to keep playing."

"But what does this stat give you? For example, Intellect gives you mana and increases its regeneration speed. But Meanness? I don't understand why people would want to level up in it."

"I don't know for certain, but from what others told me, in the mine Meanness is used only because it's the easiest thing to level up in: mix some sand into someone's food and you get a level. Just to give you a rough idea. But this stat mainly comes into full play outside the mine. After all, not everyone wants to become some great, dragon-slaying hero. Many choose to play the dark side of the game and become thieves and assassins. That's where this stat comes in handy. But, as I said, I don't know exactly what it gives you."

"Right, I see. How'd you end up here? After all, you don't get fifteen years for stealing lollipops," I asked and, seeing how Kart tensed up, I quickly explained why I needed to know this. "You see, I like to know the people that I deal with and of all the prisoners only you've been speaking normally to me so far. So that's why I decided to get to know you a bit better. Or is this subject over the line?"

"No, it's just that I thought.... that... Well, whatever — no harm in telling you the story: in real life I was one of the inner circle of a very influential person and knew very many of his secrets. When he went bankrupt, I was given a choice: either to tell all I knew or to get sealed in a capsule for the max term of fifteen years. They could not break me outside so they shut me in here; even rewarded me with a 'suitable' profession to boot: 'Informer'... You see, if I start to level up in it then probably in six months or so I will start talking about my boss in order to increase my level... And I don't want to do that, because even though he was a bit of a rogue, he always stood up for his own people and tried to help as much as he could. So it's better if I...."

Suddenly Kart started to tremble, fell on his bed and became surrounded by a faint glow. This didn't last long and soon Kart sat up and turned to me, looking rather pleased.

"Ah, I know why I like you," he smiled. "We've not had anyone new at the mine for over half a year. With you I started to increase my skill again, since no-one at the mine would listen to me for free."

"For free?"

"What did you think? People in here catch on pretty fast when making extra cash is involved. It's me rather than them who has the need to tell them something. And they have to be actually listening too. So that's how many try to make money out of me."

"If it's no secret, what are your other stats? You've probably already picked all four by now."

"Me? By now my Chattiness is up to level 19. Amiability is at level 8 – another must-have. Everyone's levelling in it, so I've joined the club. I increased Smithing to level 4, but then stopped. To be a Smith you need a large amount of ore and I spend virtually all of mine on the daily quota. I've reached level 10 in Mining, and it's not getting any higher, thankfully, since my Informing is at zero. This way I have to hand in 100 pieces of ore a day. Ah yes, Smithing is not a stat, but a profession. As for my other stats I have three levels in Marksmanship and nine in Endurance. Now I rather regret picking them. There are no real opponents at the mine, only Rats, and chasing them around is a nightmare. Even though you do get additional reputation for each tail, the amount of time you spend trying to hit one of them is ridiculous. And it's your pick that you have to throw at the Rat, because nothing else generates aggro with it. I tried throwing a bowl, a copper ingot, even a boot — all of it goes through the Rat as if it wasn't there. Throwing the pick is another world of trouble, since it often flies out of your section. And what if it hits someone walking by? Then I would be done for in the blink of an eye. So I just mind my own business and don't touch the Rats. Although my hands are just itching to go after them, to put it mildly. So much free reputation running around right under your nose, but you can't touch it. And I have just a little to go until Respect status too."

"But why would you be 'done for' right away? You'll be thrown back to level one, all your stats will turn to zero and you'll start levelling up again. What's the problem?"

"The problem is that the Game remembers the parameters of each person playing it. When a prisoner levels up his skills, he receives pleasure and he wants more and more. But when he dies, he loses all the points gained in skills and professions and won't get a new dose of pleasure until he reaches their level at the time of his death. For example, if I die, that's it. I'll never again feel the sensation I just felt from levelling up in Chattiness. Of course, I'll keep trying for a few more months and then just fade away. I'll be gripped by apathy. We already had people like that, so I had plenty of chances to observe this. When someone falls into apathy, he stops working and gets transferred somewhere else. That's the way the cookie crumbles.

"I read that the habit of gaining pleasure gives rise to Addiction among the prisoners, which on release is treated in rehabilitation centers. Everyone gets sent there once they finish their terms — it's compulsory. This is also the reason why those who regain their freedom do everything they can to avoid going back to Barliona: they will be given the same class, same profession and all the same stats, but the system would remember the last time they levelled up at the mines. You can create and delete three hundred characters, the system would still remember that you were in a prison. They would start at the first level, but in order to receive pleasure, they would have to bring all their stats and professions to their old level again. And this is very difficult. Many totally lose it, scream and attack other players or succumb to apathy. And again, they disappear from the mine. This is why ex-cons spend nearly all their time in Barliona continuing to develop the characters they had as prisoners, to avoid going back as prisoners and starting from scratch. And Meanness allows them to find their place in Barliona."

"How do you manage to avoid being set up by Bat and the others? After all, you are one of the highest level players at the mine. Level 11, right? Someone can gain several levels in one go if you die."

"It's simple. I managed to increase my reputation with the mine guards to Friendly and when someone tried to play me again, the governor gathered everyone and said that he would be very upset if anything happened to me. So it's been three months now since anyone touched me. Anyway, I've lost track of time chatting with you. We should go or we'll miss the food."

"Wait, one last thing. I discovered that I can cast healing spells, but that I can only heal someone else, not myself. Would you mind it if I healed you in the morning and in the evening? Only do me a favor: don't laugh, because the whole healing bit looks ridiculous."

"No problem, it might even be interesting: in all my time here no-one tried to heal me, most tend to want to do the opposite. Also, I've never seen a Shaman's kamlanie, so it should be interesting to watch."

I summoned the Spirits of Healing twice for Kart and, depleting my mana reserves, saw the now familiar message.

+20% to Intellect. Total: 50%
Your Hit Points have been reduced by 2. Total: 38 of 40.

What's this?

Attention, you have healed another player. You have unlocked a new stat: Healing. The higher your level in Healing, the less mana you need for healing spells and the spells themselves become more powerful. There is a chance for the spell to be cast again without mana.

Do you accept? Attention, you will not be able to discard an accepted stat once you activate it.

No, I had no desire whatsoever to become a healer, either in the mine or outside it. No thanks.

"Oooh..." said Kart, when a light wind from my spell ruffled his hair. "You know, it's ticklish and invigorating... Well, let's do it: as soon as your mana recharges, heal me. You dance pretty well too," Kart could not help smiling.

The morning meal acquainted me with a new type of dirty trick — putting sand in the food. Kart's prophesies came true. How did I miss the moment when Bat came up to me and, pretending to stumble, poured a handful of sand into my bowl?

"Oh, how clumsy of me... You're not going to

eat that, right? Give me your plate, I'll bring you a new portion," Bat was a picture of concern.

"No, thank you. I'll go myself. Thanks for the offer," Bat's showy friendliness seemed suspicious to me.

"No, no, that would be no trouble. Let me make it up to you. It wasn't nice what I did yesterday. It's just you were asking such a high price for the skins, so I acted on impulse. So, truce?"

"Truce, Bat."

"Truce."

"But I'll go and get the food myself, all the same."

When I came to where they handed out food, I showed the guard my food with sand and wanted to ask him for a new portion when I heard:

"Beat it! Each prisoner gets two portions a day: in the morning and in the evening, if he meets his quota. You've already had your first. The fact that you got sand into it is your problem. Eat it as-is."

So if I handed my plate to Bat... What a jackass...

Turning around I saw Bat smiling and shrugging, as if to say 'Ah well... didn't get you this time. But there will be others.' I'm gonna kill that scumbag.

The sand gave the food an unforgettable taste. I could eat it, but it was disgusting...

Attention: you have eaten a spoiled product: Buff gained: Energy loss reduced by 25%. Duration — 12 hours. You received a negative effect: The speed of skill gain reduced by 50%. Duration — 12

hours.

No, I'll torment him first, give him a good kicking and then kill him...

My section looked the same: ore veins, dust and Rats sneaking around. Rats were a good thing. I could do with extra Intellect and reputation.

Striking the vein without the added strength was noticeably harder. Even though I had level 3 in Mining, when the message telling me that my Energy had fallen to 30 appeared, as much as 40% of the vein's durability remained. This was bad, very bad. Never mind, tomorrow I'll be more careful. Before going to fetch the water I hunted down two Rats (+2 Rat pelts, meat and tails), first 'healing' each of them (+10% Intellect, +8 Experience, +10% Strength, +10% Stamina). Truth be told, the second Rat nearly had me when I missed it with my pick. I only had 3 Hit Points left after the fight. But that's fine: after getting some water, I finished the first vein (6 pieces of ore, +1 Experience, +5% Strength, +19% Mining, +2% Stamina). I still had 50 Energy remaining, so before starting on the second vein, I decided to show the Rats who was boss around here. The next Rat (+5 Intellect) gave me what I'd been waiting for so long.

Experience gained: +4 Experience, points remaining until next level: 75
Skill increase:
+5% to Strength. Total: 100%. Strength increased by 1. Total: 2.
+5% to Stamina. Total: 57%

And that's when it hit me. My whole body was filled with warmth, and it struck my head as if I just drunk a bottle of vodka, I started to shiver — it felt like being immersed in ecstasy. Overwhelmed by these sensations, I fell to my knees and groaned uncontrollably. So that's what the Holy Grail feels like....

Nothing else interesting happened until the end of the day. I downed 6 more Rats, bringing the day's total to 9 (+30% Intellect, +30% Stamina, +30% Strength) and crushed 6 veins (36 pieces of ore, +30% Strength, +113% Mining, +12% Stamina). Right, tomorrow I'll have to hand in 40 ore pieces. But that's fine, if I don't mess up with the food again. Also tomorrow I should raise my Intellect and Stamina to the second level, so the coming day was looking very promising.

In the evening I witnessed another set up. When the food was handed out Bat came up to one of the prisoners and saying "Hello, sweetie", started to grope him vigorously. The prisoner, more than surprised by Bat's behavior, pushed him away and showered him with choice swearwords. But he happened to push Bat in the direction of the Smithy, where picks were leaning against the wall. Pointing upwards. Bat fell on them and screamed at the top of his voice, his Health Bar was reduced by about 20 percent and the prisoner that pushed him fell and disappeared in about a minute, leaving a pile of gold pieces in his place. The governor turned up, watched the hologram of the incident, glanced over Bat, who was looking pleased with himself, turned around and left without a word, Bat gathered the pile of coins and walked away, with a prisoner entourage in tow. So, that's how dirty tricks are played in our mine... Slick bastards!

That's how things went on for four days. I healed Kart, killed nine Rats a day, after dancing for them, worked at the veins, and every day raised my reputation with the guards by 19 points through selling the surplus and Rat tails to Rine. I was now very careful with anyone standing close to me, so nothing bad happened to me during this time and no-one attempted to get all huggy. What really cheered me up was that I gradually began to save up money. It wasn't that much – only coming to 22 silver in the five days – but it was a start. If I get money things will start looking up for me. These thoughts filled my head each day as I left for work in the mine. What other good things happened in these four days? I've increased my Strength to level 4, my Intellect to level 3 and my Stamina to level 6, so I was on top of things as far as levelling was concerned. Around 50 Rat skins collected in my bag, but I was in no hurry to sell them – who knows what materials I might need for Jewelcraft? What if I needed a skin after I sold them all? I had to unlock my profession first and then decide what to do next.

Today was a significant day for me: I decided to see what Rine had for sale, so, after handing in the quota and selling the rest, I waited until Rine was less busy. What if I managed to get my hands on something useful? Didn't I have plans for a change of clothes? I did. And plans should be carried out.

"Good evening, Rine," I began, as I walked up to the dwarf. The vital necessity of making progress towards the status of Friendly with the mine staff only reinforced my habit of being polite to NPCs, which I developed over the years of playing in Barliona. After all, they could give you a quest or give you a trade discount or do something otherwise nice or useful. You never know with NPCs.

"And to you. You've done your quota and sold me everything else, so what can I do for you?" asked Rine, somewhat surprised.

"Well, I've saved up some money and decided to have a look what such a remarkable dwarf might have for sale. Maybe I'll buy something."

"Oh, in that case — my door is always open!" So, it looked like Rine was quite a salesman too. "Take a look: I have scrolls for various professions, 10 silver each, but you still have to pay me 20 more silver for unlocking a profession. I have all kinds of scrolls: Cooking, Leatherworking, Smithing and Jewelcraft. I've got any profession you want! All only 10 silver apiece too. How many would you like?"

"None, I'll stick to something more essential for now. An outfit or a new pick, for instance. The pick that you gave me is a bit of a pain to work."

"Yes, of course I have some picks. Quite a selection, to suit any taste, color or smell... Well, maybe not smell. Anyway, take a look," Rine began displaying different picks. "Here's one dealing 11 damage; this one does 12 and that one does 13..."

Rine showed me 10 picks in total, all with different levels of damage... If I understood things correctly, the higher the damage, the faster you destroy the vein, so I should choose the one with the highest – and still stay within my means, of course.

"Is 20 damage the maximum for your picks? Do you have anything higher?" I continued to test the water with the dwarf.

"Of course I do, but there's no way you can afford it. I can show it to you, if you like," Rine rummaged in his bag and took out another pick. He turned it over briefly in his hands and then handed it to me.

Well I'll be... If only I had a pick like this from the start, I'd have finished off all the veins around here!

Miner Rine's Pick. Damage: 25. +1 Mining. Energy loss when mining ore is reduced by 10%. Item class: Uncommon. Level restrictions: none.

I was all but drooling.

"And how much is this baby?" was all I managed to utter.

"Like I said, you don't have enough money for it. It costs 30 gold and you won't scrape together even one yet."

"You're right, Rine, such a pick is beyond me for now. All right, how much for a simpler one, with 20 damage?"

"That's easy enough, it comes to 10 gold," said Rine, looking at me slyly.

"Rine! This is daylight robbery! For a pick that does only double the damage of the one I already have you are asking 10 gold?"

"What did you expect? You'll work twice as fast with this pick. If you don't want it, don't take it, no-one's forcing you," Alt was spot on when he said that the moment you touched the subject of money the dwarf transformed into someone you didn't really want to deal with. What a shark.

"Rine, this is too much. Let's see the one with 15 damage. It can't cost that much.

"Of course not. It's just 3 gold. I'm practically giving it away for free here."

"And what can you sell me for 20 silver?" I could see that it was pointless to approach Rine with so little money.

"For 20 silver I can only offer you a pick with 12 damage. That's it. Here you go," Rine was about to hand me one of the picks.

"Hold it, Rine. Just hold on. Let's say I take the pick with 15 damage for 20 silver, but will tell you straight away that I'll start saving up for the pick worth 30 gold. And then buy it off you for 40. For me it's simply a must-have. You don't have much to lose: you give me a discount now and make extra profit later and I'll have obligation to you which I'll be fulfilling. I'll save up the needed sum in two months' time. Also, when I buy the pick for 40 gold, I'll return the one with 15 damage to you for free. What do you say?" I quickly blurted out, surprising even myself.

"Obligation, you say? And what if you fail to meet it?" the dwarf looked thoughtful.

"It's not like you're risking anything. If I don't keep my promise, you can take this pick back in two months' time and start selling everything to me at a triple cost and buying things from me at half the price."

The dwarf seemed to be thinking it over, weighing up the pros and cons, scratching his chin and mumbling something under his breath. I stood there, keeping my fingers crossed that he would agree. It would be very good to speed up my work by one and a half times. With that earning 40 gold in two months looked quite possible.

"All right, take it," Rine gave up, and gave me the pick with 15 damage. "And hand your money over here."

Skill increase:
+1 to Trade. Total: 2
Item acquired: Miner's pick: Damage: 15

Hurriedly giving Rine the money, in case he changed his mind, I went off and sat by the wall of the smithy. That's it, now I can take it easy for a bit. I wonder if Rine would have agreed to give me the pick with +1 to Mining right away? Hells, I should have asked for it in the first place. Bad move on my part, a real miss. What's that? I noticed that another timer had became attached to me in the meantime and took a closer look at it.

Obligation to Rine. To provide 40 gold to Rine in order to buy a pick. Duration expires in: 60 days.

No forgetting this, even if I wanted to — the system will bring it up and remind me.

There was nothing else to do, so I leant back on the wall and closed my eyes: 'Soon I will gain a second level. My reputation is growing slowly but surely, so I'm moving in the right direction. I should make an estimate of how soon I could leave the mine. I get 19 Reputation every day. At the moment I already have 99 of the 1000 needed for the status of Friendly, so that's fifty more days of work ahead of me. Altogether, that's not too bad. But then to get from Friendly to Respect I'll have to gain 3000 points, which is 160 more days. This means that in just over half a year I should be in the main gameworld. It's strange that Kart mentioned only one prisoner who left the mine. If gaining reputation is so simple, why is no-one here doing it? Or does everyone really like this place? I have to ask Kart about this.'

Kart... If we hadn't become good friends during this week, we were at the very least friendly. Kart told me many interesting things about local laws, customs and habits and in the process now just levelled up in his profession (in the space of a week it went up to level 20, which made Kart veritably ecstatic). He also advised me on how to act in any particular situation and how to behave myself around Bat and his gang.

A word about Bat. Judging by the fact that it has been four days now since anyone made any moves on me, some dirty trick of epic proportions was in the works. The happy looks shot in my direction did not bode well for me. Kart did not manage to find anything out, so all I could do was wait. I guessed that everything would become clear in due time. If Bat made an attempt to kiss me, I could try returning the 'affection' and see how he reacts to that.

"Mahan, watch out!" I opened my eyes as Kart's shout reached my ears and saw a mining trolley full of ore speeding towards me containing Bat, who was making a frightened face and screaming something at the top of his voice. 'If this whole contraption hits me, I'm toast.' I thought. Realizing that it would be physically impossible to get out of the way of the trolley, I stared as one charmed while my first death in the mine headed my way. What did Rine say? 'A very unpleasant experience?' I bet it's far from pleasant to get plastered across a wall by such a mammoth. Good-bye skill points...

Suddenly with a wild scream Kart smashed himself into the side of the trolley, overturning it on its side and making the whole contraption — Kart, Bat and the trolley — tumble away from me. In a few moments this clump of mess stopped and I saw Bat getting up. And Kart? What happened to Kart? Hells! Didn't he just cause deliberate damage?

I sprang to my feet and glanced at Bat. The fall stripped off about 80% of his Hit Points. Resilient bastard. Kart slumped on the floor nearby. He urgently needed water, otherwise he wouldn't survive. Kart's Life bar slowly but surely diminished. Fecking copper! I summoned a Spirit of Healing and ran for water.

Skill increase:
+5% to Intellect. Total: 70%
Your Hit Points have been reduced by 1. Total: 49 of 50.

'Get lost, I have no time for this!' — I waved away the message.

I ran up to the watering hole in a few seconds, but discovered there was no bowl to get the water with. Those lowlifes thought of this too. The water seeped through my hands, so I took off my robe and, having drenched it in water, ran back. Sanitation misgivings can go hang. Life is more important.

A large crowd of people formed around Kart. I pushed myself to the centre and saw Bat squatting by Kart and telling him something with a smirk:

"... told you that I'll get you one day. And now no-one can say that I provoked you. Didn't lay a finger on the governor's favorite."

Kart wheezed something in response. His Life bar was already showing only 28%. The devil take you.... I quickly poured two healings over Kart.

Skill increase:
+10% to Intellect. Total: 80%
Your Hit Points have been reduced by 2. Total: 47 of 50.

'Shut up! I'll switch you off to all the hells!' I opened Kart's mouth and started to squeeze my robe straight onto his face. The water started to dribble onto Kart, but missed his mouth – it was as if some invisible sphere got in the way and the water bounced off it, missing Kart's mouth. Friggin' hell!

"Ah, Kart's sidekick is here. Well well, my friend, you are just prolonging his suffering. And you won't get any water to him. There's nothing to put it in," giggled Bat.

I looked at the people standing around us. Although calling them people was a bit much — just a crowd of malicious prisoners, smiling sweetly and staring at Kart.

"Bat, give the bowl back! He'll die!"

Bat shrugged, as if to say that we all die and if someone goes early, that's not his problem.

"Friggin' hell, Bat! I'll give you fifty Rat pelts and bring you nine pelts a day every day for a month. For free, do you hear? Free! Give back the bowl, you bastard!"

"My dear boy, I've been at the mine nearly as long as Kart and in that time levelled up my profession of Leatherworking to the maximum level possible when using Rat skins. I buy and take them only in order to process and sell them at a higher price, and exchanging what I'll now gain for destroying Kart for some cash would be plain stupid. The entire mine contains only three people who haven't died at least once: Kart, myself and you. So get ready — you're next. Although don't fret, there's not much point touching you until you're at least level 2. But Kart's 11 levels are well worth it. He's the highest level character in the mine and made such a stupid mistake. I might as well have won the lottery."

Powerless, I summoned the last Spirit of Healing on Kart, extending his life by a few dozen seconds. I have to do something, but what???

"Take... my... bag... I... give... you... full access... Hurry..." I heard Kart's barely audible whisper.

I quickly grabbed his bag and tried not to get too surprised by what I saw inside. There was no time for that, although its contents were surprising enough. Firstly, the bag was an incredibly large one. It contained 40 slots. Compared to my 8 this was enormous. There were several Copper Bars, some incomprehensible devices, but the main thing was the

Copper Plate! Kart had a Copper Plate! And he said that he regretted investing in Smithing! There are no coincidences in this world.

Seeing Kart's Hit Points sinking to 35% made me unimaginably quick. I pushed everyone aside and like lightning flew to the mine, dipped the plate in the water and ran back. The water wasn't draining out of it. I had to make it! Kart must live!

When I returned, I didn't even have to push anyone aside — people immediately moved out of the way. I noted Bat's disappointed face with satisfaction, lifted Kart's head and carefully put the plate with water to his mouth. I made it! Only 10% of Kart's Hit Points remained. He began to drink the water in feverish gulps, slowly increasing his Hit Points and probably his Energy too. That's it, he'll live!

A few seconds went by. Kart sat up, looked at me and stayed silent. There was no need to speak, everything was clear enough.

Suddenly the governor appeared next to us. The enormous orc towered over all the prisoners, looking at us like we were little foolish children.

"What happened here?" his question, asked in a completely calm tone, made all the prisoners fall to the ground.

"We were loading the ore, Serk and Brick threw it to me on the trolley, where I sorted it" Bat began to explain. "Then something happened and suddenly the trolley started to roll; the chock probably slipped out from under the wheel. I was sitting inside it as it sped towards the smithy and was about to jump off when Kart came out of nowhere and hit the trolley. We all tumbled over and I almost died. You know Kart — he never liked me: so he probably decided to kill me. But he failed. It's just as well that my total Hit Points are a good 120. He may have stripped me of 101 of them, but I survived. And Kart fell down, which happens to anyone who inflicts intentional damage on another player. We were about to watch him die, but this jerk," he nodded at me, "found a bowl somewhere and brought water. Now Kart is alive and well and I don't know what to do. The law is the law: whoever deals damage should die and here it got all messed up."

"The law is the law. I agree," the orc waved his hand and a projection appeared in front of him.

✠   ✠   ✠

"YOU USELESS BAGS OF BONES, *hurry up with the ore loading. He could get up and go inside the barracks any time now. It's a perfect chance to finish him off," said Bat, sitting in the trolley and looking somewhere below him. "Did you check everything? It won't miss him?"*

"It shouldn't. It's aimed directly at Mahan. Boss, are you sure we won't die? After all, this is dealing intentional damage to another player," mumbled one of Bat's two accomplices, probably Serk.

"Calm down. We've taken the bowl of water for a reason. You'll remove the wedge, get stripped of Energy and collapse, and then Brick will revive you with the drink. Get it, Brick? Just try not getting the water to Serk, you know me. All right, ready? Now!" ordered Bat.

"Boss, why are you sitting in the trolley yourself?" asked Serk, preparing to knock the wedge

— 95 —

from under the wheel.

"I want to see him get splattered against the wall with my own eyes, see his surprise, his pain, and, of course, I want to be the first one to feel sorry for him, stroke his dead body, even shed a tear, if it came to it. One should level up in everything at once! Hit it!"

Serk knocked the wedge out and the trolley rolled down.

"Mahan, look out!" Kart's voice shouted and then Kart rammed into the trolley. The trolley, Kart and Bat tumbled into one big mass.

The recording ended.

✠ ✠ ✠

"I DIDN'T TOUCH KART, HE'S THE ONE who attacked me," mumbled Bat, now looking less sure of himself under the orc's gaze.

"The law is the law," the orc murmured thoughtfully. "For intentional dealing of damage to another player Kart is sentenced to being stripped of all his skills. Kart, get up."

Deathly-pale, Kart rose and lifted his head, looking the orc straight in the eyes. They looked at each other like this for several seconds and then something happened that I did not expect: the governor turned his gaze away.

"The law is the law, Kart," repeated the orc, took out his sword and looked ready to take Kart's head off.

Damn you all. Why can't people live in peace? Why in order for some to live, others have to die?

"Stop!" I shouted. "Kart was saving my life

when he rammed the trolley. He did not inflict any direct damage to Bat, so no law was broken here. And if someone has to be stripped of skills, I'd like to take Kart's place. Kill me instead — it's my fault that Kart was set up.

Your reputation with the Pryke Mine Guards has increased by 100 points. You are 801 points away from the status of Friendly.

'To hell with your reputation,' I waved away the message. 'What's the point of it if even at "Friendly" status people get their heads chopped off instead of getting helped?'

"Hm," said the orc. "A good exchange, a death for a death. But Kart broke the rules, so Kart will be the one to answer for it. As for why he did it, that's his business. Kart, are you ready?"

"Y-yes," mumbled Kart in a doomed tone.

The orc swung the sword and hit, and a small cloud appeared where Kart was standing, which hung there a few seconds and dissipated. The only sign of Kart was a pile of gold coins. All the prisoners stared at it, but in the presence of the governor no-one moved to pick it up.

"If anyone touches Kart's money, I will be very upset. Kart must pick it up himself," said the orc, turned around and left.

Suddenly Bat glowed, groaned, sinking to his knees, and started to half-moan something. A whole whirlwind surrounded him, lifting dust and hiding him from other prisoners. When the dust settled everyone saw Bat lying on his back and smiling with great satisfaction.

"Two levels!" Just imagine! I gained two levels in Meanness on Kart's account!" Bat shouted, as he got up. "That was... It was divine." Turning around Bat saw me. "You can relax now, Mahan, we won't touch you for sure until you're at least level 4, but after that..."

Kart is finished.... If he lost all his skills, that's it: as he himself said, in a few months he will wilt and be transferred somewhere else. And what do I do now? What's the point of levelling up in the full knowledge that in about three levels I would also be set up like this and sent for respawn? I looked at Bat's satisfied face and at the fact that he had only 19 Hit Points left. Gradually a plan began to form in my head.

What had Bat said? "There are just three people who have never died in this mine — Kart, Bat and me". Kart's already gone and I'll follow him soon enough.... So why wait?

I looked at Bat and began to plan my actions. Energy did not disappear immediately, but in about 2 seconds. The first strike had to come from above and from behind. The Energy will fall rapidly. The second hit must come upwards from below, so that the pick stopped over my head. By this time Energy will fall to zero and I will go down like a sack of potatoes. Correction: when hitting the second time I must lean over in order to fall forward. On top of Bat. The pick should inflict the third hit as I fell. 19 Hit Points. With the new pick I deal 19 damage, but how much armor does he have? What a pity that we don't get a strength buff with our evening meal, as it would have come in very handy right now. Bat is a Leatherworker and it's clear that he'll not be wearing low-level clothing, so it could block quite a lot of damage.

Bat turned around and headed towards the barracks surrounded by his people. Right, they've already written me off. I'm an expendable resource. Well, their mistake!

Less thinking, more doing! If Bat leaves then everything I just thought of will have been for nothing and I would never bring him down. Getting a better grip of the pick, I run after Bat. Suddenly Kiplev's song popped into my head:

Above me silence,

I ran up to Bat, swung up my pick and lowered it on Bat's head. Energy began to fall rapidly and the other prisoners stared at me, astonished. Just as well, less chance they'll interfere...

Damage inflicted. 6: 19 (Hit with the Pick + Strength) — 13 (armor)

That's some armor! But the main thing was not to stop now!

Sky, full of rain,

I sharply changed the direction of the pick's swing and took it back upwards. Bat was shouting something, the people around were shouting something, but none of this mattered any more. It's all finished for me, I just had to end it all for Bat as well...

Damage inflicted. 6: 19 (Hit with the Pick + Strength) — 13 (armor)

Energy level was at 5, my feet were giving way. Bat was falling down, this was good. I had to lean forward to make sure I fell on top of Bat. Another 6 damage wouldn't quite do it. Hells, and I was so close...

Rain is falling through me,

As I was falling down, drained, I hit Bat the third time. From above. Please let it be a Critical hit!

Damage inflicted. 6: 19 (Hit with the Pick + Strength) — 13 (armor)

That's it. It was all pointless. He survived, the bastard!

But there's no more pain.

But what's this? I was lying with my face down on something soft. It didn't feel like the ground. Something was blocking my eyes and I had no strength to lift my head and look around. Never mind, let's see if this works...

Damage inflicted. 1 (bite)

Bat's body flickered and vanished. And now it really was finished. Now I could die. There were no more people in the mine who had not died. Although, no. There's me, but soon I'll be gone too. The important thing was that I already thought of what to do with Kart to prevent him wasting away.

Suddenly I was struck with SUCH pain that I forgot all else. The world ceased to exist for me — it was replaced by pain. It tore me apart from inside, it ate away my skin and pierced me all the way through. I was pain and pain was me. I was probably screaming, wheezing, howling, but the pain would not go away; it only seemed to increase. Then it suddenly ended.

"...I repeat the question: Mahan, what happened here?" Air! It was an effort to make my body take a breath. The voice of the governor seemed like the gentle murmuring of a stream to me now. I was still alive and no longer felt pain. This was splendid. I focused on the orc. Well, would you show some emotion at last, you bastard? I'd just killed a person and the orc was standing there asking what's happened. The snow just fell down, that's what happened.

"Revenge. Revenge happened here. And this will happen to anyone who would touch Kart or me again."

"You were aware of the consequences of your action?" asked the orc. What was that? Did I glimpse a shadow of satisfaction? Or was I seeing things?

"Yes, I knew. And I already felt these consequences on myself."

"That's good if you did."

The orc once again grabbed the sword and plunged it into my chest. There was a quick flash of pain which seemed nothing compared to what I already went through and the world around me went black.

That's it. Goodbye skills.

I did not know how much time went by; something blinked and I found myself where I first appeared in the mine. Hello Pryke Copper Mine! I'm back. I took a step towards the barracks, but then fell to my knees and, as my jaw dropped, read the message that just appeared in front of me.

Quest accepted: "Revenge in the Mine!"
Description: Speak to the camp governor.
Quest type: Unique.
Attention: in connection with death and the settings of this game zone all your skill and stat levels have been nullified. Have a pleasant Game!

I simply don't get this game! What quest?

CHAPTER FIVE
THE PRYKE MINE. FIRST MONTHS.
PART 1

"COME MAHAN, THE BOSS IS WAITING for you," boomed the guard, who just a week ago had barely refrained from kicking me. Although to say that he refrained would be an exaggeration.

Nothing changed in the administration building: it still had the same paintings and carved leather-covered furniture. 'I wonder what's keeping this place so fresh and cool?' I thought. 'Is there a mage specializing in Cold spells in the mine?'

"Have a seat, Mahan!" the orc's heavy voice rumbled through the office.

I sat in the armchair and couldn't help thinking: 'How many people actually sat down in the governor's presence before? Or did I just happen to get lucky? For instance, the armchair was definitely not there during my last visit.'

"So, we'll start with the facts. First. You committed the first premeditated murder in the history of this mine. Before there were only injuries, arranged accidents, but no direct killing. Second. You tried to protect a sentient who helped you not to die. Moreover, you offered to die in his stead and self-sacrifice is very highly valued by the committee for the investigation of murders." A   committee?   What committee?

"Today a committee was called together for examining the incident involving an intentional killing of a prisoner. A decision was taken that the sentient known to you as Bat was guilty of attempted murder. You were exonerated of any guilt and it was ruled that you had a right to revenge Kart. Your action and the attempt to sacrifice yourself for another merit a reward – here you go," the orc handed something to me. I took some kind of a cloth and a message appeared before me:

Quest "Revenge in the Mine!" completed.
Reward: Miner's cloak. +1 Strength. +1 Stamina. Item class: Uncommon. Level restrictions: none.
Your reputation with the Pryke Mine Guards has increased by 1000 points. Current level: Friendly. You are 2801 points away from the status of Respect.
Experience gained: +600 Experience
Level gained!
Level gained!
Level gained!
Points until the next level: 400
Free stat points: 15

Well, I'll be... I wanted to jump for joy, but restrained myself. If the governor is a picture of calm, I should follow suit. But, dammit, this is great! Three levels, basically for nothing! And also a cloak that's quite something for a low level player! But above all – 1000 reputation almost for free! This meant a radical change to my plans for leaving the mine, making them a lot more realistic! But three levels, it's mind-boggling...

"I'm done here. I can answer any questions you have. If I remember correctly, you love asking them," said the orc, permitting himself a quick chuckle. Wow! We're making progress!

"I wouldn't go as far as 'love', but I'll ask all the same. Why is meanness flourishing at your mine? After all, this is a correctional facility. Here by default there should be no such thing as backstabbing and dirty tricks, but, in fact, if these aren't exactly encouraged, nothing is being done to discourage them... And then you see some committees getting together and making some kind of decisions. What's the sense in this?"

"Good question. A person pays for their crime by being torn away from the world he is used to and forced to work. And work hard at that. As for how that person develops from then on, that is a personal matter for each particular individual, a decision he alone can make. Some choose the path of a profession, while others an easier way. For instance, my mine contains 185 convicts who chose the shady path of development. That's from the total of 240 prisoners. This is entirely their choice and within the bounds of the mine they are free to do as they like.

The only limitation is that with this skill it is impossible to leave the mine on parole and they know it. As far as the committee is concerned, although each death in the mine is investigated most thoroughly, if it is proven that it occurred as a result of an accident, even if an arranged one, the case is closed. The trio that wanted to crush you with the trolley were found guilty of attempted murder and removed from our mine to another location."

"Is it true when they say that once the prisoners are no longer able to level up their skills they fall into apathy, lose interest in life and get removed from the mine?"

"I can hear Kart's voice in your words," said the orc. "Apathy can at times arise if a sentient is weak and cannot get over such a big loss. Such a sentient is then sent away from our mine to another place, where he can begin his development anew."

"And where is this..." I began.

"Enough! You are touching matters that do not concern you in any way. When a prisoner falls into apathy from losing all his skills, he disappears from the mine. It doesn't matter where he goes. That's all you need to know. And now – go."

"Another question, the very last one. You said that a committee was called together. When on earth did it have time to meet, if I died and respawned immediately after that? These two events just don't fit in the same timeframe."

"The standard respawning time is set at twelve hours from the time of death. The committee was gathered ten minutes after Kart's death, five minutes after Bat's death and three minutes after yours. The meeting where the decision on all three deaths was reached took forty minutes. So they had plenty of time."

Twelve hours? Yes, in Barliona that's the limitation set for respawning after death. But I simply didn't remember this time, it flew past me in an instant. Nice one. I wonder if the whole of the prison term could fly by like that. Eight years – in the blink of an eye... Eh, dreams, dreams.

When I came out of the administration building, something struck my eyes. There was a sense that something was missing from the surrounding world or, on the contrary, there was something extra or out of place, but I simply couldn't put my finger on it. Everything seemed to be there: the barracks, the smithy, the mine and the prisoners working in it, the ever-present heat and dust. Stop! Can someone tell me what happened to the ever-present heat and dust? Now I saw no such effects: the whole valley was clear and fresh. A small cloud shielded the setting sun, its burning rays softened to become pleasant and calming, and a refreshing slight breeze blew around me. Where would a breeze come from in a valley? It's surrounded by cliffs! I saw no such change when I entered the administration building, but it wasn't hard to admit that I liked the current environment a lot more. If that's the bonus for my reputation increasing to 'Friendly', I should double my efforts to get to 'Respect'. I wondered how the mine would change when that happened.

At the place of my death I found a whole silver coin: exactly half of what I had left after buying the pick. The orc probably said that he would be very upset if anyone touched my money. Although there wasn't much to take, since I put everything I had into Rine's pick with the attached obligation.

I decided that before heading out to work I would look into allocating the stat points I had gained. I had 15 free points. This was good. Adding 3 points to Stamina, taking it up to 7, I decided not to spend the remaining 12 points yet. If it took me a week to level up my skills this far, in the next few weeks I should be able to get them to an even higher level. But when the skills either stop increasing or begin to increase very slowly — or even after I leave the mine — these free points would be simply priceless.

I was quite happy with the result of the day's work: I broke apart 4 veins (22 pieces of ore, +4 Experience, +2 Mining, 40% Strength, +20% Stamina), killed five Rats (+50% Intellect, +20 Experience, +5 Rat skins, meat and tails). Now killing Rats was much easier – the status of Friendly permitted me to summon the Lesser Lightning Spirit, so before the Rats could get to me, I managed to knock some Hit Points off them. In addition, each strike of the Lightning Spirit made the Rat freeze for a few seconds, which enabled me to finish it off with the pick.

After waiting for the evening and handing in my daily quota, I started to look for Kart. There was no sign of him at the evening meal and he wasn't in the smithy. Where on earth did he wander off to?

I found him in the barracks. He lay still on the bed, curled up and howling quietly in a strange voice.

"Kart, are you all right?" I couldn't ask him

anything more stupid, but I had to start somewhere.

"Me?" replied Kart and lifted his head. Judging by the redness of his eyes, he must have got a fair bit of sand in them and had been rubbing them hard. I did not want to think about the alternative. "Of course I'm all right, what else can I be? For eight years I managed to avoid dying, survived where others bit the dust, but then you appeared and everything went to the dogs! Why the hell did I try to save you? Can you explain that one to me?" Suddenly Kart tensed up with pain, groaned and then curled up and started to howl quietly again.

"Kart, did you eat today?" I asked seeing that Kart was going into convulsions.

"No," rasped Kart. "What's the point? I didn't go to the mine today, so I have no ore to give to Rine. What difference does it make when I peg out: now or in a couple of months, when I'm kicked out of the mine?"

"You missed the mark, hot-shot. Get up and let's go for a walk," I summoned a Healing Spirit on Kart, grabbed him by the arm and dragged him away. "Walk with me and I'll tell you an interesting tale on the way. Afterwards you can tell it to someone else – after all, you are the Master Gossip!"

Kart looked at me with incomprehension, but got up and followed.

"So, here goes. The story runs like this. In a Kingdom Far Far Away there lived an handsome lad... Or was he just good-looking? It doesn't really matter. And so this lad got into an unpleasant situation – villains decided to do him in and run him over with a mining trolley. But the lad had a faithful Friend, who saved him, but at the cost of losing all his heroic might, which took him ten years to gain. And then the lad, that'd be the good-looking one, decided to help his Friend regain his heroic might, which the evil Dragon stole from him. But because he could not return the mythical strength to his friend, he decided to make his friend a renowned artisan, so that buyers would come to him from around the world and buy his wondrous wares, made with Smithing and Leatherworking crafts. You're getting the gist of this, right? As far as I can see we have no smiths here at the mine and your Smithing profession was only at level four, so we'll quickly re-level you in this. And your Leatherworking level was non-existent, so we'll be levelling that up too. I realize that a profession is one thing and a stat is another, but we'll break through all the same!"

At this point we came up to Rine. Kart started to double up again, so I poured another healing over him. Blast! My mana was at zero and we urgently had to sort out the food. It's just as well that there was still some time left.

"Ah, the die-hards have turned up. Mahan, you already handed in your quota for the day. And don't forget that tomorrow it's 30 pieces of ore that you owe me. And you Kart... Seems you've decided to play 'Who wants to be a lunatic?' game. Why didn't you go to the mine and work to get your quota today?"

Kart stood there sullenly and looked at his feet. I could see that he had no intention of answering. All right, let's play a trick and answer for him.

"Kart, your Mining is at 1 now, right? This means that today you had to bring in just 10 pieces of ore, if I'm not mistaken. Here you go, take it," I said and handed Kart my surplus. "I think this will just cover your daily quota."

Reluctantly Kart took the ore and, after thinking a moment, passed it to Rine.

"Oh, no. You can't do that. The prisoner must gather the ore himself and then hand in the daily quota to me," Rine began to argue, but I interrupted him:

"Rine, I remember our governor's words very well – the daily task of each prisoner is to bring in a certain amount of ore, determined by his Mining level. The boss did not once say that this ore could not be bought or obtained from other prisoners. Nor was it ever said that you have to work your hands raw in the mine: we were simply allocated a place for obtaining the ore to meet the quota, but whether it is mined or bought is up to us. For example, the governor personally promised me that if I find a Precious Stone, he would strike off my quota for that day. Consequently this proves that our main task is to hand in the daily quota. Kart's quota is 10 pieces of ore, and it is lying before you now. What's the problem?"

"But this isn't right..." said the dwarf, now sounding less sure. "If everyone starts to do this, then..."

"Then soon there won't be anyone to buy ore from in this mine and everyone will be sent for a respawn," the governor's voice suddenly sounded behind us. "What Mahan is proposing is not forbidden. Prisoners have a right to work together. If Mahan wishes to hand in Kart's daily quota for him, it's between Mahan and Kart."

Attention, a new stat has become available to your character: Charisma. Charisma determines the strength of the character's personality, his appeal, his ability to convince and to lead, and also his physical attractiveness. There is a chance that NPCs will offer the player unique quests.

Do you accept? Attention, you will not be able to remove an accepted stat!

Why not? In this gameworld only NPCs hand out quests and hold all the key positions. Even our governor is an NPC. So, I think that such a stat would come in handy and I'll still have three free stat slots.

A new stat has been unlocked for the character: Charisma. Total: 1

"If you take off right now, you'll still manage to get your portion of the evening rations," said Rine, after thinking a moment and taking Kart's ore. "The things convicts come up with – anything to avoid working," he mumbled to himself as he headed for the smithy.

We had won! Now my plans for pulling Kart out of the hole began to look more realistic.

"Allow me to go on with my tale, Kart," I said, when Kart returned from supper, somewhat cheered up. "As I said, our handsome lad could not return the heroic might, taken by the Green Dragon, to his Friend, but he could hunt foul beasts called Rats. And the earth was strewn with the prized skins of the

Rats. And so instead of going to the mines and hacking at the accursed ore veins the lad's Friend will be working Rat skins in the coming week and making all kinds of wondrous things out of them and so gain great happiness and esteem. And the meat of those enemy Rats can probably be cooked in a deep black pot or fried over a roaring fire, to make the Friend's life even more wondrous, because he'll become a renowned Cook, respected by all."

I paused and looked at Kart. Now I liked his look much better: gone were the pair of stupefied cattle-like eyes, where it was a struggle to find even a spark of intelligence. No, the eyes looking at me now were full of renewed hope and I could see that Kart's brain was fitfully going through different possibilities for levelling up. That's right Kart: unless you want to help yourself, I won't be able to pull you out.

"Kart, before I continue with my tale, I need to know how much money you have. Much depends on this. I only have 2 silver coins, which won't go very far."

"I have 104 gold, 25 silver and 45 copper coins," said Kart, looking in his bag. "No-one touched my money after my death, so I didn't lose anything."

"Great, then I can continue the story. And so the young lad advised his Friend not to mine veins in the near future, but to stand by the greedy Dwarf and buy surplus ore from other fellows working in the area for 11 copper coins. It shouldn't be hard to find such fellows, who'd be eager to gain some extra ever-coveted profit, since the miserly dwarf buys the ore for only 10 coins a piece. And thus, the young hero's friend will have another joy — a daily tribute and good skimmings, which he will use to develop his Smithing profession. By this time the handsome lad will have learned Jewelcraft and will take heavy Copper Ingots from his Friend in order to level up his own skills. This way they will live happily and level up ever after. And that's the end of the tale, and anyone who failed to listen well is likely to be done for pretty soon."

Attention! A new stat has become available to your character: Chattiness. Chattiness determines your attractiveness to NPCs, ability to gain trust and also allows you to be popular with crowds. There is a chance that you will talk your opponent to sleep for a set amount of time.

Do you accept? Attention, you will not be able to remove an accepted stat!

No thanks. It's quite enough to have Kart running around with this stat.

"Well, aren't you just the handsome lad," Kart said suddenly, giving me a sly look. "That's it! The patient will live! But do tell me, the hero's good friend, what the heck do you need me for?"

"Well, you see, Kart, my life is just so boring, so I just have to give myself something to do. After all, there is absolutely nothing else to do here. It's not like I should get back to work now. Instead let's go and find Rine. I have around 60 Rat pelts in my bag and we can start training you up in Leatherworking."

We found Rine in the Smithy. He muttered something under his breath when he saw us, but still came out to greet us, wiping his hands on the apron.

"What, just can't sleep? It's late and it's an

early rise for a day of heavy work tomorrow. Or you've already got the quota for the rest of the week on your hands? Or maybe the rest of the month?"

"Lay off the sarcasm, Rine. We're here on business. We want to be trained. Kart here needs to learn Leatherworking and I need to learn Jewelcraft. We also both need to be taught Cooking."

"So, they decided to get an education," muttered the dwarf, annoyed. "You just won't behave like all the normal prisoners — go to the mine, gather all the ore that you can, hand it over to me and be happy. Oh no — you've found yourselves some loopholes to get out of doing work. I don't like slackers, they're just..."

"Rine!" Kart and I shouted at once.

"What? 'Rine!-Rine!' I don't want to teach you anything until you start working properly. I don't want to and I won't."

Way to hit a roadblock. The stubborn dwarf got it into his head that we have to be put back on the righteous path. Well then — two can play at this game.

"Fine, Rine, have it your way: if you don't want to teach us, don't," I said and looked in the direction of the administration office. "Kart, what do you think? Has the governor already gone to sleep or not?"

"Who knows? What do you need him for?" asked Kart in surprise.

"What do you mean, what for? If I am not mistaken, at the mine we have, or rather had, the opportunity to learn any profession. At any time. Rine doesn't want to or simply can't teach anyone right now, so I'll go and ask the governor to teach me," I said, starting to head for the administration. Well, Rine. Your move!

"Ehh... Mahan!" shouted Rine, after I was already halfway there. "Stop! Sod you..."

I turned around and looked at the dwarf.

"What's with the shouting, Rine? It's late already, you'll wake people up," I was the very picture of surprise, but inside as pleased as the cat who got the cream.

"How can I not shout, when I have to chase those looking to be taught all around the mine? Who needs this, in the end, me or you? Come here, both of you, and I'll do some teaching. Have a look at things first. Now, let's think. The unlocking of one profession costs 20 silver coins, tools for the professions — Jeweler, Leatherworker and Cook — cost one gold each. And then there's the 10 silver for each recipe. I have 3 recipes for Jewelcraft, 4 for Leatherworking and only 2 for Cooking. This means that in total" — Rine paused to think — "I need 7 gold and 40 silver from both of you. So hand over the money and let's get to the teaching."

Skill increase:
Charisma stat increased by 1. Total: 2

"Rine, who do you take us for? Why are you hiking up the price as if you're trading on the main market square of Anhurs? Where have you seen so much being charged for teaching? Are you the Imperial University? And the tools? It's as if they are actually made of gold, the way you're asking a gold for each. They'll not fetch above 2 copper coins. However, we're prepared to take everything for 2 gold."

"For 2 gold? Mahan, you must be kidding me. I almost broke my back dragging these tools and recipes all the way from the neighboring town, had to earn the ability to teach you losers with my own sweat and blood and you're offering me just 2 gold for all this? How can I even talk with you after this? 5 gold and not a copper less."

"Rine, this is outrageous! We break our backs here in the mine from dawn till dusk, barely see the light of day and earn mere pennies! Where would we get 5 gold? If we turn out all our pockets, spend several days standing by the barracks begging, we won't gather more than 3."

"Really? You're the ones breaking your backs? You're the ones not seeing the light of day? Don't make me laugh! The end price is 4 gold, and that's final. That's as low as I'll go, beg as you might."

"Agreed! Kart, can you contribute some money here?" I looked at Kart, who was doing his best not to crack up laughing. "I seem to be all out right now."

Skill increase:
Trade increased by 1. Total: 3
Your reputation with the Pryke Mine Guards has increased by 10 points. You are 2780 points away from the status of Respect.

Having taken our money and clearly in better spirits, Rine went to the smithy and brought several items and pieces of paper.

"Right, let's get the teaching out of the way first," said Rine, making a series of movements with his hands.

You gained the "Cooking" profession. Current level 1.
You gained the "Jewelcraft" profession. Current level 1.

"You'll figure out how to use the professions yourselves, I'm not going to nanny you here. Now, take these, you're going to need them. You have to read the papers in order to learn the recipes."

You received an object: Jeweler's tools (Attention! Does not take up inventory bag space).
You received an object: Cooking kit (Attention! Does not take up inventory bag space).
New Jewelcraft recipe learned. Copper Wire. Total: 1 recipe.
New Jewelcraft recipe learned. Lesser Copper Ring. Total: 2 recipes.
New Jewelcraft recipe learned. Lesser Copper Chain. Total: 3 recipes.
New Cooking recipe learned. Fried Rat. Total: 1 recipes.
New Cooking recipe learned. Rat Burger. Total: 2 recipes.

"And don't forget," Rine said, looking at me, "in 59 days I'll be expecting my 40 gold."

Kart looked at me in surprise, so on the way back to the barracks I had to tell him of how I bought the pick and my obligations to Rine that came with it. After telling him, I had to spend some time refusing

Kart's money, insisting that I would be able to earn the needed amount. I barely managed to decline his help, but had to promise that if I failed to save up the needed sum, I would definitely ask Kart for financial assistance. Perhaps Kart is also a dwarf and just knows how to hide it well? He grips on like a leech.

I greeted the morning with joy, but decided to find whoever thought up this damned alarm clock and tell him just how wrong he was. Very wrong. And I'll be very emphatic.

As we agreed, Kart did not go out to mine. For today his timetable would keep him busy in the smithy, where he'd be levelling up his Leatherworking profession. He said that now he was able to make a Leather jacket, trousers and boots, but that these clothes gave no bonuses other than increasing armor. Today I had to look into what rings and chains I could make with Jewelcraft. Would they also come without any additional stats? That would be a pity. But I'd get to that later, now I had to focus on the ore.

After I smashed away the day's second vein, I discovered that a stone of some kind, about the size of my fist, was lying on the ground with the ore. Strange, I had not encountered one of these before. Could it be some sort of a unique bonus? That would be nice. I should show the stone to Rine in the evening, he should know what it is.

By the end of the day I could happily boast of level 4 in Mining, 2 levels in Strength and Intellect and of 58 pieces of Copper Ore, 8 Rat skins, tails and pieces of meat. Not bad for a second day after all my stats were reset.

Immediately after handing in the quota and the

Rat Tails, I decided to level up my Cooking profession, because gaining independence from the food we were handed out twice daily would have been a nice bonus. I didn't have that much Rat Meat on me, but quite enough to explore the benefits of this profession.

I opened my cooking book and started to examine what recipes I had:

Fried Rat.
* **Description: Fried Rat meat may not have a very pleasant taste, but in dire need would prevent you from dying of hunger. On use: Restores 20 Hit Points. Minimum level: 1**
* **Crafting requirements: minimum Cooking level 1.**
* **Ingredients: 1 piece of Rat Meat.**
* **Instruments: Cooking Kit.**

Rat Burger.
* **Description: Processed Rat meat. When eating, please do not think about what it is made of. On use: Restores 40 Hit Points. Minimum level: 1**
* **Crafting requirements: minimum Cooking level 1.**
* **Ingredients: 2 pieces of Rat Meat.**
* **Instruments: Cooking Kit.**

When I started to roast the meat it stubbornly refused to come out the way it was pictured in the cookbook. It was either overdone or underdone or burned to a cinder altogether. Having used up 10 pieces this way I stopped wasting my supplies and sat down to gather my thoughts. I was clearly doing something wrong, but simply didn't understand what it was. That stingy dwarf — he could have told me how to use the professions, but no, he decided to be stubborn: you'll learn for yourselves. So now I had to try and figure this out.

How do I roast the meat? I stick it onto a skewer, put it next to the fire and start to turn it slowly. I think that's how they roasted a deer in some film I once saw. I didn't know of any other methods. In the real world all food was made by the imitators and I did not level up in Cooking when I played my Hunter. Now I had a reason to regret that in all the 30 years of my life I had not once tried to find out how food is actually prepared. So what am I doing wrong? No answer presented itself and I started to go through the tools in the Cooking Kit, trying to figure out their function through their names: saucepan, ladle, frying pan, a contraption which stated that it was a meat mincer. I wonder how it cuts the meat if it only has a rotating screw and not a blade in sight. The kit contained a few other incomprehensible objects, which I did not bother to take out. What we had here was a monkey with a set of chess.

Unable to find a solution, I went outside the smithy and saw Alt. We seemed to be on normal terms, so I decided to ask him if he knew anything about Cooking.

"Greetings, Alt. Listen, do you happen to know how to roast meat properly? My attempts lead to it immediately getting crusted up and either undercooking or getting completely burned."

"Do you put the frying pan over a very hot fire?

Try reducing the heat, maybe that'll do it."

"A frying pan?" my surprise was so natural that Alt couldn't help grinning.

"Why don't you tell me how you go about roasting the meat?" he said, a hint of sarcasm in his look.

"I copy how I've seen things being roasted. I screwed... I mean I skewered the meat onto the spit and held it over the fire, turning it around from time to time. But nothing came of it."

"Nor will it. This isn't like swinging the pick, here you have to know what you're doing. Let's go inside and I'll show you. With this it's best to show once instead of explaining ten times."

Alt took one of my instruments by the name of 'frying pan' and put it over the fire. After waiting a little while, he tossed the meat which I handed him onto it and started to turn it from time to time. The smithy began to fill with quite an appetizing smell. Just a few minutes later Alt took the fried piece of meat off the frying pan and gave it to me:

"It's ready. Do you get it now?"

I nodded and, putting the meat on the table started to copy Alt's actions. The pleasant aroma of frying meat once again spread around the smithy.

"And now you turn it: see how the sides have gone brown?" it turned out that Alt had been standing near me all this time and watching my actions. I would have to find a way to thank him for the help — this was a rare thing in the mine. After the meat was completely cooked I took it off the frying pan. Now the result looked a lot like the illustration in the cookbook and I found myself almost drooling over it.

Skill increase:
+30% to Cooking. Total: 30%

In an hour I fried all the meat that I had, increasing my Cooking to 5. Almost 80 pieces of Fried Rat should have allowed me to completely bypass handing in the daily quota — I had no shortage of food supplies. And if I started to sell the meat to other prisoners, I'd probably make a profit. Strange that no-one had thought of this before.

Taking one of the prepared pieces I ate it, trying not to think that just a couple of days ago this meat was literally running around my section of the mine. No, that's life, that's the way things are, sorry Mr. Rat.

Attention! You ate a foreign object and lost your daily food buff. -1 Strength, Energy is lost 50% faster. If you do not receive a new food buff within the next 12 hours, penalties will be imposed. Have a pleasant Game!

...! Penalties like dying from your stomach digesting itself? I had seen Kart in that state and had no desire to try it on myself. But now it was clear why no-one was offering their Cooking services. Anyone levelling up in Cooking here only does it for the pleasure it generates.

As I walked around the smithy to sell the meat I had just fried to Rine, I saw a show put on by none other than Kart. He stood by the dwarf and shouted with abandon:

"Come over! Hurry! I'm buying ore surplus for 11 copper coins! Come over! Show your goods! Get your money! Only today and only here will you get this great offer! I buy ten Copper ore pieces for the price of eleven!"

With such talent, and his Chattiness stat, the guy was priceless. A crowd gathered around, offering to sell Kart their surplus. In the evening we'll have to see the results of his trading. I waited for Rine to get free and, coming up to him, first sold him all the meat, before getting down to business. If Rine bought raw meat at 2 copper, he offered only one for the fried variety, saying that I spoiled the whole lot. I decided not to argue, but made a decision not to do any more Cooking in the mine. Not only was it useless, but also unprofitable. When all else was settled, I had one more question to ask of the dwarf:

"Rine, I had this thing land in my lap today," I showed him the stone. "Can you tell me what it is? I've not come across this before: this stone must have some unique purpose."

"Unique, you say? Let me have a look," replied Rine, taking my stone. He rubbed it in his hands, handed it back to me and continued with a sly look: "Well, lad, why don't you go to the administration and see for yourself just how unique your find is. It is a good stone, of course, but it is of little use to anyone except a Sculptor. I have a small pile of stones like this. Do you want me to sell them to you at one copper at face value."

Again, I was wrong to get all hopeful in thinking that I had managed to get hold of something unique. When will I learn...

I hang on to the stone as a reminder to curb my flights of fancy, took the Copper Ingots from Kart, who was busy trading with other prisoners, and headed for the smithy. Now I had to get my head around Jewelcraft. A worm of doubt started to wear down my confidence in anything useful coming out of that either.

So, what things could I make? I opened the page with professions and began to study it.

Copper wire
❖   **Description: used in the crafting of copper rings and neck-chains.**
❖   **Crafting requirements: minimum Jewelcraft level 1.**
❖   **Ingredients: 1 Copper Ingot.**
❖   **Instruments: Jeweler's Tools.**

Lesser Copper Ring.
❖   **Description: Lesser Copper Ring. Durability: 30. Adds 1 random Stat from the main list: (Strength, Agility, Intellect, Stamina, Rage). Minimum level: 1.**
❖   **Crafting requirements: minimum Jewelcraft level 1.**
❖   **Ingredients: 2 Copper Wires.**
❖   **Instruments: Jeweler's Tools.**

Lesser Copper Chain
❖   **Description: Lesser Copper Chain. Durability: 30. Adds 1 random Stat from the main list: (Strength, Agility, Intellect, Stamina, Rage). Minimum level: 1.**

❖ **Crafting requirements: minimum Jewelcraft level 2.**
❖ **Ingredients: 3 Copper Wires.**
❖ **Instruments: Jeweler's Tools.**

At the first glance this did not look like much, but for me it was a cause for celebration. Rings with stats! In Barliona a player could wear up to 8 rings at the same time, so if I had rings with additional stats, then... mmm... Right, I must stop daydreaming, where was my 'reality-check' stone? I still had to make a lot of wire and only had 6 Copper Ingots. Too little, hells... Perhaps I should start learning Smithing myself? No, let Kart level up in that.

Making the wire turned out to be a rather involved task. After an hour of exertions I managed to make only one piece of Copper Wire. The only consolation I had from this self-torture was the message:

Skill increase:
+50% to primary profession of Jewelcraft.
Total: 50%

Another hour. I needed another hour, but the message that my Energy hit the 30 mark, the darkness gathering outside the Smithy door, and the awareness that tomorrow I'd have to bang away at the ore again forced me to stop my work and head off for a much-needed rest.

Kart pleasantly surprised me. Not only did he reach level 3 in Leatherworking, he also managed to buy 95 pieces of Copper ore for just over 20 silver.

Tomorrow he would embark upon the fascinating activity called Smithing. It turned out that my Jewelcraft needed quite a lot of copper ingots. Considering that one ingot is made out of 5 pieces of ore, I dreaded to think how much of it we would have to mine or buy.

Next evening, after handing in my daily quota, tired, I sat down for a rest in the shade by the smithy. Although my body was at full Energy and did not feel any fatigue, working at the mine completely wore you out mentally. Today I made a record: 12 smashed ore veins. If you deduct rest and trips to get water, that was an hour per ore vein. I didn't even touch the Rats today. I reached level 6 in Mining, level 3 in Strength, level 8 in Stamina and gained 67 pieces of Copper Ore. Today I still had to bump up my Jewelcraft to level 2, but I could not force myself to work again, so I sat in exactly the same place where Bat had nearly killed me and enjoyed a cool breeze. It was like being on holiday!

I closed my eyes, tried to relax and fall asleep. I'd take a short nap now and then continue working like a dog; but as soon as I began to drift off I heard a hushed conversation, which knocked any sleep right out of me.

"You reckon Bat won't be back?" asked a voice, which sounded rough, with a crack and a lisp. I don't even remember hearing one like that in our mine.

"No. It's been a while now and there's no sign of him. His gang is beginning to get worried, a few have already asked to join mine. Did any come to you?" said the second voice, which I recognized. It was one of the dwarves, who, according to Kart, headed the second largest gang after Bat.

"One or two did turn up. I even gave them a job to do to see what they're made of: to rub out Mahan. I sense that Bat didn't disappear just like that — Mahan had a hand in it. Do you remember how he downed Bat? I was watching my back for days after that: what if I'm next? Who can tell with this Shaman: everyone comes back reset to zero after respawn, but he returned with three levels."

"You're right: Mahan must be a rare scumbag. I agree that he should be rubbed out. Rine's become a real pain with the Rats already: he can barely contain his joy every day at the sight of Mahan's rat tails and puts me down for not doing the same. Can you believe that? Mahan is the only one in the mine who can cast spells and I get told off for not killing Rats. I could strangle the bastard myself."

"No worries, I set the date. It's either Mahan or them. They have three days to send him off for a respawn and they'll be in the clear. And then we'll have a chat with him ourselves, explaining that standing out from the crowd is not a good idea. We'll acquaint him with the fact that he'll have to pay us every month if he doesn't want to keep starting from scratch. But enough of him, let's get to the business at hand. If Bat doesn't return his 80 mooks should be shared. I propose we keep things simple and split them half-half."

"Agreed. Let's do it tomorrow after food."

"See you there then."

The local 'Vito Corleones' walked off and I felt a drop of sweat trickle down my back. It was good that the sun had already disappeared: I was in thick shade and they simply didn't notice me. Or they'd have rubbed me out right there and then. Hardened bastards. To plan a murder of another human being, even if it's a virtual murder, so calmly and casually is harsh. Especially if I am the human being in question and the murder is set to take place in the next three days. Hells, what should I do? Complain to the orc? There's no way he'd listen to me. He'd just label me a paranoiac and send me off to work. Kart? What would he be able to do? Nothing. But what can they do to me? Set me up? Then I'll be careful and won't be provoked. There is nothing else they can do to me. This isn't real life where you can just stick a shiv in me. 'Wow, some turn of phrase I have in my arsenal.' I thought and even laughed to myself: I know about the shiv, but not about cooking meat on a frying pan.

I got up and headed for the barracks. I had no desire to focus on wire-making, so sleep was the only other option. I would soon have to resolve the situation with that pair that decided to set some thugs on me. The sooner I do it, the better things will look for me — I really hated living in a state of uncertainty.

The morning greeted me with pleasant sunshine, a cool breeze and slight problems.

During the morning meal, the place where the empty bowls were kept turned out to be empty. When the prisoners complained to the guards, they said that there were enough plates for everyone and that if one of the prisoners took them all that's between that prisoner and the rest. They should have come earlier to get their portion. In the end the food was put straight into the hands of the prisoners. Good thing it wasn't too liquid and did not flow out between the fingers. But even this was no simple solution. The green and bubbly porridge was hot, so almost everyone threw it to the ground, screaming, waited until it cooled down and then ate it. Well, well. It looked like we weren't going to see much surplus ore being sold — people would be lucky to hand in their daily quotas. But what bastard nicked all the bowls? The answer came soon enough. When the next prisoner dropped the hot porridge to the ground, thereby turning it into "spoiled food", one of the prisoners standing nearby was engulfed in a whirlwind of light. He probably just levelled up in Meanness. I made a special note of his disgusting mug, which was now smiling at others' misfortune.

I did not have to check the temperature of the porridge with my hands — Kart shared his plate with me. The thing turned out to be quite useful and I decided to ask him to make me one as well.

In the evening, after handing in my quota, I saw five prisoners standing around the guard handing out the food and looking silently at the vat. I came up to Kart and pointed out the group to him with a questioning glance.

"Those five were unable to meet the daily quota, so they didn't get any food. Tonight they will be respawned," said Kart with a sigh. "Despite working until the very last moment, until just thirty minutes before the food stops being served, each is still short of 10 to 12 pieces of ore. It's a pity about Sakas. He's a good guy, despite being an orc."

"Hang on, you're saying just 60 pieces of ore would save them? Then why hesitate? I have 24 pieces, how many do you have left?" I gave Kart an exacting look.

"I have around 40 on me. Hang on, you want to sell them the ore?" it finally dawned on Kart. "I must be getting slow not to think of it myself," he lamented.

We made it in time. All five of them had money on them, so Kart and I were not left out of pocket. Although for myself I decided that I'd give them the ore even if they had no money. Even if I didn't really know any of them, one can't run away from one's conscience: if I had a way to help and didn't do it, it would eat me alive.

The next day witnessed a harsh set up of yesterday's bowl prankster and I discovered another interesting feature of the local cuisine. The people in the mine turned out to be quite inventive: if you buy a granite stone from Rine, crush it into crumbs and mix it into a plate of food, the meal would acquire an 'interesting' debuff. In particular, the prisoner loses 10 Hit Points every 10 minutes. Thus, if you don't want to die you have to drink water at least once an hour. With the excess water he started to lose profession and stat points. All that with six more hours of the debuff ahead. That's why the prisoner was now running around the guard and demanding a change in food. He begged, threatened, threw himself at the vat — and went right through it. When his shouts changed to screaming, the governor turned up. The orc saw a recording of some sort, said something to the prisoner, who then immediately shut up, turned around and left. Needless to say, from that evening no-one saw that prisoner around the mine any more.

CHAPTER SIX
THE PRYKE MINE. FIRST MONTHS.
PART 2

I N THE EVENING I DISCOVERED WHAT levelling up in Jewelcraft was like. It took me just an hour to make the second wire. Quickly glancing at the message telling me that I had gained experience in my main profession, I took out the next Copper Ingot... and the world suddenly stopped. A strange feeling came over me: Kart stood nearby, ladling molten copper from the smelting pot, and it froze in the air, barely touching the ingot mold. Walking around Kart and marveling at this effect, I noticed that a point of light began to form somewhere in my chest and shine out through my robe. The shining started to grow and increase in brightness, while a pleasant warmth started to spread through my body. In a few moments the light became so bright that I almost shut my eyes. When it had filled the whole of the smithy, there was a flash of light, and for a few moments I shone like the sun. I opened my eyes and saw that the world around me was so full of color that even the perpetual greyness of the mine could have vied with a rainbow in the richness of its hues. A couple of seconds went by and everything started to move again, returning the world to the familiar grey. It was simply impossible to describe the sensation that I felt at that moment — the reluctance to return from such a beautiful, colorful and wonderful world made me utter an involuntary exclamation, "Noooo!" That's when I understood that levelling up in Jewelcraft would now become my top priority. The effect from levelling up in the profession was only slightly spoiled by the swearing of Kart and other workers, who cursed as they rubbed their eyes from the bright light.

Kart also worked hard for the past two days: he had a stable supply of ore from other prisoners. Our savings diminished, but we stuck to the plan, not deviating from it in the slightest. Our main aim was to start making rings.

And that moment finally came: the day of the forging of the rings had arrived.

According to the Jeweler's handbook, the technique for making them was quite simple. You take Copper wire and wind it around a mandrel (a circular core of the correct diameter). After making two rows of ten turns, you carefully take the ring off the mandrel and wind a second piece of wire across it. You then weld the ends of the second wire and that's it — the ring is ready. Or so they say!

I killed the first four hours on winding the wire around the mandrel. You wouldn't call the result of my efforts neat even if you've had a few drinks too many. Even when it looked like I'd succeeded in winding the wire correctly, there was the problem of how to take the resulting ring off the mandrel without breaking it. I spent another four hours on this, because it meant I had to rewind everything once again. And when I finally managed to take the coiled wire off the mandrel without destroying it with my clumsy fingers, I accidentally squeezed the ring and crushed it. My agitation knew no bounds. Why is this so hard, compared to working with ore? There you just come, swing your pick a few times and get a result, but here you make one wrong move, breathe out of turn or look the wrong way and any result evaporates. At least the wire didn't break with such frequent use.

I spent a couple more hours mucking about with it and understood that it was time for a break. It wasn't working — by now I was ready to tear this wire to shreds. In the absence of any better ideas, I came out of the smithy and sat by the wall. As Kart put it, other prisoners had started to call this spot the 'Place of Shaman's Power' amongst themselves. I spent all my free time there, turning the stone I had mined around in my hands. Of course a Shaman wouldn't do something like that for no reason! He's probably communing with the spirits and the stone is his conduit into a different world... What a bunch of morons.

My first day of ring-making ended in my complete capitulation, but it did have one positive point: Kart made Rat-skin coats, trousers and boots for us. Even if these clothes gave no stat bonuses, the total increase in armor from 6 to 13, as well as the look of the outfits, made us feel a lot more safe and comfortable. At least now I no longer resembled a zebra.

The morning of the next day found me in the smithy: for the first time I was up before the alarm. It was a sign of progress and that today was the day I would make a ring. Not making one was out of the question!

I took the wire in my hands, closed my eyes and started to imagine the sequence of my actions. For a while I could not concentrate, until a Copper Wire appeared before me. I could then begin visualizing my actions, which was a lot more effective. So, I had to develop an algorithm. I would start with winding the wire around the mandrel. Where's the mandrel? Here it is. Turn after turn... no, I don't like this turn: let's unwind it. And again, turn after turn. Now it was coming out all right. No, just here it needs to be tighter. This one came out well: I was pleased with the result. Now to press a little here and hold it here – that's it! The ring came off. Now I take the second wire. It's long, but that's all right. Starting just here, holding down with a finger. The first turn was good, so we go for the second. No, this I don't like – the gap between the turns is too large. Trying again: the first turn, second, third, and on and on. That's it. Now we connect the ends of the second wire, heat and weld them. Yes, the ring is ready. So that's the algorithm that I had to follow.

The first thing that I saw when I opened my eyes was the reflection of a bright light in Kart's eyes. What's he doing here? Everyone's still asleep! And where did all this light come from?

Skill increase:
+15% to primary profession of Jewelcraft. Total: 15%
+5% to Agility. Total: 5%
+3% to Stamina. Total: 3%
Item created: Lesser Copper Ring. Durability 30. Intellect +1. Minimum level: 1

My hands were holding a completed ring, surrounded by a gradually fading glow. Did this mean that instead of imagining how to make a ring I was actually making it? Was I meant to do it this way every time? Seems a bit daft. Illogical. I should try once again with my eyes open and do everything with my hands and not my thoughts. I did, however, like the fact that my Stamina and Agility were increasing, if only slightly, with every ring I made. Did this mean that the more intricate and repetitive work I do, the more I improve my stamina and agility? Pretty good, if you ask me.

I spent just a little under four hours on making the next ring. The second wire was not as easy to twist with my eyes open, but I managed it.

Skill increase:
+15% to primary profession of Jewelcraft. Total: 30%
+5% to Agility. Total: 10%
+3% to Stamina. Total: 6%
Item created: Lesser Copper Ring. Durability 30. Stamina +1. Minimum level: 1

I had enough time to make one more ring

before the day was out. It gave +1 to Agility. Something had to be done about this — I was not a big fan of creating rings with uncontrollably random stats. Of the three rings that I made only the one with Stamina was useful, which could not be said of the others.

I took the Intellect ring and stated turning it in my hands. So why did you end up with an Intellect bonus? Was it because I made you with my eyes closed? Why don't I try and remake you?

Closing my eyes, I imagined the ring before me with its Intellect bonus. Letter 'I' appeared next to the imagined ring. Other possible stat bonuses were Strength, Agility, Rage and Stamina. A row of letters 'Str', 'A', 'R' and 'Stm' appeared near the rings. Now came the question: why was letter 'I' chosen at the creation of the ring and not any other letter? Good question, for which so far I had no answer.

But, what if...

Creating imaginary pliers, I pulled letters 'Str' and put them right next to the ring. Letter 'I' moved to the row with the others. Eh... if I could only do this with my eyes opened! I could not think of doing anything else, I left letters 'Str' on the ring and opened my eyes.

I then shut and opened them again. The message that popped up remained in place:

You used a Jeweler's ability to change stats on crafted rings. The maximum durability of the ring has been reduced by 3. The ring stat bonus of +1 to Intellect has been replaced by +1 to Strength.

Right, let's have a look at the ring properties.

Lesser Copper Ring. Durability 27. +1 to Strength. Minimum level: 1

Bingo! Watch out Pryke Mine, here I come!

I redoubled my efforts in ring-making and the first takers turned up in just a couple of days.

"Hello Mahan. Do you have a minute?" I opened my eyes and saw Alt before me, looking somewhat impatient.

"Hello, Alt! Take a seat. What can I do for you?"

Settling himself next to me, Alt took a moment to gather his thoughts and finally began:

"Mahan, a rumor is going around the mine that you know how to make rings with stats. Is that true?" I nodded and Alt continued: "That's good. Sell me 8 rings with Strength. In return, seeing as you are an old friend, I will give you one silver for each ring!"

"A whole silver!" I chuckled. "You're the very picture of generosity, Alt! But try to use your head for a moment. To produce every ring I use 2 Copper Ingots. Each Copper Ingot is made from 5 pieces of Copper Ore. The cost of ore with Rine is 10 copper and Kart probably buys it for 11. Therefore just the cost of materials for making a ring comes to two and a half silver, excluding the work itself. Can you imagine how much time is needed to make an ingot, then make the wire and then twist a ring together? And you want all that for one silver? Alt, I thought you a more reasonable guy."

"All right, so how much do you want for it?" asked Alt, somewhat befuddled.

"I won't sell a ring for less than two gold," my reply was firm.

"But this is daylight robbery! This is"

"Alt, one ring with a stat bonus costs two gold. If you don't want it – don't take it, you're the one who came to me. Just think of the benefits you'll get if you buy my ring."

Skill increase:
+10% to Trade. Total: 10%

"You're one greedy Shaman. No human kindness in you," said Alt, disappointed, and started to get up. "What benefits are you talking about if the cost of the ring will never be recouped?"

Alt turned around and was about to leave. Hang on a second! What happened to buying the ring?

"Hold a moment, Alt! Before you leave me all fraught with anger and disappointment, let's have a little chat. Have a seat again and let's make your brain do some work, Mr. Artist. Now, look: the maximum level of Strength that you can get working in our mine is 12 and the average level that most have is 9. Even if you buy only 2 rings and increase your Strength by just 2, you are set to gain a much bigger profit from it than the four gold you'll spend. In effect, for you two Strength rings mean 4 additional Copper Veins mined out a day, that is an additional 20-25 pieces of Copper Ore. Even if instead of selling it to us you sell it to Rine at 10 copper, you will be getting 4-5 silver coins a day. That's at the very least! Thus, in 40 days you'll earn back the money spent on the rings right now. And then you'll be simply working for your own extra profit. This will lead to a new pick, a larger bag, and even new rings, which will also start earning extra for you in a month's time. Think Alt, just think! By investing in the rings now, you are investing in the future."

Skill increase:
+20% to Charisma. Total: 20%
+10% to Trade. Total: 20%

I'm some talker!

"Another thing. I haven't forgotten who helped me to get the hang of Cooking, so here you go. This Strength ring I'm giving you for free. See the difference when you are mining the ore with it and without it, and then come talk to me tomorrow," I handed Alt one of the rings I had made, doing all I could to fight the thrift fiend within me, which was screaming that this was robbery and sheer wastefulness. Calm down, horned one: this is advertising!

The next day the whole of the mine knew that I could make rings with stats and the stream of gold began to flow.

Kart and I had a strict daily timetable. In the morning I went to the mine and spent a couple of hours killing rats, levelling up my Intellect, gaining Experience and getting skins for Kart, I then handed the tails in to Rine and made rings until the end of the day. Hunting Rats became sheer pleasure — after I put on eight Intellect rings I killed Rats non-stop, without ever running out of mana. My section, Kart's section and those of a couple more prisoners who, for the price of a ring permitted me to hunt there, had enough Rats for me to bring down 30-40 by noon and increase my reputation with the guards by 60-70 points every day. Kart began his mornings with making Copper Ingots, then moved on to work on Leather and finished the day by trading with other players. It turned out that clothes that he made were also in demand with the prisoners — everyone was fed up with the stripy robes. The only downside of this lifestyle was that there was practically no time left for rest.

A couple of weeks went by with such a work schedule. I even forgot that there were plans to bump me off and the date set for that had come and gone. Such thoughts were completely displaced by the daily routine. With the aid of Rats I advanced to level six, bringing my free stat points to 22. I increased my Intellect to 8 by killing Rats and healing Kart. By constantly crafting rings I brought my Jewelcraft to level 6 and also increased my Stamina to 10 and Agility to 3. The main thing was a guaranteed daily income of 16 gold coins, out of which only one was spent on buying materials. Thus the net profit was... Well, one could say it was something to be proud of. I wondered what we would do once the prisoners ran out of money, although each was probably able to pay at least 16 gold. I hoped to get about 3500 gold off all the prisoners. We did agree at the start that 30% of this money belonged to Kart, but this was a minor detail. And why did I first think that Jewelcraft wasn't a worthwhile profession?

'As soon as I hit level nine in Intellect, I will assign all my remaining stat points,' I decided and then heard a shout from the overseer:

"Mahan and Kart — the boss wants to see you right away!"

The comfortable surroundings of the administration building and the governor behind his desk were the two unchangeable things in this world. I even wondered: when the orc turned up around the mine, did he do it in person or was it a projection? I had to come up with some excuse to come here and have a look. Simply too curious! It would be pretty funny if we had several identical governors: one constantly behind the desk and the other one coming and going.

"So you've come," the familiar bass of the governor rumbled through the whole office. "You know, Mahan, you're all I hear about these days. First the killing and now it's been three weeks since you mined any ore and yet you're still alive; and also these rings of yours... Rine has already been complaining to me that it's been three weeks since prisoners brought him any ore outside their daily quota. And when Rine starts talking to me about losses, that the mine will soon go broke with prisoners carrying on like this, snatching profit right from under our noses, I have little choice but take measures, don't you think?"

The first thought that popped to my head was that Akela does not speak like this. Akela speaks in short, thought-through phrases, each carrying great meaning, but here our governor has exploded with a veritable verbal torrent. Why was that, all of a sudden?

"In three week's time our Regional Governor will be having a reception dedicated to work and productivity of all the mines," the orc continued. "And what can I show him? Only the fact that we are barely managing to fulfill the quota, the fact that no additional income is going into the treasury and that we are simply rubbish at our work."

Oh my, that got him going. And he doesn't even need to shout: his calm voice makes the hair on your back stand up and you simply want to fall down and whimper pitifully. His Charisma level must really be something else. Does this mean that we'll have to pack up our little ring business? Well isn't that just sweet?

"The reception will take place in three weeks' time. I need a present for the Regional Governor to confirm the status of my mine as one of the best. And since one of you is a Jeweler and the other a Smith, in two and a half weeks I expect you to craft an item that gives a total stat increase of 5 — a present worthy of representing my mine. Now go!"

Quest accepted: "Present for the Regional Governor".

Description: In the course of 17 days craft a piece of Jewelry which gives a total stat increase of +5. Quest type: Unique Limitation: only for Jewelers.

Reward for completion: +500 Experience, +500 reputation with the Pryke mine guards, +3 to the Jewelcraft profession. Penalty for failure: -1500 reputation with the Pryke mine guards.

Judging by Kart's surprised face he had also been given some sort of a quest. Yeah, I bet it's his first quest in all the ten years he spent at the mine. But to me, who's barely been here a month, getting quests is nothing new, and unique quests at that. Although the fact that failing to complete the quest would mean such a big reputation hit was very bad indeed. I had already started to dream of leaving for the main gameworld in the next few months.

"Mahan! " Kart began once again, as soon as we left the building. "Can prisoners really be given quests? I've not seen or even heard of anything like this in all my ten years here! This overturns all previous ideas about the justice system! "

"How come? After all, you've levelled up your reputation with the guards to Friendly. You don't get your reputation up by engaging in all kinds of dirty business, like Bat, for example. So it's no surprise that quests don't get given out to them. "

It was far-fetched reasoning, since I myself had no idea why the mine governor had presented us with such a quest all of a sudden. Why had he decided to reduce our reputation? After all, the chances of completing the quest were very close to zero. At the moment I could craft rings that only gave a +1 stat and I had no other recipes and neither did Rine — I had already asked him about this. He refused to bring in any new ones, saying that such matters have to be decided by the camp governor. Since the orc didn't give us anything when he set us the task, asking him for a recipe would be pointless.

"Kart, what quest did you get? Mine is restricted to Jewelers only, but you're no Jeweler, so you couldn't have been given an identical quest."

"Mine's a simple one: to make a total of 20 flat

Copper bars of a particular thickness and width and then ensure that your daily quota is covered for seventeen days — the entire time set aside for the ring to be crafted, as I understand it. You'll be making a ring, right? Mine also comes with the condition that your quest is completed and the item is crafted. Have you already thought of how you're going to make it? What do you need the bars for? Keep in mind that I don't know how to make them and that Rine doesn't have such a recipe, so I'll be making them blindly, by trial and error. All by myself. Mahan, we really must complete this quest, understand? If I succeed, I'll get 500 reputation! I'll gain Respect and get the hell out of here! You hear?! You have to make that ring!"

It was like being struck by lightning — "By trial and error. All by myself." So the governor is confident that we can complete the quest, or he wouldn't have given it to someone with the reputation rank of Friendly. We just have to show an ounce of creativity!

When we arrived at the smithy we were greeted by another disappointment. For some weeks now the other prisoners only approached us to buy rings and no-one tried to play any dirty tricks on us. We had become relaxed, a little too relaxed. Only Kart and myself worked there during the day and in the evening we were joined by another thirty humans, dwarves and an orc, who specialized in woodcarving. The orc turned out to be quite a decent guy — interesting to talk to and not prone to attempts at flattery aimed at getting a discount on the rings from us; he was simply holding up a conversation and was quite good at it too. When he worked the whole of his attention was taken up with the piece of wood in hand: he seemed to live it, listen to it and mumble something to it. But the items that his hands made from it were a marvel to behold! Once he was done with it an ordinary stool would turn into a work of art. It felt like a travesty to sit on something like that in anything less than a tuxedo. He had truly gifted hands! But I'm digressing... So, what happened was that the smithy was empty. No, of course it was still full of tools for different professions, but what Kart and I left there had vanished. I still only had that small beginner's bag, so I had to leave things in the smithy from time to time in the hope that no-one would pinch them. For several weeks we've not had any problems, and then this happened. Someone 'cleaned up'. This included 200 Rat Meat, 60 Rat Skins, 32 Copper Ingots and I didn't know how many pieces of processed Rat pelts, a memory that didn't slip Kart's mind, judging by the change in his expression. Although I lie: they didn't take absolutely everything: my 'reality check' stone was left behind. Scumbags.

The guards were soon called, but had little to say to us that was of any use. It was all 'Yes, we can watch a hologram of how several prisoners took out your things. And yes we can have a chat with them that stealing is bad and they'd better return it, only to get a predictable answer: everything that's not being kept in private bags is common property. 'Finders, keepers' and all that. And if Kart and I were unhappy with this state of affairs, we could, of course, fly into a rage, punch them in the face and whatnot, but in general we would do well to take a hike now, since we were interfering with the guards' break time.'

This means that we're shutting shop with the whole ring business. I had plenty of money by now and selling rings to people who are prepared to set me up at the first opportunity makes little sense. I'd rather sell them to Rine and get a reputation boost to boot. Speaking of Rine. I think the time had now come for me to give him back the owed forty gold and get a new pick. And also, as experience had shown, I had to buy myself a bigger bag, to avoid any thefts in the future.

Rine was hammering at something in the smithy.

"You again?" he was clearly in bad spirits. "What now?"

"I came to fulfill my obligation: pay you the 40 gold and collect my pick. Here it is," I said and handed the coins and my 15-damage pick to Rine. If I knew anything about him, this was certain to cheer him up. Gold was coming his way!

"Obligation? Yes, good." muttered Rine, somewhat tense, and then took out the pick and handed it to me. "Here you go. Anything else? No? Then you can stop distracting me from my work."

Item acquired: Miner Rine's Pick: Damage: 25. +1 Mining. Energy loss when mining ore reduced by 10%. Item class: Uncommon. Level restrictions: none.

No, something was definitely going on with Rine, I just couldn't put my finger on it. What got into him? The normally smiling dwarf was tense and snappy.

"Rine, what happened? You're not yourself today. I just gave you forty gold, but you're acting as if you've made a heavy loss again."

"Right, Mahan: You've got your pick, now get out of here."

"Rine, I'll give you ten gold if you tell me what happened. Do you hear this? Ten gold just for the information! Look here" and I put a stack of coins before the dwarf.

Finally! His eyes regained their normal greedy glint, he now looked focused and I was once again looking at the same old wry dwarf. I don't know why I needed this, but it felt much better that way. A barely detectable hand movement and the money on the table was gone. Rine is really quite something, I didn't even see him move!

"Once a year we have an open day at the mine. The prisoners get visitors, who tell them about the outside world. The next one is set to take place in a week's time. My granddaughter, the little squirt, decided that she wanted to see how ore is mined and how precious stones are found. She's crazy about gems, a true dwarven lass," said Rine with pride. "I'll give her a tour, that's not a problem, but she's gotten used to 'granddad' giving her different presents. And right now I can't think of anything, so I'm getting annoyed with myself: time is slipping away and I still have no present to speak of."

"Maybe you could use some help?" I uttered the standard phrase for getting a quest and silently swore at myself straight away. If the dwarf does give me a quest, where will I get him a present for his granddaughter? Right, I'll have to watch my tongue, or I'll get into real trouble.

"Do you think you'll be able to? If you manage to surprise my granddaughter, you'll not regret it. I'll give you a bag with 70 slots as a present. So, will you do it? Just keep in mind, you have just one week for this."

A bag with 70 slots? Of course I agreed to this! I'll give this quest a good think later.

"Of course I'll do it, honorable Rine. In a week's time your granddaughter will have her present for sure. I am a Jeweler after all!"

Quest accepted: "Present for Rine's granddaughter"

Description: In 7 days' time produce a piece of Jewelry that would surprise dwarf Rine's granddaughter. Quest type: Annual. Restriction: only for players with the reputation of Friendly and higher with Pryke Mine Guards.

Reward: +100 Experience, +100 reputation with Pryke Mine Guards, 70-slot Bag and permanent discount of 20% when buying items from Rine. Penalty for failure: -500 reputation with Pryke Mine Guards, permanent doubling of the price when buying items from Rine.

Five days had elapsed since I got the quests, but I had made zero progress towards completing them. I just simply couldn't think of anything. I made twelve rings every day, but not one came out with stat bonus of greater than 1. Not a single one! I tried everything I could think of to get the needed result. I remembered the moment when I made my first ring and each day tried to reach the same state, but nothing came of it. When selecting alternative stats for a ring I tried to add several letters at once, but this experiment resulted in the ring falling apart after losing all of its durability. Things weren't really working for Kart either. He was mucking about trying to make metal sheets, but they kept coming out either too long or too short or too bent or too crooked — he had to make each of them with hammer and anvil since there were no casting molds. I had no idea why I might need these sheets, all 20 of them. But enough for today. I just had to relax and have a rest. So I was sitting there, holding my stone in my hands, just sitting and staring into space. Gradually my thoughts began to gather around the stone.

It's so strange that I've become so attached to it. There was nothing special about it: in the month that I had it I had studied every centimeter of it. It was just an ordinary piece of granite, half the size of my fist, just a collection of numbers that my brain perceived as a stone. But why do I keep carrying it around with me? Why the thought of it won't leave me alone? Without realizing it I began to toss this stone up with my hand, following its flight path with my eyes. Up — down. Why do such stones even come out of ore veins? What is their purpose? Do the sculptors need them? In that case they would occur more frequently, but after smashing a great number of veins I got such a stone only once. Up — down. Although Rine really does have a good pile of them and it looks like nobody wants them. Up — down. I may not have been long at the mine, but I understood by now that nothing happened here purely by accident. Up — down. Take the governor's quest, for example. Why did he give it to us? Is it an ordinary quest for prisoners with the status of Friendly and their profession levelled up past a certain point? Up — down. I don't think so. For instance, someone like Alt has probably reached the status of Friendly and his Artist profession is at least at level six, but if Kart hadn't heard of anyone in the mine getting quests it looks like Alt wasn't given any. Up — down. Why? To deplete us of cash? That's stupid — the boss could have said that the rules forbade the prisoners from possessing more than a handful of coins and taken the rest for himself. Up — down. But he didn't do that. Up — down. Why?

Up — down.

Up — down.

Up — down.

After I tossed it up one more time the stone felt unusual. Or rather, wrong. I stopped tossing it up and down and looked at it in surprise. It was the same stone, but I could feel that there was something wrong, out of place or false about it. It was strange, but I sensed that the stone was uncomfortable in its current form, that is felt imprisoned. And this feeling was so strong that I involuntarily took out my Jeweler's burr and began to remove excess mass in order to free my stone. I understood this stone — we were both inside a prison, but the stone has a chance to escape, a chance that I could grant it. Somewhere at the back of my head a thought flashed: 'So you're talking to stones now?', but I brushed it aside. The stone was unwell and needed help, which I was able to provide. I'd deal with my mental state later.

First I needed to clean up here and file a little just here. And in this bit I had to be very careful or I would damage the stone. And in this place all the excess should be removed. This piece is all wrong as well, but this other one belongs here, but at a different angle. Now we're talking! And what do we have over here?

I don't know how long this went on for, but when I suddenly realized that the stone I habitually played with took on its correct shape I came to myself. I had to nearly shut my eyes, because the light that shone from the stone in my hand was so bright and so rich that it was impossible to look at. Gradually the glow faded and I was able to open my eyes. Several prisoners stood around me and their faces, usually covered by masks of fake amiability, were full of extreme surprise.

I felt a warmth in my chest, like that when levelling up in your main profession, and I turned into light, there was an explosion and the whole world changed color. No, it didn't change in hue, it just completely changed. Before this, levelling up in Jewelcraft happened inside the smithy and the world could only be glimpsed through the gap of the door, but this time the walls could not hide the beautiful world of the Pryke Mine. Why on earth was anyone so eager to leave this place? It is so beautiful! The colors faded, the mine returned to its usual drab state and I was pounded with a torrent of messages.

You have acquired a class ability 'Essence of things': you can now feel the essence of a thing irrespective of its appearance. Attention! This

ability does not enable you to feel the essence of things concealed by spells of 'Hidden Essence' level and higher. Ability level is determined by character level.

Skill increase:

+1 to primary profession of Jewelcraft. Total: 7.

New Jewelcraft recipe created. Precious Stone: Stone Rose. Total recipes: 4.

Precious Stone created: Stone Rose. Intellect +3. Minimum level: 5.

Attention, a new stat has been unlocked for the character: Crafting. Crafting influences all professions, determines the ability to independently learn the finer points of a profession and permits the creation of unusual items. There is a percentage chance that you will be able to independently discover and learn a unique recipe.

Do you accept? Attention, you will not be able to remove an accepted stat!

I struggled to read the flashing messages and was quietly reeling. A nice little session I just had with that piece of stone! After reading over the description of Crafting one more time, I accepted this stat. I thought it might come in rather useful.

A new stat has been unlocked for the character: Crafting. Total: 1

I now turned my attention to the stone in my hand. It was a stone no longer: I was holding a small (about half the size of my palm) beautiful stone Rose, made with such a degree of detail that one could see drops of dew on the petals. Did I really make this? Incredible! And now I have a recipe for making such Roses, which means that I can make as many of them as I like.

But there was more! More importantly, the Rose increased Intellect by three points. This meant that if it is combined with a +2 ring, I would complete the quest given by the governor. Also, if she's crazy about stones, Rine's granddaughter should find the Rose to her liking, which means that I have this quest sorted too.

"Mahan, you woke up!" Kart's happy shout put a stop to my train of thought.

"What do you mean 'woke up'? I was simply sitting here, doing some work," I said, surprised.

"Doing some work, eh?" grinned Kart, taking a seat beside me. "If you call sitting down in one position for two days while cutting something out of a stone oblivious to your surroundings 'doing some work', then yes. What's there to worry about? We brought you food, but you took no notice of it. So we had to feed you like a baby!"

Two days? I had been cutting out the Rose for two days? While being spoon-fed all the while? Must have been quite a sight! Stop! Two days?! Today was the deadline for completing the quest from Rine! What was the time?

"Kart, where is Rine?"

"He's here somewhere, taking his granddaughter for a walk in the grounds. We have a visitor's day today, so he's showing her the sights.

Kept asking how you were doing. He even came up to you a couple of times, shook his head and walked away muttering something to himself. Will you tell us what's going on?"

"Later Kart, no time now. I must find him as soon as possible!"

"You don't have to go far for that — there he is," Kart gestured somewhere behind me, I turned around and saw Rine with a little dwarven lass, who was running around our mine like a supersonic jet. She looked about ten, her black hair stuck out in two pony tails and the image was completed by a long polka dot dress. An endless torrent of questions reached my ears:

"Grandpa, when granite is found, it's handed over to you, yes? Grandpa, does granite have a soul of its own or not? Grandpa, can you show me what can be made from it? Grandpa..."

That's some granddaughter Rine had there. Suddenly they were standing right next to me and I saw a questioning look in Rine's eyes. It was actually more pleading than questioning. I nodded.

"Stay right here a minute, don't run off anywhere," Rine told his granddaughter in a strict tone and then walked over to me and whispered. "Well? Did you manage it?"

I handed the Rose over to him. Rine took a few seconds to look it over and then his face broke into a smile. He shouted:

"Where are you running off to, lass? Come here, grandpa's got a present for you!"

In the flash of an eye the little girl was at Rine's side. A fresh trail of dust indicated that she got here using her feet rather than a scroll of teleportation.

"Here, take this. I found just the present for a fidget like you," said Rine and handed the Rose to his granddaughter.

The little girl quickly snatched the present and started to examine it. She looked at the Rose for a few seconds and then looked up, her huge eyes filled with tears, and shouted: "My grandpa is the best dwarf in the whole world!" and jumped up to embrace Rine.

Quest "Present for Rine's granddaughter" completed. Reward: +100 Experience, +100 reputation with Pryke Mine Guards, 70-slot Bag and permanent discount of 20% when buying items from Rine. To receive the bag, contact Rine.

"Mahan, drop by in the evening," said Rine in a happy whisper as he hugged his granddaughter. When he put her back down, she began running around the mine, screaming: "I have a Rose! Grandpa gave me a Rose! My grandpa is the best dwarf in the world!" I could see that her parents had their work cut out for them!

In the evening I visited a very pleased Rine, took the new bag off him and headed for the smithy — the governor's quest wasn't going anywhere and I only had ten days left to complete it.

I had barely touched my work when three men walked into the smithy. Two I did not know and the third was Kart, who at this time was usually busy making Copper Ingots. Come to think of it, I did remember one of them — he was among the five to whom we sold our surplus ore after they failed to meet their daily quota. Had they come to offer their thanks once again? Of course, that's nothing to turn your nose up at, I'd even enjoy it. But this felt rather strange. When they saw me they glanced at each other hesitantly and headed in my direction.

"Mahan, we need to have a chat," started Kart.

"All right, let's talk then," I responded, in full incomprehension.

"Let's go outside, since it's a bit crowded here," Kart went on, glancing around the smithy. In the evenings the smithy, which was divided in two parts, was full. Rine was working on one end and the other was full of prisoners. Here Kart made Copper Ingots, Sakas was always carving something from wood, Alt painted his pictures and another couple of dozen people got on with various jobs. On the whole it was full of normal work activity.

"Let's go out then, if we must," I responded and followed the three outside. Kart seemed to have some unfathomable plan in the works.

We walked a few meters away from the smithy, then they all stopped and turned towards me.

"Mahan, this man's name is Bohn and he can tell you all about it himself. Should have done it a while back, really, but you were too busy all the time so we never got around to it. Go on, Bohn."

"When you rubbed out Bat, his group was thrown into turmoil; some of the people started to leave for other gangs, while others decided to go it alone. One of the latter even decided to play that joke with the plates. Rick and I," he nodded in the direction of the third guy, who had remained silent all this time, "also decided to join Grom's gang. But we would only be accepted if we sent you off for a respawn. I'm sorry, but we prepared ourselves pretty well — bought stones off Rine and crushed them to put them in your plate later. But the idiot who stole the plates messed it all up for us. I did not manage to mine my quota and if not for you I'd be the one taking the respawn trip. You helped me, even though you didn't have to. So, instead of you we put the crushed stone into that idiot's plate. As a result Grom didn't take us in, since we failed our job, and we decided to join you, because it's very dangerous to remain alone in the mine. People are wary of you here and are reluctant to cross you directly. Even Grom wanted to get to you by using someone else. That's why we went to Kart, as your right-hand-man, and asked for an audience. Kart agreed on the condition that we would watch your back. So for the last two weeks we made sure that no-one touched you and helped Kart feed you when you got stuck with that stone of yours. We only failed with your items, since we didn't know you left stuff just like that in the smithy. The probation period set by Kart had ended, so we now come to you with the question — will you take us into your gang?"

I had to take a seat. Right there and then, since I didn't expect this at all. Me, have a gang? But why am I the last one to find out about this?

"Kart, what the hell is going on here?" I forced a question out of myself.

"You still don't get it? Then I'll explain. Although I'm very surprised at how slow you are. Really, knowing you, I thought you'd be quicker on the uptake. From the moment that you sent Bat off the mine, you became a central figure for those focused on levelling up in their professions. Haven't you noticed how people have been coming to you for advice? Remember how a Leatherworker and a Sculptor had an argument over a work station in the smithy? What happened? You said that the Sculptor came first, so the place was his. And that was it, the matter had been settled, no-one said anything, your word was the law. Didn't you yourself notice how you've taken the place of the boss of the craftsmen in the mine? You may be an unofficial one, but you're still a boss."

"What the friggin' hell do you mean by a 'boss', Kart? What are you talking about? Would anyone dare to nick a boss's stash of items? I can tell you that no, they wouldn't. But ours did get nicked, the whole load of it and afterwards we were told to get lost quite emphatically."

"Mahan, you're such a naive clod," smiled Kart. "Although, truth be told, quite a few things happened while you sat there oblivious to the world around you. Remember: as long as you're making the rings you'll remain untouchable in the mine — the benefits received by the people using them are just too high. So no-one would want to get on your bad side just for a small amount of experience in Meanness. While you were 'off-line' creating, not only was all the stolen stuff returned to you, in the form of money at least, since those idiots immediately sold everything to Rine, but it was even topped up with 30 gold as compensation. And the oafs who took our things will be working for us for free in the mine, while other prisoners personally make sure they're not slacking. Official apologies and assurances of peace were relayed to you, although I believe that none of that really mattered to you at the time. And these two chaps didn't just feed you for two days in a row, but also prevented three attempts to drop some crushed rock into your food. So, I congratulate you, Mahan, you are now the leader of those who took the path of levelling up in professions."

"And what do I do with all this?" I uttered reluctantly.

"Obtain the official status of a supervisor from the orc," replied Kart and gave me a list of some kind, "here you go, this is the list of people who signed confirming that they want to be under your supervision. And that's without us asking everyone, but only those whom we were sure of. Fifty seven people in total."

Bloody hell! Do I even need this? Did anyone ask me whether I wanted to be a boss and be responsible for 57 people? All this was probably so clearly readable in my face that Kart chuckled and said:

"Calm down, other than paying a visit to the orc, there is nothing you have to do personally; your task is to make rings. Everything else is not your problem. By the way, you will automatically be receiving ten percent of the money made by each member of the gang. So you'll be paid well for your work."

"All right, I'll give you my reply in the morning. Decisions like these are not made in five minutes."

Next morning I went to the orc, handed him the list and expressed my desire to become a supervisor in the mine, in charge of the people on the list. The orc took a few seconds to examine the names, and then a chair appeared in the office and the orc said:

"Take a seat. And tell me why you need this."

For a while I sat there, unable to explain my decision. When I arrived at it during the night it seemed to me to be the decent and the right thing to do, but now, sitting in front of the orc I was not as sure. I finally made up my mind and looked at the governor.

"In short: it will make life easier for normal people."

The orc thought this over for a moment and then made a brief remark.

"He who takes a lot upon himself will have a lot to answer for. Remember this."

Your reputation with the Pryke Mine Guards has increased by 100 points. Current level: Friendly. You are 1685 points away from the status of Respect.

Attention! Changes to the description of the Charisma stat. The following skills have been added: people under your supervision receive extra Experience, percentage equal to your Charisma score.

Skill increase:

+1 to Charisma. Total: 3

After leaving the mine boss I went to the smithy to make rings. With a familiar turn of hand I wound the wire, connected the ends and ended up with a ring. It was just an ordinary ring, nothing special. How was it on the stat side?

Lesser Copper Ring. Durability 30. Strength +1. Stamina +1. Minimum level: 1

Well, yes, just an ordinary +1 ring. I threw it into the pile with the rest, took out more wire and began to make a new ring.

STOP! What the??? I ran like lightning to the pile of rings and started to look for the one I had just made. When I found it, I looked it over from every side, but nothing seemed to distinguish it from the rest: after all, I had used the same process to make them all. Where was the recipe? I opened the Jeweler's Recipe Book and, mesmerized, spent several minutes looking at the ring's description:

Lesser Copper Ring.

❖ **Description: Lesser Copper Ring. Durability: 30. 1 random Stat from the list: Strength, Agility, Intellect, Stamina, Rage. A bonus is added on account of the Crafting stat: (Crafting level) random Stat from the list: Strength, Agility, Intellect, Stamina, Rage. Minimum level: 1.**

❖ **Crafting requirements: minimum Jewelcraft level 2.**

❖ **Ingredients: 2 Copper Wires.**

❖ **Instruments: Jeweler's Tools.**

1 random stat from the Crafting skill... If Crafting increases the number of additional bonuses

on my rings then I should put the maximum number of free stat points into it. I was saving up those 22 points for a reason. Possessing a +23 ring with the ability to change the stats at any time is simply heaven for a starting player. Easy said — easy done. I stopped and opened the window with my stats.

Attention, the Crafting stat cannot be increased by addition of stat points!

What the hell?! So it looks like there is no easy way to level up Crafting. So, what to do? Eh, I wish I had the manual, I'd look up everything I need to know straight away. But now I'll have to find out for myself, by blind trial and error. I found Kart and told him about Crafting and its effect on the rings I made. I'm not sure if it was the effect of my words on Kart or the fact that he'd been trying to make metal sheets for eight days without any success, but he finally had a break-through and made a sheet with the required parameters. Pleased, Kart gave it to me and got on with making the rest; I went off to try and figure out what it was I had to do with it.

The simplest answer that came to me was to link the edges of the sheet together, polish them and get a completed ring. But how do I attach a stone to it?

I came to Kart in the evening, still without a clue of what to do with it. To my surprise he was finishing his 20th sheet, diligently banging it with a hammer. This meant that his remaining time should be free. And after we hand in the quest he'll leave the mine altogether. I should ask him to make something for me to remember him by. Although, what could a Smith/Leatherworker make? Suddenly an idea struck me: I knew exactly what he could make!

"Oh, Mahan, it's good that you came by. Just imagine — I'm finished already! Only the first one gave me trouble as I was getting the hang of it, but it was all plain sailing after that. So you better not let me down! Now it's all up to you!"

"Kart, you've done very well for sure, but I'm here with a proposal for you," I said and described my idea to Kart. "Will you make it?"

"Mahan, are you kidding me? I have no idea how to make that!"

"But you had no idea how to make the sheets either, right? And with this you don't even need to measure anything to make sure every millimeter is where it should be. Let's sit down and think how to go about it. I'm sure you'll manage it! You have plans to leave the mine in a week's time and this way I'd at least have something to remember you by."

"So you already know what you need these sheets for?"

"Not a clue. If the worst comes to worst and I can't think of anything else, I'll just connect a Rose and a ring, which should give me the needed result. But there must have been a reason why you were given the task of making these blasted sheets. We just have to figure out how to use them. So, I can do the thinking and you can work on my request. All right?"

Skill increase:
+10% to Charisma. Total: 30%

"You have a deal; I should be able to get to grips with the first part easily enough, but the second might present difficulties. That's all right though, it's for me to worry about now?"

"Correct. By the way, tell people that from today I am able to make +2 stat rings: they will cost 5 gold per ring. If anyone wants one, they know where to come."

"Need you ask? I'll be the first in the queue! You're making some for me, right? Selling these rings should be easy as pie. You already have a week-long queue for that, so keep making them, I'm going to need the money now," Kart smiled, looking pleased. Yes, he's one foot out of the mine. I envy him... How will I live here without him?

Leaving Kart to get on with my request I headed to Rine. My idea needed stones, if I didn't know what to do with the sheets yet (they just wouldn't form a ring, and there was twenty of them), then at least I knew where I was with stones.

"Hello, Rine. How's your granddaughter — did she like my present?" I began as I came up to the working dwarf.

"Oh, her parents heard no end of the stories about her rose. She runs around with it all over the place, doesn't go anywhere without it. Remembers me fondly for it too. What can I help you with?"

"I'd like to buy twenty granite stones off you. I seem to recall that you were prepared to sell them to me one copper a piece."

"You may as well remember something I told you a year ago!" Suddenly I seemed to be speaking to an altogether different dwarf. "What about inflation?

And taxes? Do you know how much we have to pay for all these stones lying here? I can't sell them to you for a copper a piece. Each stone now costs 1 gold, and that's at a discount for you as a loyal customer."

Thirty minutes of arguing with the dwarf had zero effect. A gold for each stone and that's that. I didn't even level up my Trade by one percent. It was impossible with someone this stubborn. Dammit, hadn't I been promised a 20% discount on all goods after completing that quest for Rine?! Hard-hearted dwarf!

"All right Rine, it's a deal," I gave up. "20 stones at 1 gold each. But I'm going to be the one to pick them out!"

"Of course you'll be doing that," said the dwarf, satisfied. "Like I have time to dig around that pile. Pay 10 gold for the privilege of choosing the stones and off you go. You know where the pile is."

"Rine, what is this? Are you trying to make a business out of exploiting me? What's with these prices? 10 gold just for digging around the pile?"

"Yes, why are you so surprised? We're going through a crisis right now, on account of dire shortage of Copper Ore; which we have you to thank for, by the way. So we have to get inventive just to avoid going broke."

"Rine, I thought no alcohol was sold at the mine, where did you get some? I'm prepared to pay 30 gold for a bottle."

"What are you on about? What alcohol?" the dwarf asked, surprised.

"What do you mean, what alcohol? The normal kind that you drank before I came to you and that completely clouded your brains. All right, you forgot that I made the present for your granddaughter. These things can happen to a dwarf: I've heard all about it. But what shortage are you talking about? Yes, we are now buying virtually all the surplus ore, but during the last month the average level of the Mining profession at our mine increased from 9 to 11. Everyone started to hand in 20 more pieces of Copper ore every day. And aren't you the one who collects all the surplus left after the processing? I only need half an ingot for a wire — what happens to the other half? Kart can't re-smelt it, there's a clear limitation there, but then our kind and, more importantly, thrifty dwarf takes the remains of the bar for himself, right? Absolutely free of charge too! And that happens with each item made in the mine! You make more in leftovers than you ever did in unprocessed ore that was sold to you as surplus! And I bet you have no trouble making new copper bars out of the unused bits. Just try and tell me this isn't so! I know you, you won't lie to my face — if the income of the mine hasn't increased from the time I started to make the rings I'll pay you 60 gold right now, just to dig through that pile. Well, Rine, don't you want to earn a lump sum? But if I am correct, taking 10 gold just so I can go through the pile is simply a disgrace, Rine. A big dwarven disgrace!"

Skill increase:
+1 to Charisma. Total: 4
+1 to Trade. Total: 5

"All right, but it's still one gold per stone from

you, Mahan," mumbled the Dwarf, annoyed. "That's not a whim of mine, that's the price set by our boss after you made that Rose."

I left Rine to himself and headed for the pile. I needed just eight stones for my idea, but I did not want to take any chances and decided to have some backup. I turned each stone in my hand, trying to listen to myself, but didn't feel anything particularly supernatural. It might be that to start seeing the essence of things I'll have to walk around for two weeks with each stone, as I did with the Rose, to understand what it really is. So I picked twenty stones at random and went over to my Shaman's Spot. It was time to set my plan in motion.

CHAPTER SEVEN
THE PRYKE MINE. FIRST MONTHS.
PART 3

I N THE EVENING I WITNESSED a somewhat entertaining auction. A large crowd of prisoners were arguing amongst themselves over their turn for buying rings with a +2 stat bonus. At some point someone shouted that he's prepared to pay 5 and a half gold for a ring if he's served before the rest, the crowd went quiet for a few seconds and then all hell broke loose... In a couple of hours Kart brought me a list of the people in the queue, which made for quite a shock when I looked at it:

> ❖ **Dirk. 4 Rings with +2 to Strength, 11 gold per ring.**
> ❖ **Grom. 4 Rings with +2 to Strength, 11 gold per ring.**
> ❖ **Alt...**

Altogether the list documented an order for 94

rings worth 800 gold in total. With my current level in Jewelcraft this meant four to five days of intense work. The opportunity for such profit was not to be missed.

In the morning I spent a couple of hours on creating the Rose, reducing it three times in size and then trying to combine it with an existing ring. I then tried to repeat this with a ring as it was being created. Then I simply tried to screw the Rose on top of a ring, but all to little effect: the number of stats did not increase. The ring had +2 and the Rose had +3, but when I combined them it did not result in a +5. I only got +3 Intellect, whatever I tried to do. After a couple of hours of experiments I gave up. I had jumped the gun when I thought that the orc's quest was as good as done. Things turned out to be not that simple: the ring (my plan was to make a gem ring) just wasn't happening. Well, technically it was, but only with +3 Intellect. When I changed the Rose's Intellect to Strength in order to have something useful in the mine, the Rose turned to stone dust and the ring reverted to its +2 bonus. A pity. I spent a few more hours creating my third Rose, but making it in the original size this time, put it on the table, spread the metal sheets around it and then tried to think. But the thinking wasn't going too well and I just stared at the sheets like I was seeing them for the first time. Not a single thought appeared in my head. After a while I felt that there was someone else in the smithy aside from Kart and myself. I reconnected with reality and turned around.

Alt stood by the table and looked at the sheets, mumbling something under his breath.

"Mahan," he turned to me, when I came up to greet him and ask what he was doing here. "I came here to buy some paints off Rine and saw your sheets on the table. Tell me, have you already picked a pattern for your chain?"

"My chain?" I asked in surprise.

"Aren't you making the Regional Governor's Chain? Before my imprisonment I saw several pictures where town governors sported these chains, made up of connected shaped metal sheets, with the symbol of the city at the bottom. So if you see the Rose as the symbol of the province," said Alt and started to shift the sheets around the table, "and connect the rest of these, you'll end up with quite a nice-looking chain. But you'll have to cut something interesting out of these sheets, to go with the Rose, or it won't look right. That's the kind of chain regional Governors wear."

'I need a present for the Regional Governor to confirm the status of my mine as one of the best.' I remembered the boss's words. Then I finally guessed that the orc knew what we had to do, but had left it to us to figure out the way! That's why Kart's task was to make the sheets. I'm such a blockhead! Why did I get all hung up on the rings? I can also make chains, I just completely forgot about it — because of the high demand for rings crafting chains didn't make a lot of sense. I would probably never have remembered if it hadn't been for Alt.

"Alt, would you like to get a couple of rings with +2 Strength?" I asked Alt and, seeing his immediate interest, continued, "You're entirely correct, I need some sort of a pattern that could be cut out from the sheets. I can cut it out, all right, but I can't draw it. You're the only one that can draw in the mine, so I need your help. On each sheet you'll draw a picture for cutting out and I'll give you two rings for the job. Deal?"

Skill increase:
+10% to Charisma. Total: 40%

A rather pleased Alt headed off to do his drawings, while I spent several hours on making the rings and instructing Kart, who was having real difficulty with my request. Certain elements came out well, but problems arose when it came to combining them: Kart was short of another pair of hands: to support here, bang there or twist over here. But, swearing and cursing the day he ever agreed to do this thankless task, he did not give up. 'Promises have to be kept," repeated Kart under his breath after he ruined another set of crafting materials.

Towards the end of the day I had more of a chance to do some work for myself. I leant on the smithy wall and took out one of the stones. I then closed my eyes and tried to feel what this stone wanted to be. I sat like that for a few minutes and understood that this stone just wanted to be a stone, since I wasn't getting anything else from it. But what if I tried a different approach?

I closed my eyes again and tried to draw with my imagination the shape that I wanted to get. It was slow going at first, since the shape constantly blurred, first becoming a Rose, then a pick, a couple of times there was even a Rat looking at me out of my imagination, but I forced these visions away and started again. I knew the result I was going for and I just had to force my brain to picture it. At last the desired object made an appearance: I was looking at a 3D image of the item. Now came the interesting part. I imagined a piece of stone next to this image and tried to combine them, connect my image to the stone. At first the stone and the item repelled each other like two repelling magnets, but my insistence and obstinacy did the trick. The virtual shape connected with the virtual stone. Pleased with the result, I opened my eyes.

Class ability "Change of essence" acquired: you are able to change the essence of a thing. Attention! This ability only works with inanimate objects and does not permit a change of essence in objects protected with spells of the 'Essence shield' level or higher. The level of the object whose essence can be changed depends on the character level.

Only now could I feel the wrongness and falseness of the stone. And I knew why — I felt the essence of the stone, which now wanted to be the object whose essence I had just imprinted. Just think what this could mean for future crafting work! I quickly removed all the unwanted bits from the stone and looked at the message telling me that I created a new Jewelcraft recipe and a Precious Stone with a +1 to Stamina. I had also increased my Jewelcraft by 9%, but it was strange that the discovery of this recipe did not lead to an increase in Crafting. So, Crafting does not increase with items made using a known creation path, but only with truly unique objects. All right, something to remember for the future. The main thing is that I managed it without getting stuck for two days like last time. I had to create just seven items for my idea to come to life.

All of the following day I used the newly created recipe to make things I had conceived out of the stones, although I destroyed almost half of the stones while I was at it. Changing the essence of some stones made them crumble to dust. They probably really didn't want to be what I suggested they should become. It was their choice and it was just as well that I had some extra stones. I gave the crafted objects to Kart, explaining their purpose, and then began to make the rings — the waiting list was still there and people were already asking when it was going to be their turn.

Two days later Alt brought the sheets marked with the drawings. I spread them on the table and examined the designs. On one hand Alt certainly had talent — each sheet depicted some kind of a flower, many had intertwining leaves, some even had dewdrops and one flower sported an ant. On the other hand Alt was very far from getting the plan off the ground: when I asked him how on earth could any of this be cut out, he shrugged and said that his task was to come up with the concept and mine was to bring it to life.

Arming myself with cutters, files and metal canvases, I began the crafting work, removing millimeter by millimeter from the sheet. The smithy was filled with such an unpleasant and irritating squeaking that Kart grumbled, suddenly remembering that he had many things to do in the barracks, and I soon found myself alone. At one point I lost my concentration and made a wrong move, and the sheet simply broke into several pieces. I looked at the other sheets in puzzlement. Does this mean that if I make a mistake the sheet will simply fall apart? On one hand this is understandable: 20 sheets were too high a number for the Chain; but on the other, if I had to proceed like a minesweeper, the speed of my work would be drastically reduced. And I only had five days ahead of me.

I fastened the next sheet in a grip and began to work it with even greater care. I cut off the excess pieces by micrometers not millimeters this time, and then...

"Mahan, how long are you going to be making that infernal noise?" Kart returned to the smithy, looking far from pleased. "You're disrupting everyone's work — the whole mine is echoing this awful sound you're making, it's enough to make your ears bleed."

I jerked the canvas in surprise and once again was left with a pile of broken pieces.

"Hey, why are you destroying the sheets?" asked Kart, surprised, when he saw me going through the shards. "That's not what I made them for. Look, that's the second one you've broken. Just can't get the hang of it?"

I shook my head, took the sheet with one of the simplest drawings and went off for a think. I was doing something wrong, but what...

I closed my eyes and created a sheet in my mind. I was surprised how easy that was: probably by now I was used to doing these things. The drawing on the sheet took a bit more effort, but in the end I also imagined it on the metal surface. I had a three dimensional model of the sheet that I could begin to work with. As I touched the sheet to cut out the pattern it curled into a ring. Right, this piece of metal contains the essence of a ring, but for some reason I'm not feeling it. I'm probably not high enough level for that. It means that if I start to cut out the drawing, this sheet will fall apart like the others. What a stumbling block.

As soon as I unbent the ring back into a sheet, at the edge of my consciousness I heard a sharp sound of breaking metal and my virtual sheet broke into many pieces. I opened my eyes and saw the shards of the bent sheet in my hands. So if I'm crafting in my mind, the same thing is taking place for real? Which means that I created a ring out of the sheet and then broke it. It's quite convenient actually, the fact that I don't need to work with my hands, definitely something to look into. This didn't happen with rings made from wire: I built their model in my head or deformed them, but nothing happened outside my head. So why was it happening here? Was it because I was holding the primary material in my hands? I really must get to the bottom of this, as this ability will be very useful later in the game.

With my mind rested I got back to work. I had 17 sheets left and I needed 15 for a decent chain. This meant that at the most I had two more attempts to get my head around the rules.

Another sheet appeared in my mind.

So, each sheet contains the essence of a ring.

But what if we try to replace it with a different essence? I sketched out the drawing separately in my mind and tried to combine it with the sheet. Once again, this had an effect like repelling magnets, I applied a bit of pressure, there was a bang... and I was left with only 16 sheets — and just one more try. I could not ask Kart to make additional sheets — this could fail his quest, as he was clearly told to make no more than 20 sheets. If he made more, his quest would fail.

The next sheet flew apart when I set aside virtual crafting and once again tried to cut it with normal tools. Right, now I really am like a minesweeper, no room for a mistake. I just had to decide whether to make it normally or by crafting it in my mind.

I left the sheets alone for four days. I completed all the rings on the list, increased my reputation by 56 points with the help of the Rats, now I had 1629 points remaining until Respect. The time set aside for the quest was running out, but as soon as I thought of making the chain, I was seized with involuntary shaking. I was afraid that I would fail and because of me Kart might not gain his freedom. The less time remained the greater this fear grew. In the end I got myself into such a state that I began to doubt whether I would be able to complete the quest at all.

Kart kept quiet, without hurrying or bothering me needlessly, since he saw the state I was in. Even the new people joining the queue for the rings started to come only at the end of the working day, not to get in the way of the 'mad Shaman'.

Tomorrow I have to hand in the quest to the

orc.

"You know, Mahan," Kart said as he sat next to me. He looked at the sheets laid out on the table in the shape of a chain with the Rose at its head and continued: "I think that you should not stress so much over this. Even if you don't manage to get this done, the last month had shown me that it is possible to live in the mine not just by using other people, but by your own efforts. When I leave prison I plan to try my hand at blacksmithing. You wouldn't believe how much I came to enjoy swinging the hammer and seeing a result on the other end. Here at the mine we have a good chance to train ourselves up in this, so if we don't manage to complete the quest tomorrow, it's not the end of the world. Life will go on. You'll continue making the rings and when you reach the limit of your current professions, you'll start to level up in Smithing and Leatherworking. So you should not see being unable to complete the quest as losing. You have to look at the bigger picture and not just single out certain details, even the really painful ones."

Heaving a deep sigh, Kart supportively patted me on the back and went to the barracks. At that moment I sensed that Kart had given me an enormous clue, but what was it? I played back our conversation several times in my head and for a while could not understand what it was that struck me. Then it hit me: *"You have to look at the bigger picture and not just single out certain details."*

I looked at the laid out sheets with the flower drawings on them and suddenly understood it all. Looking at the big picture! I sat myself down comfortably, closed my eyes and began to form one sheet after another in my mind. It was difficult and took a while, but I felt that I was on the right track. When the fifteen sheets presented themselves before my eyes, I added the Rose to them. Now I could begin. What I did before could not be called anything other than doing violence to the sheets — I bent them, forced some incorrect essences on them. It was all wrong. What I needed was to be found on a different plane.

I mentally removed the flower drawn by Alt from each sheet and moved the sheets aside. They were only getting in the way. The main work had to be done with the drawing and not with the sheets. I took the first flower, once again admiring its beauty, and began to make it three dimensional. I looked at the resulting model from all sides, correcting it here and there, adding details that were not visible on the initial drawing. After some time instead of a flat projection of a flower I was looking at a beautiful 3D flower, surrounded from all sides with broad leaves, dew drops rolling down them. Yes, that's the result I needed. Such a flower would look amazing together with my Rose.

I repeated this operation with the rest of the drawings and combined them into a chain, putting my rose at its head. The result was magnificent, but it was just a see-through projection. The main task still remained: to make the physical chain. I took the sheets that had I put aside, put them in the same order as the chain and then slowly began to bring them closer together. If I had been able to close my eyes in this design mode, I'd have closed them for sure — my nerves were that tense. This was the moment of truth, a make or break. Now I could even lose my Rose.

The chains combined instead of breaking and the sheets began to flow into the images of flowers, giving them physical form. Yes! I did it! I turned the resulting chain in front of me a few more times and opened my eyes. Although the daylight was fading, I was surrounded by light: a chain made of flowers shone brightly in my hands.

Item created: Kameamia (item name given automatically). Intellect +6, Stamina +5. Item class: Unique. Minimum level: 10.
Skill increase:
+1 to Crafting. Total: 2
+1 to primary profession of Jewelcraft. Total: 8
Attention! This item cannot be repeated. There is no recipe.
You created a unique item. Your reputation with all previously encountered factions is increased by 100.

I put the Kameamia in the bag and went to get Kart. We had to go hand in the quest, no matter what time of night it was. Such matters couldn't wait until morning.

"Mahan, what the heck's gotten into you?" asked Kart when I dragged him to see the boss. "It's the middle of the night, the orc is probably fast asleep by now. And we'll turn up just to tell him that we've failed the quest. He'll be cranky already from being woken up, but when he sees us empty-handed he'll tear us to shreds in the blink of an eye. Come to your senses!"

Ah yes, Kart doesn't know what I just did, so much for having faith in me. Never mind, let's surprise him.

"Kart, we can't wait until the morning. Trust me. We really can't..."

"It might have occurred to you that the night is not the best time to interrupt my thinking." The familiar bass of the governor seemed even comforting on some level. I took out the Kameamia from the bag and put it on the boss's table.

"We did the quest. Even overdid it somewhat. Now our mine can confirm its status as the best around."

The orc silently picked up the chain. I was sure that for a few moments a shadow of a smile passed over his lips, but it quickly vanished barely leaving a trace.

"Yes..." the orc didn't say anything more for a couple of minutes as he held the Kameamia in his hands and then lifted his eyes and asked: "You are still here? I thought that being in the administration after sunset was forbidden."

Quest "Present for the Regional Governor" completed. Reward: +500 Experience, +500 reputation with the Pryke mine guards, +3 to the Jewelcraft profession.
Level gained!

I have 1029 points remaining until Respect, so

now if I get busy with the Rats and increase my reputation by 50 points a day, I should be able to gain Respect in 22 days. Less than a month! It now looks like I'll end up in the main gameworld less than three months from the time I arrived in the mine. And it doesn't really matter that for another three months I'll have to live in some kind of a settlement. What's important is that I'll leave the mine.

Suddenly there was a melodious ringing and a light appeared above Kart's head.

"You've decided to leave us, then?" hummed the orc, looking at Kart's mystified face. "The transfer committee will be reviewing your case today. I expect you tomorrow evening with all your things."

Kart's last morning in the mine was a very busy one. He ran around the place like crazy, trying not to forget anything — to say good bye to some, to collect ring orders for me from others. He didn't spend much time around me: just brought all of his 400-strong stash of ingots and immediately ran off. I sensed that he was leaving me for dessert. That was fine: if I'm the pudding, I'll prepare a little cherry to put on top. I went to the smithy and spent several hours trying to make new rings for Kart, which I could now make with a +3 stat bonus, thanks to levelling up in Crafting yesterday. Kart was a Warrior, so, keeping this in mind, he could use five rings with Strength and three with Stamina. It occurred to me that I should make some for myself tomorrow too.

I was almost out of the smithy, when I slapped my head and returned to my work station. Why was I only thinking of rings? What about a chain? I keep forgetting about it, but another +3 stat bonus for beginners is quite nice.

I'd been making Copper Wire practically on an industrial scale (about 200 pieces) and now, taking a piece out of my bag, began to study the recipe for the chain. There was nothing complicated there, it was a simple neck chain made up of small rings linked together. No coiling required, which was just as well: I knew I could make it for sure. After a few hours of work I connected the ends of the chain. That's it: perhaps a little crude, with some rings slightly bent (although, truth be told, they were all bent), the chain still did the job and gave a +3 stat bonus. It didn't really matter what it looked like, one could always wear it under the coat. I took a moment to think this over and decided that while Kart was still busy I could make myself a chain like that as well. This time I'd probably be faster too, since my hands would remember the process.

It didn't really go any faster. It was several hours of the same monotonous work (creating rings and then connecting them) which I could not speed up at all. By the time I was done with my own chain people started to return from the mine and Kart would show up soon enough too.

"You know, getting ready to leave here is not as simple as I thought," said Kart when he finally made his way to me. "Ten years is enough time to gain a good number of connections, habits and traditions. In some way it's a pity to let go of all this. It turns out that habits are terribly strong things. Who knows where I'll be sent and how people will treat me with this damned prisoner mark. Sakas will replace me as your right-hand man, handling various matters. You can rely on him completely, I had time to make sure of that. By the way, I've finished your order for you. Will you be taking it now?" Kart hastily changed the subject.

"Of course I will. Or you'll be gone together with it and there'll be no finding you in the rest of Barliona."

"Then here you go," said Kart and handed me the items. I had a look at their properties.

It was a leather coat. At first glance it could have been made by any Leatherworker. Its distinguishing feature, however, was a copper chainmail tunic that Kart had inserted into it. He had spent about a week working hard at it. It may not be as good as a steel or mithril one, but we had to start somewhere. Six Precious Stones that I gave Kart were skillfully added to it in the form of buttons, making it look much nicer than a standard one. I was initially worried that there would be the same story with the buttons as with the Rose and the ring, and they'd just not combine, but it all came out just as I wanted it.

Kart's Rat skin leather coat. Durability: 60. Physical damage resistance: 18. Socket bonus: Precious Stone buttons adding +6 Stamina. Item class: Rare. Minimum level: 6.

Damn! Why doesn't Kart have Crafting? An additional stat bonus would have fit right in on such a coat. Well no point regretting the impossible.

Them there were the leather trousers. The remaining two buttons went on the trousers, increasing their Stamina by 2.

Kart's Rat skin leather trousers. Durability: 50. Physical damage resistance: 12. Socket bonus: Precious Stone buttons adding +2 Stamina. Item class: Rare. Minimum level: 6.

There were leather boots too. Kart couldn't think of what to do with them, so he gave them extra durability with some copper chainmail.

Kart's Rat skin leather boots. Durability: 50. Physical damage resistance: 12. Item class: Rare. Minimum level: 6.

I immediately put on the new gear and had a look at my stats. With eight rings giving +2 Intellect and with what Kart just gave me, the stats should have been something to look at.

11 Stamina, 3 Agility, 5 Strength, 27 Intellect, 42 Armor and 27 free stat points... At level seven not too bad at all.

"This one's from me," continued Kart, taking out another item. "It's just too strange: looking at you banging on random stuff, like stones and picks. It isn't right for a Shaman. Sakas, who's a Woodcarver, and I did some work and this is the result." Kart handed me over an object of some kind.

I took it and could not believe my eyes. It was a tambourine, with a wooden frame that had Rat skin stretched over it. I was so happy I was speechless — why hadn't I thought of asking Kart to make me one of these before?

Shaman's Tambourine. Durability: unbreakable. Description: Using a Shaman's Tambourine during kamlanie decreases Spirit summoning time by 20%.

I now even looked like a real Shaman. I'll make myself some +3 rings tomorrow and will become a real Shamanic beast! Ah yes, the rings...

"I also have a present for you," I said, taking out the rings and chain. "Made them today, they're +3 each. There's also a chain — yours is the first one I made. I'd have added some stones to them, but the Rose stubbornly refuses to be combined with rings and using buttons for this doesn't seem right. So I'm sorry the rings are only +3."

"Never mind, it's an excellent gift too, thanks for everything. Now it's time to take our leave," we stood next to each other in silence for a few minutes. We didn't feel like talking, on account of the 'lump in the throat syndrome'. I would never have thought I could get so attached to anyone, and now it was difficult to part ways.

"All right, we're men after all. We'll live to see another day!" said Kart, glanced around the mine and went on, "When you get out, find me. It would be easier to serve the rest of our time together. I plan to stop in Anhurs, I have an acquaintance there. If you leave me a message at the 'Wild Horse' tavern, I'll find you. Deal?"

"All right."

Lost in thought, I watched Kart walk off towards the administration building. I had met him just over two months ago, which is not that long, really, but enough to get to know someone. And I liked him quite a bit as a person, so I will miss him a great deal at first. Never mind, we'll make it through somehow. When I leave here, I will definitely seek him out. The door closed behind Kart and I went off to see Rine — from this day on I would have to work on my own. Although... I did have around fifty subordinates and a new 'right hand', Sakas. I'd have to ask him what exactly the right hand of a supervisor in a mine does.

CHAPTER EIGHT
THE PRYKE MINE. FIRST MONTHS.
PART 4

A FTER KART LEFT I DECIDED TO SPEND the first day in my section of the mine, just swinging my pick for a while. I knew I had enough ore to last a lifetime — the thieves working for me provided a stable supply and my bags also contained around 130 pieces for a rainy day, but I wanted a break from making rings, having grown tired of it. Of course, I'd have to make myself some +3 rings and think of how to make one with a precious stone. Inserting a stone into a ring was a good idea, but it needed a special kind of stone: neither the Rose nor buttons would work. That was something to think about. All of this would come later, but right now I just wanted to swing my pick. On the way to the mine I saw the prisoners' surprised faces and decided to keep quiet about my ability to make +3 items for now. I felt that as soon as this information was leaked, I'd be facing a new list of people wishing to buy a ring or two. First I had to sell all my +2 rings, of which I still had twenty left. No point throwing them away. I would hold off making new rings: for now I had enough money and, since changing my surroundings wasn't likely in the near future, I needed a change in activity or I might just go mad. Thus, pick on my shoulder, I headed for my 20 veins. Eight rings with +2 strength, a chain with +3 and the clothing that Kart made me meant that it should take me at most four hours to smash these 20 veins without a break for water. I'd spend some time doing physical work and then see what could be done with rings and chains.

I made a plan for myself: to increase all four main stats and Mining at least to level 9 in my remaining month in the mine. Free stat points were good, but I had to be very careful about how I spent them. As long as I was able to level up with Copper Ore, my task was to increase my stats this way. I wouldn't be able to level up in Jewelcraft with rings and neck chains — level 11 needs new recipes, but there aren't any in the mine. Of course, I could invent something, like with the Kameamia, but the chances of doing that were so little that I didn't even want to try. When Kart left, he passed the reigns of ingot production to Sakas, so I wouldn't have to spend any time making them. It might still take a couple of weeks for Sakas to get his Smithing to level 6-7, enabling him to make the number of ingots I needed, but I had a supply of them for now, so it was fine. My 'gang' also included leatherworkers, so the issue of what to do with all the Rat Skins was solved as well. I really didn't want to spend time on levelling up additional professions.

Mining ore turned out to be even easier than I had thought. One hit of the pick took off half a percent of Durability and in five minutes the vein flickered and disappeared. I checked my Energy level, which had gone down to 94 units, and then moved on to the next vein. Now I understood why the prisoners were so eager to buy the rings: if it took me an hour to smash all 20 veins, it should take 2-3 hours for the rest of the mine. And then — you either went to rest, or... went to Rine or to the governor with a request to expand your section of the mine. In a 12-hour working day you could smash about 60-70 veins. So now a prisoner got 320-350 pieces of ore on average. At the twelfth level of Mining, you had to hand in 120 pieces. The remaining 200 pieces of ore could be sold for 40 silver, which was 10 coins short of a gold piece. That's a good raise for the pension, I chuckled and continued to bang on the vein. This meant I could sell the +3 rings for at least 15 gold.

I finished my tenth vein and started to call on the Spirits to heal the Rats. When they ran up to me and attacked, I diligently kicked them and, wincing from the bites, used this to level up my Stamina and Agility. Although with my level of armor Rats could only cause me 1 point of damage, the pain was almost unbearable. When the Rat died, a message appeared before my eyes:

Attention, a new stat has become available to your character: Endurance.
Endurance determines a player's ability to reduce any damage from an opponent by (Endurance /10) %. If the player is under a debuff

that has "duration: until death", it is replaced by "duration: 24 hours". There is 1% chance for the player to receive a one minute buff 'stone skin', which additionally reduces sustained damage by 10%.

Do you accept? Attention, you will not be able to remove an accepted stat!

This time I had to think very hard. On one hand Endurance did not increase my damage, so if I picked it, I would have only one slot left for a combat stat. For a Hunter, Warrior and so on this was Marksmanship, for Intellect-based classes it was... I didn't know what it was. I didn't remember which stat increased damage for mana-dependent players; it would have to be something like Immunity or Amplification. As for Endurance... All right, you can't have too much armor.

A new stat has been unlocked for the character: Endurance. Total: 1

Attention! Special conditions for Endurance stat used in prisoner capsules: for each 5 units of Endurance the level of pain felt is reduced by 1%.

I even froze for a few seconds, letting the last phrase sink in. So it looks like there was a perfectly lawful method for getting back in the game while bypassing the sensory filter issue. You just have to endure quite a lot. What can I say... Rats, you're really out of luck now. I looked around my section. Today seven Rats had spawned there. One I'd already killed. 'I have to be very careful with the others to make them last as long as possible,' I decided, and summoned a Healing Spirit onto the second Rat. Then the harsh levelling up in Endurance commenced.

I managed to make the six Rats last about three hours and when I was done with them, I gave a sigh of relief. Yes, acting like a masochist is no easy or pleasant matter, but the result — in the form of a 15% increase in the Stamina progress bar, level four in Agility, level five in Strength and level three in Endurance — was worth it.

When I finished with the veins, I increased my Mining to level 8 and handed in my daily quota soon after, noting with some pleasure the astonished expression on the dwarf's face. Ah yes, of course, if the Shaman has came back to the mine, there must be something going on. What about the rings, chains and stone cutting? He's probably up to something... After I handed seven Rat tails and some ore surplus to Rine, my reputation increased by 15, leaving 1014 points to go until Respect. Now I had to decide what to do next. I had a crazy idea of asking Alt to draw some playing cards and open a casino at the mine. 'I wonder if there'll be a reputation penalty just for the idea or they'll wait until the first game.' I chuckled to myself. The next thought was more realistic: if not cards, why not carve some chess pieces for myself? I know how to play and even enjoy it at times and I have no reason to believe that playing chess would be prohibited. After all, it would be evidence of moral reform in us degenerates and would improve the relations within the workforce. We might even make a betting totalizator for this. But no, not worth the dent in the reputation. One thing made me less than happy

— I could not bring myself to make a chessboard and pieces out of granite. So I had to go to Rine with a petition.

"How are you, Rine? I've been so busy that haven't had time to ask after your health: please excuse my tardiness," I started to say, a stupid smile on my face, as I came up to the dwarf. Yeah, right: just a couple of hours ago I came and handed in my daily quota, and now I'm back again with the 'How are you?' and 'How's your health?'. How unbelievably stupid.

"Mahan, why do you always approach me in a roundabout way? Why not try being straight-forward? Tell me, what have you cooked up now? It's always these word games with you," interrupted me the grumpy dwarf.

"I'd like to make a chess set for myself, but our stones are no good for that. You travel to town — can you buy me several pieces of something inexpensive, but nice-looking? Just don't ask what — I'm not much of an expert with the stones yet. I know there's diamond, very strong and expensive. But that's all I know about precious stones."

"The stuff you come up with!" grinned the dwarf, thinking over my request and scratching his chin. "So you want to have some semi-precious stones presented to you. Who was it that shouted through all the mine that practically every vein had a Precious Stone in it and that Mahan was the best at finding them? Who threatened to bankrupt the mine, selling the stones at face value? Even bought a top-class pick from me; I all but gave it away to you, and now you throw your hands up and go: I didn't find any stones, please bring me some, kindly dwarves. Even remembered my health all of a sudden." Having had his fun, the dwarf became serious. "I can't make decisions like that. The list of the goods brought here is approved personally by the mine governor and he's the one that checks to make sure I've not bought anything extra. So it's the other place you want with questions like that," he nodded in the direction of the administration building.

I sighed in resignation, and went to my favorite place. The orc couldn't stand it when people came to him with requests. If I asked him to bring me some Precious Stones I could get into trouble, which I'd very much rather avoid. To endure an extra month in the mine for the sake of a chess set? Thanks, but no thanks. I'd rather make them out of stone or ask Sakas to make the pieces out of wood. With these thoughts I started work on making +3 rings. If I had time on my hands I had to spend it well and equip myself in the best way possible.

After I'd made the rings, I had around four hours left until the end of the working day and I decided to go to Kart's section to continue levelling up Endurance — the Rats in that section were still untouched. I was even curious: was my access to this section now removed or left in place until it was assigned to some other prisoner? I decided to quit guessing and, for the second time today, headed in the direction of the mine.

I still had access to it, but the Rats let me down. The section had only one representative of the 'grey tribe', whom I tried to avoid hitting altogether. I even tried to heal it, but my healing had no effect on the Rat. I could only stretch the 'pleasure' of Rat bites for forty minutes, which got my Endurance up to 5. It was disappointing that I could not really feel the 1% reduction in pain. Now all that remained was going back to the Smithy and getting on with making rings for everyone. I looked around Kart's section and decided to smash some more veins. I didn't have much left (just 34%) until level 9 in Mining, which meant around 13 Copper veins. The three hours until the end of the working day were enough for me to get through them.

When I started on the fourth vein something caught my eye. I turned around, bewildered, and saw a Copper Vein that looked very different from the others: it was larger and had a rich greenish tinge. I walked up to it, perplexed, put my hands on this pile of rocks and looked at its properties:

Large Copper Vein. Spawn chance: 0.01%. Required Mining level: 9 and above.

That's some stroke of luck! My eight levels in Mining and my +1 pick made it just possible to meet the requirements. With a better grip on the pick I readied to smash this pile of stones and see what it might drop. If an ordinary Copper Vein produced 5-6 pieces of ore, this one should give all 10 or even more. Let's see now. With my level of Strength and Mining such a pile shouldn't be much of a challenge.

In my eagerness I got carried away and went at the vein forgetting all else. A hit and then another and one more. What's that message?

Energy level: 30. Stop, you angry Shaman!

Ah, this is my pre-set warning, put in place to prevent a stupid death from loss of Energy. It's been a while since I saw it, why did it pop up now? I came to and looked around. What the...! My Energy level was 30, while the Large Copper Vein Durability was at 40%. How long had I been hitting it for? Suddenly the horn signaling the end of the working day sounded through the mine. Wow, was I at it for nearly two hours? I went to get the water to restore my Energy and continued to smash the vein. 'Just like my first day in the mine,' I chuckled; the first Copper Vein also gave me a fair amount of trouble. I spent another hour reducing the vein's durability to 5% and then sat down for a rest. My Energy level was sufficient to continue working, but I was mentally worn out: it's been a while since I got stuck like this with one ore vein. Only one thing puzzled me — why didn't Kart tell me about this kind? Despite such a small spawn chance, in his ten years of work such a vein had to appear at least once. The only explanation was that he never tried to smash it. He had to meet the daily quota, so getting distracted by such a strange and labor-heavy vein was pretty much pointless.

I sighed and went back to hitting the vein. 4% Durability. I wondered what dropped from veins like this. If smashing it needs such an unbelievable amount of effort, it must contain some sort of a bonus. 'Could it drop a chest of treasure?' I chuckled to myself. 'Yeah, right, and then some Pirate Flint would pop up, kick my ass and take the chest away from me.' 3% Durability. 'But I'm not going to give him the chest. When Flint gets close I'll knock his wooden leg from under him with the pick. And then run like hell. A one-legged Flint won't be chasing me very far. Damn, but what about his parrot? Named Iago, I think. He can fly and can shred me to bits. So I'll have to give up the chest.' 2% Durability. 'Well, he can kiss my ass — the chest's mine. As soon as the parrot flies up to me, I'll send a Lesser Lightning Spirit at him. Or a couple of them. Or maybe a dozen, all at once. Now I have a Tambourine, thanks to Kart and Sakas, so Iago hasn't a chance. If the lightning doesn't get him, he'll die from laughter, looking at me dancing around with it.' 1% Durability. 'But while I'll be dancing with the tambourine, Flint may have time to hobble over. He'll have me then. Maybe we can share? Split it half-half, like good mates — they can have the chest and I all its contents. That should make everyone happy. Right, that's how we'll do it then.'

When the vein's Durability Bar flickered for the last time and the vein disappeared, I involuntarily took a better grip of the pick and turned around in expectation of Flint, flinging it at the messages that were popping up.

Experience gained: +5 Experience, points remaining until next level: 476
Skill increase:
Mining increased by 1. Total: 9
Strength increased by 1. Total: 6
+20% to Stamina. Total: 57%

Working this hard is bad for you, I thought as I caught my breath and realized that no Flint was going to appear. My senses and the deepening shadows told me that the food would stop being served any time now; I had to run fast or I wasn't going to make it. I quickly gathered all that was dropped by the vein, without even taking a look at what I'd got — that could wait after the food was sorted out. Examining all the loot in the twilight wasn't the best idea anyway. Gripping my pick, I ran at full speed to the place where food was handed out. I got there just as they shut shop. The overseer in charge of the line was already packing away when I ran to him, the first empty plate I could grab in my hands.

"I've handed in the quota, I should get my food now," I fired at him, catching my breath.

"Food is handed out in the course of two hours after the bell is rang," replied the overseer and continued to pack. "The two hours are now over, and no food is to be handed out. Sorry, Mahan, my instructions on this are very clear. If you're unhappy about any of this, you're welcome to appeal to the mine management. Right now I have enough to do as it is."

Without a minute's loss I headed to the administration building. I no longer cared that the governor didn't like to be bothered with requests — I may not survive the ten hours until the morning meal. Although no, I'd probably survive if I restored my Hit Points with Fried Rat every thirty minutes, but the sensations in my stomach would still be there and I'd be looking at a long sleepless night.

The boss was sitting behind his favorite desk and reading some papers. When I entered the office, he looked at me questioningly and lifted an eyebrow.

"Today I personally met my mining quota and handed it in to Rine, but didn't make it in time to get the evening meal. I was told that to get my portion I had to ask you for permission. So, that's why I'm here," I said all in one breath, once again feeling uncomfortable under the orc's gaze.

"The food stops being handed out two hours after the ringing of the bell. After that no food is handed out to the prisoners," the orc's heavy voice rang through the office. "I can't give you food even if I really wanted to: there simply isn't any more in the mine. Now go, I still have a lot of work to do."

Dumbfounded, I came out into the muggy air of the mine outside. The boss just sent me off to die. Me, with my Friendly reputation, the one who made the Kameamia for him. This cannot be, it's just illogical! But perhaps this isn't about logic? Perhaps the orc doesn't want to help me because he knows that I will manage to find a way out by myself, just like with the Kameamia and the copper sheets made by Kart. But what is the way out then?

I headed for my favorite thinking spot instead of the barracks and fitfully began to go through what I could do to remain alive in the next ten hours. Firstly, I really must make myself some Fried Rat, because I can't heal myself and would have to restore my Hit Points constantly. Secondly... What the other thing was I really had no idea — except to quickly think up a painkiller of some kind, since there was already an unpleasant tingling in my stomach.

Drawing a blank on that one, I went to make the Fried Rat. I didn't have that much meat on me, since I stopped collecting it: selling it to Rine for a couple of coppers when I had a couple of thousand gold on my hands would have been... strange. Now I was very glad I'd saved one 40-unit pack of meat for a rainy day. And today it was raining cats and dogs, all right...

I laid out all the needed ingredients and started to fry. Unlike that first time, when I was only learning and my Cooking level was low, now the fried pieces of meat looked quite appetizing. So juicy and golden, with a pleasant aroma too. 'What a pity this isn't beef,' I thought in passing, 'or I'd make an excellent marbled steak right now.'

I cooked the first lot and started on the second and then tried to eat a piece, because the pangs in the stomach were starting to get to me and my Hit Points were gradually diminishing. 'And so the race between the mine restrictions and my meat supply commences,' I chuckled and bit into the piece. Mmmm, tasty stuff!

Attention! You ate a foreign object and lost your daily food buff. -1 Strength, Energy is lost 50% faster. Bonus for ingesting improved food: You have been freed from penalties related to food intake for the next 30 minutes.

Buff gained: Strength +1, Stamina +1. Duration — 12 hours.

Hit Points restored. Total Hit Points: 190 of 190.

What?! What did I just eat? I grabbed the second piece of Fried Rat and looked at its properties.

Fried Rat. Description: Fried Rat meat may not have a very pleasant taste, but in dire need will prevent you from dying of hunger. Crafting bonus: the food has a pleasant appearance, smell and taste, increasing your Stamina and Strength. Special features of the Pryke Copper Mine location: You have been freed from penalties related to food intake for the next 30 minutes. On use: restores 20 Hit Points, +1 Stamina for 12 hours, +1 Strength for 12 hours. Minimum level: 4

10 hours. If the buffs last 30 minutes, I need 20 pieces of fried meat. I'll make it...

My sleepy, red eyes watched the overseer getting ready to serve the morning meal. I've made it — although I did fall asleep a few times just to wake up from an excruciating pain in my stomach. Then with some effort I'd shoved another piece of Fried Rat into my mouth, swallow it without chewing, clearly understanding that I could not afford to fall asleep. Now all that remained was to get my morning food buff and forget this whole incident like a bad dream. If not for Crafting, which allowed me to ignore the penalties for 30 minutes at a time, I'd...

I woke up around midday and decided not to go to the mine: I had plenty of ore, I had levelled up my Strength yesterday and although the probability of finding another Large Vein was small, it scared me somewhat — what if I got carried away with work again? The thought of increasing my Endurance through Rats after yesterday... made me shudder. Not now, thanks. I took out my bag to see how much ore I mined yesterday. Right, this I already had, this too —

ah, here's the new stuff. Wow, 22 pieces; not bad for one vein. And what's this? I don't remember seeing this before. A stone about three or four fists in size was lying in my bag. What are its properties?

A piece of untreated Malachite.

Short and clear. A piece of untreated Malachite. Such a neat phrase, but I forgot my nightly food problems in an instant: our mine had Precious Stones!

I suppressed the first impulse to run to the orc and slam the stone on his table and began to think of what could be made from this piece. I did not see any principal difference between granite, from which I cut the Rose, and Malachite, so my task was to think of something interesting, cut it out of this piece and then take the result to the governor.

I sat around for two hours and could not think of anything good. I had no idea what could be cut from Malachite. My imagination turned out random ideas of what I could make: a toad, a tree leaf or our boss. And why not — he's also green and would look really good made from Malachite. I immediately discarded these thoughts: I had enough of our governor in flesh and blood and having his face stare at me in Malachite as well was too much. When I began my third round of thoughts edging towards a green orc looking very interesting in Malachite, I headed off to sleep. 'That's it, my brain is overloaded and I can't think any more. It's time to rest.'

With a sigh of relief I lay down on my bed and closed my eyes, but a green orc appeared again and I kicked at him angrily in my mind. What is it with the orc apparitions? There was one small comfort — the orc that had appeared to me looked nothing like our boss. The virtual orc stood, holding enormous yatagans in both hands, and his face was so frightening and distorted by anger that it was impossible to look at him without a shudder. I never saw so much fury in someone's eyes. It seemed that every line of his face was speaking of insatiable blood-lust, making the orc an embodiment of rage. Blood rage. The unusual battle garb, almost completely covered with spikes and huge studs, scabbards for the yatagans, attached to the back, hair tied in a knot and heavy boots, with snarling wolves on their tips — all this gave this orc a very colorful and eye-catching look. The figure was so detailed and clear and the orc himself was full of such a warlike spirit that the viewer was involuntarily filled with respect for such a warrior. One could fear him or hate him, but one would respect him. This was a true Warrior of his tribe. Maybe I really should make one from Malachite? It would make an excellent figurine.

As soon as I thought this, a piece of Malachite appeared next to the orc, but to my surprise it was much larger than the warrior. Strange, the actual piece of Malachite was not nearly as big as the one that appeared in my imagination, or was it a hint that the orc's figure should be small? If yes, then it would explain the comparative size of the orc figure to the piece of Malachite. But what should I do with the leftovers? Should I give them to Rine as usual? My toad-demon of greed — that very same one that I decided not to carve — would strangle me bare-handed. Perhaps I should make several orcs? As if reading my thoughts the number of orcs increased to eight. At first they all stood in a row and then began to mix together, forming a figure that resembled the Malachite stone in form. 'What on earth would I do with eight orcs?' a thought flashed across my mind, but I barely noticed it, being fully absorbed by the creative process. When the figures mixed together and became completely still, I combined them with the projection of the Malachite. Yes, they all fit perfectly, as if they were made for each other. Now I just had to separate the figures and enjoy the result.

I couldn't tell how much time it took me to separate the figures in stone, but it felt like a good while. When the last orcs joined the row, I sighed in relief: all I had to do now was remove the excess pieces of Malachite from the figures that had been left there after the separation and polish. As soon as I began on the first figure, I was taken out of the design mode, as I've been calling it for some time now, by a rough push on the shoulder.

"Mahan, you all right there?" I opened my eyes and saw a heavy figure of an orc looming above me. The thought rushed by: 'I didn't even get around to polishing you, so what's with the pushing?' Seeing the orc was so unexpected that I even backed off, putting my hands in front of me.

"Mahan, maybe we should call the boss? Why are you crawling away from me? You haven't hit your head, have you?" asked the orc in surprise, and I finally came to myself. It was Sakas, our Woodcarver and my new right hand as the local supervisor. Damn, I'll go stark raving mad with these orcs. Why of all the prisoners in the mine, with just one orc among them, it's this orc that had to be the one to snap me out of it? Some 'plague of orc' we have here.

"Thank you Sakas, everything is all right; I just got lost in my thoughts," I replied as soon as I caught my breath from such an unexpected coincidence. "Why are you pushing me: did something happen?"

"It's just there's only thirty minutes left until they stop serving the morning meal and you were sitting there without any sign you were going to budge any time soon. We brought food to you, but you wouldn't even eat from a spoon. So we got worried and decided to push you awake."

One of these days, when there won't be a friendly human (or orc) nearby, I'll starve to death with my approach to crafting items. I thanked Sakas and, quickly finishing the food, returned to my design mode and started to remove unwanted details from my orcs.

I freed the legs and body of the figure from excess Malachite, but spent quite a lot of time on the orc's head, or rather on his eyes. Even in the virtual mode I just couldn't manage to make them really fierce and savage. I needed some kind of a template, to emphasize the specific feel of an orcish gaze. And then I remembered the moment when I was playing my Hunter and we made a raid on an orc settlement to steal their totem. The gaze of the orc leader when we tied him up and dug up the totem in front of him was exactly what I was going for now. And how much money and items we got out of them in return for that totem... That's one fond memory right there. But I digress. Concentrating on the figure I made several additional cuts. Right, now I've got it. One close look at those eyes was enough to make your skin crawl all over the place; you wanted to stop whatever you were doing and quickly put some distance between you and this mad orc. I took note of the image of the stone in my memory and opened my eyes. It was evening. So it seemed like it took a whole day to create one of these figurines. No matter, the result was worth not rushing it and doing it properly.

It took me eight days to make all the figures. I completely forgot about levelling up my reputation and the fact that I might have left the mine in just twelve days' time if I continued to kill Rats. I was fully immersed in the creation of the orcs. When the last figure took its place in my mind, I put them in a row and began to examine the result of my labor. I was very pleased with it: eight warrior-orcs, menacing and fierce, strong and mighty. What struck me was that all the orcs had different faces, despite me using the same template for them. They had similar features, but some had longer fangs or more deeply set eyes and so with each of them. I smiled, surprised, and thought that if I had an army like that when I left the mine and if they were all my level or a few levels higher than me, I'd be a force to be reckoned with in Barliona. Soon everyone would know the dread band of orcs and their Shaman leader. Now I just had to make my figurines from real stone. I laid out pieces of Malachite before me and, taking each piece in turn, entered the design mode and imagined how the shape of the stone was changing in line with the orc figure. This took me a few more hours and when I completed the last orc and opened my eyes all my figurines were right there before me. All together they looked even more fierce than in my imagination and, despite their small size (about a thumb in height), were so detailed that you felt they could come to life any moment and start destroying everything in their path.

Congratulations! You have entered the path of recreating the Legendary Chess Set of Emperor Karmadont, the founder of the Malabar Empire. Wise and just, the Emperor offered his opponents to settle disputes on the chess board instead of the battlefield. Each type of Chess piece was made from a different stone. Pawns: Orc Warriors from Malachite and Dwarf Warriors from Lapis-lazuli. Rooks: A Battle Ogre from Alexandrite and a Giant from Tanzanite. Knights: A War Lizard from Tourmaline and a War Horse from Amethyst. Officers (Bishops): Troll Archers from Emerald and Elf Archers from Aquamarine. Queens: An Orc Shaman from Peridot and Elemental Archmage, a human, from Sapphire. Kings: The head of the White Wolf Clans, an orc from green Diamond and the Emperor of the Malabar Empire, a human from blue Diamond. The Chessboard: black Onyx and white Opal, framed by white and yellow Gold. Numbers and letters on the chessboard: Platinum.

After the death of the Emperor the chess set was destroyed. Now it is only up to your skill whether Barliona would again see this truly great wonder of the world — the Legendary Chess Set of Emperor Karmadont.

You have created the Malachite Orc Warriors from the Legendary Chess Set of Emperor

Karmadont. While the chess pieces are in your possession, each minute you will regenerate 1% of your Hit Points, Mana and Energy in addition to your standard regeneration; Strength is increased by 10%.

Skill increase:

+1 to Crafting. Total: 3.

+1 to primary profession of Jewelcraft. Total: 12.

You created a Legendary Item. Your reputation with all previously encountered factions has increased by 500.

I could barely keep up with the appearing messages and so took little notice of my surroundings. There was plenty to see though — I was enveloped in a pillar of light, some melodious solemn music played and a rainbow was flashing periodically above the orc figurines. The world of Barliona welcomed Legendary Items.

"Mahan, the camp boss wants to see you right away," the shout of the guard sounded through the mine as soon as the pillar of light around me faded. I put the figurines in the bag and headed off to the administration building.

Contrary to his habit the orc was not seated behind his great table, but was studying a painting on the wall that was usually covered by a curtain. I always thought that the curtain covered a window... I stood myself quietly by the table, reluctant to break the silence and waited for the governor's reaction.

"The race of orcs in its long history had many great warriors and fighters of its own. We are born warriors, live like warriors and die like warriors. This is our fate. But even among us there are those whose names are remembered for centuries. The Eight Great Warriors, whose deeds have been forever imprinted on the memory of my race. Look at them," said the orc without turning around. I stood by him and looked at the painting. It was split into eight parts, each of which depicted an orc. Well I'll be... I was looking at the very same orcs that now lay as chess pieces in my bag.

"These Great Ones are the pride of my people. Just a couple of dozen minutes ago an announcement shook the world of Barliona: one of the Great Jewelers in Barliona had created the Legendary Malachite Orc Warrior chess pieces from Karmadont's chess set. Our world has several billion souls, but I think I know whom the troubadours are shouting about in every square," the orc turned around and looked me in the eye. "A Legendary Item had just been made in my mine; what it is remains unknown. This has been put into all the reports and sent to all the relevant authorities. This object was created by you, which has also been included in all the reports. You have only two crafting professions — Jewelcraft and Cooking. I doubt that you've cooked up the Legendary Fried Rat."

After a few moments of silence the governor continued:

"A word of warning. In this world you can only steal money from player's bags. But there is one exception to this rule. It does not apply to Legendary Items carried by the player either on himself or in his bag. If you carry an item on yourself, it has a 10% chance to be left behind in place of the dead body. If the item is in the bag, with the sufficiently high level of shady skills it would be possible to pick it out of the bag. Remember these words."

Message for the owner of the Legendary Item!
In the event of your Death there is a 10% drop chance for the equipped Legendary Item. If the Legendary Item is in your sack, there is a 10% chance that it could be stolen by another player using the 'Theft' ability. Requirements for stealing a Legendary Item: (The level of Meanness of the thieving player / Level of your Character) > 0.5.

It was just as well that I was next to a wall, so instead of falling down I simply leant on it. What the mine governor just said completely changed my subsequent life in the Game. First of all, I'm a dolt. If I'd bothered to unlock Leatherworking and Smithing, the orc wouldn't have me against the wall now. Secondly, the very fact that Legendary Items could be stolen... This explains the reason why people level up in Meanness in the gameworld: why go through tedious crafting and boss raids when you can simply steal. And steal not just any item, but a Legendary one. Thirdly, as soon as other players find out that I'm the Jeweler who made the chess pieces it'll be the end of me. There are enough people in Barliona hunting for Legendary Items even without those trying to level up in Meanness. If without Meanness it's impossible to take the figurines off me directly, it's easy enough to make me practically beg to be relieved of them. As soon as I get out of the mine, a red band would be tied on me, allowing people to kill me without any penalties. This would only work outside the town, but either way a player that kills me will not have any PK (player killer) tag debuffs imposed on them. Now this meant that, aside from every death being very painful until I sufficiently raised my Endurance, it looked like with this 10% chance I was likely to lose my chess pieces too. And all of it would be strictly lawful: if you don't want others to hunt you — sit out the rest of your prison term inside a town, not daring to set your foot outside. Because as soon as you do, you have to be ready for an open season on your hide. So if anyone at all found out that I was the owner of these figurines, there'd be hell to pay. The hunt will begin, followed by torture and killing. There is no ban on torture either. In normal capsules the players don't feel a thing — they're even curious to watch themselves being skinned alive and will make fake faces to simulate excruciating pain, while in real life they'd scream their heads off if you just step on their toes. A bunch of perverts! Thus, I can't tell anyone that I have these figurines — at least until I level up somewhat. But the orc wasn't ordering me to show him the chess pieces. He was just warning me of possible dangers. I automatically opened my bag to get the orc figurines. Shameful as it was to admit this, but I wanted to boast. In the three months that I spent on the mine this was my third serious work as a Jeweler: the Rose, the Kameamia and now these chess pieces. It was, of course, strange that I could make such things at level 7, but it was certainly pleasing. I took out the figurines and put them on the table. Next I'd have to get the mine governor to write off my daily quota: I had no need of it, since other prisoners handed it in for me, but for the sake of principle...

The orc carefully picked up the first figurine. Usually he was calm as a rock, but now he looked shaken and inspired at the same time, holding the figurine in his huge hands so carefully, you'd think it was made of air and he was afraid to crush it. Suddenly he spoke, looking at the figurine in his hands:

"This is Pandyar the Killer. Five thousand years ago the orcs of the Trapp Clan were attacked by spirits. These possessed the orcs, gaining control over them, and then killed every living thing, savoring the agony of their victims. In the course of a week the body of the orc possessed by a spirit completely burned from the inside, after which the spirit would leave this body and move on to possess another. It was impossible to exorcise the spirits, but it was possible to fight them: if the orc died the spirit that possessed him died with him. When 90% of the tribe became victims of the spirits and those that remained had nowhere left to run, Pandyar the Killer, using the only mind-shielding charm that could protect him, stood before the army of spirits in the Pass of Fear. Alone against several thousand of his brothers and sisters, against his followers and against his teachers. The fight lasted several days. Pandyar killed two of his brothers, his father and destroyed nearly two thousand orcs. The Trapp tribe ceased to exist, but thanks to Pandyar some orcs survived, giving the world the Great Clan Chief two generations later. Shaine mor, Pandyar Kahandr (Orcish: Rest in peace,

Pandyar the Killer)", the governor said suddenly and put the Pandyar figurine on the table and picked up the next.

"Grichin the Unbreakable. Around three thousand years ago the orc tribes were gripped by internal strife. Clan went against clan, tribe against tribe. The dark elves of Aldora decided to take advantage of this situation — they invaded our lands and began to systematically exterminate my race. Ten orcs under Grichin's leadership stood in their way, having sent messengers to all the clans to warn them of the coming danger. Everyone in Grichin's band understood that they wouldn't survive and that the elves would wipe them out in a few hours, but they could not abandon the women and children fleeing from the nearest settlements to their fate. They met the elves in the Thunder Ridge Pass. In the meantime the leaders of the tribes agreed to lay aside their enmity, united and moved as one to meet the invaders, but these were nowhere to be seen. When the warriors of the united orc army approached the Thunder Ridge Pass, they saw Grichin pinned to a tree with spears, yatagans strapped to each hand and in full battle gear. His unseeing gaze looked in the direction of the pass, where the elf army stood. As the orcs prepared for battle, the elves sent out heralds with flags of truce, bearing the tale of what had happened in the pass. Ten orcs had held off the elves for three days — three heavy days, fighting off wave after wave of elf attacks. When only Grichin remained alive, he charged in attack, breaking through the ranks of the elves, through the personal guard of the elvish battle commanders and, despite his wounds from arrows and spears, managed to destroy almost all of the elven King's command post. Grichin died and the elves, stunned by his deed, self-sacrifice and rage, nailed him with spears to a tree, showing respect for the great warrior. The orc died, but remained undefeated. Shocked by Grichin's fierce strength, the dark elves of Aldora swore an oath of friendship with the orc people, and for thousands of years since have been our brothers, ready to die for orcs and for whom any orc would give his life. Shaine mor, Grichin Parkat.

"Leite Doubleblow, Varsis the Furious, Vankhor Heavyhand, Grovor Dreadshout, Ksor the Merciless, Duku the Bloody," the orc continued to list the Great Orc Warriors and the deeds that earned them their place in history.

Your reputation with the Pryke Mine Guards has increased by 200 points. Current level: Friendly. You are 314 points away from the status of Respect.

I gathered the pieces back into my bag and looked at the governor. His face was once again inscrutable and he continued in his usual calm, chilling voice:

"Each of these warriors was known for his incredible Strength, so when their figurines or images are collected together they increase the Strength of their owner. I believe you've felt this already. And now go, you still have much to do. You don't have to hand in your quota tomorrow, I'll warn Rine."

The next day I decided to spend on my own

precious self and remake my chain and all my rings. The third level in Crafting allowed me to make +4 items, so it was worth spending some time on this. Buying another twenty pieces of granite off Rine, I decided to experiment in creating a gem ring. It was stupid, having the ability to make stones and rings, not to try to combine the two into one. I decided to make something like a wolf's fang for my chain and a stone cut diamond for each ring. It should look pretty good. And if anyone's bothered by the fact that the cut diamond will be made of granite rather than real diamond, that's their own problem.

First I had to create a new Jewelcraft recipe. 'I'm thinking of such things so casually already,' I chuckled, 'create a new recipe — as if that's nothing special.' I spent several hours in the design mode trying to imagine the forms of a royal diamond and a wolf's fang and then embodied their essences in stone, destroying about nine stones in the process. They just didn't want to become cut diamonds. As soon as I was finished with the stones, there came the expected message that I learned new Jewelcraft recipes — Precious Stone: 'Stone Cut Diamond' and Precious Stone: 'Stone Fang', each adding +3 to a Stat. Before the day ended I made eight rings and a neck chain, inserted the stones in them and was now enjoying the result.

Lesser Copper Ring. Durability 27. + 4 Intellect. Bonus for inserted stone: +3 Intellect. Total: +7 Intellect. Minimum level: 7
Lesser Copper Chain. Durability 27. +4 Intellect. Bonus for inserted stone: +3 Intellect.

Total: +7 Intellect. Minimum level: 7

Yup, I was some cheater: to have +71 to Intellect and 27 unallocated stat points at level 7 was sheer outrage. And it wasn't a problem that all my ring bonuses were with Intellect, since I could change them at any time, either to Strength or to Stamina or a mixture of them all. Surprisingly, my Hunter only had four +20 rings, which had to be bought for a steep price from a Jeweler, and the rest were just +10 rings. This really was an outrage, but if I was the one getting up to it — all the more reason to be pleased.

I spent the next seven days levelling up my stats, using Rats and mining to increase my Strength to 7, Stamina to 11, Intellect to 9, Agility to 6 and Endurance to 7. In seven days I brought down 87 Rats, after I resumed patrolling other prisoners' sections, so I was only 86 points away from level 8 and 140 points away from Respect. If I was to translate that into Rats, I had 70 of them left to kill until I could leave the mine. Four days at the most.

The day barely dawned when all my plans were ruined by the shout of the overseer:

"Mahan, the boss wants to see you right away!"

The orc's place was surprisingly crowded. The owner of the office stood by the bookshelf and was leafing through a tome. The sight of the enormous six-foot-tall orc holding a small book in his hands was so unnatural that I struggled to suppress a smile. 'Why is he not at his usual place?' I wondered and looked in the direction where I usually saw the mine governor.

The huge and very comfortable chair wasn't

just occupied, but also surrounded by a detachment of impressive-looking guards. And these guys are still alive? The boss must be getting old. The place behind the orc's table was occupied by a plump, short-armed man with a fat glossy face. It would have been easier to call him a toad — one that's been blown up to the size of a dwarf. I realized who graced us with his presence when I saw the Kameamia around this character's neck: the Regional Governor was visiting the mine.

The Game Developers always give the NPCs a behavior pattern and temperament that corresponded to their appearance. I wondered what the inspiration behind this NPC was: did his creator remember his mother in law at the wrong time or did he just have a weird sense of humor? Whatever the case may be, I had every reason to believe that the Regional Governor was a rare bastard and that it was dangerous to get involved with him. If what the boss recently told me about the chess set was true, I can probably guess on whose account this weird creature came here.

"So that's who made my Kameamia?" when I heard this Governor's voice, I once again silently swore at the developers. They sure knew how to troll. They decided to make a play of contrasts — this picturesque toad spoke in a high squeaky voice, smacking his spittle-filled lips at every word. I had to muster all my self-control to endure the start of this acquaintance and not break out in stupid laughter. I tried to concentrate on what he was saying instead.

"I decided to put all my business aside and come to have a look at the name behind my

Kameamia. Come closer and accept my gratitude. I know how to value those who are capable of bringing joy to their Governor with truly Unique Items. Or even Legendary ones," he stretched out his hand with his palm facing upwards, fingers slightly bent.

I didn't get it: was he asking me for alms?

"I believe that such a master must grace my town with his presence. So, what do you say? Ready to move to my town? I can arrange this. All you have to do is say that you're the Great Jeweler who makes Legendary Items and give them to me. Well, don't just stand there! I'm waiting to see your handiwork," the Regional Governor jerked his hand impatiently, dispelling any remaining doubts. He thought that this was the cue for me to fall to my knees, kiss the floor to honor of my benefactor's arrival and immediately confess: 'I'm that Jeweler and here are the figurines, please take them'.

"I am waiting! Don't you want to get out of here? Be careful, I am very easily angered," squeaked this man-like ridiculousness.

So, it looked like this toad of a Governor decided that the prisoner who made his Kameamia is none other than that mysterious Jeweler. Damn, looks like I'm in a pickle. And it all makes sense — did he make the chain? Yes he did. A unique one? A unique one. Did he create a Legendary Item in the mine? Yes he did. So the chess pieces were mine for sure.

"Yes, I did recently make a few crafted items," I replied and saw the regional governor's eyes fire up. He almost jumped off the chair, wishing to quickly run to me and snatch, take and appropriate everything I had. The orc narrowed his eyes, piercing me with his gaze. What? You didn't expect this did you? Yes, that's what I'm like.

I dug around my bag and took out eight +2 rings that I've not yet sold to other prisoners and handed them to the Governor.

"That's all that I know how to make. They're only +2, since I'm not a very experienced Jeweler yet. After I do more learning and levelling up, I'd make some for +3 or even +4. Isn't this what you came for?"

The Governor gathered my rings and began to examine them. Gradually the happy glow on his face faded into a picture of disappointment. He stood there a moment, wrinkling his brow in disgust, and then threw my rings on the table and wiped his hands with a handkerchief.

"Cheap rubbish!" hissed the Governor. "Why did you give me trash that could be bought in any Jeweler's shop? I clearly told you that I need the Malachite Orc Warriors from the Karmadont Chess Set! Do you have them? Are you the one who made them?"

A-ha! We are no longer quite so sure that I'm that Great Jeweler. Very good. Time to move in for the kill. I barely opened my mouth to state my refusal, but the orc beat me to it.

"The limitations of the Pryke Copper Mine do not permit prisoners to reach level 13 in any of the professions. The message of the heralds stated that the Malachite Orc Warriors were created by a Great Jeweler. A level 12 Great Jeweler is..."

"But he made the Kameamia!" screamed the Governor, interrupting the orc. "Even if it's made from cheap materials, it's still magnificent! What else could he create if not the orc figurines?"

"The figurines were made from Malachite. No Malachite was ever brought into my mine," replied the orc.

"This is my mine! You hear, you ugly orc mug? Remember: this is my mine, not yours!" shrieked the Governor as he jumped on the chair.

"No Malachite has been brought into your mine. Ever." replied the orc, unperturbed.

"Then I want to get the item that he created," a calmer Governor now turned to the orc, ignoring me altogether. "Even if it's not the chess pieces, I will not allow him to own a Unique Item. Moreover, he should go pack his things — I'm taking him back to my castle. I have no intention of letting a Jeweler capable of making Unique and Legendary Items slip away from me."

"Prisoner Mahan cannot leave your mine at your behest," replied the orc, also completely ignoring my presence. "Neither I nor you may break the law. Neither I nor you may take a prisoner's possessions by force. That is also the law."

"I'm the law here!" screamed the Regional Governor, breaking off the orc and spraying spittle in all directions. "If Mahan didn't make the orc chess pieces, he must create all the rest! He must! Only I should possess such things, because with their aid I could open..." The Governor suddenly fell silent, glancing from side to side, got his breath back and went on. "I shall await this man in my castle! Today!"

"Prisoner Mahan cannot leave your mine at your behest," repeated the orc methodically. Yeah, this guy will make a decent parrot, come to think of it. He's so green and big — a typical Ara. He just lacks a tail, but attaching one is no problem.

The Regional Governor lost it. Big time. For about ten minutes he was screaming at our boss that an oaf like him could only work in a mine, preferably as a prisoner. The Governor didn't forget to favor me with some of his attention either, revealing to me a joyous piece of news: I was a slug and pathetic parody of a human being or not a human being at all, but a cross between a gnoll and some unknown vile creature. At last, having screamed his fill, the Regional Governor ordered for a transport portal to be opened and, saying that he won't forget what happened here in a hurry, left the mine. If that's the role this NPC is playing, I became curious about how things were going with this province's economy. Or did the developers put a wise advisor next to each ruler like this?

Nothing unusual happened until the evening. Twenty Rats took me forty points closer to Respect, Sakas started to produce 12 ingots a day and, in general, I had no reason for giving the Regional Governor's visit any further thought. It was a really strange episode of my imprisonment, to be honest. He came, threatened, shouted and left. What's the point? In my thoughts I was already at the meeting of the release committee, but then I was summoned to the mine boss once again.

This time there was no-one else in the office besides the orc. I was even glad of this — he wouldn't summon me without a reason, so I'm probably in for a bonus of some kind.

To my surprise the boss started to speak to me in protocol-steeped intonations:

"According to the Emperor's decree, each mine in our province must provide at least one prisoner for mining Malachite at the restricted-access Dolma Mine. Provision requirements: random selection from prisoners of level 7 or above with at least level 9 in the mining skill. On my mine we have forty eight sentients like that and the selection process picked out the prisoner known to you as Sakas. According to point 6 paragraph 15 of the provision on prisoners in the Malabar Empire, I am questioning other candidates on whether they wish to take the place of the chosen candidate. Here is the situation. The Dolma mine contains Large Copper Veins, from which Malachite is mined. The task of the prisoner is to mine 20 pieces of Malachite in the course of two weeks. The mine contains aggressive Rats, so there is a chance that the prisoner might be sent for respawn and be stripped of all his stats. If this happens, he returns back to his mine. As in our mine, there are sections containing veins; no-one has access to these except for the prisoners, so the section would have no immediate guard protection. But if the prisoner, being attacked by a Rat, manages to run back to the main part of the mine, he will be helped by guards and healers."

The orc fell silent for a few moments, and then continued in his usual Akela voice:

"The level eight orc known to you as Sakas has ten levels in Mining and nine in Woodcarving. He put pretty much all his free stat points into Agility, so he doesn't have much of a chance against the Rats. I am asking you: do you want to take Sakas' place?"

"Why did this decree suddenly come out?" I asked the orc, baffled, as I thought over his words.

"The reason is simple: the crafted Malachite figurines. The Jeweler profession became very popular in Barliona in the past week. Practically one out of ten sentients is now aiming to become a Jeweler. The mines meet the demand for ores well enough, but they cannot do so where Precious Stones are concerned. Now everyone's rushing to buy up Lapis to make the Dwarf figurines, but you have to train yourself up before you're able to work that stone. You have to learn by making Copper Rings and working with Malachite and only then can you start making things with Lapis. It is possible to mine Malachite in our province, but only prisoners are able to do that, because Dolma is not one of the free mines. The Emperor ordered for one prisoner to be taken from each mine and sent to mine Malachite. Sakas is guaranteed to die in that mine, but you have a chance of surviving and completing the task. Now it's your time to choose: will you take Sakas's place?"

"What will happen if I complete the quest?" I asked the orc, although I've already made my decision.

"Nothing except for my Respect. My respect, not that of the Pryke Mine Guards. Everything else you already have," said the orc, in what seemed to be a quiet voice, but his words echoed through the office like thunder. So it means that if I accept the quest now, I'll not get anything except for the uncertain Respect of the orc?

Quest available: "Bloody Malachite".

Description: In the course of two weeks, while fighting off Rats, mine 20 pieces of Malachite from Large Copper Veins in the closed Dolma Mine. Attention! The Rats are aggressive! Chance of Malachite drop: 100%. Quest type: Rare. Reward: Respect of the Pryke Mine Guards, Respect of the Pryke Mine Governor. Penalty *for failing the quest: resetting of all stat points.*

"And what will happen if I accept the quest, but fail to complete it in time? Assuming the Rats don't get me first?" I decided to clarify a point of concern.

"If the prisoner fails to complete the quest within two weeks after its start, he is left for the Rats and all his skills are reset."

I couldn't help smiling. Resetting of all stat points. Is that what it's called now? If you fail the quest — you get eaten by Rats. If you get too carried away with mining ore — you get eaten by Rats. If you fail to run to the guards in time — you get eaten by Rats. What great prospects. Do I even need this?

"In that case I'll pass. I have no reason to risk everything that I've already achieved. I have too much to lose."

You have rejected the "Bloody Malachite" quest.

Your reputation with the Pryke Mine Guards has fallen by 300 points. You are 400 points away from the status of Respect.

The orc looked at me for a few moments, then

said in a chilling voice, "This is your choice. You may go."

As I left the mine governor, I tried to convince myself that things didn't turn out all that bad. I could weather an extra month in the mine to avoid risking my Crafting skill. So that was the price of Crafting — a month of freedom. Otherwise I had no way of knowing if I'd be able to raise it to its current level again. A pity about Sakas — he could make some really good things. I'll have to look for a Smith again, and if Sakas gets 'lucky', a new deputy too.

I sat in my favorite spot, lost in thought. On one hand, what I did was sensible and smart, guided by the principle 'every man for himself'. On the other hand... I felt so rotten inside, it was quite beyond words. It looked like I was no better than people like Bat and other prisoners who were only capable of seeing their own advantage in everything and levelling up in Meanness. Perhaps I shouldn't have passed over such a nice stat? It'd come in handy now.

I got up and went to the barracks. I'd try to sleep all of this off. But as soon as I came up to the building I saw that I made a mistake — just then Sakas came out of the barracks with a face full of resignation. That's right — the guy's given up and is mentally ready for respawn. What kind of a bastard am I?

"Sakas, stop!" I shouted, to my own surprise, and caught up with him. "Where are you off to?"

"According to the Emperor's decree..." began the orc, but I cut him off:

"I know all about the Emperor's decree already. When do you go?"

"Now. I was even freed from work today so I could prepare for it. Although what's there to prepare for? Unlike you I don't have that many things: my tools are always with me and what I craft I immediately sell to Rine or present to the mine governor and there's little point in stealing unworked wood — Rine doesn't buy it. So I'm ready now. Ah yes, I've made another dozen Copper Ingots this morning, had nothing else to do, really. I'm sorry it's not much, but that's all I could do. Here you go."

Sakas handed me the ingots and, downcast, headed to the administration building. So even knowing that he's heading for certain death he still thought of someone else first?

"Just hold on a minute!" I shouted again, catching up. "Tell me how much time you have left?"

"You mean time in the mine? I almost gained Respect and my plan was to make a few things, present them to the governor and leave the mine. If you mean how much of my prison term I have left — I have to stew here for another year and a half." Pausing for a few moments, Sakas asked: "Tell me, do you think Smithing will still be in demand after I come back? It would be difficult to get my current professions up to their present level, but I had a chat with Kart when he was reset. He told me of your idea with the professions. You'll need a Leatherworker or a Smith, right?"

"Of course it's still in demand. Let me see you off. Perhaps you could take my rings? I've made some +7 rings recently and I think you could use them. No-one would read their properties without your permission anyway. You need Strength, right? Eight rings and a chain will give you +63 to one or to a collection of stats. Just say what you need and I'll make it straight away."

As we walked to the administration building, the somewhat cheered up Sakas planned what rings I should make him. In the end we decided on 5 rings for Stamina, to add 350 extra Hit Points, and another 3 rings and a chain for Strength, to help with fighting off the Rats and smashing veins. We came into the mine governor's office together.

The transport portal shimmered in the middle of the office; the Dolma mine was probably on the other end. The orc met me with a chilly look. My refusal had probably lowered his opinion of me, quite a lot. But I'm sorry, I can't help that — I need to get out into the main gameworld. I don't see any other way than sending Sakas to his death. Finishing the last of the rings there and then I gave them to Sakas.

"Here, take these. I hope they help," I said, but then the heavy voice of the governor broke the silence:

"Prisoners cannot take items to the Dolma mine that have been in their possession for less than a week. The portal would not let them through, so you can take your rings back. They're no use to Sakas."

Well, I'll be damned! What is this? I mechanically put the rings back on my fingers and looked at the shocked Sakas, who slowly headed towards the portal. Looking at him I understood that I'd be regretting what I was about to do for the rest of my short, but probably very exciting, life. Right up until the moment when the Rats eat me.

"Sakas, stop! Let me at least shake your hand for good luck," I stopped the orc and, when he hesitantly stretched his hand, jerked it, pulling Sakas away from the portal and clearing a path for myself. Before I dove in, I looked at the governor, who stood there, silent, and said:

"For the record: I agree to take Sakas's place," and not waiting for a reply, I closed my eyes and stepped into the transport portal. A pang of cold, some slight disorientation and I found myself next to a lop-sided sign, where time-faded letters proclaimed: "Welcome to the Dolma Copper Mine".

"The name and title of the mine!" The abrupt scream came from behind, and seemed to throw me in the air.

I turned around and couldn't believe what I saw: an enormous, three-meter-tall ogre, dressed in the Imperial guard uniform, stood before me. But ogres are meant to be wild, they are something that people hunted! How can he be here and in Imperial uniform too?

"Mahan, Pryke Copper Mine! I came from our mine to dig for Malachite," I blurted out.

Quest accepted: "Bloody Malachite".

Description: In the course of two weeks, while fighting off Rats, mine 20 pieces of Malachite from Large Copper Veins in the closed Dolma Mine. Attention! The Rats are aggressive! Chance of Malachite drop: 100%. Quest type: Rare. Reward: Respect of the Pryke Mine Guards, Respect of the Pryke Mine Governor. Penalty for failing the quest: resetting of all stat points.

CHAPTER NINE
THE DOLMA MINE
PART 1

'WHAT AN IDIOT! I AM ONE crazy dimwit! Did that conscience that I swept under the carpet sneak-attack me? Wanted to play the hero, eh?' These nice thoughts about my own dear self ran through my head as I headed to the local trader.

The resident dwarf named Lish was the spitting image of Rine: small and beardless, he looked at me with the same sly smile as I went through his goods. While I was at it, instead of actually looking at Lish's goods, which at a glance were the same as Rine's, I focused all my attention on the arriving people, who had started to turn up one after another.

"Pryke mine must be going through tough times if that's the best it can send us." said Lish after a while, when I started to lose interest in his wares altogether. "What's with sending us level sevens instead of twelve? At least you're not the only one, or it would have been too sad for you lot."

The dwarf continued to grumble, but I wasn't listening. *'At least you're not the only one...'* Lish's words stuck in my mind. Does this mean that Sakas went through with me after all? Or did he go after me, but came out here first? I was getting confused.

"Which way did the orc go?" I asked once Lish stopped talking.

"What orc?" was the dwarf's surprised response.

"What do you mean 'what orc?' The one from the Pryke Mine," now it was my turn to be surprised.

"We've had four people from Pryke Mine today and you're the fifth, but there weren't any orcs among them," the dwarf said, killing off my last shreds of comprehension. So, aside from me, there's four other prisoners from my mine here? Who are they?

"Hey, Mahan, if you're not going to buy anything, take a walk and look around. It's still a couple of hours until the prisoners are gathered and told the rules, so you have time to wander round and get your bearings."

The surroundings weren't much to look at — everything was old and worn, there wasn't even a smithy, where I had first intended to make some copper wire to kill time. At a loss what to do with myself, I decided to have a closer look at the prisoners that Lish said came from my mine.

"Pryke Copper Mine!" I shouted as loud as I could. "Anyone from Pryke Copper Mine, come over here!"

In a few minutes three humans and a dwarf walked over to me. They came up separately, which meant that they didn't know each other. The hard and grave looks that they shot at other prisoners including myself indicated that they were also shocked by the news that several sentients came from that mine. What else? There wasn't much else to say about them, it was time to go and break the ice. I placed a lot of hope in my level four in Charisma: that they'd not tell me to get lost right away and at least hear me out. It was time to see whether or not I made a mistake by investing in this stat.

"Greetings all," I began, when they all gathered. "Let's introduce ourselves. My name's Mahan, I'm from the Pryke Copper Mine and, being perfectly honest with you, I don't know any of you. Are you sure there hasn't been some mistake? The Pryke Copper Mine is this wonderful place with an administration office full of crafted objects, an orc governor, don't know his name, and dwarf Rine, either a trader or head of supplies. Is that the Pryke mine you hail from?"

"My local monicker is shitty, so call me Clutzer," said one of the humans that had come up. He was quite thin and not very tall, with shifty eyes and an inconspicuous face. Someone like that had to be playing a Rogue, I thought. All he was missing was a couple of daggers and he'd be ready to go. "That's some pretty shit you're shooting about the mine, Mahan. Rine, the grody orc, the mine, all's there, but I just can't grok ya. What rock did you crawl out from under? We never had you at our mine, for real. And you're acting like an underboss."

I was taken aback by this speech. No-one spoke like that at the mine, but here we had a veritable well of gangster lingo. The only non-human in the group put an end to my total bewilderment.

"I'm Eric, to keep things short," said the dwarf. "I also don't know you, Mahan. I've not seen any of you before either. I was promised that if I mined 20 pieces of Malachite, I'd finally go into the main gameworld. I have another half a year to go until Respect, but I'm fed up with waiting, so I was happy to jump at this proposal. With my level 12 in Mining, getting 20 pieces of Malachite will be a walk in the park."

"I'm from Pryke too. You can call me Karachun. I was also promised that I'd be released from the mine if I get the Malachite. And, by the way, like the rest it's the first time I've seen you Mahan and you Clutzer..."

"Hey, Clutzer's my nick!"

"It's all the same to me," continued Karachun. "It's not like I ever saw you at the mine before. There were two hundred and forty prisoners there and I know each of them. None of you were ever among them. Period."

"Leite," said the last man. "Same as the rest — not seen anyone and don't know anyone. So, what should we do? I also have 12 in Mining and character level. As far as I see, that's what you need to end up here. I too was promised parole if I gather the Malachite."

"FALL IN!" the ogre's shout rang through the mine and we started to gather into one big crowd. No ranks formed — everyone stood like a bunch of sheep in front of the ogre, shifting from foot to foot. We needed our sergeant here from boot camp — he'd sort them out fast.

"Attention everyone! I'll explain the rules of the Dolma Mine for the first and last time," began the ogre.

"First. From today and for the next two weeks there are no restrictions on food and drink — you can use them any time as much as you want. From tomorrow morning food will be constantly available by the entrance to the mine; whoever needs it can come and use it.

"Second. Dolma Mine has only one section, about two by two kilometers in size. It contains about three thousand Large Copper Veins, which are renewed daily — so there'll be enough for everyone. Guards have no access to the mining section, so if a Rat attacks you, you either kill it yourself or run out of the mine all the way here. The mages will arrive here tomorrow — they'll provide protection.

"Third. Rats. Ours are big, fat and have a bite to reckon with. So keep your wits about you. Each Rat has its own habitation zone, about 40 meters in diameter. If you kill the Rat — you're free to work within a 20-metre radius. There are 1-2 veins in each zone, so you have plenty to work on; and remember — a new Rat appears in about an hour, so don't get carried away with work, and keep your eyes open. If you get eaten, you'll go home to your mummy," a murmur went through the ranks of the prisoners, but the ogre quickly cut it off: "Silence! I'm not finished!

"Fourth. The territory of the mining section is very well-explored within one kilometer from the entrance. What lies beyond is known only in part, so my advice is: if you want to live, don't go too far. You can work alone or form groups. If you form a group you won't be able to leave the group until the time set for this task runs out; a group has to hand in the sum of the Malachite pieces to be mined by all its members. To make it clear from the start — loners have never survived in the mine for more than two days. About the groups. If anyone dies and leaves the group, the number of Malachite pieces that the others have to mine is reduced by 20. If the deceased had Malachite in his possession, it remains where his body was and can be picked up. And remember: if a group of five people, for instance, gather twenty pieces of Malachite and one of the group dies and is removed, the amount of the gathered Malachite is reduced as well — by the share of the one removed. In the described example, the group will be left with 16 pieces instead of 20.

"Fifth. If by some miracle you manage to get 20 pieces of Malachite and stay alive, you'll still have to remain here until the two weeks run out. During that time you can mine Malachite for yourself. The countdown starts in the morning; there are no sleeping quarters in Dolma, so you sleep right on the ground. No-one will wake you up, so if you're lazy you'll pay for it in two weeks — your time for mining is limited.

"And sixth. The Rats drop Skins, meat and there is some chance of various fangs, tails and other items that alchemists need. So if you get lucky you may even make a profit when you leave.

"Now you're free to go. Next time I want to see you either with the 20 pieces of Malachite or in two week's time when I'll be personally sending you to the mine as Rat food. Dismissed!"

There still remained a couple of hours until the evening and so I decided to do some scouting around the mine. I was curious what was out there, what was meant by a common section, how many Rats were running around and, in general, maybe I should try smashing a vein. 'It's true that fools think alike', I noted to myself, because after the ogre's speech almost all the prisoners went to the mining section. Of course: the sooner you start, the sooner you'll finish.

The section was separated from the rest of the mine by a glimmering veil, beyond which nothing could be seen. 'So here's the veil that the guards cannot cross', I guessed. This means that the mining section itself is like a Dungeon in the main gameworld. But if that's the case, getting together a standard Dungeon group is a must — a tank, a healer and three DDs (damage dealers, fighters specializing in damage). My gut feeling told me that there must have been a reason why there were five of us from our mine, and a good one at that. The dwarf will be the tank — he's small and thus harder to hit, plus he should have some special bonuses for tanking, if I'm not mistaken about dwarves. I'll be the healer, even though I really hate doing that, and the rest of the gang will go at the Rat from the sides while it gnaws on Eric. I'll have to put this proposal to them. I was walking up to the veil with these thoughts when suddenly some prisoner tumbled out of it with a terrible scream. He immediately got back on his feet and ran towards the guards and then THIS THING appeared from the direction of the mining section.

The THING was the Rat, but about the size of a small pony, around a meter in height and about 2.5-3 meters in length, tail and all. Is that supposed to be a Rat? It's a Horse! The animal stopped, surprised at seeing so many people, then something seemed to click in its head and it unhurriedly trotted after the prisoner that had just appeared, completely ignoring all the others. 'Ah, the Rat has an aggro-list (a list with the data about each player that enters the mob's perception zone. The mob attacks the player at the top of that list. In order for the mob to switch to a different player, the latter has to re-aggro it: generate a greater amount of threat than the first player on the list).' The thought flashed by, 'this means the others have nothing to worry about.' What happened next I could only explain as an act of subconscious reflexes, since these were by no means conscious actions on my part.

"Eric, grab it, I'll heal! Clutzer, Karachun, Leite, wait five seconds and then hit it from the sides! Don't come at it from behind or it'll slash you with its tail! Now!" I shouted frantically. I don't know what moved Eric: my shouting, my Charisma, reasons of his own, or Mars moving into Capricorn, but after my cry, he ran up to the Rat, took out his pick and made a good swing at it, shouting: "Aaahh, you bastard!" and hit.

The Rat made a high-pitched squeal, stopped and immediately reacted to Eric's attack: it made a sharp turn ending in a bite and his Life Bar was diminished by a quarter. That foul vermin — how much damage was it dealing? If Eric is level 12, he must have 60 points in his stats; he's bound to have put some of them into Stamina to avoid his Energy going down too quickly during mining. So to take off a quarter of hit points just like that was quite a lot. Now it was my move.

All these thoughts rushed past in less than a moment. Eric barely had time to scream in pain as I got my Tambourine out of the bag. Thanks again, Kart and Sakas, for making me this wonder. Now, to begin.

I selected Eric and started to hit the Tambourine. I decided to take no notice of how it looked like from outside, my task was to get Eric back up. I started with my usual song:

The Shaman has three hands...

Yes! Eric's Hit Points went up.

"Waste that Squeaker!" shouted Clutzer and attacked. Right, things should get easier now.

... and behind his back a wing...

Yes! Eric's doing a good job too, not screaming from the Rat bites, standing there, teeth clenched, and taking it.

... from the heat upon his breath...

Yes! Why is it just Clutzer hacking at the Rat? Where are the others?

... shining candle-fire springs.

"Karachun, Leite, you need a special invitation?" growled Eric through his teeth. Good: if he has time to look around, he's still with us.

"Take that, you bastard! Rub out that grey-furred biter! Karachun, away from the tail, or it'll get you!" our shouts echoed through the mine.

"Eric, turn its head to the mine! The tail!" I shouted when I saw that the Rat was hitting other prisoners with its tail. I wasn't exactly worried for them (it's not like the tail was going to kill them), but I had no intention of sharing the loot. Who knows what the local system for loot allocation was. Things were rather interesting with this in Barliona — in some cases the loot went to the person who hit first, in others to all those who sustained damage. So we shouldn't take the risk — there's not a lot to go around as it is. By this time I had little doubt that we'd bring it down.

The Rat continued to throw itself at Eric, biting him again and again. It was surprising that the dwarf didn't fall down: when such a mass jumps on you, it takes some skill to stay on your feet. Eric stood there, teeth clenched, and hit the Rat, whose life bar was falling slowly but surely.

The Rat's sides were flanked by Clutzer, Karachun and Leite, who hacked at the Rat like it was a vein: taking an aim, hitting and looking at the result.

"Die already!" — Eric screamed wildly, jumped and made a devastating blow to the head. He probably scored a crit, because the Rat fell on its front paws and remained motionless for some moments. It's concussed, a guess hit me, and since Eric's health was at full, I decided to see how I would fare as a fighter. I selected the Rat to summon a Lightning Spirit on it and shuddered. Oh hell: level 14, 1000 Hit Points in total of which around 400 still remained!

Damage inflicted. 8: 36 (Lightning Spirit Damage)/2(level of opponent /Character level) -10 (Inner resistance to Spirits).

Dammit! What about all those Strength rings? Why did I ever take off all my gem rings? At least I didn't take the neck-chain off. 'Damn, just hope my mana will last,' I thought angrily, again selecting Eric and summoning another Healing Spirit. The Rat had recovered and started to chew on our tank once again.

When only 20% of the Rat's Hit Points remained, it suddenly began to increase in size, its eyes started to become bloodshot and its fur took on a bloody tinge.

"Mahan, give me all you've got, it's going berserk!" Eric's shout filled me with dismay.

Grey-furred damnation! When berserking, mobs inflict 100% more damage, pain and general unpleasantness. If it scores a critical hit, Eric's had it! And I only have enough mana for 4 more Healing Spirit summonings.

"Hit it with all you've got! Let's do this!" I shouted and started to summon the Healing Spirits.

A Rat attack hit = minus 30% to Hit Points, a Healing Spirit on Eric = plus 10% Hit points. A Rat attack hit = minus 30% to Hit Points, a Healing Spirit on Eric! Plus 10% to Hit points...

Skill increase:
+1 to Charisma. Total: 5

The Rat suddenly flickered and disappeared. Yes! We downed it! It took more than a minute to bring down a Rat. Between the five of us! Trying to fight it alone is just pointless. It'd eat you in the blink of an eye. I looked at Eric and saw that he was surrounded by a whirlwind of light. That's right — he's reached level 13! That makes sense, we weren't attacking the Rat as a group and the prisoner it was chasing probably never touched it after seeing all its

Hit Points, so all the experience for the Rat went to Eric alone.

I'll be damned... during the fight my Hit Points went down to just 20! I hardly even noticed! I urgently needed to find a Shaman mentor, or I'll bite it while I'm busy healing others. After getting some water, which was thankfully nearby, I restored my life and mana levels, and then had a look what the Rat left behind. No-one other than Eric was able to pick up the loot, but we could look all we wanted. There wasn't much to look at, though. Rat Skin, 3 pieces of Rat Meat. That's it. Nothing special, really; so much for getting my hopes up that our tank would get something useful. And he was our tank, because I was sure that after a demo of the Rats the number of people wishing to mine Malachite alone would plummet dramatically.

The majority of the prisoners started to disperse. There were still about two hours left until the end of the day, but no-one else wanted to risk going to the mine. That Rat really did leave an impression on everyone.

"I'm thinking that we should form a group," said Eric, when there was no-one else around. "I played Barliona before going to prison. I was a tank then and this time round too I fell back into my old habit and started to level up my Warrior as a tank as soon as freedom was on the cards. If each Rat has one thousand Hit Points and they take off fifty with each hit, you won't get far without a healer here. Mahan will heal and you three do the killing. We'll choose a section, kill the Rat, smash the vein together, get the Malachite and move on. This way we'll complete the quest. I don't see any other way."

"You got it, shorty," agreed Clutzer "Them's some crazy Rats, can eat ya like nuthin', groddy buggers. So I'm in with the group thing."

"Agreed," nodded Leite, "but let's decide now how we'll share the Malachite we mine. It won't be good if someone splits as soon as he gets the 20 pieces. I can do without any 'happy surprises'."

"If you make a group you won't be able to quit it just like that, and the amount of Malachite for the quest would still be based on all of us," replied Karachun. "I'm fine with just one of us lugging this Malachite around, as long as we get the right amount of it. I say we group up too. That Ratling was just too big. If one of these spawns every hour, we'll never get the assignment done by ourselves."

"What about you, Mahan?" Eric looked at me, "Do you agree? This won't work without your healing. If you're in, then form the group: you were the fastest to react to the Rat and knew what to do, so you'll be the raid-leader. I've got one more question for you now: where did you get such a short name, like NPCs have — just five letters? We're all walking around with half-sentence tongue twisters and have to shorten them to usable nicknames, but when I first saw you I thought you were an administration representative — your name is that different from the rest."

"I agree that we should form a group and will send you an invite in a minute." I said, "I have an immediate proposal — we've downed the Rat and there's still enough of the day left before dark. There's five of us. I propose we take a walk to the mining section and smash at least one vein. We should start today. As for the name — before I was put into the capsule the operators gave me the chance to choose my own name rather than use a random one. That's why my nick looks like that."

I selected Eric, Clutzer, Leite and Karachun in turn and sent them each a group invite.

You have created a group.
4 people have joined the group.
Attention! Changes to the 'Bloody Malachite' quest. The amount of Malachite to be obtained has changed. New amount: 100.
Loot distribution: Each man for himself. The type of loot distribution cannot be changed in this location.

Well, well. The time had now come, I thought, to allocate the remaining 27 free stat points. Of course it would be nice to save them until I leave the mine, but if a Rat eats me, they'll be of no use anyway. I put on my Intellect rings again and began to increase my stats.

Let's think. For starters, I need to put about 7 points into Stamina, so I could summon a couple more Spirits. Damn, with this limitation I'll have to allocate my stats in a way that's far from optimal. Total: Base Stamina of 17, with the items going up to 26, thus at level seven this would be enough for 30 or so spells. 'At this rate I'll be a tougher tank than Eric,' I smiled to myself. Right, next — Strength. We'll have to be quick about smashing the veins, so 10 points to Strength would be just right. 10 points remaining. Intellect or Agility? I only need Agility for professions and it's of no use to me right now. So, it's Intellect. Although, stop. Why don't I try to put a couple of points in Charisma? Since I'm a RL — a raid leader — it could be useful.

Attention, the Charisma stat cannot be increased by addition of stat points!

I see. Same as Crafting. A pity, would have been good to increase my level of influence over others. I'll have to level up in it as the circumstances permit. Putting the 10 remaining points into Intellect and increasing it to 18 at the base and 82 with items, I opened up the group interface and examined the stats of the rest of the group.

Eric. Warrior. Level 13. Stamina 40, Agility 15, Strength 30, Rage 8. Yes, I was wrong, the tank overshot me in Hit Points by quite a lot. But that was good: the thicker his hide the easier it'll be.

Clutzer. Rogue. Level 12. Stamina 25, Agility 15, Strength 40, Rage 6. I guessed the class right with our slang connoisseur. I was also glad to see that he had enough Stamina: a smaller Energy loss meant more time for mining the vein.

Leite. Warrior. Level 12. Stamina 25, Agility 10, Strength 45, Rage 7. This also made sense. In a mine you didn't need Stamina that much, especially if you're a Warrior, so the emphasis was made on Strength, to mine the ore quicker.

Karachun. Warrior. Level 12. Stamina 25, Agility 10, Strength 45, Rage 7. Leite's clone, by the looks of it.

If they all have level 12 in Mining, they

shouldn't spend more than four hours on a Large Copper Vein, even if they go at it alone. And if all of us start smashing a vein — it should be finished in an hour at the most; this could mean about 10 veins a day. To sum up: it should take us 10 days to complete the quest. If not for the Rats it would have been easy enough. But the Rats...

Looking at the others I saw Eric staring into empty space and mumbling something under his breath. That's right, he was also checking his interface. It's good to play with someone who knows what they're doing. The rest were walking around nearby. Fighters — can't expect too much of them. They don't need to clog their head up with extra information, like who has how many Hit Points left. That's what the tank and the healer are there for — all they have to do is stand aside and swing their picks.

In a couple of minutes we were all ready to head for the mining section. A picturesque view appeared before us: an enormous plateau where in places plies of stone — Large Copper Veins — rose above the ground. It was very quiet, only the faint rustling of the wind and occasional squeaking of Rats could be heard above the section. The visibility was quite good, so we could see how the rather plump Rats were scampering around here and there. The area that we entered didn't have a Rat any more, but it did have a vein, which we surrounded and began to smash. The sound of our picks echoed through the mine. For a moment we stopped and looked at the Rats — the loud noise could have made them nervous and inquisitive where these five potential meals came from. The Rats didn't look startled and continued to scurry around their zones. Great — around forty minutes was left until the one we killed respawned and we continued working on the vein. Our aim was Malachite.

After a while an agitated squeak told us that the Rat had respawned and that it wasn't happy. By then the vein's Durability fell to 20%, which meant that it really did take us an hour to smash it. Great!

"Eric, grab it! Fighters don't attack without my command," I shouted an order, as if it was an old habit.

"We fight the Rat like the last time: Eric hits it on the face, the fighters stand on the sides and practice their Mining skill on it and I stand back and do the healing." Maybe I shouldn't have declined the Healing stat. You just stand there without doing a thing, hitting your Tambourine and singing songs, while the rest are doing all the work. On the one hand the role of the healer is well-respected, and, in view of the sensory filters being turned off, could even present a way of avoiding extra painful damage. On the other hand, this really isn't my thing. I just don't like being idle. I healed Eric once again, restoring all Hit Points, selected the Rat and summoned a Lightning Spirit on it. Let's see what happens this time, when I'm levelled up and with all my rings on.

Damage inflicted. 113: 246 (Lightning Spirit Damage) /2 (Opponent Level /Character Level).

WHAT?!
Repeating the kamlanie for summoning the

Lightning Spirit, I once again saw:

Damage inflicted. 113: 246 (Lightning Spirit Damage) /2 (Opponent Level /Character Level).
Experience gained: +80 Experience, points remaining until next level: 396
Skill increase:
+1% to Intellect. Total: 43%.
Achievement earned!
Bane of the Animal World level 1 (10 animal kills until next level).
Achievement reward: damage dealt to Animals is increased by 1%.
You can look at the list of achievements in the character settings.

Silence fell on the mining plot. I looked at the remains of the Rat, and the others looked at me, without saying a word. So it turns out that with the rings I don't just become a cheater, I go into godmode: ten Lightning Spirit summonings and the Rat's a toast. A couple of levels more and it'd take only 4 or 5 summonings.

"Mahan, is there something you want to tell us?" Leite broke the surrounding silence.

I was quiet for a moment and then said, "It's the rings. I'm a Jeweler and can make rings and neck chains for myself; with a bonus for any stat. You want to hear the rest or can you guess?"

"How much do you want for a ring?" Eric asked straight away. "I understand that you don't give them away for free but you do sell them, right? I've got to have a bonus like that."

"At my mine I sold them for 15 gold. I think that would be a reasonable price here too."

"Have a heart! Aren't we all working in the same group at the same job? Can you make it at least 5 gold a piece?"

"All right, let's make it five, I can live with that. My aim is to get enough Malachite, not to turn this place into an auction house."

"Excellent; now show us what you have," Eric began to get his money out, "We need rings with Strength. Do you have some with Stamina too?"

"I have everything, since I can change the stats on the rings."

"WHAT?" Eric stopped in his tracks. "How? I heard about this — in my old clan the guys who did Jewelcraft said that there was a feature allowing you to change stat bonuses by decreasing the ring's durability, but to get it you had to go through a ton of quests, go somewhere and study something. How is a prisoner able to do all this — especially with a level 7 character? A short name, such abilities in Jewelcraft... There's something you're not being straight about, Mahan — you're holding something back. Well, to hell with it, pass those rings here."

I moved to give Eric the rings and was surprised by a message popping up in front of me. From Eric's expression I guessed he was seeing the same thing.

Attention! You cannot transfer items or money to players from parallel Pryke Mines.

So they really were from the Pryke Mine, but

from some parallel version of it. I couldn't give them the rings, remaining the only cheater in this mine. So that's how things can play out!

I turned to the other group members and saw that we now had a few problems. It was clear enough what to do with the Malachite, but we had never discussed how the loot from the Rats and Copper Ore should be split. What if something unusual dropped from a Rat? Who would get those bonuses? Such matters should be settled from the outset, in good time.

The Rat dropped standard loot: a Rat pelt and a couple of pieces of meat. All of this lay unclaimed on the ground as we stood around it, looking at each other in silence. No-one wanted to lose out on the loot, but neither did anyone want to look like the bastard who'd just grab everything for himself. Everyone was silently waiting for proposals from the others. Well, since I was given the honorable title of raid-leader, I should be the one to get the ball rolling.

"Right, I see that we've found ourselves in a bit of a pickle with the loot distribution, yes? I propose a simple solution: I take what drops from the first Rat. The second Rat is Eric's, third — Clutzer's, fourth — Karachun's and fifth — Leite's. If a Rat drops something unique, this bonus belongs to whoever gets lucky with his turn. The others have no claims against him. Otherwise we'll argue until we're blue in the face about who should be getting what."

"Eric's already got his from that first Rat. If you two swap places, the second Rat is yours, the next one will go to Clutzer and so on," replied Karachun. "I like this approach. If someone gets lucky, he gets lucky. I won't have a problem with that."

When all agreed that they were happy with this loot distribution method, I picked up the loot from the Rat and put it in my bag. Just a bunch of cheap stuff, but if there's a lot, it'll be enough to live on.

"Mahan, what's with the miming? Do you think this is a talent show or something?" asked Leite. Everyone continued to look at the place where the loot had just been.

"I don't get it. What are you on about?" I asked, surprised.

"You bent down, didn't take anything and then pretended to put something in your bag. And the loot's still on the ground, exactly where it was. Don't ask us to pay for the mime performance, we just can't put a price on talent like that. You're faking it pretty badly, man."

I really didn't get it. I again opened up my bag and looked at what I put there. Well, yes, there's the pelt and the meat. I didn't have any meat at all before, so there was no mistaking it.

"Looks like you're the ones playing jokes. I already took my things and put them in the bag. The spot you're looking so intently at is empty, as it happens. So if anyone's seeing anything there, go ahead and take it all, I'm fine with that."

"Don't be a smartass, Mahan. You better not be pissing about with us," said Clutzer and pretended to pick something up from the ground and put it in his bag. "An extra pelt's not gonna rip me pockets."

Without saying a word, Leite and Karachun repeated Clutzer's silly movements. Are they trying to start an aerobics class here? Or did they actually get their loot? Eric continued to stand there, gazing at the spot where the loot fell.

"So, now it looks like each of us got his own loot from the Rat." He began. "This means that even if we are in a group, the loot drops for each of us individually and cannot be seen by the others. Only the Malachite is shared. Or is it the same for the Copper Ore too? We have to finish off the vein and find out whether each will get his own or we'll be sharing the ore in turn, as Mahan proposed with the Rat. This approach is to my liking too. If lady luck smiles on me with some bonus, it would be just for me and no-one else." Then Eric also bent down, picked up his loot, invisible to the others, and turned to the rest of us.

"What's with the standing around? We have an unfinished vein to mine; at this rate a new Rat will spawn, while we're faffing around here. Off to work, you loafers!"

We returned to the vein and quickly finished it in 10 or so minutes. It gave 22 pieces of Copper Ore and 1 piece of Malachite. The Ore turned out to be shared, so we gave the first lot to Eric. The next one would be mine. Not bad, considering that it takes us about an hour to get through a vein this size.

Experience gained: +1 Experience, points remaining until next level: 395.
Skill increase:
+5% to Mining. Total: 61%
+1% to Stamina. Total: 58%
+1% to Strength. Total: 55%

All these floating messages brought me little joy. At the Pryke Mine a Large Copper Vein provided 5 experience points, but here it gave only 1. Did this mean that the more people in the group the less Experience and stat increase you get? Unfortunate: more people means less stuff to go around. Still it's better than working alone.

We all agreed that the mined Malachite would be kept by Karachun. It was now clear that we'd complete the quest without unduly exerting ourselves and that our exit to the main gameworld was practically guaranteed. Definitely something to be happy about, but I also wanted to solve the problem with the rings — how could there be such a savage restriction without any possible workaround?

We smashed another vein, destroyed two more Rats and headed off to the common zone. We had barely passed the threshold separating it from the section with the veins when we were surrounded by a crowd of prisoners. People awaited us impatiently for the last two hours to see for themselves that it was possible to leave the mining area in one piece. I had little desire to recount our exploits and replied to questions with vague mumblings, but this quickly turned into Clutzer's moment of glory. He wove an embellished tale of our battles with Rats, although I could barely understand a word he was saying: "The sheisty Rats, for real, like, got their cards all mixed up, and our mate Mahan's one badass shaman," and so on. I wondered if he was the only one who could understand what he was on about.

"Hold on, Mahan. I'd like to do a few experiments with transferring rings," Eric stopped me as I was about to head off and look for spot to sleep. "If we can't hand over items directly, perhaps it's possible to outwit the system. Shall we try?"

Eric seemed to have read my thoughts about the rings, so I agreed right away. It would have been interesting to find a loophole in the restrictions: after all, this was my job before I ended up here. I made a decision to follow Eric's suggestions:

"Right, so we can't transfer the rings directly, we've tried that already. Although, try and give me a ring now. Nope, it's not working. All right, moving on. Throw it on the ground. That's not working either: when you're not holding the ring, I can't see it at all. Then try throwing it away rather than throwing it down: imagine that you're getting rid of it like trash. No, that's no good. Are you sure you chucked it without regretting it? All right, what next? Let's try to give the ring to someone from a different mine, perhaps the transfer would work through intermediaries."

Using other prisoners didn't work either, nor using the dwarf trader, nor, truth be told, any other of Eric's ideas: the system totally blocked the transfer of items that were created outside Dolma. Hmm, maybe that's the problem, that the items were not made here. We have to check this out.

"Eric, hold on. It's my turn to brainstorm. I think that the ring should be made here. At first I'll make it from the materials that I have. I've made them before, actually, but we weren't grouped up then. If transferring them still won't work, we should make ingots from the ore that we mined today. Although here we have two things against us: I'm not a Smith, and can't smelt the ingots, but even if we find a Smith, there's no smithy in Dolma, so we've no way of getting the ingots made. Otherwise it's a very good idea."

"Don't you worry about a Smith and ingots. I'm a Smith and will make those ingots for you. We don't even need a smithy — I always have a smelting pot with me, same goes for ingot mold and coal. Fire isn't a problem — see those torches the guards have? So try and make it from your materials, while I go and prepare everything for smelting."

I didn't spend that much time making the ring — Eric hadn't even finished heating up the coals. When I'm back in Pryke, I'll have to ask Sakas to carve a wooden mold that I can pour melted Copper into. I'll try to make a whole ring then, or all the ones made from wire will get worn out soon and break. But, what am I on about? I'll not be coming back to Pryke, there's nothing for me to do there. I changed all the stats to Strength and handed the ring to Eric. It didn't work. A pity, now there was only one chance left. I gave the ore mined in Dolma to Eric and headed off to sleep, leaving him to do the ingots. It was too late to wait for the results of the smelting and then spend time making the wire and rings. Tomorrow, all tomorrow.

In the morning I had barely opened my eyes when a pleased Eric handed me eight Copper Ingots. He did it. 'Dwarves are such bores these days', the thought flashed in my head as Eric recounted the tale of how he made the ingots. 'Do I really need to hear about all the difficulties he had to overcome or that he didn't sleep all night? Well done, I applaud you, have a pie as a reward, or something. A pie!'

The thought of food woke me up completely. There are no restrictions on food in Dolma, so I won't get a penalty if I eat what I cooked myself. With my level of Crafting the meat I cook should taste great and come with a bonus or two. I should do that right now, the rings can wait.

As I drifted away with thoughts of how I'd be frying the meat and the potential bonuses involved, I mechanically took the ingots from Eric and spent a few baffled moments looking at the message that popped up:

You received an item from a player from a parallel Pryke Mine, created by him using a shared resource. Attention! After you leave the Dolma Mine this item will be removed!

Great! So if the ore is shared, items made from it should also be shared: this means we can pass them between ourselves. A disgruntled inner hoarding hamster grumbled that now I'd have to work for free and give away rings for nothing, but I silenced him very quickly. You can't buy freedom! 'Well... Technically you can, but I don't have that kind of money' I thought with a sigh.

I didn't spend a lot of time on cooking. I used a torch as a cooking fire and very soon the meat turned into something very appetizing. I saw the hungry looks of my group and tried to share the meat with them, but it was impossible — the meat was not shared, so items made with it could not be handed over. Not the end of the world, I thought, enjoying the tasty and juicy Rat meat.

Buff gained: Strength +3, Energy loss reduced by 50%. Duration — 12 hours.

Eric told the others that we had found a way, albeit a temporary one, for transferring things, so we decided that while everyone was smashing the veins I'd be making rings and only lending a hand with the Rats.

And we got started on the grind.

Just by making the rings and without touching the vein I received experience each time it was smashed, so in terms of levelling up I didn't lose anything. One Rat — one Ring. This cycle continued for four hours until I ran out of ingots. After that I could take a rest and do some swinging with the pick. Making wire in the absence of the special instruments was a real pain in the ass, but the result in the form of four Rings with +4 to Strength was worth it. With enough ore the whole group would be covered in rings in four days' time and we'd complete our job way before the set deadline.

When a Rat gobbled up yet another player, whose scream of woe and pain echoed through the whole mining section, we had a visit from a delegation. All the other prisoners formed five groups of nine people each, but only one of these had a healer, which did not prevent it from losing three people by this point. Two more were Rat food after deeming themselves to be mighty tanks. So that's minus five already — all on the first day. The Rats here seemed to have the run of the place.

The visiting delegation proposed that Eric and I should become Ratcatchers. He'd tank and I'd heal, while the nine-strong group hit the Rat and then quickly switched to mining ore. In payment each group would give up one piece of Malachite a day. Taking a time-out we went to talk it over with the rest of our group.

"So that's how it is," I said, having described the proposal to them. "On the one hand it will take us longer to smash a vein and we'll be making eleven or even ten instead of twelve pieces a day, if Eric and I are distracted by other Rats every hour. It will take us about twenty minutes to help all five groups. Then we'll be smashing our vein for forty minutes, then our Rat respawns and it's rinse and repeat."

"These bastards bite like hell..." grumbled Eric under his nose. "When I was playing a tank, I had never heard of sensory filters being turned off in Barliona. But here you can feel every bite and every push. You stand there, teeth clenched, only thinking how not to scream in pain. Just today I increased my Endurance stat by fifty percent, and if I hadn't trained it up before on our Pryke Rats I'd have made a pretty rubbish tank. But then we'll have five additional pieces of Malachite a day... Dammit, I'm in!"

Karachun, Leite and Clutzer also agreed to carry on working while Eric and I hunted Rats in the neighbouring sections. I didn't even tell anyone yet that I also got experience for smashing the veins despite not hitting them myself, so the group would be glad of the additional experience and loot. Eric would be the one to generate aggro with the Rat, so all the extra bonuses will go to us. I must definitely remember to tell all the others to go and pick up all the loot — Rat pelts and meat — all around the mining section after we finish work for the day. Or any other useful drops, if they get lucky.

That was our first day. After I finished the rings we got through another seven veins and Rats in our zone and then Eric and I showed a total of twenty nine Rats how unwelcome they were in the mine. Which is very unwelcome indeed. This day was when I came into my own. Two Rats later I reached level eight and put all my free stat points into Intellect; and when I reached level nine I truly started enjoying myself. We did the right thing by agreeing to hunt the Rats. One thing was disappointing: the experience gain from the Rats decreased with each level. At level nine each one gave a measly 20 Experience points. A pity, but not much to be done about it: the more you grow, the slower you grow. Eh, why didn't I start to level up in Leatherworking? So many skins going to waste. But the 18 pieces of Malachite that lay in Karachun's bag after the first day of work, which also included the two from yesterday, placated my inner hoarding hamster and greed-toad, making them nice and accommodating. We had six days to go before completing the quest.

CHAPTER TEN
THE DOLMA MINE
PART 2

O N THE THIRD DAY OF WORK WE LOST Karachun. It was stupid and banal, but a fact's a fact — only four of us remained now. And I was the only one to blame for this. And it all started so well...

On the second day I went up to level 10, after which a Rat would yield only 10 Experience Points. Such misers this lot, I should give them the slip. I'll work a couple more weeks and then leave for sure. When I reached level 10 I started to hunt the Rats alone — there was no longer any point in taking Eric with me, a discovery that came easy enough. When we went for one of the Rats, the group which we came to help took too long to get their act together, so Eric and I were left alone with the beast. Generally that was nothing to worry about: I had Eric's back and he carefully dodged the bites, so it was all right. About ten seconds later, seeing that the crowd wasn't going to come and join us, I started to summon a Lighting

Spirit.

Damage inflicted. 198: 291 (Lightning Spirit Damage)/1.4 (Level of Opponent /Character Level) -10 (Inner Resistance to Spirits).

Wow! I was right to put all of the new 15 points from the last three levels into Intellect! In the four seconds it took me to summon the Spirit I stripped off almost a quarter of the Rat's Hit Points. The rest was a piece of cake. Two Lightning Spirits on the Rat, one Healing Spirit on Eric, a Lightning Spirit on the Rat and we're done. Thus came the immediate question: why distract Eric from mining Malachite? With the next Rat I asked Eric to back me up, focused and started to aggro the Rat.

Damage taken. Hit Points reduced by 38: 80 (Rat bite) — 42 (armor). Total: Hit Points: 212 of 250.

Aw! Grey-furred damnation! How can Eric stand this? Intently banging on my tambourine I started running away from the Rat, circling around its whole territory. And why not? No-one's forcing me to stand there and enjoy the 'bite therapy'. The Rat ran after me, managing to bite me from time to time, but now it was a lot less frequent or painful. By the time the Rat finally died, I increased my Endurance skill by a good 40%. Not bad, considering that I caught only three bites, reducing my Hit Points by 120 in total. Damn, so much was taken off by Spirit summoning — practically half of the health I'd just lost. Fine — once

I become a real Shaman, I'll sort out this nuisance. For now I made use of another Dolma Mine perk — the ability to heal my own dear self. One could not do that in Pryke, but here you could heal yourself all you wanted. Only one thing was bad — first I completely healed myself and then 10 Hit Points was taken off me for summoning the Spirit. Not much to be happy about, right? Where's the logic behind it? First a Spirit comes and then heals. The developers probably included this feature for a non-initiated Shaman as something of a last chance, otherwise when you only have 2-3 Hit Points left you wouldn't be able to do any Spirit summoning if the Hit Points were taken off first. But here you first summoned, got healed and then paid the price in full. I consoled myself with this thought and sent Eric off to smash the vein and started hunting the Rats. That's how the second day ended, without any sign of the coming trouble.

In the morning of the third day in Dolma, after successfully dodging some Rats in our section, I headed to the sections of the other groups. During my third round of this the Rats died quickly and without a problem. There was only one drawback — after the last Rat I was completely depleted of mana, because as your level increased so did the amount of mana you spent per spell. If at level one I spent 4 mana and 2 Hit Points on summoning Lightning and Healing Spirits, now it cost me 40 mana and 10 Hit Points. So with the last Rat my mana ran out and it had to be finished off with picks — at least the group I was with was quick enough to lend a hand. I should have gone for a drink to restore the mana, but Rats already began respawning between the mine exit and the place where we were now working, and I had to kill at least two to get to the water. I looked at the Rats scurrying about and decided not to bother, because the mana would get recharged by itself in about fifteen minutes. With my level of Intellect this wasn't a problem, so I slowly headed in the direction of my group. I had rings to finish — just three more to do and the whole group would be fully ringed. 'That's some ambiguous word I used there,' I smiled and, with all the mana that had managed to recharge by then, summoned a Healing Spirit on myself. That last Rat made an extra effort at biting me, the grey bastard. Then suddenly a shout sounded though the mine:

"Mahan, help! Rats!"

Dammit! I quickly picked up the pace and rushed towards my group. I ran without even thinking that all I could hit the Rat with was my pick.

When I got there, I had a surprise waiting for me in the form of two oversized Rats. The Large Copper Vein, which the group was mining, was located at the intersection of the territories of three Rats; and although we already killed one of them, the other two got their chance. So now one of these was absorbed in enthusiastically gnawing Eric, who habitually dodged it and was doing all he could to attract attention of the second Rat, which set its sights on Karachun. As far as I knew, the dwarf didn't have any special tanking abilities, so he could not pull the other Rat away.

"Mahan, heal me, quick! Leave me alone already!" shouted Karachun taking swings at the Rat. 'Why aren't you running away, you dope? Why are you just standing there? Haven't you ever played before? You can't run away from this section, that's clear: the Rats have already respawned on the sections between here and the exit. But why stand there and keep hitting it, not allowing Eric to take the aggro off you? That's just stupid!' Karachun only had 90 out of 250 Hit Points left. You need to run! These last three days all of them reached level 13, but invested in Strength, putting their hope in me and Eric. Looks like that was a mistake.

I selected Karachun, and started to summon a Healing Spirit. It'll be all right in a moment, I thought trying to calm myself, but then I saw a message that made my heart sink into my boots:

Low mana level! You cannot summon a Healing Spirit. You need 40 points of mana for the summoning. Current mana level: 18 of 970.

"Noooo!" I shouted, grabbed my pick and flew at the Rat. "Leave him alone you grotty beast! I'm the tasty one! Eat me, damn you!"

Current mana level: 26 of 970.
Karachun's Hit Points: 50 of 250.

"Karachun, run from it, don't just stand there! I can't heal you now — no mana! I need a few more seconds! And don't hit it — you're not letting us take the aggro off you!" I screamed, doing all I could with the pick to pull the Rat. But it was no good. With my level of Strength it was practically impossible. And Karachun himself was hitting the Rat like stupid, as if he didn't hear us. These Berserkers. Stop hitting it already, you fool.

Current mana level: 34 of 970.
Karachun's Hit Points: 10 of 250.

'Please, Mr. Rat, leave him alone already! He's really not that tasty! Look at Eric, he's plump, small and juicy. He's doing all he can to make you like him, just look at him!'

Current mana level: 42 of 970.

At last. Two seconds. I need just two more seconds to summon the Healing Spirit. 'Hold on Karachun!'
The Shaman has three hands...

Attention! You cannot summon a Healing Spirit on this target. The target is dead.

I fell to my knees. A pile of Malachite and five rings was all that remained of Karachun. That was the end of his quest for freedom. Where's that Rat? I'll tear it apart with my bare hands...

Critical damage inflicted. 406: 2*291 (Lightning Spirit Damage) /1.4 (Opponent Level /Character Level) — 10 (Inner resistance to Spirits).
Experience gained: +10 Experience, points remaining until next level: 640

The second Rat we brought down just with our picks. When it died silence descended on the mine. The other groups even stopped working to stare at the spectacle — levelled up players just bumped off their partner, giving him an extra three to four months in the mine... Yeah, there was enough to stare at, for sure. All in all my heart felt so sick that I wanted to howl.

We didn't do any more work that day. Eric picked up all the Malachite, money and rings left over from Karachun and put them in his bag, joking that's he's next on the list, after which we cleared our path of Rats and came out. The rest of the prisoners, knowing the futility of trying to mine Malachite with Rats around, followed us. There was little desire to repeat Karachun's fate.

No-one talked to each other for the rest of the day. I, because I felt guilty, Eric probably because he was unable to pull the Rats off him, Leite and Clutzer... I don't know: probably simply out of solidarity. There was nothing to say, really: the seemingly ideal plan for obtaining Malachite had fallen through. I hoped to have it done within six days, but now...

In the evening I noticed that Karachun's greyed nick with message 'Dead' next to it was still part of the group and selected the 'remove' option.

Are you sure you want to remove the player from the group? Attention! If the player is removed from the group the amount of Malachite needed for completing "Bloody Malachinte" quest will be reduced by 20 units. Following removal the

**player will not complete the "Bloody Malachite"
quest.**

Cancel! Cancel! Cancel!

"Everyone come here! Eric, get the Malachite
out, let's count it!" I shouted in a voice that had a bit
more life in it now. If all of the Malachite remained
then there was a chance that Karachun would
complete the quest — even back at his mine. I just
had to get the others to agree to it!

The amount of Malachite was exactly what
Karachun had on him — 42 pieces, including the
pieces that we were due today for our guard work. So
Karachun's share didn't vanish! Damn, I just couldn't
remember what the ogre said about those who died —
did they leave the group straight away or only after
being removed? What happened to the quest in this
case?

"In the normal game," said Eric, after I shared
my guess about Karachun with the others, "even if
the player is killed in battle with a boss, he still gets
experience and access to loot. The same happens with
quests — if he dies in the middle of one and his group
completes the quest, he completes it too. If the same
rules apply in the mine... Guys, even if they did put
me in the can for five years, I don't want to be a
bastard. Of course, Karachun's no angel if he ended
up in the mines, but we should give him a chance.

"I'm down with that," replied Clutzer.
"Karachun was a sharp dude. And in general we have
no right to deny him the opportunity of getting into
the main gameworld. That'd be just wrong. I agree
with Eric — we should give him a chance. At least

we'll have a clear conscience. I'm ready to put my money where my mouth is."

Silence once again descended on the mine. If even Clutzer started speaking like a normal human being, we should definitely give Karachun a chance to complete the quest with the rest of us.

The next three days went by without any major incident. Our work gang of three kept a very close eye on where the Rats lived and I always kept a reserve of mana, so everything was under control.

A few good things happened: in total we already had 87 pieces of Malachite, 25 of these coming from our 'Rat catcher' pay; I levelled up to 11, which unfortunately meant that I started to get only 5 experience points per Rat, so level 12 wasn't really going to happen in the mine. I increased my Strength and Stamina by 1, bringing up their base value to 17 and 18 respectively. My mining went up to 11 and was on a sure path to level 12. My 'Bane of the Animal World' achievement reached level three, increasing the damage I dealt to animals by three percent. I put the five new stat points into Stamina, because Spirit summoning now cost me 11 Hit Points each time. In general, everything was going well until our sharp-eyed Eric spotted some strange object in the distance.

"Leite, have a look over there: what do you see?" said Eric when we were getting ready to leave for the day. We smashed 10 veins today, systematically working our way from the entrance, but to our disappointment not a single Rat territory contained more than one vein. No luck today. As a result we moved almost four hundred meters away from the entrance, leaving ten respawned Rats behind us. Like it or not, we had to hack our way through them on the way back. In the meantime Leite was looking in the direction where Eric pointed.

"That's the mountain on the horizon, as usual. It's been here from day one, what did... What'd you see in it?"

"Don't look at the mountain; do you see that black spot all the way at its base?"

"No, I don't. It's probably a shadow that's fallen in a strange way — it's almost evening now," Leite was a picture of incomprehension.

"Shadow my boots! Haven't you ever played Barliona before?" said Eric, indignant. "I'd give a tooth, preferably one of Clutzer's, that it's not a shadow, but a cave entrance. And if this section with the Rats is a Dungeon of sorts, the cave is..."

"Is the home of the local boss," I finished his thought. Eric was right, if the dot that he saw really was a cave, it must hide a bonus of some kind, protected by a boss. But what use was that to us? Our task was to gather the Malachite and then get the hell away from the mine, not play 'tag' with bosses.

"Why get all worked up? We hand in the Malachite and split," said Clutzer, as if reading my thoughts.

"Don't you understand? We'll finish the quest tomorrow, hand in the Malachite, and do what exactly for the next seven days? Just warm the ground with our backsides, without even checking that place out? We're all level 13, except for Mahan, who with his rings could easily pass for a level 19. Tomorrow we'll hand in the quest, reach Respect, pack some food and head off to the cave. Even if we die on the way there, all that would happen to us is that we'll end up in our mines before the rest — reputation does not get reset. In the main gameworld you'd need a week at the most to reach level 12. There are quests there! So, in essence, we've got nothing to lose: if we die from Rats or from the boss, we'll return to our mine and leave it straight away. If we kill them, we'll collect all the bonuses. The ogre did say that we'll take with us everything that we loot here. We all have to decide on this, but I believe that we can't let a chance like this slip away."

I didn't know about the rest, but I had some thinking to do. On one hand, I've died before and, although painful, it wasn't exactly fatal. But on the other hand, there was something that made dying in the mine very undesirable — the Crafting stat. If I died, it would get reset too. Though I completely agreed with Eric about the rest (with my Hunter it only took me a couple of days to reach level 10), levelling up in Crafting again would not be that easy. I also suspected that I would not be able to make the chess pieces if my Crafting was too low. Damn, again we had a situation where 'the honey is sweet, but the bee stings'. And this time the sting was a big one.

"Let's decide tomorrow. We still have to get 13 more pieces, hand them in and make sure the quest is completed. We can talk after that," suggested Leite, to everyone's agreement. Once we had fought our way to the exit, we went off to do some thinking.

Unable to come up with anything to keep myself busy, I headed to Lish. I only had a look at his wares once, and in a great hurry. A more thorough browse through his stores would be good, in case there was something useful.

"Ah, what people grace us with their presence today," said the dwarf, happy to see me. Unlike Rine, who was always working, Lish was always sitting on a log. I wondered which of them was a wrong type of dwarf: the one always working or the one always sitting.

"What fates bring the Rat Terror of Dolma to call on my humble person?" So Lish knows how to sneer too. I think I like our Rine better.

"I thought I'd come and have a look what I can buy from such an esteemed dwarf, but I see that he's busy taking a rest. I'll be off then," I've practiced this phrase on Rine, except in his case it was 'working' instead of 'taking a rest'. As usual, the phrase worked like a charm: Lish immediately jumped to his feet.

"What do you mean 'I'm busy'? All I do is wait around for people to come and start buying my wares. But they only come to sell the ore — they don't even look at the goods."

"Why look at them if all the dwarves have the same wares? Whether it's back in my mine or here or anywhere else. I didn't see anything of interest on the first day — nothing I've not seen with Rine, who sells things in my mine — although he'd probably have more goods than you. Quite a lot more."

"What? You didn't even look at my stuff properly and are trying to talk it down already? I've got at least ten different picks. And what about boots and jackets? Have a proper look, will you?" Lish got all worked up, taking out his wares from a large bag and laying them out right there on the ground. I couldn't get a reaction like that out of Rine. My skills must be growing, by and by.

Jackets, trousers, boots, picks, beginner recipes in a separate stack: in general, all the standard stuff, as with Rine. There wasn't a single item with stat bonuses, the only difference being in the level of armor (in clothes), durability and strength of damage (in picks). I shook my head and looked at Lish. Ehh... a pity, I thought he might have had something of interest. But this...

Seeing my disappointed face, Lish seemed to lose heart. Now it was his turn to give his wares a joyless glance-over, though he was praising them as the best in the world just a minute ago; he was looking more downcast every second. Well, sorry — if you don't have anything, you don't have anything.

"No, Lish," I decided to speak only the truth, harsh as it might be for the dwarf. "You have the same stuff as everyone else — the same clothes, the same picks and the same recipes. But to Rine I even went for Precious Stones, which I needed for my Jewelcraft. Now there's someone that can get hold of anything," I decided to finish off the dwarf, embellishing things somewhat. Just a little. I decided not to say that Rine told me to get lost with these requests. But that doesn't matter.

I turned and was about to head off only to be stopped by Lish's happy shout:

"Mahan, hold on! Why didn't you say right away that you do Jewelcraft? I have something here that I rarely bring out, since I hardly ever come across Jewelers. Have a look," Lish rummaged around his bag and I read a message that appeared in front of me:

Attention! You used special properties of the Trade profession: you are being offered non-standard goods.
Skill increase:
+1 to Trade. Total: 6

Lish took out a scroll of some kind.

"Here I bought a couple of Jewelcraft recipes a while back, but haven't managed to sell them to anyone. I'm sorry, but I can't let them go for less than 20 gold a piece — that's how much I bought them for. And I'm not going to sell at a loss."

"Agreed. No-one's in the business of losing money. But let me have a look at what recipes you have first, or I may already have them and won't be able to get my money back."

"Look, by all means. It's not like you can activate them while they're still mine," said Lish and handed me the scrolls.

So, what did we have here...

Greater Copper Ring.
- ❖ Description: Greater Copper Ring. Durability: 80. +2 random Stats from the main list (Stamina, Strength, Agility, Intellect and Rage). Minimum level: 8.
- ❖ Crafting requirements: minimum Jewelcraft level 8.
- ❖ Ingredients: 2 Copper Ingots.

❖   Instruments: Jeweler's Tools.

Bronze Wire.
❖   Description: used in the crafting of bronze rings and neck-chains.
❖   Crafting   requirements: minimum Jewelcraft level 10.
❖   Ingredients: 1   Bronze Ingot.
❖   Instruments: Jeweler's Tools.

Bronze Ring of Strength.
❖   Description: Bronze Ring. Durability: 100.   +2   Strength. Minimum level: 10.
❖   Crafting   requirements: minimum Jewelcraft level 10.
❖   Ingredients: 2   Bronze Wires.
❖   Instruments: Jeweler's Tools.

Aside from the Bronze Ring of Strength, there were also Bronze Rings of Stamina, Intellect, Agility and Rage. So, if Copper Rings gave random stats, starting with Bronze they were pre-set for each ring. Great, but how is it implemented? Will I have to learn through trial and error again? Doesn't matter. Seven Jewelcraft recipes for 20 gold each... These dwarves have it made.

"I'll take them. Here's the money."

New Jewelcraft recipe learned. Greater Copper Ring. Total recipes: 8

After learning the other recipes and losing 140 gold, I went to sleep. Having suppressed my greed-toad, my inner hoarding hamster was happily examining the new recipes, while the toad was left to weep over the spent gold. Never mind, oh green one: we still have about two thousand gold left, so things aren't that bad. Recipes are always useful. Now I just had to figure out where to get hold of Bronze Ingots and whether to go for that boss or not. If that boss was even there. Why would there be one in a mine for prisoners? Our task was to gather ore, not hunt down bosses. But then again, those Rats must be here for a reason. So it remained an open question. Tomorrow we'll be finished with the Malachite and then see.

We mined the 13 pieces of Malachite ourselves and had no need of the pieces we were owed for Rat clearing. This made all the groups very happy, but at the same time very downcast. They still had four to five days to go before they were done, so although the extra Malachite was good, they saw that this could also mean the end of my guarding duties and the Rats would be gnawing at them now.

At the end of the working day, we cleared the Rats on our way out of the Mine and headed to the lop-sided and worn administration building. That's it, the quest was completed and we could take a rest for the remaining seven days. Wonderful.

"I told you that the next time I wanted to see

you was when you hand in your quota!" the ogre's
roar shook the office. Unlike the Pryke office, there
were no paintings, curtains or a big table with a
throne-like chair here. The furnishings were quite
Spartan, nothing extravagant: a simple table and
chair. That was it.

"There's a reason we're here," I replied for the
others as the raid-leader. "The assignment has been
completed — Eric bring it over."

Eric took out the pieces of Malachite and put
them on the table before the ogre. And why not? He
told us to hand it in to him, so that's what we're
doing. With each piece that Eric laid on the table, the
ogre's jaw dropped lower and lower. By the last piece
he turned into something altogether unrecognizable.
Eh, if I could only take a screen-shot of this — I'd win
more than one contest with this picture: a shocked
ogre. Such a sight was worth seven days' work.

"Here are the hundred pieces, including
Karachun's share — he's gone for a rest just now. So,
is the quest completed?"

The ogre nodded, still standing and quietly
staring at the pile of Malachite.

**Quest "Bloody Malachite" competed.
Reward: Respect of the Pryke Mine Guards,
Respect of the Pryke Mine Governor.**

There was a melodious chiming and a glow
appeared above our heads. Hello main gameworld, I'll
be seeing you soon. But first I had to settle the matter
with the boss. Some thought also had to be given to
the other groups — it wasn't right to ditch them just

like that.

"'You have become the fifth fastest team to meet the Malachite quota in the entire history of the mine," the ogre finally recovered himself, stepped away from the table and headed towards the exit. "Wait here."

A few minutes later he was back, carrying some objects in his hands. Wow, does this mean that we'll be getting some rewards now? Great! It's nice to join the ranks of the fastest miners. But my greed-toad started to fidget again — if not for Karachun's quota, which we were working off today, we would have completed the quest yesterday and taken an even higher place. Damn, why didn't they tell us this was a competition? We'd have worked even faster or asked for two pieces of Malachite from the other groups for protection.

"According to an old decree of the Emperor, if a group of Malachite miners becomes one of the fastest five, they are to be given a reward for their work. Karachun will receive his in his mine — I'll send it today. Now, to deal with you lot."

The ogre started to give out the rewards. Eric received some kind of a shield, at which he stared like the ogre at the Malachite before. Impressive — when he equipped it his Hit Points immediately increased by 130. So, this little shield gave at least +13 to Stamina. Not a bad bonus for a beginner tank. And if you take into account that it should provide a fair amount of armor, it was really priceless.

Clutzer got two daggers. They had no Stamina bonus, but his face soon resembled Eric's. What did they all get, really? My hands were itching to take it all and have a look.

Leite received a sword. He was good and restrained himself, only his eyes widened a little, but immediately returned to normal. The sword didn't have any Stamina on it either, since the Hit Points didn't increase, so it probably came with a Strength bonus.

When the ogre came round to me, my inner hamster stood on its hind legs, lifted and folded its front paws and, drooling and wagging its tail, watched the approaching ogre expectantly with love-filled eyes. Such a sell-out!

The ogre handed me something resembling a Tambourine and a stick with a knob on the end. And that's it? A shadow of disappointment even crossed my face: I already had a Tambourine, although I had to use my hand to hit it since it came without such a stick. I don't remember what it's called, I should have a look in the properties. Ehh, the others got a shield, daggers and a sword, and all I got was this shoddy Tambourine. I took it from the ogre and checked out the properties.

Shaman's Tambourine Trala with a Mallet. Double-handed item. Durability: unbreakable. Description: Using a Shaman's Tambourine Trala during kamlanie decreases Spirit summoning time by 50%. The penalty for summoning all Spirits is decreased by 50%. When the Tambourine is in Shaman's hands: + (Character level) Intellect. The Mallet can be used as a blunt weapon: Damage: (Strength * 2). Tambourine and Mallet can be combined with other items. Item class: Scaling.

Level restrictions: None.

The inner hamster fell on its back in complete rapture and its legs waving in the air. Scaling items were incredibly expensive, costing up to several hundred thousand gold. Only a handful of NPCs sold them in the whole of Barliona and they could not be sold to other players or NPC-traders. You could only throw them away. But what nutter would dump an item with stats that increase with each new level? Or an item that could be combined with others? If I wasn't mistaken, 'combination' meant adding drawings to the Tambourine to increase its stat bonuses, inserting some crafted Jewelry, adding enchantments to it or making something from the stick with the knob — I forgot what it's called again. There is a lot you can do with an item that could be combined with other items. I understood my hamster, whose legs were still ecstatically treading air, very well. Players would do anything to obtain such an item, and here it practically dropped into my lap. Though, truth be told, if not for the 25 pieces of Malachite for our guarding duties, we'd have never made it into the top five.

When we left the ogre, Eric immediately turned around and said to everyone:

"Guys, don't even ask me what I just got, as I won't tell you anyway. Sorry, but if the rumor spreads through Barliona that I have such a thing," he glanced at the shield, which he was still holding, "I'll never be able to level up my character in peace. Every PK-er (Player Killer) will see it as his duty to send me for a respawn, stripping me of part of the experience. I don't need this, so please just forget I was given anything. I advise you to do the same — the fewer people know what you've been given, the easier it'll be for you."

I was in complete agreement with Eric: although I was extremely curious what the others had got, I didn't really want to tell them about my Tambourine. It was just as well if no-one knew anything. No-one could look at the properties of my items without access, which I had no intention of granting anyone. But still, what on earth did they get?

The next morning we had another visit from representatives of five remaining groups. If you removed all the congratulations and other idle chatter, the actual essence of their request, and it was a request, sounded like this: please help with the Rats until the groups finish their mining. Each of us will get a Malachite piece daily and I, as the main Rat-hunting manpower, would even get two.

We all agreed and continued to work in the mine for the next five days. Each group smashed twelve veins daily, providing everyone with 3 pieces of malachite and me with level 12 in mining. The Rats did help me, after all, to reach level 12 and I spent 3 stat points on Stamina and 2 on Intellect; I also reached level 4 in the Bane of the Animal World. To top it off I was given two pieces of Malachite a day for my guard duty. So these five days were well-spent and I even managed to make a good profit. The only disappointment was that the Rats didn't drop anything other than meat and pelts. No alchemical goodies dropped either for me or any of the group. At least that's what they told me.

At last on the fifth day all the groups of prisoners completed the quest, leaving us two days for the trip to the cave and back. If the length of the mine was two kilometers and Rats were located at forty-meter intervals, we had to get through about fifty Rats. That was quite a lot, even for our currently strong group. In the end we did decide in favor of going after the boss.

"Well, have you decided?" asked Eric two days after we had received our rewards from the ogre. "We have to make our minds up faster: there's only five days left and I wouldn't want to go on the last day if we decide to do it after all. Otherwise we might get locked up here with the Rats and die for certain. With the little presents from the ogre we'd run there and back barely noticing the boss. We'll just knock him over as we're passing through."

"Well, that's quite a snazzy getup they gave is, for sure" said Clutzer. "If there's more like it in the cave, we'd get totally decked out."

"Mahan, we can't go without your Spirits. You with us? Come, you've got nothing to lose anyway. So, we'll die, and you'll level up to 12 in a week. But this way we have a chance to gain something, possibly something really valuable."

"Eh, Eric. Do I have to tell you that I wouldn't swap my Crafting for any potential bonuses from a level 15 boss? What other level would be there, if all the Rats are level 14? The boss would have to be 1-2 levels higher. Or even 3 levels; this means that the cave has a level 17 mega-Rat, just sitting there and waiting for us to show up, all dapper and smart, and take away all its goodies."

But maybe I should stop thinking logically? If we don't go to the cave, what is the probability that I would really regret it? It's substantial, quite substantial, even. Well then, maybe I should just tell logic to get lost? It's not making life any easier. Do I want to go? Yes, I do. Then what's the problem?

"I agree. It would be good to go and have a look at what's there. Maybe there isn't even any cave and you were just seeing things," I said. "We'll go as soon as we finish helping the others get the Malachite."

Come what may, I decided then and there the time for our expedition had come. When they heard about the Boss and that there was a chance of dying none of the other prisoners agreed to come with us. We were fine with that — all the more loot for us.

I stocked up on Fried Rat, in case I needed it to restore my health — what if my mana ran out and my Hit Points were close to zero? Anything can happen. No such luck with water — we didn't have any canteens or any other large vessels. Even Lish didn't have any for sale. However, from what I understood of the local rules, even if we had some, they could only be used by their owner and no-one else. Never mind, we'll just have to hope that my mana restores quickly enough.

And so, on the morning of the sixth day, after selling all the remaining meat, skins and ore to Lish to free up bag space for potential loot, we headed for the mining section. Our objective could be spotted on the horizon, but first we had to try out the items we received from the ogre in the field. I didn't summon the Lightning Spirits on the first three Rats and was essentially watching from the sidelines how the group quickly dispatched the poor animals. While they were at it, the Dolma mine saw the emergence of three more fearsome Rat vanquishers. Eric, holding the pick in one hand and the shield in the other, took hardly any damage and the Rat's Hit Points started to fall very quickly when Clutzer and Leite went at it from the sides. Judging by their pleased faces, everyone in the group liked this method of attack and so we split into two parts — they dealt with one Rat, while I went ahead and pulled the next one that stood in our path. In just an hour we arrived at the spot and were faced with the standard shimmering veil of a Dungeon entrance/exit. Eric was right — our section did have a boss and we were standing before the entrance to its lair.

"Right, let's agree on the way we'll go about things from the start," said Eric. "Since no-one except for Mahan has ever played in Barliona, I'll go through the main rules of fighting a boss. We come in together, then I immediately go a couple of meters ahead and you stay put and see what's going on. Mahan, you're in charge of immediate support: summon the Spirits as soon as we come in. Who knows what's on the other side, so it's best to play it safe. Next. Clutzer and Leite — attack only on Mahan's command and only targets which I'm already hitting or those called out by Mahan. No attacking things at random and don't even bother with the other mobs that'll be swarming around — it's my job to pull them all to me and keep them there. And remember: I don't have taunt yet (tank ability to take the mob's attention on himself), so if someone suddenly goes for you, crouch, cover your head and take the hits. You can scream something if you like, but on no account hit back. Or I won't manage to get it off you. Mahan, you stand a short distance away from me. Healers often generate aggro, so be prepared to call a Lightning Spirit and command the others to hit your mob. That's the first part. Any questions on this?"

"What kind of a boss do you think is in there?" I asked Eric.

"The question is off-topic, but still relevant. Most likely it's a level 18-20 Rat in there, with some unpleasant abilities. So, if there are no questions on the first part, I'll move to the second. All bosses have special abilities, which they use to hit either the tank or the whole of the group; so it is essential that Clutzer and Leite listen to what Mahan says. And you," Eric looked at me, "need to make quick decisions — whether we stand together to spread damage between everyone or scatter in different directions. There is no guide for this boss, so we'll proceed like when gaining the "First Kill" achievement: at our own risk. I know this about Rats: they like using poison on anything crossing their path. If this boss also uses poison, we're not going to have an easy ride. We don't have any antidote and if there is no time limit on how long the poison lasts we could end up kicking the bucket. So, Mahan, your mana regeneration is our only hope for making our way to the mine exit through all the Rats. I think they'll respawn by the time we kill the boss. Another point — all poisons have a serious weakening effect, so there is a chance that the boss will start bouncing around the rest of the group. Be ready for that."

"The boss will start to do what?" asked Leite in

incomprehension.

"I mean it will stop gnawing me and go after everyone else in turn. In that case we'll follow the plan I just described — you sit, shout and stop hitting the boss. I'll keep the boss facing away from the entrance. Don't approach it from the tail if it's a Rat, or any other boss we might get, for that matter, we don't need to take any avoidable damage. Only hit it from the sides. With the loot, I think we will each pick up our own, but if something happens and loot becomes shared, I propose we can agree now how we split it. I know we shouldn't count our chickens and all that, but I don't want to start a job without talking through all the details."

"I propose a simple solution," I said. "If an item has an Intellect bonus, none of the others here would find it useful, so it will go to me. If something will add Rage, naturally, it's not something I'd even look at. Again, with bonuses to dodge, parry or armor it's clear that that thing should go to Eric. If it's Strength or Agility, then Clutzer and Leite will have to draw lots. If an item would suit all or none or if some alchemical or other useful items drop, we'll choose the owner by casting lots. Everyone knows 'Rock-Paper-Scissors'? We'll use that, since we don't have any dice. We could, of course, toss coins, but that would take longer. There are four of us, I always play with Eric, Leite and Clutzer. Then the winners will play amongst themselves. I think it's a good idea for sharing the loot."

When all agreed, Eric continued:

"And now, the last point. I don't know how the fight will play out, perhaps the boss will kill us all and we'll each return to our own mine, so I propose that after we get into the main gameworld we find each other and form a clan of our own. I'd add you in my friends list right now, but this function is currently disabled — until the moment of our release, as far as I understand. We seem to play well together and each has a unique bonus; either way, I still have four years of time to do, so I have to sort out my life in the main gameworld. That would be easier to do together. Near Anhurs there is a tavern called 'The Jolly Gnoom', the innkeeper there is a gnome named Rothfronda and we can meet at her place. If Mahan has to be stuck in a settlement for three more months, after that time I'll be waiting for you at the tavern every Tuesday and Thursday. You need about five thousand gold to create a clan, but with Mahan's rings I don't think that should be a problem. We could buy the ore — though it's better if we mine it ourselves at the free mines — and Mahan would make rings and neck-chains. It shouldn't take us more than a month to come up with the money. In a Jewelry shop ordinary +2 Bronze Rings cost around 30 gold. Silver +5 rings are about 60 gold each and gold rings, which give +10 to a stat and can have enchantments put on them, cost a few hundred."

"Strange, I always thought that being a Jeweler wasn't exactly popular in Barliona. If making rings generates so much money, why aren't half of Barliona's population Jewelers?" I asked Eric, surprised.

"Try figuring this one out for yourself. For example, I've been playing for several years, but I never heard about such a thing as Crafting; and the fact that it allows you to increase the number of stats in the crafted items is huge. This will sell; and, going back to Jewelcraft, even +10 rings are very useful up to level forty. However, from level forty onwards, when you have two hundred stat points, the 40 points you can get from gold rings don't make that much difference. They will be a drop in the ocean and the result wouldn't be as noticeable as it is now. With each level the effect of the rings diminishes. Of course, the clans that go on raids or capture other clans' castles take great care to be better even by +1, so that's where people tend to level up in Jewelcraft. For the majority of players though, being a Jeweler is just a low-level diversion. In my old clan the people levelling up in Jewelcraft usually got as far as making bronze items and then gave up, because Silver Ingots are already expensive, to say nothing of the Gold ones: with just a couple of free mines producing these metals making rings is simply unprofitable. Thus everyone is just saving up to buy some gold rings once and for all and be done with it. Mithril rings and above are the prerogative of the top players and clans — I don't even know where you can buy these. So your +4 Copper Rings will sell like hotcakes, and if you make your way to Silver, you'll have buyers queuing up."

'Right, so when they were putting me in the capsule they didn't give me such a bad profession after all,' I chuckled to myself. I had to reach the level where I could make Silver rings. So far I haven't told anyone that in my case rings and chains turned into combined items into which stones could be inserted, but if we formed a clan I'd have to show my cards.

This would mean that everyone would have to be made the same kind of gear as I have. Still, that could wait — now we had a boss to get through.

"The clan gets my vote. As soon as we get out, I'll make sure to add everyone as a friend and we'll form a clan. But now, let's go. We've been hanging around here too long already. Clutzer, Leite — ready?" I saw them nod and looked at Eric. "Well, dwarven tank — lead on."

"We all come up to the veil, form a line and step in on the count of 'three'. Ready? Then it's countdown time. One. Two. Three."

I got out the Tambourine and the Mallet and stepped through the shimmering entrance.

CHAPTER ELEVEN
THE DUNGEON

A S SOON AS THE SHIMMERING VEIL disappeared, Eric took two steps forward and put out his shield, Leite and Clutzer stood either side of me, their new weapons in hand, and stared ahead intently. We were ready to repel any attack, but for some reason no-one was attacking us. It seems that I was again slow on the uptake: why would there be mobs right at the Dungeon entrance? They are all further in. I barely moved myself forward when a message popped up:

Message for the player! A new territory has been discovered: The Mushu Dungeon. The probability of finding a valuable item from an ordinary opponent has increased by 49.999%, Experience received is increased by 20%.

I couldn't help smiling when I read the message. Only quest items had a drop rate over 50%.

As a rule, the greatest probability of other items being dropped was exactly 50%. We've discovered a new territory, which meant that no-one's been through this Dungeon before us. Unless I was mistaken, the first explorers had the greatest likelihood of getting loot. We already had the chance of items dropping off the Rats in the Dolma mine; keeping in mind that it had increased by such a high percentage, this original chance amounted to just 0.001%. And despite it all the ogre told us that there was a possibility of getting additional income. Some joker he was!

The place where we found ourselves strongly resembled a tunnel: the three meter high corridor disappeared into the distance. At intervals of also about three meters lit torches cast strange shadows on walls made of roughly hewn stone. There was a sense that the passage had been dug out with picks and any further work on the walls was deemed unnecessary. Only the floor was more or less even, so you did not have to trip at every step. After about fifty meters you could barely see anything, even with the help of the burning torches. It looked like the developers had imposed a visibility limitation to make going through the Dungeon more interesting. Once in the tunnel, I immediately noticed a strange green bar appear before our eyes.

"Careful as we go," I said and an echo went through the passage: "...go..., ...go...". "This place gives me the creeps." The strange bar started to fill with red as echo made its way around the tunnel. Eric gave me a reproachful look, put his finger to the lips and we slowly went on to the sound of the dying echo. As soon as the echo disappeared and the bar became completely red, a strange rustling sound came from down the passage, growing louder every moment. It wasn't even a rustle, but more like a myriad of little legs hitting a stone floor. In about ten seconds we saw a wall of incomprehensible something moving at us from the depth of the corridor. When it was about forty meters away we could finally see what it was: a giant worm, which took up the whole of the corridor space and was moving towards us with the implacable certitude of a real full-track tank. The entire perimeter of its body sported small appendages with which it pushed itself against the walls as it moved forward. So that's what had been making that disgusting rustling sound! The worm's head had no eyes, but sported an enormous round opening — about a meter and a half in diameter — that served it for a mouth. The whole of this mouth was full of long teeth, making it resemble every type of shark at once. The moment I spotted the beast heading for us it became clear to me that we'll never kill it, because it would simply crush us with its mass and then eat us, and our expedition for extra bonuses would end before ever really starting.

"To the exit, move it!" I shouted and run up to Eric, who was getting ready to take on the beast, pulling him towards the shimmering veil. "That's not the way to deal with it! Out, before it crushes us all."

We sped to the exit and again stepped through the shimmering veil. As soon as we were back in the mine grounds I shouted:

"Everyone back off from the exit and get ready! That bastard could follow us out!"

We set ourselves at the edges of the Dungeon

exit and started to wait for the weird beast to come out. A minute went by, then two, but the thing never appeared. That's right, it won't set a foot (or appendage) outside the Dungeon. As soon as we left the Dungeon the red bar disappeared, which gave me an idea about what to do with the pseudo-millipede.

"I think I'm too freaked out to jump this beaster...." Clutzer ventured.

"No need to jump it," I cut off any disputes, when I saw Eric preparing to explain to us that we had to go back and finish off this thing before it crawled away. Everyone looked at me in surprise and Eric asked:

"You think of something?"

"That's right. When we came in, did everyone see a status bar before our eyes?"

The others nodded and I continued:

"When I started talking an echo spread through the tunnel and the bar started to turn from green to red. And as soon as the bar turned completely red this thing went for us. Something tells me that we've got to make our way towards some point very quietly and carefully, without disturbing this sleeping beauty. If we don't make any noise, we'll get there. If we make a din this wonderworm will be on top of us again and swinging our picks under its nose is totally useless. It'll swallow us whole, totally disregarding our epic efforts."

"All right then," said Eric, "but in about three minutes I'll still go in and check if that thing has crawled back where it came from. And then come back right away to call the rest of you. And if I'm not back... Well, it won't be very nice if we all came in and it was right there. Best if it's just me..."

Eric's explanation was a bit muddled, but I got him. Why risk everyone if we have a specially trained tank, whose role dictates he should always go first.

The beast wasn't by the entrance, so five minutes later we were all again standing at the start of the Mushu Dungeon and getting ready to clear it out. The bar took its place before our eyes, all green as before.

Very slowly, with each taking care not to make any extra noise, we moved forward. We walked for about 10 meters: the bar wasn't turning red, and the tunnel remained completely silent. 40 meters... 60 meters...

A hundred meters from the entrance we came to a fork: the corridor split into two passages, equally illumined by torches. The others gave me a questioning look. Fair enough, I was the raid-leader and it was my call to decide which way to go. If I guess right we'll bypass the worm and it'll be 'well done' to everyone. If I guess wrong — it'll be the raid-leader's fault, not that of the group.

I silently indicated the left passage. I know that good heroes never turn left, but now I had a feeling that this was the direction we should head.

We carefully made our way along the corridor and after some time came to an enormous cave. Well, well. Tough luck. That THING was lying right in the centre of the cave, about twenty meters from us. We stopped dead at the cave entrance, examining this creation of the developers. Now we had the chance to have a proper look at the wonderworm, but did we really need all this?

Tunnel worm. Level: Inaccessible. Hit points: 45 000 000.

Inaccessible level meant that the beast was at least thirty levels above me. There's no point in even trying to bring this one down. Because it's totally useless.

I looked around the cave. It was large — about thirty meters wide, its ceiling spanning out of sight. The 'wormie' was nestled in a special hollow in the floor and paid no attention to the guests that just dropped in. We carefully turned around and headed back. They're right when they say that turning left leads to a sinister end. You should only go right! In about a hundred meters the right corridor was blocked by a thick grate, with bars you couldn't even squeeze your head through. We spent a few minutes searching for hidden levers, locks or secret stones, but it was no use. In a fit of anger Clutzer grabbed the grate and started to shake it. 'At least it's not making any noise', a thought flashed in my mind, but then there was a rattling sound, the green bar turned red by about 30% and Clutzer was holding a long metal rod. Glancing in surprise from the rod to us and then to the newly-made gap, Clutzer very carefully put the bar on the floor and then wiped the sweat from his forehead. Had it been any louder, it would have started an echo in the corridor and the lovely worm would have dropped in for tea. Still, we got away with it.

We squeezed through the gap and went on. Just a few dozen meters later the corridor took us to a cave or, to be more exact, a giant hole. The bottom of the hole was about three to four meters deep and was full of stakes pointing upwards. The hole itself was about twenty meters wide, so jumping over it wasn't an option. We didn't find any hanging bridges, ropes from the ceiling, grips or levers to help us get to the other side. What a snag! One cave with a worm in it and the other full of spikes. How do we go on from here? The fact that we were meant to go on was clear from the passage at the opposite end of the cave.

When we came back to the fork, I explained in gestures: 'we're taking a break' and then sat down for a think.

There's no way that the Tunnel Worm was the local boss. Otherwise it would be a rather silly Dungeon — a single boss without a crowd of mobs. It had been a mistake to leave the hall with the worm without first examining it properly. What if it was hiding a lever that was key to getting through the second cave. We had to be thorough.

I gestured the others to stay put and once again headed for the cave with the worm. Once there I carefully made my way along the wall, mindful of any movement from the beast — in case it got curious about who decided to pay it a visit. But all was quiet. When I got to the opposite side of the cave, I discovered a strange device on the wall that looked like a crossbow. Is this what we should use to bring down the worm? But where were the arrows? Besides, it wasn't meant for normal arrows, being large enough to hold a spear. If not a spear... Perhaps we could use that rod that Clutzer tore out of the grating. It was about the right size. We had to try it. Judging by the lever on the crossbow, I couldn't load it by myself, we needed the whole group for this, and as soon as we shot the worm, we'd be able to hide in the alcove next to the crossbow. It's decided then: that's what we'll do!

I went to fetch the rod, gestured the others to follow me and brought them to the cave. We carefully made my way to the contraption and, gritting our teeth from tension, managed to lift the crossbow and load it with the rod. It was now or never... When everyone hid themselves in the alcove I pressed the trigger.

You wouldn't think it's possible to go deaf in virtual reality, but this is probably exactly what happened to me a moment later. As soon as the spear hit the worm, it flinched, lifted its front end and screamed. Although no, that's not right. It SCREAMED! The deafening roar filled the whole Dungeon and our green bar instantly flashed red and disappeared altogether. Well, at least we're making some progress.

Letting out another scream the worm started to race around the cave. If we weren't in the alcove we'd have been immediately flattened, since the beast's speed was insane. A couple of moments later it discovered the exit and sped off in search of the attacker. The cave was filled with the scraping sound of the monster racing down the corridors. Suddenly and clearly we heard the creaking of metal, a piercing roar from the worm, a loud thump and... the Dungeon was filled with silence.

Experience gained: +350 Experience, points

remaining until next level: 480.

If the message was anything to go by, the Tunnel Worm had roared its last. We carefully left the alcove and started to examine the cave. If we were to go ahead we first had to make sure we've not missed anything of value. The said things of value were promptly found in a small hollow in the middle of the cave. Clutzer took out a couple of items and a bag of gold and then laid it all out on the ground. I looked at the item properties.

Leather Belt of the Sorcerer. Durability: 50. Physical damage resistance: 20. Stamina: +2. Intellect: + 5. Item class: Uncommon. Minimum level: 10.

Chainmail Pauldrons of Strength. Durability: 50. Physical damage resistance: 60. Stamina: +2. Strength: + 5. Item class: Uncommon. Minimum level: 10.

We dividing the coins into four equal piles, each of us receiving 53 gold. Not bad for the first mob, not bad at all. The belt with Intellect I could take for myself, but the pauldrons suited both fighters at once. So we had to cast lots with 'Rock-Paper-Scissors', which resulted in Leite becoming the happy owner of the pauldrons. We equipped the new gear and went on, curious to see what happened with the worm.

Continuing to move with care, we came to the place where the way was blocked by the grate. Small broken pieces of the bars sticking out of the ceiling were the only reminder that it had ever been there. Some green slime was dripping off them — probably the monster's blood. Trying not to step in the puddles of slime in the wake of the worm after it had crashed through the metal obstacle, we came to the cave with the hole. At the moment its size was measured by a unique unit called '1 worm'. Pierced by the spikes, the familiar-looking worm formed a bridge of sorts across the hole. It must have gained an impressive speed when rushing through the corridors to fly over such a distance. In any case, this was the cause of that last deafening roar.

Now we just had to carefully make our way to the other side of the hole. Eric went first.

"Watch out for the slime!" he shouted, flinging the slime off his boot with his pick. "It immediately reduces item durability by 5 points"

The body of the worm was soft and repulsive to the touch and the motionless appendages it used for moving around were enough to make you gag. Sinking to our knees in the carcass and carefully avoiding the item-degrading slime, we got to the other end of the cave and went on.

A few dozen meters later Eric, who was walking ten paces in front of us, gave a cry and started to fend something off. Every second his movements became slower and slower. In the end he froze altogether. Strange, what on earth happened to him? Even more strange — his Hit Points started to go down. I summoned a Healing Spirit and carefully approached Eric — and immediately jumped back: thin and almost invisible webs were hanging from the ceiling and Eric was covered in them pretty much head to toe. What would we do without a tank?

"Clutzer, Leite — we have to get Eric out! Careful, there are webs here! This is what we do: I grab Eric and get tangled like him, Leite grabs me and Clutzer grabs Leite and pulls the whole train out of the web."

"I'll leg it first. We'll all buy it if the healer kicks the bucket," replied Clutzer, ran to Eric and grabbing him by the arm started to pull him back. He managed to pull our tank for a total of three steps before he himself froze like a stone statue.

"Mahan, just make sure you don't get tangled yourself," said Leite before following Clutzer. Two more steps. There were only four steps to Leite, but they had to be made through the web. I'll not be able to pull all three of them out. I'd manage one step at the most and then the corridor will sport four wax figures with gradually falling Hit Points. I wondered if they were in pain. Something must be gnawing at them if their Hit Points are diminishing. Anyway, time for some quick thinking. I went over to the edge of the space with hanging webs and looked up. The whole ceiling was dotted with small cocoons from which the webs were coming out. All right, let's see now what's inside these things. I selected one of the cocoons and summoned a Lightning Spirit.

Damage inflicted. 348: 348 (Lightning Spirit Damage) /1(Opponent Level /Character Level).

Experience gained: +10 Experience, points remaining until next level: 470.

Skill increase:

+3% to Intellect. Total: 43%

There was a muffled squeak and a smallish spider fell to the floor, legs in the air. So, that's where the web was coming from and these cocoons were actually spiders. Just how many of them were there?

It took me twenty minutes to make my way to Eric, having first pulled out Leite and Clutzer. I almost completely drained my mana reserve, summoning lightning and healing Spirits in turn. In these twenty minutes 72 spiders got me up to level 13 and my base Intellect to 38 points. If it wasn't for the Tambourine, which reduced the penalty for Spirit summoning, I would have simply ran out of mana. After freeing everyone from the web I sat down and closed my eyes. That's it, I need a rest — in the next 10-15 minutes I'm pretty much useless.

"Mahan, get up. It's been half an hour already," Eric shook me awake in what seemed like moments after I closed my eyes. "We have to get going. And here's your share," Eric gave me a bunch of stuff. I put the items in my bag without even looking at them. Now we had to think of a way to get through the web and not get sidetracked by digging through the loot.

Coming to the edge of the area with the hanging spider webs, I stopped and started to examine the ceiling carefully. I just couldn't believe that the developers would design a Dungeon that could only be completed if there was a RDD (Ranged Damage Dealer) in the group. What about the freedom of choosing the group?

"What are you trying to see there? It's not staring, but hacking you have to do here. We tried jumping through ourselves, but the Clutzer got caught in the web again. Good thing he had at least one leg free, so we could pull him out. There's no other way — only fighting through."

A way! Of course! This could be an unusual type of labyrinth! One that was hanging from above and must not be touched. We just have to find the starting point.

The corridor in this place was just four meters across, so I found the spider-free bit of ceiling soon enough. Damn, could I be right with my guess?

"Eric, come here. Let's try an experiment."

I told the others of my hunch. We spent some time arguing the probability of my being right or not, after which Eric said that I was a brainless fool, and he's prepared to take a risk to prove it. But if I don't pull him out, he'll find me and let me know exactly how wrong I was. Fists clenched, I watched Eric stare carefully at the ceiling and walk in zigzags around the corridor. In a few places he even walked in our direction, but then quickly turned and moved further away. Thirty minutes later we heard Eric's happy shout:

"Mahan, you were right! There's a way! Take care how you move, keep your arms close and you'll get through no problem. It's just fifty meters away!"

'What a strange Dungeon,' I thought, moving along a web-free passage. 'Instead of a bunch of mobs you get some weird worms, holes with spikes and spider-web labyrinths. But where's the boss and his entourage? Do any even exist?'

The next cave answered my questions. Right in the centre of a round cave, about forty meters in diameter, was a two-meter-tall spider, bearing a strong resemblance to a tarantula. Yes, an overgrown tarantula. I selected the spider and looked at its properties: it's important to know what you're dealing with.

Black Guardian of the Queen. Level: 19. Hit points: 250 000. Abilities: Leap, Summon Spiderlings, Web.

The glowing skull above the spider's Hit Point bar indicated that we were looking at the first boss of the local Dungeon. So, aside from him, there was also a Queen of some kind — probably at the end of the passage that could be seen on the other side of the cave. At last we'll have a real fight, instead of all these 'agility games'.

"Right, let's see what we have here," Eric said after we all had a good look at the spider and retreated back a few steps. "It doesn't have poison attacks, which is already a huge bonus. The Web's clear enough — it will slow us down for a while or get us stuck to the floor. If it's the second, we'll need help getting free of it. The Summoning of Spiderlings is clear enough too — it'll summon a crowd of little minions and we'll have to kill them fast. But I have no idea what 'Leap' is supposed to mean with this boss. It could jump at any of us (in which case you must fall down) or at me or at a particular area. Whatever — we'll take it as it comes. One thing's bad — the bastard is level 19, which means the Queen will be level 21-22. We may have reached fifteen already, but the difference is noticeable. So, Mahan, don't waste your mana, I'll be taking serious damage here. Do you remember what I said before entering the Dungeon? Only hit it from the sides, listen to Mahan and if the boss goes for you — sit down and cover your head; I think that's it." Eric sighed nervously and glanced at the spider. So, I'm not the only one who can feel afraid.

"Let's go," said Eric, getting a better grip on the pick, and then, hiding behind the shield, ran towards the spider with a wild scream: "Waste that hairy bastard!"

The Queen's Guardian didn't wait for our tank to run up to it and start showing it who's boss. As soon as Eric was in the cave, the 'Leap' ability status bar appeared above the boss, took two seconds to fill and the tarantula jumped at him. Hit! The tank was thrown at the wall and then slid down it, remaining motionless for a few seconds. Judging by the 'Dizziness' debuff, he took a big hit. Minus 230 Hit Points, almost 25% per one attack — and that's despite Eric having a good armor with his shield and Endurance.

"Leite, Clutzer — let's go!" I shouted and started to summon a Healing Spirit on Eric. The battle commenced.

We've figured out the 'Leap' ability quite quickly. It turned out that the boss was unable to use it against players standing right next to it. However, it did take us two more hits against the wall to discover this — after it used this ability against me. I took the first hit a minute after the start of the battle. The Queen's Guardian did not otherwise hit very hard and many of its normal attacks Eric caught with the shield, so the tank's Hit Points never slid below 90%. I even summoned a couple of Lightning Spirits, taking off 244 Hit Points each time. And then the bar of the 'Leap' ability started to charge above the boss's head for the second time. Eric got a better grip on his shield, crouched, readying to take the hit, but the tarantula turned its head towards me and lunged forward... At first I felt an excruciating pain: it was as if a giant sledgehammer struck me on the chest. I came to myself in mid-flight, noting with detached interest how my legs and arms were waving in the air like a comet tail. A thought flashed in my head that it must look quite nice from outside, but making contact with the wall knocked me out once again. When consciousness returned, I started to summon a Healing Spirit on myself right away. I lost 65% Hit Points and 2 points to item durability in one hit. At least I didn't drop the Tambourine and the Mallet as I flew. So, this disgusting cockroach (I don't give a damn that a tarantula is a spider) likes to attack everyone in turn then? Catching every fourth hit is unpleasant, but survivable. With these thoughts I watched how a minute later the 'Leap' bar started to charge above the boss's head again. Leite or Clutzer? Should I place some bets while I'm at it? Hit!

I came to myself on the ground. Again, Hit Points were down by 65% and item durability by 2 points. Dammit! All my stuff will break at this rate! Why did this piece of filth go for me again? Why not Leite or Clutzer? Struggling for an answer, I decided to save my mana. In those two minutes we had only damaged the boss for 15% of its Hit Points, so I had to make sure my mana lasted the whole fight. I ran up to Leite, took a place by his side and started to apply my Mallet vigorously to the boss's carcass. Just 30 Hit Points per hit, but the sea is made up of drops too. When the 'Leap' bar started to charge above the boss for the fourth time I crouched. Is it me again? I even closed my eyes waiting for the blow, still going at it with my Mallet. The bar filled up again in two seconds, the boss screamed and lunged forward, toppling Eric. Hit! The Queen's Guardian crashed into the wall, causing it to lose 5% of its Hit Points, froze for a few seconds and then came back to its place at the centre. A debuff appeared on the spider 'Damage taken increased by 10%. Duration: 1 minute.' So that's it! The 'Leap' ability works only on those using ranged attacks and if no such players are present the boss rams itself into the wall and lands itself with a 'bonus' that's quite good for us. Great!

In the next three minutes we left the spider with only 60% of its Hit Points. This was quite easy: you just stand there and hit it, like an ore vein, no running around needed. It looked like the developers didn't think through the boss's fight mechanic all too well — nothing too exciting.

You should never count your chickens too early...

As soon as the boss's Hit Point bar fell below sixty percent, it lifted its head and started emitting a sickening screech. Nothing happened for a few seconds except the spider ramming into the wall one more time, but then came a shout from Clutzer:

"Incoming! The beast called its minions!"

I looked around and cursed through my teeth. Yeah, right — some uninteresting boss this was. Totally boring. It comes with three additional 'uninteresting' level 15 little spiders with 300000 Hit Points each. That's more than the boss itself! How are we meant to kill them?

Judging by Eric's cursing, he'd also spotted the new spiders and was trying to get his head around the situation.

"Don't get distracted by the new spiders, they're mine!" shouted Eric, after coming to some decision and running up to the spiders that just descended on us. Hit! Airborne Eric was indicating with all his flying glory that the boss's 'Leap' ability had just recharged. Dammit!

The three spiders and the boss started to inflict some serious gnawing on Eric. I had to summon Healing Spirits one after another and if this continued, I'd be out of mana in a couple of minutes.

We held out for one more minute, after sending the boss off for another hearty meeting with the wall. 'No, this is definitely not working,' I decided, when Eric's Hit Points fell below 40%. Hitting the other spiders was useless, we'd never kill them all, but neither could we leave them on the tank — he's get eaten. But, what if...

"Eric, I'm taking the new spiders! Don't touch them! Kite!"

I used the kite tactic quite a lot in Dolma when I went Rat hunting. You summon a Lightning Spirit and run away from the Rat and then summon another. The more you run the less damage you sustain. Eh, this'll hurt... Three Lightning Spirits went at the spiders and I sped through the cave, running away from them as fast as I could and counting the seconds until the next leap of the boss.

Seems the spiderlings aren't that nimble! They don't run that fast and keep together, so no danger of them scattering through the cave. If I could only slow them down in some way, but how? When only five seconds was left until 'Leap', I ran up to the boss — I really didn't fancy taking any avoidable pounding. As I ran away from the spiderlings my mana recharged, Eric wasn't taking any extra damage and the spider minions didn't catch up with me, so soon enough we found a way to deal with them.

I ran up to the boss a second before the 'Leap' bar appeared above it. The tarantula turned in the direction of the three spiderlings and launched forward. Hit! With the boss it was the same story: minus 5% to Hit Points, plus 10% damage taken, but the spiderlings made our day. They stayed stuck to the wall, wriggling their legs. It seemed that the boss's hit had lodged them in place. Good — now they won't get in the way.

The boss summoned its minions two more times: when it crossed the 40% and then the 20% Hit Point threshold. After getting them stuck to the wall in the same way, I couldn't wait to see the boss's third ability: Web.

Well, we didn't wait in vain. When the Black Guardian had only 10% of its Hit Points left, we finally experienced this ability.

"BEWARE," a calm low voice echoed through the cave.

So this Dungeon even came with a warning. Such warnings are put in place when a boss is about to start using particularly unpleasant abilities, which have a good chance of ending the whole raid.

The tarantula froze and its body started to shiver, something raised up on its back and it started spewing out bits of web.

"Heads up!" I could not think of anything more original. "We continue hitting it, but keep an eye on the falling webs!"

"The minions are coming!" Clutzer's shout was full of desperation.

"Eric, try to pull them! We'll hit the boss with all we have! There's only 9% left, we've got to bring it down!"

Leite failed to dodge one of the falling webs and was immediately wrapped up. And not just wrapped up, but also losing 10% of Life every 10 seconds. What a snag!

"Clutzer, get Leite out or he's toast. No touching him, only daggers!" I shouted, summoning Healing Spirits non-stop on Eric and Leite in turn. I was wrong to berate the developers: the last phase of the boss was worthy of admiration. If I was playing in the main gameworld, I'd even applaud them, but now when with my death the Crafting stat was at stake, I was beginning to feel ill at ease. Had it been a mistake to come here after all?

Clutzer got Leite free after about a minute. The boss was still at 4% Hit Points, Eric had 30% of his Hit Points left, Leite had 20, Clutzer — 60 and I — 40. I only had enough mana for two more Healing Spirit summonings. That's where things became interesting.

Thirty seconds before the boss's leap, Clutzer got stuck in the web. We didn't have any strength or time to get him out, so I shook my head when Leite looked at me questioningly. We had to take the risk, or we'd all had it. With the remains of my Mana I healed Eric and let my hands drop helplessly. That's it. I was completely and utterly empty. Attacking with my Mallet was of little use, so I watched the others and dodged the falling webs. At least they didn't get you stuck to the floor, or there'd be no escape from this sticky rain.

Hit! Eric remained on the floor — the web had got him in the end. The wild chirring of the boss echoed through the cave, after which it crashed on the floor. The last lot of spiderlings still running about fell on their backs and the ones on the walls grew still, the web fell off Clutzer and Eric and silence enveloped the cave.

"This trip's getting way too freaky to keep with it, for real," came Clutzer's muffled wheeze and I was hit by an avalanche of messages:

Experience gained: +600 Experience, points remaining until next level: 1170.
Level gained!
Skill increase:
+ 2 to Intellect. Total: 40.
+2 to Stamina. Total: 29.
+2 to Endurance. Total: 9.
+1 to Agility. Total: 7.
Free stat points: 10.
Achievement earned!
Tough as Nails. level 1 (4 boss kills until the next level).
Achievement reward: damage dealt to all bosses increased by 1%.

My first thought after reading the messages was that I was getting slow: I never allocated the stat points I got for the spiderlings. The additional five points of Intellect would have helped a lot in this battle. To avoid repeating the mistake I immediately put all the stat points into Intellect and then had a look around. Our loot had to be somewhere nearby. My mana was gradually recharging, so I started to summon Healing Spirits on the battle-worn group, which camped in the middle of the cave and appeared to have no intention of going any further.

"Clutzer, get up! Our loot is here somewhere, let's look for it. Do you think we swatted that cockroach for nothing? And anyway, what's up with you people? We just brought down a boss! We did get knocked about a good deal, but we're all alive! Let's go — you're not going to give up half-way, are you?"

"Mahan, we barely managed to kill this one and you're saying we should keep going," said Leite, despondently. "The next one would gulp us down without as much as a glance!"

"Quit being such crybabies! You've all gained a level! Now we'll get some new gear too. We'll take this whole place out! Get up and let's go! Time's a ticking and tomorrow we have to be at the exit to start off for the main gameworld, but you're sitting here and sulking," I saw that my words were having little effect and barked: "On your feet! Fall in!"

All three of them sprang up and stood in a line.

"And now suck it up and go find that loot! Dismissed!"

Skill increase:

+1 to Charisma. Total: 6.

'Yes, Reflexes are a terrible thing,' I thought as I watched the others searching for the loot. When the united world Government was formed, it made year-long army training compulsory for all eighteen-year-olds. If you failed to take part, the best job you could hope for was being a street cleaner. During this training obedience to the commander's voice was hammered into you well and good; there was little need to say anything — even half asleep you'd carry out orders just to avoid the disciplinary unit.

Clutzer was again the one to find the loot. Did he have a nose for it or something? Aside from 120 gold each, from a small chest in a hole in one of the walls, the other items included:

Leather Bracers of Intellect. Durability: 50. Physical damage resistance: 20. Stamina: +2. Intellect: + 6. Item class: Uncommon. Minimum level: 13.

Mail Bracers of Strength. Durability: 50. Physical damage resistance: 60. Stamina: +2. Strength: + 6. Item class: Uncommon. Minimum level: 13.

Mail Bracers of Strength. Durability: 50. Physical damage resistance: 60. Stamina: +2. Strength + 6. Item class: Uncommon. Minimum level: 13.

Mail Bracers of Stamina. Durability: 50. Physical damage resistance: 80. Stamina: +8. Item class: Uncommon. Minimum level: 13.

There were no questions about who should get

what. As I put on the new bracers I thought that there was only one bad thing about this Dungeon: all the items we got were of the Uncommon type, distinguished from common ones only by a relatively small stat bonus, +8 in our case. Now, if we got Rare or Epic class items, then... but I was drifting off to the land of dreams again. I might as well have remembered Legendary or Scaling items.

We didn't come across any obstacles on our way to the next boss. It's not like you could call a swarm of Rats that attacked us as soon as we moved down the corridor much of an obstacle. Eric was a living wave-breaker against a sea of level 5 Rats. They had just 500 Hit Points each, so we pretty much mowed them down. As usual, there was a 'but' — these kills yielded no experience. After the battle was over we simply divided the loot into four piles of approximately same size, without even looking at what they contained, and moved on. We didn't have that long until we had to return to the Dolma mine.

The second boss put a smile on our faces. Quite literally.

We kept moving until we came to the den of the boss — this time it wasn't sitting on the ground, but hovering in the air. A snow-white cross between a dragonfly and a scorpion hung about a meter above the ground. It had the body and the wings of a dragonfly and the head and pincers of a scorpion. You had to ask — what was the developer smoking when he came up with this one?

White Guardian of the Queen. Level: 19. Hit points: 200,000. Abilities: Mighty Blow, Laughing

Gas, Frenzied Whirlwind.

"Right, it's debriefing time," Eric began, as the most experienced raider. "The 'Mighty Blow' should target either myself alone or anyone next to the boss. We'll have to check; if it's the latter we'll have to run away from the boss when it uses this ability. Frenzied Whirlwind will be like that Tarantula's Web, saved for the final phase of the battle. Mahan, you'll have to be careful how you spend your mana. What this Laughing Gas is — I have no idea. If we draw a parallel with the real world, this thing," he nodded at the dragonfly, "lets out a gas that will make us laugh. Knowing the kind of maniacs the developers tend to be, we can suppose that we'll be laughing until the time we take an antidote or die. We don't have an antidote, so, Mahan, your Spirits will have to sort it all out. This Guardian has fifty thousand Hit Points less than the spider, so it won't be ramming itself against the wall. At least it doesn't look like we'll have to deal with any additional mobs. Everyone ready?"

"Let's do this," Eric said again after we all confirmed our readiness. "Waste that winged bastard!"

I wondered what would happen if the next boss had a tail — would he shout "Waste that tailed bastard"?

We made quite a lively start. Every Mighty Blow only hit the tank, taking off 30% of his Hit Points, but if Eric caught the blow with his shield, the damage was laughable. The dragonfly didn't fly around the cave and we didn't have to run after it, so our combined damage was respectably high. In a couple of minutes only 60% of the boss's Hit Points remained.

And that's when the fun began:

"BEWARE."

I didn't really see what the dragonfly did, but suddenly the whole cave was filled with plumes of green smoke. I managed to hold my breath in time and looked at the others. Eric wasn't breathing, continuing to take the dragonfly's blows, Leite seemed to be behaving normally, but Clutzer...

Just a couple of seconds after the smoke appeared Clutzer started to laugh uncontrollably:

"Leite, can you believe it? We're whacking a dragonfly. He-he. A flying buzzing fly that thinks it's a dragon. Ha-ha. A fly! Can you imagine — a buzzing fly! Buzz-Buzz!" Clutzer started to grimace, using his arms to imitate antennae, and tried to headbutt the White Guardian. After a few seconds Leite cracked up and joined Clutzer:

"You're some funky dragonbuzzer, man!"

Right, we'd lost our DDs and the boss still had 60% of Life left. We had to snap them out of it, but how? I jumped to Leite, turned him to me and prayed that the developers turned off the 'deal damage — go for respawn' setting in the Dungeon and started to slap him about the face to return him to his senses. Leite looked at me with glassy eyes:

"Mahan, you're here too! He-he. We're swatting some flies here, haha, but shhh!" Leite dropped to a whisper and pointed to Clutzer. "See that dung bug over there, with the huge antennae? I'm gonna chop them off in a minute."

What to do? I was fighting off spasms as my

body began to run out of air. Eric, red from holding his breath, was already at 40% of Hit Points, but any Healing Spirit summoning would mean I'd join our DDs, who were now chasing each other, the boss all but forgotten. At least they're not using weapons and just sticking to headbutts. I looked around in desperation — it can't all end so badly, just can't!

Small mushrooms by the wall caught my eye. Not even the mushrooms themselves, but the shining rainbow that hung above each mushroom. Nearly fainting, I ran to the mushrooms, fell to my knees and started to eat them. All or nothing! I just managed to put a mushroom into my mouth before feverishly starting to breathe in the air. Two seconds, nothing happened, then five...

"Mahan!" Eric's shout was full of desperation and then turned into crazy laughter. No more tank. I grabbed the mushrooms and ran to the laughing group, calling Healing Spirits on my way. Eric was really getting demolished. Each hit of a pincer took off 10% of Hit Points, but this just made him laugh even harder. At least he wasn't trying to chase Clutzer and Leite, who had now started to hide from each other behind the mass of the hovering dragonfly. I ran up to Eric and managed to stick a piece of mushroom into his mouth between the blows, hoping that it would neutralize the poison. This really wasn't a good time to see the bar of 'Mighty Blow' starting to light up above the boss. It would bring Eric's Hit Points down by 30% in normal battle and one didn't want to think what it'd do now. Realizing that I could already be out of time, I began the summoning chant, half-expecting to see a message telling me that the Spirit cannot be summoned on a dead target.

Hit! The clank of the blocked attack told everyone in the vicinity that it had been caught by the shield.

"Mahan, I'm all right, get the others out!" Eric's shout took a great weight off my shoulders. Now the dragonfly's days were numbered. If the mushrooms allowed you to ignore the Laughing Gas, we just had to eat some quickly enough. As soon as Leite and Clutzer came to themselves the green clumps of smoke in the cave disappeared. We'd survived the 'Laughing Gas' ability, launched at 60% of Life: if this boss had a similar design to the tarantula, this ability will be used two more times — at 40 and 20 percent.

I was right. When we heard the warning, Clutzer and I ran for the mushrooms, leaving the others to work on the boss. I took a mushroom to Eric and Clutzer gave one to Leite, so we survived the following explosions of the laughing gas without any losses. The last phase didn't present any problems either — the boss started to spin, dealing damage to the whole raid with its wings and pincers. On one hand the damage was quite substantial, taking off 10-15% Hit Points in 5 seconds, but on the other, in these 5 seconds I had time to summon 4 Spirits, completely healing the group.

Experience gained: +600 Experience, points remaining until next level: 570.
Skill increase:
+1 to Intellect. Total: 51.
+1 to Stamina. Total: 30.
+1 to Endurance. Total: 10.

"Well, you 'dragon-buzzers', there should be a chest around here somewhere," I decided to poke fun at Clutzer and Leite, who went to search the cave straight away. I could bet a farm that Clutzer would be the one to find it again.

"Mahan, come here! Your advice is needed," came Leite's shout, potentially making me a farm-less RL. Like some little kids — can't they do anything without me?

When I came over and had a look at the loot chest, I made a mental apology to all the others. Well, well. The developers had compensated for the fairly easy battle mechanic of the boss with a very tricky access to the loot chest. There was a small corridor, about three meters wide, that went about twenty meters deep into the rock. At the very end of the corridor was our chest on a plinth, but the floor in between was covered with one big bright-green puddle. There were some small islands in it, but only at the end of the corridor, by the chest. Leite carefully touched the puddle with his foot and immediately jumped back with a scream, tearing off his boot, which was smoking; it soon evaporated right before our eyes.

"The puddle... Durability... The boot..." Leite said, perplexed, standing on the stones with his bare foot. So that's it! The puddle destroys item durability. You live and learn; I should make a note for myself that such puddles exist. Nevertheless, it's important to try everything out for yourself. I took out one of the old rings, carefully touched the puddle with it and then put it on the ground. That's right, destruction in progress: the ring's Durability fell by 2 units per second, it smoked and hissed and then disappeared altogether.

"Maybe we should just leave it?" asked Eric, as he watched my experiment. I don't want to lose what I'm wearing now for some unknown stuff in the chest.

"I agree. Losing that boot was enough for me," Leite concurred.

I looked at Clutzer. If he was also against it we'll be moving on. I wasn't too eager to take the risk either. Clutzer glanced at us and started to take off all his clothes, mumbling something under his breath, until he was wearing his character's birthday suit: an undroppable loin cloth.

"Mahan, I thought you had the smarts, but you just totally don't get it" said Clutzer and stepped into the puddle. Minus 10% to Hit Points.

"Heal me already!" shouted Clutzer and headed off to the chest in some giant leaps. He really wasn't bad at making a fly-like impression. He grabbed the chest and hopped back.

"Like I'll leave the loot to some tools! In the can they'd mess you up for stuff like this," mumbled Clutzer, wrinkling from pain, but clearly pleased. He acquired a minute-long debuff, taking off 10% of his Hit Points, so I focused on healing the hero of my inner zoo. The hoarding hamster put up posters of Clutzer all over its designated space and together with the greed-toad they demanded for him to be made an authorized representative of their family.

Eric opened the chest, glanced inside, swallowed in excitement and looked at the others in shock. I examined the loot and understood why:

Mardvir's Leather Boots. Durability: 200. **Physical damage resistance: 70.**

Stamina: +10. Intellect; + 16. Magic, fire, cold and poison resistance: 30. Item class: Rare. Minimum level: 13.

Rurok's Chainmail Boots. Durability: 200. **Physical damage resistance: 100.**

Stamina: +9. Strength: + 16. Magic, fire, cold and poison resistance: 30. Item class: Rare. Minimum level: 13.

Rurok's Chainmail Boots. Durability: 200. **Physical damage resistance: 100.**

Stamina: +9. Strength: + 16. Magic, fire, cold and poison resistance: 30. Item class: Rare. Minimum level: 13.

Halik's Chainmail Boots. Durability: 200. **Physical damage resistance: 130.**

Stamina: +26. Magic, fire, cold and poison resistance: 30. Item class: Rare. Minimum level: 13.

It took us a whole hour to get to the last boss. There were no more bosses, but there were swarms of Rats, Spiders and Millipedes attacking us at every step.

In the end the final boss of the Dungeon appeared before us.

A two-meter-high Rat sat at the centre of its den and waited for us to pay it a visit. The shimmering transport portal was immediately visible right at the end of the cave. Would it take us straight to Dolma? Good if so, no-one really wanted to go back the same way.

**Queen Aiden. Level: 22. Hit points: 400 000.
Abilities: Phase 1: hidden, Phase 2: hidden.**

"What do you say, Eric?" asked Leite.

"In the normal gameworld I'd not go in here without the manual," said the tank at last. "Hidden abilities mean only one thing — they are chosen randomly from the whole multitude of different boss attacks. If you don't study all of them and pass an exam on boss abilities with the raid-leader you won't be able to join the raid party. There is only one such boss in my memory and we spent almost a week preparing for it: we researched, read up, even bought a virtual boss trainer, to work through different combinations... Imagine this: one hit of the boss has to be let through because it heals, and the other avoided at all costs because it kills instantly. If you don't know which attack does what, you won't get very far. It's the same here. If we attack the boss now, there's a 98% chance that we'll die. But we do have the 2% chance of bringing that Rat down.

"I'm not going to go for the last boss," I said after some thought. "In case of the other bosses I thought that we had a good chance of beating them, but here I'm convinced that we're looking at a suicide mission. If we will be making a clan, I may as well tell you what a respawn would mean for me. I've levelled up to level 3 in Crafting, which allows me to add 3 additional stats to the rings and to the stones I insert into them. Yes, you can attach stones to rings as well, don't be surprised — have a look at mine," I opened viewing access for my rings. "If I die, I'll be useless to the clan, because Crafting levels up through the creative process and there's nothing simple or easy about it. You cannot add free stat points to it, I've already tried. That's how it is. Risking this for items, even if they're incredibly good for our current levels, but set to become disposable junk a couple of weeks after we get out... is stupid. I don't believe that we'll get Scaling Items from the Queen. We already had some incredible luck with loot from all the other bosses."

"I agree with Mahan. We'll make a clan and go on so many raids that we'll get more than our fill," said Leite, supporting my reasoning.

"Yes, I understand that you're right," Eric agreed reluctantly. "It's just we're the first to go through this Dungeon and if we manage to down the Queen, we'll get the 'First Kill', an achievement that only about ten thousand people in Barliona managed to gain. It's divided into two parts — one is connected to a particular Dungeon and the other simply shows that we have it. When I was playing I never dreamt I'd get a chance of getting this achievement. Even though a new Dungeon appears in Barliona every half a year, only a very limited number of clans gets 'First Kill'. The kinds of wars that are waged over this are really something else. I once saw a broadcast of one of these battles, when the fighters of the Phoenix Clan, including hired players, protected the entrance to a new Dungeon. Almost three hundred level 130 players defended against the united forces of the other clans. They held out for just thirty minutes, but in these thirty minutes the Phoenix raid group became the first to complete this Dungeon. Hellfire, the leader of the Phoenix Clan, later said that in these thirty minutes the clan had to pay around a million gold to the fighters hired for the defense. Just imagine! A million gold to gain an achievement! And here we have a chance to do this at level 15! Completely for free! Yes, the risk is great, it's highly likely that we'll fail. But, dammit, I'd really like to try!"

"What are other advantages other than kudos points?" asked Leite with some interest now. Did Eric really manage to persuade him?

"The clan which has players with the 'First Kill' achievement receives some bonuses from the Emperor the entire time that such a player is in the clan; I don't remember more exactly. The player himself receives a gift from the Emperor for each such achievement, which is presented by the Emperor in person. Can you imagine what that means? Getting to the Emperor is even more difficult than getting out of the mine or even out of prison itself, and in this case he's the one that invites you to the meeting that takes place five months after the achievement is gained, exactly the day before a new Dungeon is announced. At the same time, each person has a right to invite two others with him to the audience. The bidding for such a place on the black market starts at one hundred thousand gold and it would hurt your brain to even imagine what figure it eventually reaches. This is what's going through my head when I'm looking at the Queen. On one side of the scales — Mahan's Crafting, and on the other a visit to the Emperor with two guests. So that's what I'm saying — we all have to decide on this."

"This is what I reckon" said Clutzer, "Wasting Mahan would be lame. But if we let the Rat go, we'd feel like suckers. So my proposal is this..." Clutzer laid out his plan. Put into human language, his words were leaving me more and more gobsmacked. The proposal had logic in it, even if it was the very crazy kind. It was somehow... unconventional. And looking at Clutzer you'd never tell that he was hiding such a twisted mind. I'll have to find out what he was doing time for.

"Madness, complete and utter," said Eric, when Clutzer finished. "But the weirdest thing is — it might just work and I think it's our only chance to down that Rat. Leite, what do you think?"

"Clutzer's a funky dude, but his idea is something else," agreed Leite. "I agree, it could work, but at such a price... What the heck, I'm in."

"Then let's go to the positions proposed by Clutzer and begin. Clutzer — you're first, Leite's second and I'll come at the end. Mahan, your job is to stay put and not stick your head out. We start in exactly five minutes, I'm putting the timer on. Can everyone see it? Great, now to positions — as soon as the countdown's over, Clutzer starts us off. May whatever powers are out there help us."

I selected the Queen and put it into the frame in order to constantly monitor its Hit Points. As I went to my position I heard Eric mutter, "The stuff you come up with, you sodding dragonbuzzer."

I put myself in the designated position and looked at the timer. It was still three and a half minutes until the insane battle. Whatever the outcome, tomorrow I'll already be in some settlement in the main gameworld. A settlement is good: it means quests, achievements and faster levelling. I'll have to think about what to do in the remaining seven and a half years of my imprisonment. First I'll have to create a clan — it's very difficult to survive in Barliona on your own. Then I'll have to find Duki, Sushiho and Elenium, old acquaintances that I played with before, and suggest they join up with me. They're good guys, without hang-ups and haven't let me down once in the five years that I've known them. I will need access to the outside world, to the manuals so I'll need reliable players from the outside.

In the meantime I could not decide on my main goal. To be more exact: I did have a global goal, which consisted of me somehow getting my hands on a hundred million gold. But what I had to do to reach that goal remained unclear to me. What methods did I know for earning money? Stealing a clan's vault, selling a place for an audience with the Emperor, finding a treasure or making something incredibly rare and useful. All of this had to be done on an industrial scale. Perhaps I could sell the Orc Warrior chess pieces, but I doubted they'd bring in a lot — you needed the rest of the set. And my greed-toad would never forgive me. If a full chess set grants access to some place, losing a chance, even a very slight one to get to this 'place' was unthinkable. Forty seconds. Then there's Marina. If she's a free artist, I'm sure she spends a lot of time in the Game. It would be good to find her and tell her to her face that promises should be kept. I'd just take her by her...

BEWARE.

It began.

Clutzer's Hit Points, viewed in my frames, immediately fell to 50%: he probably got hit by some ability. Just a few dozen seconds went by and then the whole Dungeon was filled with a wild scream of the Queen. Clutzer's plan worked! The Rat's Hit Points quickly started to plummet, but Clutzer was now on his way back to his mine: he was the first to go for respawn. Then it was Leite's turn. The Queen was down to 60% after which Leite's Hit Points started to diminish fast. The Dungeon was filled by another piercing scream of the Queen and Leite followed Clutzer. The two minutes that the Rat needed to get close to Eric left its Hit Points at only 40%. Well, well. Now's the moment of truth. Eric ran past my hiding place with the Queen a few meters behind him. Just a few seconds went by and only one player remained in the Dungeon — me. The Rat's Hit Points went into a supersonic plummet: 35%, 30%, 15%, 1%, 1 Unit.

BEWARE.

I leant closer to the wall. The niche in which I sat may not have been the best shelter, but it was much better than catching who knows what in the open.

An explosion! A wave of air swept through the entire Dungeon, pushing me into the wall. I think I lost consciousness, because when I opened my eyes the Dungeon was filled with silence and a collection of messages hung in front of me:

Experience gained: +800 Experience, points remaining until next level: 1170
   Level gained!
   Free stat points: 5.

Achievement earned!

The First Kill of Queen Aiden of the Mushu Dungeon.

Achievement reward: the reputation with all encountered factions will increase daily by 5 units.

Message for the player: in five months' time you will be teleported to an audience with the Emperor. You may take two companions with you; for this you will have to give them the invitation letter in the course of five months. You may obtain the invitations in any branch office of Barliona Bank.

A small number 1 wrapped in some flowers appeared next to my name. So that's the general part of the achievement seen by all. I was free to jump for joy and shout 'Hurrah!', but to be honest I didn't feel any particular pride in earning this achievement. I had nothing to do with this; it was earned at a great price — the respawn of the whole group. Keeping in mind that our sensory filters were turned off, everyone must have felt some unforgettably unpleasant sensations before returning to their mines. Not a lot to be happy about, really. All I had to do now was find the loot, pick up the dropped gold and jump in the portal. The Dungeon was completed.

I headed for the cave that contained the Queen, remembering Clutzer's idea. Translated into human language, it sounded like this:

"This is what I'm thinking," said Clutzer, "We can't let Mahan die, since it'll be very unprofitable. But if we leave the Rat behind we'll be making a big mistake. Here's my proposal — we have to lead the Rat through all the three traps that we found in the Dungeon: the cave with the slime, the corridor with the web and the hole with the spikes. I'll have a chat with the Queen and invite her for a walk in the cave with the slime, stripping myself beforehand. I've already been there, so I can guess what will happen — most probably I'll end up going back to my mine through a respawn. But then the Queen should feel quite bad from the slime and the level of its Hit Points should fall quite significantly. Then Leite takes the Rat and travels with it to the hanging webs. He'd run along the spider-free space as far as he can and when the passage comes to a turn, he'd jump straight into the web, to guarantee the Rat getting stuck. Yes, Leite would immediately repeat my feat and will end up back in his beloved mine, but the Rat won't be doing so great either. It will get stuck and the spiders will get busy mobbing it for a piece of its Hit Points. If the Queen manages to get out, Eric's task is to take it to the hole with the spikes, stand on the edge and wait for the royal Rat to ram into him at full speed. If he manages to dodge — good for him. If not — not a worry, as long as the Rat lands on the spikes. That'll be the end. As for Mahan, there is a very good niche between the hole with the spikes and the hanging webs, so he can hide there the entire fight. His task is to survive, pick up the gold that would be left behind us, and make us guaranteed profit when we form the clan."

This was a rough translation of Clutzer's speech, because reproducing it word for word is beyond my slang skill. We really have to teach him to speak like a normal person, without all this 'for real' and 'money where your mouth is'.

The money left after Eric lay right on the edge of the hole. So he didn't manage to dodge the enraged Queen. There was nothing left at all of the web labyrinth — the Queen cleaned out the little spiders to the last leg. But for Clutzer's money I had to jump after taking off all my gear: it fell right on the opposite edge of the slime corridor. In all honestly I was amazed by Clutzer. If the first time he didn't know that it would be painful, agreeing to go into this puddle again would require considerable willpower. I opened the chest with the loot and, having taken the money, I even chuckled: I currently had a little under six thousand gold. Enough to start a clan for sure. I examined the loot and immediately set aside three chainmail items — they were for the others and there was no point in looking at their properties. But this leather item was mine, so what bonuses did it hold?

Terrisa's Leather Gloves. Durability: 300. Physical damage resistance: 90. Stamina: +15. Intellect: + 25. +1 to a random stat (must be chosen when equipped). Magic, fire, cold and poison resistance: 30. Item class: Epic. Minimum level: 14.

I stared at the description in disbelief. Even if these gloves were meant just for a level 14 player, I'll never be parted from them, at least not until I found some better ones. I put them on and saw the message:

Attention player! Please choose a stat that

you wish to increase from the following list: Charisma, Crafting, Endurance.

Of course it'd be Crafting, what else could it be?

Accepted. Current item description: Terrisa's Leather Gloves. Durability: 300. Physical damage resistance: 90. Stamina: +15. Intellect: + 25. Crafting: +1. Magic, fire, cold and poison resistance: 30. Item class: Epic. Minimum level: 14.

I put the remaining items in the bag and headed for the transport portal. Now I'll come back to Dolma and then to Pryke and tomorrow I'll be in the main gameworld. With gloves like these the idea of making money on an industrial scale seemed a lot more realistic. I involuntarily closed my eyes as I stepped through the portal. Hello Dolma mine. I was looking forward to the expression on the ogre's face when he saw the achievement I just earned. I wondered whether I'd have to put on decent clothes in five month's time or if they would hand them out before the reception. And do I even have time to think about any of this? Why am I still surrounded by a strange glowing cloud through which I can't see anything? And what happened to the frames of my group? The surrounding cloud dissolved and I was faced with a wall of black and a loading bar slowly coming up to 100. I had a feeling that I was back in the world of 2D games: no 3D graphics, just the location loading bar taking its time, since the servers are old and are groaning under the traffic, slowing everything down. I turned my head this way and that, but the bar stayed in front of my eyes. Damn, where the heck am I?

CHAPTER TWELVE
THE RETURN

T HE PROGRESS BAR REACHED a hundred percent and the black veil dissolved. So, where on earth was I? The status frames of my group and the Queen vanished — it felt like they'd been completely wiped out. Fine, I'll figure it out later. I looked around. Neither Dolma nor Pryke nor the glimmering Dungeon exit/entrance veil was anywhere in sight. The even surface on which I stood was made of a uniform grey material and was smooth to the touch, as if it was grey polished marble. There were no joints. Strange — who would work on such a huge piece of stone? I couldn't see much else, as the light was really poor. If I was asked to describe the lighting, I'd have said that it was something between a moonless night and a foggy evening, a very distinct type of twilight. The visibility was bad, but I noticed a shadow of a building of some kind. I clearly had nothing to lose, so I cautiously headed towards the dim outline, half expecting some sort of a trap. It was eerie, walking around like that. Silence, not even a breeze. Alone in the twilight. All that was missing was a vampire to complete the picture.

The sharp sound of a siren stunned me for a few seconds. It was then replaced by a metallic female voice:

Intruder in the technical section detected. The player capsule is being identified. Player capsule identified. Player capsule is being disconnected. Capsule disconn.....

A flash of light illumined everything around me, I automatically closed my eyes and then, after some blinking, saw the door of my capsule opening. 'E-ehh... What on earth...? They're letting me out already?'

It took me a few seconds to realize that the capsule lid really had slid sideways, but had then became stuck in a half-opened position. I could have squeezed into the gap if not for one 'but' — the ceiling was just ten centimeters from the capsule. The process of my disconnection from the capsule had began: wires, tubes and various devices started to come away. Long-term immersion capsules do have their drawbacks: it takes a good while for you get in or out of one of them. The majority of the other players use medium immersion capsules in which you can stay up to 24 hours. The capsule analyzes the player's state and comes with a safety measure that warns the player when it is time to have a break, giving him fifteen minutes to reach a safe place before being disconnected. There were also the normal virtual reality helmets, but I don't know who used them, since they don't provide full immersion.

When the mask covering my face slid off, I could lift my head and stick it outside the gap between the lid and the capsule. I felt like a high-tech Dracula impersonator. The place where I was had a strong resemblance to a crypt: it measured a meter by a meter and was three meters in length. The wall at my feet was completely solid, so with some difficulty I turned my head in the opposite direction. This made things much clearer. So that's where all the prisoners were kept... A great wall of shelves, separated into cells, spanned from floor to ceiling. Fifty levels, and I counted up to sixty-seven cells on each, beyond which I could not see. Mind-boggling! Real economizing on space, time and money for keeping prisoners. Another image popped into my head: Neo from the 'Matrix' film also wakes up in reality like this after eating that pill. He was also covered in wires, and I only lacked a plug in my head to complete the resemblance. Also, unlike him, I had normal control of my body. So, if this was like in the film, I'd be flushed down a drain, where Morpheus and Trinity would pick me up. That was a pretty ridiculous train of thought right there.

There was nothing left to do but lie back in the capsule and wait. I could have tried screaming in an empty storage room for prisoners, but there was little point in that, since everything was probably automated around here. It was much more likely that the opening of one of the capsules came up somewhere on the system and a bunch of people have already started running around like ants and thinking what to do next. That's right, they've got to earn their lunch money somehow. I didn't notice when I fell asleep, so I missed the moment when the capsule began to shake. 'Sleeping in an opened capsule isn't all that comfortable', I thought to myself, as I moved around in the cramped space, trying to loosen the stiff muscles. The life support systems were turned off, there was no muscle massage and the bed was uncomfortable. Put me back in Barliona already! I don't think I like this reality! I rubbed my sleep-clogged eyes and felt that something was missing. Eyebrows! I had no eyebrows! I felt the back of my head and discovered that I had no hair on my head either. I didn't look anywhere else, supposing that my whole body was now totally hairless. Damn. Is this change permanent or just while I'm in prison? I didn't relish the prospect of spending the rest of my life in a wig. Finally the shaking stopped and I noticed that I was no longer in the crypt, but was being transported somewhere along the moving ceiling. 'They could have at least closed the lid — what if I dropped out?' I thought. In a couple of minutes the transportation was complete, there was some more shaking and all went quiet. The capsule was probably put on the ground.

"Prisoner!" there came a shout. "We're opening the lid. Don't make any sudden moves. Once out of the capsule — hands behind your head, face on the floor. If you fail to comply we will use deadly force! Is that clear? I don't hear an answer!"

Welcome back to the real world, baby.

"Yes, I get it! As soon as I leave the capsule, I lie on the floor, hands behind my head! I'll not give you any problems, so no shooting," who knows, what if I accidentally slipped and they shot me full of something unhealthy and incompatible with life.

"Attention! We're opening the lid" — which was followed by the screeching of the screwdriver, swearing, then the screwdriver again, and a minute later the lid fell to the floor with a sharp bang.

"I'm coming out!" I shouted and carefully got up. There were three technicians in white coats, one guard with a gun aimed at me, and a small mountain of various technical equipment. At least there weren't any women around.

"Come out, hands behind your head, face on the floor! Move it!" shouted the guard, wiping the sweat off his face with his hand. The guy's scared! Really scared, which means he could shoot just out of fear. I carefully stepped out of the capsule and leant on the lid, steadying myself as my head began to spin. Well I'll be! Was that just from changing my position? I nearly fainted, as my vision went dark. So much for them saying that the capsules provide all you need and are completely safe. But here I've spent three months in one and my head was swimming in circles. I dreaded to think what it would be like after eight years. When my head cleared somewhat, I carefully got down on my knees and lay on the floor, face-down. Damn, it was cold!

"Pablo, take the handcuffs and cuff him. I'll cover you," sounded the guard's muffled whisper. "Damned automation, couldn't wait for the police to get here. They promised to be here in thirty minutes. Until then we're on our own. What if he's violent? Why did this crap have to happen on my watch?"

"Hey, you" that one was for me now, "hands

behind your back!"

Behind the back means behind the back, I wasn't going to argue. There was a click of closing handcuffs and an immediate sigh of relief from the other four. They've done it. They caught the malicious criminal, cuffed him and could now go and have their coffee.

"You can sit down, but you better not try anything." Ah, so there are some decent people still around. I rolled on my side and sat down, propping my back against the capsule. By the looks of it I was in the laboratory where the prisoners were taken once they served their term.

That's how we spent the next two minutes: I sat and watched the technicians and the guard, who never took his gun off me. The whole crowd stared at me in silence, too scared to move. Although no — one of the technicians was vigorously reading something in the hand-held communicator.

"Your floor is so cold here. I'll catch a cold and die and you won't be getting any medals for that," I decided to break the long silence. "Can you please at least bring a blanket I can cover myself with?"

"Yeah, right, you don't want a coffee to go with that too?" asked the guard roughly, but was elbowed by one of the technicians.

"Peterson, the guy's got a point — sitting with your bare ass on the floor is a pain", the reading technician looked up from his device.

"Get up," he said, addressing me now. "I've scanned through your file, waste collector killer. You seem normal enough, even handed yourself in. How are you feeling, by the way?"

"I'm frozen, my hands are uncomfortable and though I may be clean I'd give a lot for a hot shower. You have no idea what it's like to live in a dusty mine for three months," was my honest response.

"Ah, so he's the one?" said the guard, surprised, and lowered his gun. "That's why I thought his face looked familiar. He was on all the channels a couple of months ago. Some mess you got yourself in, man. I know someone who works at the building management service and he said they had to do so many repairs that the officials had a panic about how to pay for it all."

"Yes, I know. They hung all that debt on me. In total I have to pay off a hundred million game gold or serve out my entire eight-year term."

The guard and the technicians even whistled on hearing this figure. I had to admit — that was some debt that I was landed with. They stayed silent for a while.

"What should we do, Roberts?" the guard asked the senior technician.

"Not much for it. You're not going to try anything funny if we take the cuffs off? They'd be a bother in the shower."

"Like I'd even think about it. Do I look like I need more trouble? I still have over seven years of time to do and have no intention of adding to that," I assured him.

"Turn around," said Roberts and unlocked the handcuffs. Peterson automatically aimed the gun at me, but a few moments later relaxed and put it back in the holster.

"The shower is straight ahead, the soap and

the rest is provided. Everything's disposable. Hurry up. In and out."

I never thought that a shower could provide that much pleasure. I stood under the water and relished every moment and every drop, until they started banging on the cabin and telling me to get out. I changed into the underwear offered me by the machine, returned to the common room and sat on the sofa, wrapping myself in the blanket that was on it. Now you can send me anywhere, I'm ready.

"Why did you leave the game?" asked Roberts, perching himself on a chair nearby.

"How should I know? The mine where I was working had a Dungeon with a portal. I jumped in the portal and ended up in some technical location. Then there was a flash of light and I was here. That's it."

"So you're the one behind it all? You sure got all our admins in a panic. There was a lot of swearing going back and forth on the intranet — they were trying to find out who left around an entrance into the technical location." For a while Roberts was silent and then went on: "But you did well. Not everyone can earn Respect in three months; just a couple of people did that, in my memory. And completing that Dungeon without any hints ensured that all five of you gained a place in Barliona's history. All the top guilds are incensed that some prisoners have made it into the pioneers' hall of fame. On the forums they are saying that several clans swore to hunt you down — meaning that you'll all end up in a clan one way or another: either as members or on their blacklist."

"What do you mean, 'all five of us'? There were only four," I asked in surprise.

"Well, yes, just four went through the Dungeon, but the achievement was earned by five. That's what it said in the achievement. You figure out how that's happened yourself."

Karachun! I never removed him from the group! He remained there in the frames. This meant that Karachun also earned this achievement along with the heightened interest of all the leading players of this world. Some 'favor' we did him, and ourselves too, for that matter. Players like Hellfire from Phoenix don't like taking no for an answer. He'd offer you to join his clan so that he could add this Dungeon to his collection in the race between first pioneers, and if you refused, he'd be very upset. Being on the black list of the top guilds is a pretty unpleasant business — they kill you at every opportunity and you won't be able to buy anything from them, even at an auction. There were probably some other downsides I didn't know about, but which could be found in the manuals. Stop! How does Roberts know that I and Mahan are one and the same? It's a prosecutable offence to dig up this information!

"Roberts, where did you get the information that I went through a Dungeon or that I've earned Respect in three months?"

"You're a bit slow not to figure this out yourself. You said that you were in a Dungeon. Out of all the mines only Dolma has a Dungeon. That's one thing. The other is that only people with Respect get sent to Dolma, as a test to see if you're ready to work in a team. Moreover, prisoners from all the parallel mines get sent there."

"By the way, what are these parallel mines?" I

asked Roberts. "I met a couple of guys on Dolma who were from a parallel Pryke mine. But why?"

"Because it's unprofitable to keep more than 250 prisoners in one mine. That would mean weakened control. And multiplying mines isn't an answer either. Why take up the extra space? That's why they introduced parallel ones — we have to put you lot somewhere, in the end. They have the same governor and the same quota collector, but the rest is separate. It's simpler that way."

"All right, but that still doesn't explain how you connected me and the Shaman."

"Ah, yes. Aside from what I said, there's the main thing. Just think how this sounds: Shaman Mahan, who entered the hall of fame and prisoner Daniel Mahan, who's been through a Dungeon. You really think it's so hard to guess that you're him?"

I'm such a fool! My bad to start suspecting a good guy like that of anything.

"I'm sorry, I didn't think properly. You mentioned hints: is there some way for me to get access to them? After all, I've left the mine now and will be living in the main gameworld, where you're totally lost without the manuals."

"You may as well ask for access to the forums," laughed Roberts. "Of all the documentation, prisoners only have access to the legislative statutes. Although..."

I missed a heartbeat as I waited for the decision. If Roberts helped me, the game would immediately become considerably easier.

"If you're brought a new capsule model, it contains access to manuals and the internal game forums by default. It's just that for prisoners, it's disabled with a jammer. And it's not a program, but a small nib in the capsule hull... It might even get knocked out during transport..." said Roberts, staring into space, but then snapped out of it and went on: "I owe you a thank you, by the way, for helping me to spend time with my grandson!"

I gave Roberts a look of surprise. What's he on about?

"When you fouled up that lake, my children remembered that their old man lived out of town. They came to visit straight away, although I've been inviting them with little success for three years before that — asking them to bring the kid and let him run around in the grass. They're making him all high-tech — he even goes to the bathroom with a handheld and he's just four! He should be playing with blocks and soldiers, but he's chattering about image manipulation. They're really spoiling the kid! Well, never mind, I've lost track of time with you here. You need to go rest," said Roberts, getting up from the chair. I wrapped myself in the blanket, got comfortable and closed my eyes, unexpectedly and immediately dropping into sleep.

"Where is he?" someone's worried voice woke me up.

"He's asleep, where else would he be? He's spent three months in the capsule, so he's catching up on his sleep after all that time," Roberts's voice replied.

"What do you mean 'catching up on his sleep'?"

"Ah, it seems you don't know this. The in-game sleep doesn't provide adequate psychological

— VASILY MAHANENKO —

relaxation, so every three months prisoners are disconnected and allowed to have normal sleep. Ten hours of sleep is just enough for the next three months. As far as the subject himself is concerned, he just suddenly wakes up the next day in the game."

"So what's with this one, then?"

"That's not our problem. For some reason his capsule got disconnected from the game and the automated systems transported him to the rehabilitation centre and even broke the lid during transportation, dammit. So we're waiting for a new capsule and installation technician. Then we'll put the prisoner back in and..."

I didn't hear the rest. My eyes closed and I was once again in the kingdom of Morpheus.

"Get up," I was once again brought back to reality. For a few moments I had to fight to open my eyes. It was so good to just get some sleep, without hurrying anywhere or thinking about handing in the daily quota. Beautiful! I looked around the room with sleepy eyes and then focused on the people standing next to me. Bah! I knew one of them! That's the technician who put me in the capsule. He was the one cracking jokes at the time: 'in you jump', and all that. Now I could have a better look at him — despite an ordinary face that you could come across anywhere, his appearance made me smile. First of all, the unbuttoned lab coat had a sweater underneath. In the three months of my imprisonment little had changed in the world of fashion — this sweater was very expensive and very popular among the progressive youth. It could be worn at minus forty as well as plus thirty degrees, as the internal temperature control system ensured comfort within that range. The sweater could change color and texture at the owner's whim, and could even feel different — from smooth to fluffy. Aside from the sweater, Peter (as his electronic ID told me) wore classic trousers. The trousers were thoroughly ironed with creases and tucked into old, dirty and worn army boots. If each thing looked normal by itself, together they created an unforgettable image. Knowing modern technicians, perpetually bearded, in ordinary sweaters, work trousers and boots like these, I concluded that Peter had made a considerable effort to dress up. At least, on top. But he had never got around to the bottom half, or had just forgotten about it in the process. The fact that he was getting ready for something could be seen from his fairly good haircut, which must have been done in a salon several days ago. Why several days? Because the two- or three-day-old stubble completed the image of a technician getting ready for a date of some sort. Despite his somewhat comical look, you could guess that something unpleasant had happened to Peter. The vacant stare, frozen facial expression and the fact that he bumped into every available corner as he left the room, all pointed to that. I even became curious about what had happened to him.

Surrounded by the police, I entered the room where the technicians were already preparing the capsule for me. So my unexpected odyssey into freedom had come to an end. The policemen sat themselves on the chairs by the entrance and I headed for the capsule.

"Ah, you're here already," said Peter absent-mindedly, when I stood myself nearby and coughed quietly. "Take off your capsule and get into the clothes."

It looked like something really did happen to this guy. How could they send him to work in a condition like that? Unless I was mistaken, every morning all the technical personnel underwent express-examination, and, depending on its results, were issued the permission to work. The Corporation didn't keep any 'zombies', that is employees who'd play all night and then come to work to catch up on their sleep. By the looks of it in his current condition he'll end up calibrating my capsule so 'well' that I'll end up inside some goblin's body. I looked questioningly at his partner.

"Take no notice," was the reply to my silent question. "It's just our Petruccio's been through some tough times. His girl dumped him about an hour ago. Just before we came here. Yes, Petruccio? You want me to toss you that spanner? And pass me that thing as well please."

I see. So if one guy was struck by misfortune, the other would be making fun of it. What a 'wonderful' partner to get stuck with.

"Peter, is everything all right with you? You're not looking too well. What if you make a mess of the settings and I end up 'enjoying' it for the next eight years."

"Yes. No. It's all right. Yes. Everything is fine," he said, somewhat absent-mindedly. He then swore quietly, reset the settings and started again.

"Peter! Just look at you — you better leave off all this playing around with the settings!"

"Leave... Leave! Leaving!!!! I've had it with everyone!" shouted Peter. "I don't leave people, they leave me! I've been going out with a girl for three months and thought she liked me. I thought she was interested in my work, because she asked about it from time to time, When I told her that I'll be putting the 'waste collector killer' himself into the capsule, she even asked me to give you a present — to let you choose your own name. And then what? Today, when I was called out here, I looked at the prisoner information and then called her, because I thought it would make her happy to know that the prisoner to whom she made the gift of the name was about to enter the main gameworld. I thought I'd make her happy... When she heard this news about you, she said that it was all over between us. Why? What did I do wrong? Can you tell me?"

I looked at the technician in surprise, getting myself more comfortable in the capsule. So then, the ability to choose my name wasn't the choice of the technician, but the idea of some flighty girl. Flighty?

"What was her name?" I thought to continue the conversation, but Peter silently turned and walked away from the capsule. Yeah, poor guy. I know for myself: when you get dumped, you can even lose interest in life. And he's got a crappy work partner as well.

"Marina," his partner replied for him. "Personally, my feeling is that she left him because of you. Of course that's none of my business, but I've been trying to get Petruccio back to normal for the best part of an hour now. He even thought to jump under a car once he finished talking to her. When we get back I'll take him to a psychologist; he's my partner after all — we've worked together for some years now. But I have a strong hunch that you've had a hand in this. She even asked for you to be given the chance to choose your own name and then left Pete as soon as she heard about you. Is there anything you'd like to say?"

Dammit! Was it really the same girl?

"You don't happen to have her picture on you? I know a certain Marina, who's very similar to this one in the way she does things. She also ditched me just before I went to prison."

The technician turned the screen of his communicator and I saw Peter embracing a rather attractive girl. The same one whose wager got me stuck in Barliona for eight years.

"No, that's not the one," I spoke in neutral tones, trying not to betray the agitation that engulfed me. "She's pretty. Maybe you should tell Peter to fight for her? What if something happened to her: a bad mood or she got up on the wrong side of the bed? You never know with women."

"That's what I intend to do. On our way back I'll try to talk some sense into him and snap him out of it. That he's started screaming is already a good sign — if he's visibly taken offence it means he's coming back to normal! Well, good luck to you, man," said Peter's partner, put the last pipe in place and closed the lid. There was a flash of light and I was back in Barliona.

I opened my eyes and found myself inside a room. I had a quick glance at my stats, my bag and my character — everything was still there. I held my breath as I went into the settings and selected the forum. Before it was inaccessible, but now...

Welcome to the in-game forum of Barliona. Please read the rules...

Thank you Roberts! A big heartfelt thanks!

The room contained a small table and two chairs. 'One is probably for me', I thought and tried to get myself comfortable in it. If I'm correct about the sequence of events, now I would be meeting the committee for parole from the mine; they'll read me the riot act and decide what settlement to send me to.

Right, while no-one's here I could do some thinking. So it appeared that Marina was looking for me. But what for? To pay her debt and become my girl for a month? Yeah, right, that's really 'essential' in the virtual world. Barliona had firm restrictions on physical sexual contact between players. You could not even completely strip yourself: loin cloths, as well as chest wraps for women, could never come off. The only exception for this were special Tolerance Houses, located in each large city. Local brothels. In these a player could do anything his perverted mind wished — only imitators worked in these houses. But if two players voluntarily entered such a house, they could have contact with each other. Truth be told, I've been to such places myself a few times, especially when I started to play. Elf maids, dwarven lasses, worgen ladies and orc women... Everything exotic! According to official statistics, in Barliona the brothels were the second most popular destinations, after the Dungeons. The figures, however, didn't specify that the comparison was made between only one Tolerance House and all of the region's Dungeons.

And, as always, there was a 'BUT'. I had no idea whom Marina was playing. Perhaps she's a hardcore player and had chosen an unusual race for herself — kobold, lizardfolk, goblin or something else even more extreme. In Barliona, aside from just playing, you could make it a goal to prove yourself a good player. For this purpose unique races were introduced, with deadly racial bonuses, aggressive mobs in starting locations or negative reputation with almost all the factions. Just so you could prove that you could play such a character. When a player decided to test his strength that way, the old character didn't even get deleted, but simply disabled. If the attempt was unsuccessful, the player could have his old character back. What if Marina was a kobold? I don't think I'd... dare to go with something like that into a brothel. Although I would like to meet and have a proper chat: I don't like girls who get what they want by selling their body. Why did she treat Peter like that? He seemed an all right guy. If we meet, I'll tell her exactly what I think about all this.

My thoughts were cut off by a portal that appeared in the room, from which an energetic young man of about twenty emerged, with a sharp professional look about him: in a suit and tie and a neat haircut.

"Good day, Daniel, let me introduce myself: I'm Alexis, the junior assistant of the parole secretary, and here to read you the minutes of the meeting of the committee on your parole," he fired off. "Thus, under article 78 section 24 of the Penal Code, you have the right to be relocated to the main gameworld. Because you were in prison less than half a year, your place of settlement will be chosen at random. To determine the place of your settlement you must return to your mine, where the destination will be chosen. The incident with your going back to the real world has been examined, it has been noted that you have conducted yourself in a correct manner, and a decision has been made that no punishments will be imposed upon you.

"In response to your unasked question — you ended up in the technical location by accident. It should not have happened, and the portal has since been removed. During your time in the main gameworld you are barred from accessing any gambling establishments, such as casinos, races and other official games of chance. You may use the auction house only in Anhurs, but for no longer than one hour a day — so use this time wisely. Visits to Tolerance Houses are permitted, but there are some small restrictions: no more than 24 hours a week. I will remind you that you cannot deal damage to another player as long as you have the armband on you, but if a player attacks you, you have no such limitation against him.

"That's it from me. Do you have any questions or requests? No? That's great. Here is your portal, have a happy game." Another portal appeared next to his, which led, as I guessed, to the Pryke mine.

Alexis checked that my portal was stable and then with a sure step disappeared into his own, leaving me alone. Wait! What was that? I saw some boy run in, looking like he'd been dragged away from his toys, quickly read out the committee's decision and run back to continue playing.

Weird. What about a chat? Or about setting me on the right path? Great justice system we have here! But he did make me chuckle: no more than 24 hours a week in a Tolerance House. That's some high standard our lawmakers set. I don't even know if I'll manage it.

There was little else for me to do but jump into the portal. So now I'll return to Pryke and the orc will allocate the place of settlement for me. So far, so good. I'll have time to say good bye to all my fellow prisoners. I'll hand things over to Sakas — now he can be the head of our craftsmen 'gang'. 'I mustn't leave any unfinished business,' I thought as I headed back to Pryke.

I stepped into the mine and took in all its beauty. It was worth it too — if the sun stopped burning and the dust disappeared once my reputation reached Friendly, now the mine was full of colors. Blue sky, green grass in the common part of the mine — there were even flowerbeds. Is that how the orc and Rine see it? Or do they have Exalted programmed into them (which would take me 12 thousand more reputation points to reach) and see the mine as some sort of a resort?

"Mahan? What are you doing here?" I heard a surprised shout of one of the guards.

"I got bored without you lot and decided to come back," I replied to the overseer and was surprised not to get a rude response. Instead he offered to walk me to the administration building and get things sorted out with the orc.

The governor sat at his table, inscrutable as a statue.

"Shaman. Who got Respect not thanks to, but in spite of his actions," said the orc. Once again hairs stood up on the back of my neck. There was something very life-affirming in this calm, low and confident voice. I'll miss it when I get out. "Your place of settlement will be appointed in the evening. You can go."

"I'd like to become a Shaman. Where can I learn this?" I decided to ask the orc. Barliona had a rule that any NPC could be asked about profession or class trainers. If they knew about it they'd tell you and, if not, would point you in the right direction. Why would the orc do less than any guard in the capital?

"A Shaman... What do you know about Shamans?"

The question was so unexpected that I struggled with an answer.

"Shamans? Firstly, I'm a Shaman. We can summon Spirits with which we can heal or cause damage. We also have to go through an initiation to stop losing Hit Points for summoning. We have a Tambourine, we sing songs and dance dances. I think that's it."

"Although you're a Shaman, you have no idea what it actually means."

"Being a Shaman," began the orc after a pause, "is not about dances and songs. That is all superfluous. Shamans are those that speak to the Spirits. To be a shaman is a great responsibility. Are you ready for it?"

All I could do was nod in agreement and mumble something incomprehensible. I just hoped the orc would tell me a place where I could find a Shaman trainer. I never thought that he would start to tell me anything of his own accord. Was that the effect of Respect on him? Quite a useful thing it was, then.

"If you're ready, then listen. There are six steps in a Shaman's development. Currently you're on the lowest one." The orc began to describe each step and I went to the manual and started to read. Although he described everything very well, you remember information better when you read it. At least this was true in my case. So, what do we have for Shamans in terms of leveling?

0. Uninitiated Shaman (Aglarat bo-oh). A step zero Shaman can summon lesser Lightning and Healing Spirits. Offerings do not decrease the penalty for Spirit summoning. External attributes: none. The next step is reached by Shaman Initiation (the initiation may be attempted once a month).

1. Initiate Shaman (Yabagan bo-oh). The first level of initiation; the Shaman is able to summon Younger Elemental Spirits. The Shaman embarks on the search for his Totem (Spirit Guardian). To decrease the summoning penalty by 50% you must perform the following weekly offerings to the Spirits: milk or tea. External attributes: Shaman's Tambourine. The next step is reached by finding the Totem.

2. Elemental Shaman (Hayaltyn bo-oh). A Shaman with a Totem. A second step Shaman can freely communicate with common Elemental Spirits. To decrease the summoning penalty by 50% you must perform the following weekly offerings to the Spirits:

bread. External attributes: Shaman's Cloak. The next step is reached by successful completion of a trial (the trial may be attempted once every three months).

3. Great Shaman (Sheraete bo-oh). The third step deals with the strengthening of the powers acquired during the previous stage. The Shaman strengthens his link with the Spirits and is able to communicate with the Great Elemental Spirits. The Shaman no longer needs a Tambourine to summon Spirits. To decrease the summoning penalty by 50% you must perform the following weekly offerings to the Spirits: roast meat. External attributes: Shaman's Staff. The next step is reached by successful completion of a trial (the trial may be attempted once a year).

4. High Shaman (Tengeryin bo-oh). A Shaman of the fourth step can communicate with Supreme Spirits of Higher and Lower Worlds. No penalty for Spirit summoning. External attributes: Shaman's Hat with deer antlers. The next step is reached by gaining Exalted reputation with Supreme Spirits of Higher and Lower Worlds.

5. Harbinger (Tabilgatai zarin bo-oh). For the fifth step the Shaman has completely mastered all the Shamanistic powers. The Shaman gains the ability to be transported to any place, levitate, communicate with any being either in physical or spirit form throughout Barliona. No penalty for Spirit summoning. External attributes: none.

I didn't remember any of it, but realized that I must go through the initiation as soon as possible.

"But first you need to go through the initiation," said my former governor, as if reading my thoughts. "Come, we don't have that much time until your allocation," a portal appeared in the governor's office. Did that mean that I could become a real Shaman right now, instead of waiting three months until I leave the settlement? Great!

The portal took me to the mountains, right by the entrance to a dark cave. The orc appeared next to me, holding a gnarled staff and wearing a strange cloak with feathers and a hat with horns. Now I really was surprised. The Pryke Mine Governor was a High Shaman! This piece of news was quite mind-blowing. I could bet all my gold that his Totem was a Wolf Spirit. Definitely a White Wolf Spirit. But why is he stuck here in the mine? There aren't that many High Shamans, even among the NPCs. I quickly looked in the manual to check. That's right, only 3381 players ever reached that step. There was no data on the NPCs, but I was sure that the numbers were similar. I made a note for myself to make a special effort to find out why the orc was in the mine. The developers wouldn't have put him here without a good reason, so there must be a story behind it. To be honest, I liked the orc — he was a very colorful personality, so I would have liked to find out more about him.

"Whom did you bring, brother?" sounded a voice that made me jump in my place. It seemed that the wind itself was speaking — the voice came from all sides at once. Was this some kind of a Spirit?

"I have brought a Seeker. He is on the path to find himself and it is our duty to aid him," replied the orc.

"Is he ready?"

"No-one but the Spirit of the Forest knows

this."

"Will he find what he is seeking?"

"No-one but the Spirit of the Mountains has this knowledge."

The orc continued to refer to different Spirits and I stood nearby and listened, savoring every moment. The designers of this class really outdid themselves. Of course, they may have gone a little 'over the top' with 'brother' or 'no-one but the Spirit', but it was still beautiful and interesting! The class role play for Shamans was top notch! The initiation of the Hunters was not as interesting — you had to find a master bowman, go through a class quest line and then come and accept the honorable title of the Hunter. Although with this the difference was that as a Hunter I went through this quest chain at level five to ten, levelling up in the process. With my fourteen levels going through a quest chain like 'kill 10 mobs with the aid of enchanted arrows' would feel a bit stupid. However, bringing down twice as many mobs would seem well worth a scene like this one. I know that many players complain about unnecessary insertions from the world's history or about NPCs playing their characters to the full. All of this slows down the levelling process and increases game time — everyone is eager to become someone great, so they don't pay any attention to these trivialities. But I'm not in any particular hurry for the next eight years, so I can easily spend an extra half an hour and enjoy a beautiful spectacle.

The orc lifted his hands and started to whisper something. A whirlwind began to form in his hands, which stabilized a minute later and turned into a two-meter tornado. I only had enough time to think that Shaman really wasn't such a weak class if it could do things like that and then heard the orc's voice:

"Bow your head, little brother. You are seeing the Great Spirit of Air, that has come to witness your initiation."

I went down on one knee and bent my head. I decided to trust the orc's words completely. If he tells me to bow my head, I will. If he tells me to jump on one leg, I will. I'd even jump into a chasm, if he tells me. I was sure it'd be a test.

"Are you ready, Seeker?" the Spirit's voice echoed in the mountains. If I previously thought the orc's voice could make you tremble in your bones, I was wrong. The Spirit's words made my whole body quiver, as if it was resonating with the surrounding world.

"Y-yess, r-ready," I managed to utter, controlling the jittering of my teeth.

"To become a real Shaman, you must prove that your spirit is steadfast, that your spirit is pliant, that your spirit is strong, that your spirit is gentle. You must enter the cave, where four trials await you. What you do with each — is a choice that your spirit makes, let it guide you. If you fail even one trial, your initiation will be postponed by a month. Every shaman has the chance to become a Harbinger, but not all take this path. It is up to you alone whether you become a real Shaman.

Quest chain received: 'The Path of the Shaman'.

'The Path of the Shaman: Step 1'. Go though

the labyrinth of trials.

0 of 4 trials completed (next attempt in 30 days).

"Enter the cave and trust in your spirit. It will help you make the right choice," was the orc's parting advice to me.

I rose to my feet and cautiously headed to the dark cave. Was I to go through this trial in the dark? However, as soon as I crossed some unseen threshold the cave was filled with light and four passages appeared, followed by a message:

Information for the player! You have begun the quest 'The Path of the Shaman. Step 1'. You have two attempts for completing the trial; if you fail, you can attempt the trial again in a month's time. If your first attempt fails, press the red stone by the entrance to make your second attempt. Have a pleasant Game!

I quietly swore under my breath. This just spoiled the feeling left by the previous beautiful scene — with two attempts even an idiot would be able to get through four trials with the help of the manual and the forums. Speaking of which...

I sat on the stone, brought up the forum and began to study the process of the Shaman initiation. This wasn't just simple, it was elementary: four rooms with a particular situation played out in each. You had to perform certain actions, depending on the situation. That's it. The forum described what should be done in detail, so I had no reason to expect any difficulties. I could understand the reasoning of the developers — if you make the Shaman initiation complicated and difficult no-one would play this class. It would be easier to run around as a Hunter or a Paladin. I got up and went to the corridor labeled '1', which brought me to a closed door.

As soon as I stepped into the room I felt my head spin a little. Well, that was normal, since the place was turning by 180 degrees. In order to exit it you had to choose one of the available paths. So, what did we have here? The room was divided into two with a partition. One side of the partition contained a hole, from where a fawn's head was sticking up, on the other a wolf was growling, teeth bared, its paw caught in a trap. If the forum information was correct, this was simple: it was a test for gentleness of Spirit; you had to take out the fawn and leave the room without a second thought. Easy said — easy done. I carefully took the trapped animal out of the hole and left, that's all there was to it. What did Shaman initiation have to do with any of this?

Quest update — 'The Path of the Shaman. Step 1': 1 of 4 trials completed.

Corridor number 2. A turn of the room and this time there was only one path to the exit.

There was an ordinary five-meter hole filled with water. A centimeter-wide bridge spanned across it. It was more of a tightrope than a bridge. You felt lucky not to see it sagging under its own weight. This was simple too — a trial of the pliancy of the Spirit. Walking across the tightrope was practically impossible and the Shaman's task was to humble himself and simply swim across the hole. Nothing difficult, but everyone recommended leaving this room for the last. Otherwise the remaining trials would have to be tackled while wet. Well, never mind. I left the room, water running off me, and saw the next message.

Quest update — 'The Path of the Shaman. Step 1': 2 of 4 trials completed.

Corridor number 3. Again there was only one way out.

Ten human statues made of stone, clubs in their hands, stood in my way. Test for the strength of Spirit. You had to walk through the statues, taking no notice of their blows — a perfectly 'suitable' trial for free players whose sensory filters have been turned off. Now I'll have to feel all of this on my hide. Damn, when I read up on it, I had an immediate dislike for this trial. It hasn't really been designed with prisoners in mind. I clenched my teeth and managed to walk to the other end of the room. Damn, that hurt a lot. Even Rats didn't bite this hard. My Endurance went up by no less than 10% while the statues tenderized me head to toe. Having hit me, each statue crumpled into dust, which settled on me layer after layer. Wet and dusty, I started to resemble a dummy, but the message that appeared next told me I had not endured this in vain:

Quest update — 'The Path of the Shaman. Step 1': 3 of 4 trials completed.

Now all I had to do was show steadfastness of Spirit. Corridor number 4 took me to a room with a mixed pile of rice and peas in the middle. I was glad to see a bucket of water next to the pile, which allowed me to wash the dust off my hands and face. They were right about taking the trial with the water last — at least you'd come out clean. The fourth trial simply involved separating the mixed pile into two within an hour of entering the room, making a pile of peas and a pile of rice. It was a test of your nerves and endurance. I crouched and set to work. In this test I could beat any free player: they never spent a day in a mine, forced to swing the pick, or they'd know what steadfastness of spirit was all about. The dust falling off me stuck to the rice, but I decided to take no notice of this. I had to work and not get distracted by silly details.

It took me forty minutes to complete the last task. R-right... Somehow the process of initiation into a Shaman didn't impress me that much — all the trials were made for noobs (beginner players). As I left the room, I saw the predictable message:

Quest update — 'The Path of the Shaman. Step 1': 4 of 4 trials completed.
Quest completed. Seek out the Shaman trainer.

I headed for the exit and saw the red stone mentioned in the first system message. If I pressed it, I'd have to go through the trials again. I was almost out of the cave when I remembered the orc's parting advice: *"trust in your spirit. It will help you make the right choice."* I stopped. Just now I really trusted only my brain and the forum, but in no way my own instincts or feelings. Did I want to do everything as it was written in the player FAQ? In truth — no; as I completed the tasks I felt that something wasn't quite right. I sat down again and began to scan through the forums for any kind of a hint of what I did wrong. Yes, the task was completed, but I had a nagging feeling that I had done it all wrong and if I left the cave now, I'd only see disappointment in the orc's eyes. It took me over an hour to read everything through, but I still could not lay my doubts to rest. The only message that stood out from the rest was from a lady Shaman with a funny nick of Antsinthepantsa: "Shamans! During this trial forget that you have a brain. Thinking is for Mages! We have to feel, this is our strength!"

I sat there, staring into space for a few minutes, but not a single thought appeared in my mind, now slowly boiling over with tension. Shaking my head, I got up, went to the red stone and pushed it down full of inexplicable anger. You can all be sticking your advice where the sun don't shine!

Information for the player! You have used the quest resetting stone. Attention! You have only one attempt left to complete the trials in the quest 'The Path of the Shaman. Step 1'.

Quest update — 'The Path of the Shaman. Step 1': 0 of 4 trials completed.

I got ready to head to corridor number 1.

Something told me that the trials had to be taken strictly in sequence or it wouldn't work again. Or rather it would work, but not in the way I needed it to.

The room turned around and again I found myself standing between the fawn and the wolf. The forums clearly stated that if you freed the wolf, it would eat the fawn and after leaving the room you'd have failed in the task. The wolf had to be freed in an unusual way: there was a stick lying by the entrance and you could use it to knock the wolf out for a minute, quickly free him and leave the room. It was important to do this before the wolf recovered, otherwise he would kill the unfortunate player straight away. I looked at the fawn one more time. He was sitting in that hole and seemed perfectly fine. He wasn't screaming or fidgeting or making wild frightened eyes. What if he had a nest in there? Maybe that hole was his home and I'd be taking him away from it. With the wolf it was a different story. It's not much of a life with your paw in a trap. You could understand why his teeth were bared: at this moment I was the personification of all his pain. If I approached him, he'd try to tear my throat out. And, most importantly, his properties were inaccessible: I had no way of telling if he'd eat me in one bite or I'd have enough time to dodge. I closed my eyes and listened to myself. What to do? I really didn't want to go to the fawn and was feeling really sorry for the wolf — my whole soul wished to free him. Soul? Could that be the spirit to which I should be listening?

I walked towards the grey wolf. The fawn may have a chance to survive in a fight with the wolf, but the wolf had no chance if he remained in the trap. The choice was clear, but now I had to find a way of getting him out. Baring his teeth and giving out a muffled growl, the wolf lowered his pointy ears to his head, made the fur on his back stand up, crouched on his hind legs and did all he could to show that, once I crossed a certain line, he would attack me. He didn't care that his front leg was trapped — he intended to fight for his life to the bitter end. A real fighter. I couldn't help feeling respect for him — many would have broken by now in his place. I took a closer look and saw the expression of animal rage on the massive muzzle. Wow, so wolves were able to express emotions. I never knew. Or had this been added by the designers to enhance the overall effect?

I left that question for later. Trying not to take any notice of the wolf, who was getting ready to eat me, I sat right at the edge of the safe zone and began to examine the trap. Well, well. What a pervert you had to be to come up with a thing like that. The wolf's paw was clamped in five places at once — each toe separately, and one clamp on the whole paw. At least there weren't any teeth or springs — just gripping jaws with safety catches. All that had to be done to free the wolf was bend open five clamps, fasten them and lift the jaws. However, it became immediately clear that you couldn't open this trap from a distance by using a stick or some other tool. You had to do it with your hands, exposing your neck to the wolf.

I looked into the wolf's eyes, which were pulsing with rage, and couldn't think of anything better to say that the incredibly stupid phrase I read in the book about Mowgli: "We are of one blood, you and I!", then I closed my eyes, sank to my knees and crawled over to free the wolf. I wondered if my skills and stats would be reset if he ate me now and I was sent for a respawn. They shouldn't be, since technically I had already left the mine. I stretched towards the trap and started to unbend the first clamp, feeling the hot breath of the wolf above my head. I was so tense I could hardly breathe, and my hands were shaking, but I didn't stop my efforts to free the trapped beast. Now I knew that 'heart sunk into my boots' was not just a nice turn of phrase, but quite a real physiological trait. At least in my case. A few seconds went by and I was still alive. Did it actually work?

I rejoiced too early in thinking that the trap didn't feature any teeth. It did. When I unclenched the first latch and lifted the first clamp from the wolf's toe, he suddenly howled and then with a muffled growl bit me on the shoulder. There was an instant stab of pain, I screamed something and cowered, expecting the wolf to lunge at me and finish me off. A few moments later I opened my eyes and looked around — the wolf was in no hurry to attack; he growled quietly and periodically waved his tail nervously. I was off the hook. I turned over the clamp and saw why he'd bit me — there was an enormous jagged spike under it. When I lifted the clamp, I pulled it out, causing the wolf incredible pain. So that's how he repaid me? Pain for pain? I shifted my eyes to the shoulder bitten by the wolf. Well I'll be... Blood! For the first time ever since I started playing Barliona, whether as a Hunter or as a Shaman, I saw blood on a player! There were very strict rules about depicting it in the game: it was never shown. At least, they've not shown it before, but now I saw all too well now the red liquid was pouring from my shoulder in a thin stream. After removing the other clamps and freeing the wolf's paw from the trap jaw, I got up and, swaying slightly from sudden light-headedness, went towards the exit. The wolf bit me every time I took the clamps off his toes. Both shoulders, having received two bites each, were losing a good deal of blood — enough to fill a whole bucket. I never thought I could have that much blood in me. Not that this really mattered. The wolf sat himself by the trap and started to lick his paw. He would heal his paw and snack on the fawn, and the fact that I failed the trial wasn't that big a deal. The main thing was that I did what I thought was right. I glanced around the room with the sitting wolf and the fawn's head sticking out and headed towards the 'fascinating' walk along the tightrope.

Things looked exactly the same in the second room — the tightrope and the five-meter hole with water. The forums made no mention of how to walk along this tightrope — people only boasted about how many meters they managed to get across. I couldn't help chuckling — even here people were competing to outdo each other in the length department. The wounds from the wolf's bites were beginning to close and the blood was only appearing in small drops now, so I decided to ignore it. Brushing away all my thoughts and freeing my mind, I headed for the tightrope. I'm a tightrope walker. I'm a butterfly, gracefully fluttering above a candle, without singing its wings. I'm.... I'm a wet and angry Shaman, who's climbing back out and stubbornly continuing to fall off the tightrope again and again. The water made the wounds on my shoulders open up again and the blood began to flow in a sure treacle, coloring the water in the hole red. I climbed out of it once again, probably for the hundredth time now, and decided it was time for a break. Every fiber of my body felt that I was meant to walk that tightrope, but I just couldn't do it. It was too thin and too awkward. Placed as it was right at the water's surface, the tightrope simply refused to be conquered. And the water too, crystal clear at the start of the trial, was now an embodiment of a vampire's dream: the red was so bright that you felt like all the water had turned to blood. I involuntarily glanced at my shoulders, which continued to bleed as before. Strange. My head wasn't spinning any more, but judging by the amount of the red liquid that drained out of me, it was a bit more than a couple of buckets. 'If the wounds close with time, I think I should stop and give them a chance to heal. They get wet and open up in the water and the constant moving about doesn't help either... It's decided!' I sat by the obstacle, closed my eyes and tried to relax.

I woke up from the back of my head hitting the floor. Wow, I relaxed so much I even fell asleep. I looked at my shoulders. At last! There was a dried crust and no more bleeding. I carefully got up and approached the tightrope once again. Creepy stuff! The blood did not form a crust just on my shoulders, but also in the hole, producing a rough red film on the surface, like in some horror film. I shuddered, but, discarding unwanted thoughts, focused only on the tightrope and stepped forward. First step. Second.

Third. Fifth. It was like walking on a watery mattress, springy and reliable. No thinking! I must keep moving. I walked to the opposite end, stepped on the solid surface and looked back. I did it! The crust of blood formed a springy film on the water, which allowed me not to lose my footing and fall. So the wolf bit me for a reason, didn't he? Was all this part of the intended design? Then why didn't I get the message that I had completed even one trial? Baffled, I shrugged and went towards the exit. 'If there is no message, I'll just do what I believe to be right rather than what's written in the instructions. I can't do any worse for it.' With these thoughts I entered the third room, where I was met with ten stone statues.

The first time I simply walked past every statue in turn, with all of them giving my back a hiding with their clubs and staves. Was that worthy of a Shaman? I think not. A Shaman should speak to the Spirits and a Shaman must praise his ancestors. I suddenly understood what the orc was doing when he was examining the Orc Warriors from the Karmadont Chess Set. He was honoring them! For him, as a High Shaman, these were not just figurines, but the embodiment of his ancestors, the Spirits of his people in a way. I looked carefully at the closest statue. She was a girl of nineteen, if not younger. What I first thought to be a club was a carved staff. She wore a simple dress of a shepherdess, a rough cloak and a large bag across her shoulder. On the plinth beneath the statue there was a simple sign: Yalininka Silverwing. But it was this sign that made me bend my knee and bow my head. In the history of the human race there were not many women of whom even orcs spoke with respect. To be exact there was only one: healer Yalininka the Great — it would be hard to find a better word to describe her. She was unsurpassed, having saved tens of thousands of lives. When she saved the Leader of Forest Elves from what was thought to be an incurable poison, he gave her silver wings that allowed her to travel the breadth of Barliona by air. For twenty years this silver lightning flew around the world and where she went sickness disappeared. When Yalininka was finally laid to rest, mourning was declared throughout Barliona. Everyone wept — humans, haughty elves, bloodthirsty orcs; even goblins, who were thought to be an extinct race, came to put flowers on her grave. The Great one was worthy of this. The day of her death was declared by all races to be a weapon-free day, and for two thousand years now no-one has broken this law.

When I played my Hunter one of the quests involved collecting a bouquet of flowers to put on Yalininka's grave and to say the words that now flew off my lips:

"Rest in peace, O Great one! You will forever remain in our memory."

There was a loud bang, as if a cracker had gone off next to me, and I was enveloped in a cloud of dust. I got up and went over to the next statue. You have to be proud of and honor your ancestors, instead of showing your arrogance and disregard for their blows. I wasn't celebrating that I had found a way through the statues while avoiding the blows. Right now I was filled with pride for the race which I was currently playing. I made an effort to swallow a lump in the throat and walked on. Warriors, Emperor Karmadont, two archmages and other great people in the history of the human race fell to dust before my bowed head. Why did it have to be like that? Only dust remained of the statues, which now settled in a three-millimeter layer on my body. When the last statue crumbled, a tear ran down my cheek, only to be immediately absorbed by the dust. Wow, that one really got me! I had to snap out of it and move on, or I'd miss the settlement allocation. As I left the room, I turned once again and made a low bow to the empty plinths: it didn't matter that the statues were no longer there — their Spirits were certainly still in the room, and you had to respect your ancestors!

I already knew what to do when I approached the fourth trial. Last time I discovered that dust from the statues stuck to the rice. I took a handful of the grains, rubbed them in my dusty hands and lowered them in the water. May a goblin bite my ass off if I'm wrong. The rice sunk to the bottom and the peas remained floating on the surface. Very good. When I lowered the last handful of seeds into the bucket I felt quite satisfied. Now I really was finished. And this time the sorting only took five minutes, instead of forty, as before. I fished out all the peas and wanted to pour the water out next, but the bucket started to visibly shake and in a few moments green shoots began to appear above it. First there was one, then two and soon a thick green carpet loomed about fifty centimeters above the bucket. Well I'll be — the rice had sprouted. Each stalk became thicker at the end, so now the top of the sprouted bush somewhat resembled an umbrella. When the rice stopped growing, I carefully touched one of the stalks with my finger. This stalk pushed itself noticeably above the rest and its top opened up like a flower bud. An image of a Bear cub then appeared above the carpet of green. It was so cute and cuddly and clumsy that a smile broke across my dusty face and I tried to pat this wondrous little beast. There was a sharp and loud roar of a large bear and a hit taking off 10% of my Hit Points was the result of my attempt to touch the projection. At least there wasn't any blood this time, which meant it was only needed for the first and the second trials. I touched the stalk one more time, the projection vanished, the bud closed and the stem shrunk and came to resemble all the rest...

So what was all this about? What is this Bear cub that attacks good people, like myself, for example? I touched the next stalk. This one had a Tiger cub. The next — a Rhino. A Kangaroo joey. An Owlet.

A Wolf cub.

If all the previous animals didn't interest me that much, this white and fluffy bundle of joy, which chased its tail with such a grumpy expression because it could never catch it, was simply begging to be patted. Damn, this was going to hurt again, but I just couldn't help myself. I closed my eyes and stretched my hand, expecting another pang of pain. His fur was so soft and pleasant to the touch! I opened my eyes and saw that part of my hand next to the projection of the little wolf became transparent. With this hand I could pat the little cub, who was whining with pleasure and had no intention of biting me. At least I'd got some joy from going through all these trials. Although the stuff with the statues was good too.

After playing my fill with the wolf cub, I removed my hand, which immediately took on its old appearance. I was about to touch the stalk to return it to how it was, but was stopped by a message:

Quest accepted: 'Searching for your Totem'. You have chosen your Totem: White Wolf. In order to begin your search, seek out a Shaman trainer.

The stalk closed of its own accord and rejoined the rest, leaving me standing there with an outstretched hand. This was really something! Can I really get a little wolf cub like this? Right, isn't the orc a Shaman trainer? I have to run to him straight away so he can explain everything and tell me what to do. Who cares about initiation? This fluffy bundle was worth much more to me! I jumped up and ran to the exit, but something stopped me right by the door. There was again this stupid feeling that I'd not done something right or left it incomplete. Did I make a mistake in choosing the wolf as my Totem? If that was the case, would I be able to change it later? I opened the manual and started to look for the relevant information. Damn! If a Shaman chose a Totem for himself, he had this Totem for the rest of the game. It was impossible to change it or to make it go away. All you could do was incarnate part of the Totem into reality and walk around with him as a companion. You could even ride him, since one of the Totem's functions was transporting the player around. I really liked the wolf, but, again, this was something external rather than internal. I had to return and look through the whole of the 'zoo' once again. If I didn't find anything, I'd stick with the wolf. I sat myself by the bucket and started to open stalk after stalk, paying careful heed to my instincts.

Fifteen minutes later I came across something that made me freeze. A Dragon. It might have been small, but it was a real dragon! You only heard rumors about them. They were described in the manuals, but no-one had ever seen a live one. At least I've not come across anyone who had. At one point someone even put together an exploration raid into the mountains, hoping to meet some dragons, but it was a total failure. I carefully stretched my hand. He was smooth and nimble, with a sharp ridge. I instinctively took a handful of peas from the pile next to me and gave it to the little dragon. The projection of the dragon coiled around my phantom hand and began to munch noisily. When the peas in my hand ran out, the little dragon flew up and squeaked vigorously. He sure liked that! I got a new handful of peas and stretched it to the hungry flapper. I never thought that feeding animals could be so much fun. When I get out I'll make sure to get a couple of cat-imitators.

Once all the peas were eaten, the little dragon gave a satisfied yawn, curled up and appeared to fall asleep. The stalk started to close and a new message appeared before my eyes:

Changes to the 'Searching for your Totem' quest. You have changed your Totem from White Wolf to: Black Dragon. In order to begin your

search, seek out a Shaman trainer.

When I left the room the feeling on incompleteness was no longer holding me back. Who cares if I failed the initiation — I could go through it again once I leave the settlement. Choosing a Dragon Spirit as a Totem was very cool. Although I still had to figure out how to get him. The manuals didn't say much about it: find a trainer, he'll tell you what to do. I didn't look at the forum yet (I could do that later) — I had lost enough time as it was with my second go at the trials. Now I had to come out and disappoint the orc with my news.

I left the cave and walked up to the orc, who continued to hold the Great Air Spirit in his arms. Reluctant as I was to disappoint them, I had no choice — the orc looked at me attentively and waited for me to speak. I would tell him the truth, what else?

"I was unable to complete the trial. After my first attempt, everything I had done felt wrong, so I went through the trial again. In my own way, contrary to everyone's advice. So, all in all..." I spread my arms and shrugged, "I didn't manage it."

The orc was silent and the hurricane-like voice of the Great Air Spirit echoed through the mountains:

"A Shaman's spirit must be firm. You have doomed the fawn to death, by freeing the wolf, but you have doomed the wolf to life by releasing him from the trap. His entire life a Shaman must make hard decisions, which will make some perish and save the lives of others. And the Shaman must feel the immovability and firmness of this decision with his whole being; otherwise he would be unable to hold his own before the Great Elemental Spirits.

"A Shaman's spirit must be steadfast. A Shaman must understand that decisions that he takes now will affect him later in life. If you had swum across the hole with the water, you would not have been able to collect the kind of dust you needed for the future trial. Again and again, you steadfastly forced the water to submit to you, fusing with your own blood. You didn't know this, but felt that you were doing things right. Feeling is what sets Shamans aside from other classes.

"A Shaman's spirit must be gentle. A Shaman who forgets his ancestors is hard-hearted and blind. The Spirits would not heed his calls and he would not be able to grow into anything greater than an Elementary Shaman. This is the limit for those who do not honor their ancestors. You honored your ancestors and they believe in you, Shaman.

"A Shaman's spirit must be pliant. The direct, immediately apparent solution is not always the right one. Dividing the seeds is only part of the task — only a real Shaman can understand their real purpose. You did it, so I gave you the ability to choose your own Totem. All other Shamans get a random one.

"I have finished. You have brought me joy, little brother. From now on you are an Initiate Shaman," the whirlwind in the orc's hands quickly started to dissipate and just a dozen seconds later was gone.

Quest update — 'The Path of the Shaman. Step 1': Quest completed.
Character class update: Shaman class has been replaced by: Initiate Shaman. Seek your

**trainer for learning to work with Younger
Elemental Spirits.**

I looked at the orc.

"Teacher," I bowed my head respectfully,
"Please share some of your wisdom with me."

"I cannot teach you, little brother," said the orc.
"By the decision of the Shaman Council I have been
stripped of this ability. You will have to seek a more
worthy teacher. Old Shaman Kornik lives in a
settlement near Anhurs. Find him, he will help you.
And now we have to get back, the allocation
procedure should begin any minute."

**Class quest chain accepted: 'The Path of the
Shaman'.**
**'The Path of the Shaman: Step 2'. Find
Shaman trainer Kornik.**

The orc called a portal and we returned to his
office. Again a stupid question popped into my head:
who was in charge of the mine while the orc was
away? No, I won't ask it — what if he takes offence
and allocates me to some dump? I need to get to
Anhurs. Kornik lives there somewhere, and Kart too,
and the 'The Jolly Gnoom'. In three months' time I
have a chance to find everything.

There was a bang and a transport portal
appeared in the orc's office. That's it. I'll enter it and
find myself in some village, where the local head...

The man that stepped out of the portal stopped
my thoughts in their tracks. He was short, fat, toad-
like, with a Kameamia on his chest. The Regional

Governor had arrived in Pryke. What does he want here?

"Can't you allocate these stinking prisoners without my help?" he started to squeal in his disgusting voice, not even looking in my direction. "This one should be stuck in some piss-hole village, like the Big Hogspoo..." The Regional Governor stopped because his gaze finally fell on my person. I'm buggered! Can it be that the allocation is not handled by the orc, but by this humanoid cross between a toad and a Governor? That's it — a Govertoad!

The Governor stood there for a few moments having never finished saying 'Hogspoons', and then an unpleasant smirk appeared on his face, he even rubbed his hands and then started to spit out words:

"I told you that I wouldn't forget how you refused to give me that Legendary Item! How you treated your Governor! To my castle! Immediately! I am allocating my castle as the settlement for Mahan, the former prisoner of the Pryke Mine. Into the portal! Now!"

Attention! In the next 2 months and 26 days you have the opportunity of living in the castle of the Governor of the Serrest Province. You may leave the castle for no more than 48 hours, following which you will be teleported back. Have a pleasant Game!

I looked at my former boss. Was this a joke? 'A Shaman's spirit must be steadfast,' the orc's gaze seemed to say. 'You have to get through this, little brother.'

'What the hell?! 2 months and 26 days under the power of the Govertoad? No problem! We've been through worse,' I thought and, resolute, stepped into the portal. Good-bye Pryke Mine. I hope — forever.

END OF BOOK ONE

KARTOSS GAMBIT

THE WAY OF THE SHAMAN
BOOK #2

(preview)

CHAPTER ONE
AT THE FRINGE OF THE EMPIRE

I boldly stepped into the portal and prepared myself for long struggle with the Governor. The three months I would be forced to spend entirely in his power were no cause for celebration, but I had no intention of surrendering, crawling on my knees or cowering like a kicked dog before this fumble of the developers. That sweaty toad can kiss my ass and forget about the Orc Warrior figurines, for all his attempted bribery: peace, love or lots of dough.

Potential use of physical force against me wasn't much of a worry. I was sure that the freed prisoners couldn't be casually punished or tortured – we did have rights, after all, even if these were somewhat curtailed. It was worth bearing in mind that the system was fully aware that the sensory filters were disconnected, so I had little to worry about and... What on earth is this?

To the player located in a prisoner capsule! You have earned 'Respect' with the Pryke Mine guards and are being transferred to the main gameworld.

You have the option of taking part in the adaptation scenario: 'The Governor's Castle'. Time to be spent at the location 'The Governor's Castle': 2 months 26 days. Role taken: 'Castle craftsman'. Conditions: eight hour work day, a weekly salary, the results of the daily labour go to the Serrest province; every seventh day is a holiday, development of crafting professions (up to level 30 inclusive) – at the expense of the Governor.

Reward for taking part in the adaptation scenario: Respect with the Serrest Province, two items of the 'Rare' class.

Should you decline, you will be sent to a random settlement in the Malabar Empire and your reputation with the Serrest Province will fall to the level of 'Hatred'.

Do you wish to take part in the adaptation scenario 'The Governor's Castle'?

Judging by the shimmering portal that surrounded me I wasn't going to be taken anywhere until I made the choice. If that's the case I had time to think about it, weighing up all the pros and cons.

First. An adaptation scenario... How much more adaptation can I need? I get it already – I'm a loser and a wretch, who only gets handed truckloads of compulsory adaptation instead of the standard game and normal communication with other players. That is definitely a minus.

Second. There's the close proximity to the Govertoad, even if just geographically. I'm sorry Mr. Digital NPC, our encounter was a mistake and mutual love is definitely not on the cards. You just wanted to use me... Right, my thoughts are getting in a mess again... In any case, the Governor's personality amounts to two fat minuses.

Third. I am a business-like person and should think things through rationally. It would be foolish to simply walk past such a pile of freebies: the salary, the development of an unlimited number of professions, the character level being my only limit. I could be learning Smithing, Alchemy, Enchantment, Cartography and level up in many other things at the same time, all justified by the conditions of the scenario. Definitely a double plus.

Fourth. If I refuse, I'll get Hatred with Serrest. This is a clear minus or rather a plus towards taking part in the scenario. There are just forty provinces in Malabar and to lose access to one of them is a very short-sighted choice.

I think that's it. I don't know about anyone else in my place, but for me the choice was clear. I didn't want to limit my freedom by one holiday a week. If that's the case, I'd say 'Good luck' to the Govertoad, who'd have to make do without me. I was all but crestfallen when I jumped into the portal with the flashing message that for two months and twenty six days I'll be stuck in the Governor's castle. Things turned out a lot less dire – the system gave advance information of the scenario, naively thinking that I would go for it. After all, it came with so many freebies and big bonuses... They can dream on!

I confidently selected the 'Refuse' sign, small as it was next to the larger 'Accept', and in an instant the world was filled with colour, sound and the fragrant scent of a pine forest.

To the player located in a prisoner capsule! You have declined to take part in the adaptation scenario and were sent to the settlement of Beatwick. Time to be spent at the settlement: 2 months 26 days. Maximum time you can spend outside the settlement: 48 hours. If you are found outside the settlement beyond the allotted time, you will be teleported back into the village and a record of violation of the parole conditions will be made. Three violations annul your parole and you will be returned to the mines to serve the remainder of your prison term.

Have a pleasant game!

Compulsory quest accepted: 'Visiting the Village Headman'. Description: go to the headman

of Beatwick to be allocated living quarters for the next three months. Deadline for completion: 12 hours. Penalty for failure: 3 violations.

I made a few steps towards the village visible in the distance, but was stopped by another message:

Your reputation with the Governor of the Serrest Province has fallen by 22000 points.
Current level: Hatred. You are 12000 points away from the status of Enmity. Due to receiving a maximum negative value, your bonus for daily reputation gain is invalid.

So they did land me with that after all. That's right – I knew what I was signing up for: the maximum value in negative reputation. Although... A negative reputation is a reputation nonetheless. In Barliona there are four levels of negative reputation: Mistrust, Dislike, Enmity and Hatred. From Neutral reputation to Mistrust there are minus 1000 points and to Dislike another 3000. Then it's minus 6000 until Enmity and 12000 until Hatred. I was given the maximum in one go! When I played my Hunter, I managed to get Exalted, the maximum positive reputation, with only one faction and that only after playing for a couple of years, while now in just three months I went straight to Hatred! Yes, of course a Shaman knows no half-measures, with reputation it has to be at the maximum, with crafted items – only Legendary ones and with girls only those who get you locked up in prison. Just one thing was bad: now Serrest was lost to me – as soon as I get spotted by the guards there, I'd be immediately sent to prison 'to assess the situation'. Then it's spending a day in the preliminary detention cell and then teleportation to the borders of the province. The next time I'd spend two days in the cell. After that it's three and so on without a limit. The most unpleasant part was that a reputation like that is almost impossible to improve — you need the personal intervention of the Emperor.

Visions of the lost carefree life in the Govertoad's castle floated up on the fringes of my consciousness, but I quickly dispelled them and headed to Beatwick. At the first glance it was a pretty standard average village; judging by the chimneys it had at least seventy households. The wooden houses, roofed with wooden shingles, the barking of dogs, happy shouts of children running around after a madly screeching cat that had something tied to its tail — all of this was a picture of normal village life, which I remembered from the times I had gone to visit my parents. The enormous stockade of thick logs around the entire perimeter protected the village from the dark forest that stood about a hundred meters away. The strange expression 'forest of masts' involuntarily popped into my head — the trunks of the pines, as straight as spears, shot up into the sky, hiding the sun with their thick canopy and creating deep twilight in the forest. Fallen pines, shrubbery and hazel thicket, together with other kinds of trees, made the forest quite literally impassable. Only rare paths, probably hacked through by the locals, lead into the depths of this wonder of nature. Despite such surroundings, life was not restricted to the interior of the stockade – up until the very edge of the forest there rolled wide yellow fields of some kind of cereal crops, green meadows, where cows and sheep grazed and the hundred-meter-long vegetable patches that had villagers bent over them with their hoes. The village theme was played out to the full. Thick black smoke and the ringing blows of a hammer came from the smithy that stood near the road to the village. Great: there was a place here for levelling up. The only drawback for me was the red band on my head: without it Beatwick would have all but rolled out a red carpet for me as a free citizen of the Empire. Right now though, I'd be lucky not to get dogs and pitchforks.

I took a deep breath in the fresh air and headed at an unhurried pace towards the village, looking out for any special aspects of local life. My main task was to find the local Headman and 'register' my presence in the village. If I only knew where to look for him. This was no Pryke mine, where the orc always sat behind his desk – here the Headman could be running around anywhere.

As I made my way towards Beatwick, I tried to take note of every detail that could be of use in the next three months.

I saw how the smith, large as a bear, came out of the smithy, lifted a small barrel of water and, breathing out a loud 'Eehh!', emptied it over himself, snorting and giving off a lot of steam. He stood there for a couple of seconds giving me an unfriendly stare and loudly breathing in the cool air, then he lifted the anvil from the ground as if it was a feather, shot me one more glance and disappeared back into the smithy. With that I felt my plans for levelling up in professions take a nosedive: I hate heat. For me it's better not to work at all than be sweating buckets, my tongue hanging out as I gulp in the sizzling air.

A group of three bearded men were actively swinging the scythes and giving me extremely unfriendly glances. Their small foreheads, menacing and, at the same time, unintelligent eyes made them look very similar to Neanderthals, whose pictures I remembered from history lessons. They only lacked some animal skins on their backs, otherwise they'd be a spitting image of them. When I walked by them I could hear muttering that didn't sound at all like Barliona's common tongue. I could bet that these three had some kind of a quest connected to them: either they were the quest givers or they would provide some kind of related information. If I asked the locals, it would probably turn out that these guys weren't from around here.

An interesting-looking tree caught my eye...

"Watch out!" the clear voice of a child tore me away from contemplating the local sights. I turned towards the source of the sound and opened my mouth to ask what happened, when my forehead was struck with something large, hard and very painful. Bam! The peaceful county landscape was enriched by the image of a flying Shaman, sending curses on anyone and everyone. My flight came to a stop almost immediately – inside a fresh haystack. With some effort I dug my way out of the green entanglement, spitting out grass and brushing it off my coat. What the hell!? I habitually looked at my Hit Points, and cursed once again. 40% of my Hit Points were gone! What have I done to deserve this? The answer came soon enough, but left me somewhat perplexed. It was a huge cartwheel, tied around with a rope and framed with metal sheets. Riiight. Something like that could send you off for a respawn in no time!

"Are you all right?" a small out-of-breath boy, his face red, flew up to me, barely older than seven, by the look of it. "I was... my tooth... the wheel! It's so heavy! And there you were! And it rolled the wrong way! Took my tooth with it! And then – 'Bam!' And you're flying! Into the grass – 'Whack!' Did it hurt?" He was looking at me with such concern and guilt, trying to tidy up his messy ginger hair with fidgety hands, that I was totally unable to get angry at him. "You won't tell mum, will you? Our blacksmith is good at pulling teeth, but he's so busy all the time, so I have to do it myself," the little boy started to explain, fitfully gulping in air between words and flashing the gap where his tooth use to be.

"Now I have no tooth, like Bald Bobby," the kid continued to chatter and it dawned on me that the wheel that sent me flying was the local replacement for a dentist, when the smith was too busy.

"You really won't tell mum? Otherwise she'll not let me out by myself again, only with my sister! And she's such a bore – that's not allowed, don't touch that, keep away from the dogs! Yuck! How can you be so boring? I remember how we went to the forest..." It seemed like part of this NPC's settings stated that if silence lasted for more than a minute he'd immediately vanish from the face of Barliona. It didn't matter what the topic was or whether anyone was listening – he just had to keep talking. "Right, stop!" I interrupted his tale of venturing into the forest and gaining victory over the great vicious rabbit, "Do you know the village Headman? If you take me to him, I won't say anything to your mum," I could use a guide at the start, and the boy must know each and everyone in the village.

"The Headman? Who doesn't know him? Everyone does! Five coppers and I'll take you to him right away. He's always hiding, so you can hardly ever find him," the kid was grinning and stretching his small hand towards me, with an expectant look.

"Here you go, you young extortionist," I threw five copper coins into his hand and they immediately disappeared, as if they had never existed. Of course, I could have made the boy take me to the Headman for free, but five coppers weren't going to break the bank and this way I might get some kind of a quest out of his parents (or a good hiding, if it turns out that one mustn't give the kid money under any circumstances.)

"What's your name, then?" I asked the young rascal, who was fussing around the fallen wheel and trying to decide which was the best side for getting to grips with it.

"I'm Clouter," the lad replied quickly and started to redden from the effort of trying to lift the wheel.

"Quit fibbing, there isn't a name like that. Let me help," I came up to him and put the wheel upright. It really was heavy. "Where will you roll it now?"

"I'm Clouter," said the little guy insistently, wiping his nose with his sleeve, "I don't like Aftondil. I won't be called that. Everyone has good names, only I've got a stupid one. I always get a beating for it from the Straighters. No need to roll it, just push it that way, it'll get there by itself." Aftondil... no, Clouter pointed towards the village, "with luck it won't hit anyone on the way."

"And who are these 'Straighters'?"

"They are from the neighbouring Straight street, Al Spottino's gang. Watch out!" Clouter screamed after the rolling wheel and shouted to me: "We'll meet down the-ere!"

Clouter tripped up a couple of times, tumbling down the hill, but immediately got up and continued running after the wheel, shouting at the top of his voice. I chuckled at his goofiness and was about to follow him when I was suddenly turned around, lifted off the ground and thrust into the enraged bearded face of the blacksmith:

"Why are you bullying Clouter, you thug?" before I could answer anything, the blacksmith took a good swing and sent me flying again. It's not like I was expecting a royal welcome, but this was too much. These flights were beginning to wear me out with their frequency! I got up from the ground and quickly glanced at my Hit Points. Oh boy! I only had 18% of Life left! A blacksmith's punch hit much harder than the wheel! I saw that I might not survive a second blow and started to summon a Healing Spirit on myself.

"What's with the dancing? You're a warlock!" It was just as well that the Tambourine sped up the Spirit summoning – I managed to completely heal myself only a second before my next flight. This was some blacksmith! Strong as a bear. I tried to get up, but my feet gave way and I slumped to the ground, seeing a semi-transparent message appear:

Dizziness! You lost concentration for 10 seconds.
Skill increase:
+10% Endurance. Total: 60%.

"Stop, Mr. Slate!"

"Leave it, Clouter, stay out of the way. Can't you see that we've had a killer-warlock drop on us?"

"He's no killer! He helped me to bring the wheel back to the village and he wanted to see the Headman!"

"The Headman, you say?" Slate loomed over me and then with one hand lifted me off the ground. No-one would believe me if I told them that I got caught between a Slate and a hard place in Barliona! Quite literally. "What did you want from the Head?"

"I'll be living here for three months," I croaked through a half-strangled throat. Well, well! Playing as a Shaman I was beginning to discover Barliona from a completely different angle: I would have never thought that if you press on the throat, the player would start to croak like that. He won't be getting suffocated, but a line would appear stating that he didn't have enough air. But the rasping is not something I noticed before. The blacksmith let go and I fell on the ground like a sack of potatoes.

"Going to live here, eh? Then why are you loitering here, as if you're trying to snoop around? There's no Headman around here," without waiting for my reply the blacksmith turned around and went back to his smithy. By the looks of it, my first encounter with Beatwick residents was far from a success.

"Don't be upset," fired off Clouter. "Mr. Slate is nice, he just probably failed to make something today and that made him all cranky. Let's go together, I've finished rolling the wheel. See where it's crashed into the fence? It can stay there."

By the wooden gates I found the local guards – two red-nosed men with puffy eyes. They were doing their best to stop themselves falling to the ground by propping themselves up against their spears. They clearly weren't doing so because they were tired or spent too long at their posts, but from uninhibited imbibing of spirits. The scent of syrupy homebrew wafted a few dozen meters away from the duo, and several bottles strewn across the ground were clear pointers to what the brave upholders of law and order were really up to. You couldn't say much for their overall appearance either: a short chainmail that reached down to the middle of their beer bellies, sitting on top of a simple tunic, studded thick trousers and worn bast shoes made the guards' appearance so 'terrifying', that even if an enemy decided to invade the village he was doomed to laugh himself to death first.

"Halt! Hic! Who goes there?"

"I'm on my way to the village Headman, I was sent to live here," I gave the simple reply. It looked like the local Headman was someone well-respected, so referring to him might open many doors.

"To the Headman, eh?" the second guard started to mumble in a drunken voice. "Tell him that the gates are in safe hands, we're watching them like hawks. No enemy will get past us!" the guard straightened out, showing what a strong warrior was guarding the village. He was so overwhelmed with emotion that he lost his balance, he took several steps backwards, hit the stockade with his back and slid down, having lost his support from the spear.

"Hold it, Wilkins!" the second guard hurried after him, totally forgetting about the unfairness of things like balance and the force of gravity. I shook my head in resignation at the sight of such guards and headed into the village, but here I caught sight of the opened gates, which had previously been hidden by the plump guardsmen. They were made of common wood, but one side had been scarred by the four-digit claw of some unknown monster. Moreover, this had been done from the side of the village, as if someone wanted to make an opening into the world outside. I wondered whether there was some quest connected to these gates. Was it to find and destroy the monster? I had to offer my services to the Headman.

"What happened to your gates?" I asked Clouter, when we approached a large house located right in the centre of the village.

"Nothing's wrong with our gates."

"But what about the marks that look like they were made by some claws?"

"That's a prank played by the Straighters. Each night they sneak past the dosing guards and cut the gates with knives. Anyone getting caught gets dragged in front of the Headman and anyone who doesn't gets a ton of honour and respect. For example, I've never been caught yet!"

"So how many times did you sneak to the gates?" I asked, disappointed, and just trying to keep the conversation going now. That could have been such a great quest!

"So far zero times, but I didn't get caught either, right?" the kid gave me a toothless smile and pointed towards a brightly-painted house. "We're here now. The Headman's sitting inside, as usual." He then took off so fast that all I saw were his flashing heels. "And don't forget," Clouter shouted after running a good distance and turning around, "Not a word to mum about the wheel!"

"So you've been sent to live with us?" the Headman asked me, as he carefully rolled up the paper and hid it in a draw of his table. As soon as I set my eyes on him it was clear — this was someone who liked order, a pedant and, at the same time, an NPC who was very sure of himself. I couldn't say why, but his appearance really put me in mind of one of the advisers of the Malabar Emperor. He had the same commanding face, framed by a short goatee, and penetrating watchful eyes that took note of every detail; in general, he was a complete picture of one of Barliona's good officials. He was the complete opposite of the Govertoad and it was no surprise that such a leader had the respect of the people in the village.

"Yes, for almost three months."

"No need to stand, take a seat. We have to decide what you'll be doing here," the Headman gestured me to an armchair and then leant against the back of his own, looking at the ceiling, as if trying to think of how I could be of use to his village.

I sat in a soft and rather comfortable armchair, which was clearly not of a local make. It was strange that the house of an ordinary NPC should have such furniture, Headman or no. Reluctant to interrupt his thinking I began to examine the village leader's 'office'. It was a separate room in a residential house. An enormous wooden table, like that of the Pryke Mine governor, stood in the middle of the office and was a prime example of a well-ordered work space: everything was in folders and neat piles, with nothing out of place. He really was a pedant. A few modest-sized glass cabinets with books and scrolls, a fireplace and a luxurious thick carpet were the other furnishings of the local leader's office. I was about to shift my gaze back to my host, when it was caught by a relatively small painting: there was the Headman, two grown men, an attractive young woman and a smudge of paint that covered the fifth person in the picture.

"We have no inns, so we'll have to assign you to lodge with someone. I think Elizabeth wouldn't mind, her house has been on the empty side for two years now," the Headman began to fill out a paper, which he then handed to me, "here, please relay my request to her. Furthermore, before I decide what type of work to appoint for you, I need to know what you can do and the level of your skills. I need exact numbers."

I opened my stats and began to read out my professions and their levels. It's just as well that he didn't demand that I should tell him all my stats — I was reluctant to reveal that I had Crafting even to an NPC.

— SURVIVAL QUEST —

Stat window for player Mahan:					
Experience	285 of 1400.			**Additional stats**	
Race	Human				
Class	Beginner Shaman			Physical damage	57
Main Profession	Jeweller			Magical damage	555
Character level	14				
Hit points	680			Physical defence	230
Mana	1850			Magic resistance	60
Energy	100			Fire resistance	60
Stats	Scale	Base	+ Items	Cold resistance	60
Stamina	58%	30	68	Poison resistance	60
Agility	24%	7	7		
Strength	55%	18	21		
Intellect	16%	56	185	Dodge chance	6.40%
Charisma	40%	6	6	Critical hit chance	2.80%
Crafting	0%	3	4		
Endurance	60%	10	10		
Not selected					
Free stat points		0			
Professions					
Jewelcrafting	61%	12	12		
Mining	61%	12	13		
Trade	25%	6	6		
Cooking	20%	5	5		

"A Jeweller, a Miner and a Cook," said the Headman thoughtfully. "Totally useless professions in our parts. We have no Precious Stones, you'd have to buy them in town, which is two days' travel away on a cart. Mining might have been useful, but we have only one vein, by the smithy, and it's worked by our blacksmith Slate every day. You're not advanced enough to work an Iron Vein in any case. You could, of course, travel to the Free Lands. That's not far from here. You can get Tin and Marble veins there, but our forest is a dangerous one. Few would go there without decent protection. The Cook profession doesn't even bear mentioning: our Mrs. Potts can teach any cooks — even one of the Governor's — a thing or two. So that's that."

Free Lands nearby? Where the heck did I end up? Is this place really in the middle of nowhere?

"You don't happen to have a map of the Empire? It would be good to know where I was sent to serve my free settlement time," I asked the Headman. He squinted, giving me a long piercing look, and then replied,

"There is a map." He cleared the table, took a scroll out of one of the drawers and unfolded it. It was an enormous map of the Empire, about a meter by meter and a half. Where did he get such a wonder?! Such a map costs around ten thousand gold! "We're here," the Headman pointed his finger at the very edge of the border with the Free Lands. I bent over the map and quietly swore under my breath. 'Middle of nowhere' would be putting it mildly.

After the unification of all the countries took place and one language was adopted, the real world was split into five large regions, along the continents: Eurasia, Africa, Australia and the two Americas. In parallel with reality, five great continents were formed in Barliona, with each being divided roughly into three zones. For example, on our continent there was the Malabar Empire, Kartoss and the Free Lands. Malabar was where the players lived. It contained the main resources, quests, factions, cities, including the capital, and also some yet unexplored lands. Thus the area where I now found myself had not been completely mapped yet — even on the Headman's map it was sketched out very roughly. Kartoss, the Dark Empire, headed by the Nameless Dark Lord, was about five times smaller than Malabar in territory, but still caused a great deal of trouble with its constant incursions and raids. But you had to give this Empire its due: it abounded in unique objects and resources, which were often sought out by high-level players. It is interesting to note that both a raid group of a hundred players and a loner that secretly snuck into Kartoss had equal chance of getting loot. It was impossible to play on the side of the Dark Empire, although many times the players signed petitions and held demonstrations, asking to be permitted to play for the dark side of Barliona. The Corporation kept promising to develop this feature, but, as far as I knew, nothing was ever done in this direction — Kartoss remained the realm of the Imitators. And, finally, the third zone on every continent, which took up almost sixty percent of all the areas accessible for play: the Free Lands. Rare independent towns with their own reputation rating, villages made up of two-three dozen houses, great forests, endless steppes, impassable bogs and mountains that rose up to the sky. In the fifteen years of Barliona's existence only thirty percent of the Free Lands territory had been mapped, with the rest remaining a veiled mystery. Naturally, there were some enthusiasts who dropped everything and dedicated themselves to exploration and travel, but they either failed to produce maps of the explored areas or chose not to share them with the rest. Or, which is most likely, they sold the maps for crazy money to the leading clans. For the majority of players the territories of the Free Lands remained uncharted. One could only guess what quests and achievements they contained, although the Corporation representatives have repeatedly encouraged the players to stop battling Kartoss and explore the Free Lands, saying that these held the 'best bonuses' in the Game. The developers even placed all the new Dungeons, opened every half a year, inside the still unexplored parts of the Free Lands, to give players an incentive to spend their time on making their way there. But I digress, a lot...

I had been sent for settlement to the farthest reach of the Empire, on the border with the Free Lands, which here took the form of impassable woods, bogs and mountains. There were no towns or villages. On the map, almost exactly by the spot labelled Beatwick, there were several icons indicating free mines in this area. I should go there and check them out. However, what really dampened my spirits was that the nearest Imperial town, Farstead, was a really long way off. Two days on a cart is not exactly next door, if I understood the scale of the map correctly. Considering that I cannot leave Beatwick for more than two days, a visit to Farstead was out of the question.

"Had a good look now?" inquired the Headman and then rolled up the map and put it back in his table. "We may not be in the centre of the Empire, but there's still plenty to do here."

"Do you have any assignments for me?" I asked out of habit, knowing full well that the red band on my head wouldn't make me seem particularly trustworthy in the eyes of any NPC. I had to spend around a week in the village for its residents to get used to me and get less wary of me and only then start seeking out any quests. But there's no harm in trying.

"Of course there are, but I can't give them to just any stranger," replied the Headman, confirming my thoughts. "First live here for a little while, make some contribution to the village and then there'll be assignments for you. Although... there is one. Recently a pack of wolves has appeared in the woods. They've become bold and started raiding the herds. The shepherds said that they are lead by an enormous Wolf. If you do away with the Wolf, we can see about other assignments. In any case, it is high time for that pack to be culled, it's no good for it to be roaming the woods in such numbers. But bear in mind – I won't take your word for it. I will need proof.

Quest available: "The Hunt for Grey Death."
Description: A pack of wolves lead by an enormous alpha wolf has appeared in the lands around Beatwick. Destroy 10 Wolves and the great Grey Wolf. As proof that you've completed the

assignment bring back Wolf Tails, which have 100% drop rate from each mob. Quest type: Common. Reward: +100 to Reputation with the Krong Province, +200 Experience, +80 Silver. Penalty for failing/refusing the quest: -100 to Reputation with the Krong Province.

"I'll take it. I'll go after the wolves tomorrow, first thing in the morning," I said as I accepted the quest. "But I have a few more questions. How many..."

"Wolves first, questions later." The Headman cut me off in a tone that indicated that the matter was closed. "Now Tisha will take you to Elizabeth, to whom you must remember to give the letter. Go on the hunt tomorrow and after that we'll talk. Tisha!" called the Headman, and a couple of moments later the girl from the painting flew into the room.

"Let me introduce you, this is my daughter Tiliasha. This is Mahan, he'll be living in our village for three months. Take him to Elizabeth, he can stay with her."

"Just call me Tisha." The gentle voice of the girl was in tune with her beautiful appearance. "Let's go, I'll show you the village," she then moved gracefully to the door and gestured to me to follow her.

Quest 'Visiting the Village Headman' completed.

It was a large village. From the side of the hill I counted around seventy houses, but in actual fact there were one hundred and three households. Quite a lot, especially by frontier standards. The village followed a standard layout: the central square, where the Headman's house stood, and three streets: Straight, Crooked and Serpentine. The kids from these streets were always in the process of trying to establish who was the best and strongest, so fights were fairly frequent. Tisha also told me about the gates — a year ago her father carved three claw marks into them in order to put some fear into the kids, who were really beginning to get out of hand, making it look like there was a werewolf in the village. But the plan somewhat backfired: everyone was too scared to set foot outside their homes for a whole week. So he had to come clean about it. Then it became a tradition among the youngsters: if you wanted to prove yourself — you had to carve some claw marks into the gates. During the day the gates were guarded by a couple of drunkards, who were no good for any other job in any case, but at night the more serious guards took their place — either her brothers or hired hands, free citizens of the Empire, same as myself. The same in all but the red bands, that is. I couldn't stop myself from asking if there were any free citizens in the village right now, and was very disappointed to hear the answer that the last such person came through the village half a year ago.

Tisha's own story turned out to be quite interesting. She had come to the village together with her family just two years ago, immediately after the death of the previous Headman, Elizabeth's husband. Before that Tisha used to live in a large city. Her father held quite a high-ranking position, because a carriage use to take him away early in the morning and in the evening a large crowd of richly dressed people would gather at their house, lock themselves in the study and hold long discussions. Then something happened and father gathered the household and came here to the edge of the Empire.

"So the gates are guarded at night by your brothers? All three of them?" the thought of the painting with the smudge wouldn't leave me alone — something was amiss here. From the time of my initiation I had decided to put more trust in my instincts.

Tisha's face darkened, she fell silent and walked for a while through the village without saying a word. She then regained control of herself and said in a serious voice:

"No, not three, just two. But they only do it once a week. Never ask me about my third brother. I don't remember him myself, but we do not speak about him in the family. All that I know is that he betrayed our kin and our homeland and father banished him from the family forever. Not a word more about him. We're here. Elizabeth lives in this house," Tisha turned around and quickly vanished around the turn in the road. Oops. Looks like all my ambitious plans to seduce her have just been destroyed. Now I won't get anything other than a mere greeting out of her until I increase my reputation. A pity. But, in general, she did share some very interesting information with me. Banishment from the family is a very serious act for an NPC. I can't imagine what had to have happened for a former high-ranking official to personally banish his own son. Once I level up my reputation to Friendly, I will certainly ask the Headman about the painting myself. I'd bet my life that the story behind the banishment is quite a complicated one and must have a quest attached to it. Assignments like these are exactly in Barliona's style — improving players' social skills by reconciling families.

"But you said you wouldn't tell mum anything about the wheel," an upset child's voice pulled me out of my thoughts. "You promised!"

"Firstly, I promised no such thing and, secondly, I have no intention of telling anyone anything. What are you doing here?" it took a little while for me to spot Clouter hiding under the porch.

"What do you mean? I live here. With my mum and my sister," replied the boy, crawling out of his hiding place.

"Then it's you that I've come to see. Is your mother home?"

"She's home, all right," Clouter looked around, gave it a thought and started to crawl back under the porch. "But I'm not going in there. It's buckwheat for dinner and I hate it. If mum sees me, she'll take me by my ear and sit me at the table. I'd best stay here for a while."

"How can I help you?" a low woman's voice made me look up from Clouter's hiding place. Judging by the squeaking of the floorboards the kid was trying to signal me that he wasn't there and that I really had no idea where he might be. With a wise mother's smile Elizabeth looked under her feet and then asked a completely unexpected question: "Excuse me, I wonder if you've see a ginger boy around here? I've baked his favourite pie, but it will get cold soon and won't be as tasty. I'll have to give it all to Dawnie, like the porridge."

"You gave the porridge to Dawnie? For real?" after hitting his head a couple of times on the floorboards, Clouter ran like lightning from his hideout and stood before his mother, eyes shining. "Is it a blueberry pie?"

"Of course, it's the blueberry pie, just as you like it. Run along while it's still hot, you rascal," Elizabeth ruffled his hair, as the kid ran past her and then turned to me again, "So, how can I help you?"

"I was sent to you by the Headman. He said that I could come and live with you for three months. Here are the papers," I handed Elizabeth the letter. If her behaviour with her son was so natural, I shouldn't have any major problems with this NPC.

"Three months, eh?" muttered Elizabeth, scanning through the paper. I couldn't help wondering what the Headman wrote in there. I didn't manage to have a look in his house and then was too busy talking to Tisha. What if it gave me a boost to Intellect? You never know. "The nights are warm at the moment, so I can give you the summer house. Is that all right with you?" my landlady looked me over. "Are you going to live here as a freeloader or as a help?"

Was there a quest in this for me? It may be for free, but a quest is still a quest!

"I don't like being a freeloader. If you need anything done, just tell me and I'll do it: whether it's fetching the water, chopping wood or digging the garden..."

"No, my labourers can do all that well enough. The Headman said that you aren't new to cooking,"

Elizabeth paused and I froze in expectation. A profession-based quest! It's a dream for any player! You can't even imagine the kind of bonuses you can get there! Elizabeth hesitated, but then appeared to come to a decision and said: "I'm not a rich woman, so I can't feed another mouth. You will be completely responsible for feeding yourself?" she then glanced at my red headband and added: "I also ask you not to come inside my house uninvited."

Attention to the player! You have been denied access to the main house of Elizabeth, the widow of the former Beatwick Headman. If you breach this restriction, one violation of your parole conditions will be recorded. Have a pleasant game!

Elizabeth turned around and went into the house, leaving me on the porch in a state of complete depression. I had already gotten all excited about getting quests and a friendly attitude to me... How could I have forgotten my red-band status? With that any NPC will treat me warily and with suspicion. A former criminal, what do you expect? What if I start killing everyone left and right, or pickpocketing and nicking their money? Who knows with these ex-cons! So it looks like earning levels wasn't going to be such a simple task after all. And I had all these plans to gain a dozen or two in the coming three months by doing various quests... A pity. I'll have to do something about that, that's certain. And as soon as possible too.

The summer house, kindly provided to me by

Elizabeth, was astounding in its simplicity and Spartan feel. Its entire collection of furniture consisted of one bed, which took up half of the free space. That was it. There was the earthen floor, which remained cold even in today's heat, grey wooden planks for the wall and narrow windows right by the ceiling, which had trouble letting even the moonlight through. Great place for spending the next three months. I threw myself on the bed and started to make plans, just to keep my brain occupied.

First. I'll have to do the quest with the wolves first thing tomorrow. Extra experience and reputation with the Krong province should help me win Elizabeth's trust and move into the big house. I had little desire to be stuck in this cage for three months.

Second. I had to solve the problem of how to visit Farstead. Getting there on a cart wasn't an option — it would take too long. So I had to find another way. The Headman said that a caravan travels to that town from time to time. I had to make an arrangement with its leader to buy a scroll of teleportation from Beatwick to Farstead. The return scroll I could buy there. Judging by the distance to the town, the scroll could cost around eight or nine hundred gold. It's quite a lot, but I had to get to the Bank of Barliona and get my hands on the possessions of my former Hunter character. There should be at least eleven thousand there just in gold, not counting all the leftover equipment. Even if all of it mainly had Agility bonuses, I could use even that. It would be like plate mail compared to what I had on now.

Third. I had to find out about the mines that I'd

seen marked on the Headman's map. He did warn me, of course, that it's dangerous to go it alone there, but I really mustn't let an opportunity like this get away. If I understood correctly, the closest deposits of something or other are located a couple of hours' walk from Beatwick. 'I don't really feel like sleeping, so if I left now I'd be back by the morning. This will also give me a better idea about what I can count on in terms of levelling up professions.

Fifth... there is no fifth, I'm done planning.' Now is the time for action — to go and look at that mine. But first I had to look through my bag, since I haven't really had time for it until now. After the Dungeon it was quite full of things I haven't even looked at. I threw the contents of the bag right on the floor, lit a rushlight, put it into a small hole in the wall and began the inspection. There were the chess pieces. It was a pity that each Orc Warrior took up an entire slot in the bag. The thought of having to drag all thirty two figurines with me left me somewhat stumped. Where on earth will I get a bag that big? Then there were seven rings with a +3 stat bonus and four rings with a +2 bonus. They were the ones I failed to sell at the Pryke mine and were now outdated. There was no point of keeping them for later for a potential sale at an auction. Junk like this wouldn't even sell for five gold. I'll have to offload them with a normal NPC merchant. I didn't even look at the chainmail gloves, dropped by the last boss of the dungeon. These belonged to the members of my future clan and I had no intention to turn into a rat. Why expose myself to extra temptation? What if I liked them and didn't want to part with them? Twenty three pieces of Malachite, one hundred pieces of Copper Ore and sixty eight Copper Ingots would all come in handy for levelling up my Jewelcrafting until I solved my ore supply issues. There was my old friend, the Mining Pick. And, finally, there was the large pile of various skins, tails, meat, claws and other junk, which had dropped from the rats and spiders of the Dungeon. I had to fight the impulse to gather it all up and sell it off without even looking at it — the first completion of a Dungeon gave quite a good chance to get a considerable bonus even from simple mobs, so I didn't want to throw away something potentially useful. As I sorted through it all, I set aside a Spider Eye, horrible in its look and feel. Its properties remained unidentified, and I did not have the Wisdom stat, which would help in this task. It's not like I needed it in any case. It was much easier to go to mage NPCs in any town and identify the object for a couple of gold. I also set aside twenty two Rat Tails with "Used by Alchemists" property and twelve Spider Mandibles, with the "Used by Armourers" property — I would go around the relevant shops trying to sell these goods later. Just look at my thoughts running ahead — 'go around the shops'. I haven't even sorted out the teleportation scroll, but I'm making all these plans for the town anyway. The rest turned out to be total trash, with only the Rat Meat being potentially useful for levelling up in Cooking.

After going through the items, I put them back in the bag, got a solid grip on my Mallet and went out into the night. The owners of Barliona know very well that many of the game's players only appear during late evenings. For this reason the nights here are very light and generally have very good visibility. I took a couple of steps form the door and cursed. Just my luck! It looked like Beatwick was on that unique list of places where the rule about lighter nights did not apply. Pitch black darkness covered the village like a blanket and it was impossible to see anything even a couple of meters away. Thus my plan to go to the mine fell through quite thoroughly. I had no desire whatsoever to trudge around in this dark. I sat on a bench, leant against the wall and closed my eyes. There was an almost complete silence that seemed to arrive in the village together with the dark, broken only by the rustle of the forest and the quiet chirping of crickets. There were no dog noises or shouts from crowds of NPCs, which were now peacefully sleeping in their houses. It was an ideal night to go out by yourself and breathe in the crisp, clean air, which contained hints of pine resin, fir needles and a tangy whiff of an animal. An animal?! I immediately opened my eyes and saw just a couple of meters away an indistinct cloud, out of which two red eyes were staring at me. What the...? I selected the indistinct cloud and tried to see in its properties what I was dealing with.

Object properties: hidden.

Hidden? How's that? Concealing a mob's properties was impossible in Barliona. Or at least it was until just now. The entire game is built upon the ability to read them, which allows the players to devise combat strategies with the mob or a boss. I had to get into the manual or on the forums to see who is able to hide their properties and whether this was even possible. But that's for later, right now I had other matters to deal with — what does this thing in front of me want? I had little doubt that its intentions were anything but nice and friendly. As a rule, in Barliona if a mob is aggressive, it's sure to have red eyes. Neutral or friendly mobs would have eyes of any other colour but red. The two red lamps looking straight at me did not make my immediate future look very promising.

Trying not to make any sudden movements, I got up from the bench and started to shift sideways towards my door. I had to cover just a couple of meters. With every small step I took the strange thing also shifted sideways, always keeping a meter and a half in front of my face. I don't think I'm liking this anymore. Maybe I should attack it first? Attack is the best defence, after all. I was about to summon a Lightning Spirit on this incomprehensible something, but then my hand slid against the door knob. The thought of testing which of us was tougher was evaporated in a second — a door, despite its humble status, was a great obstacle against mobs. No-one abolished the principle of 'My home is my castle' — even in Barliona.

I carefully slid my hand behind my back, slowly lowered the door handle and quickly dropped inside the house. Immediately turning around, I tried to slam the door shut with my whole weight. Just as I was making my first move the beast lunged forward and began to push hard on the closing door from the other side.

Damage taken. Hit Points reduced by 30: 260 (Door hit): 230 (Physical defence). Total Hit Points: 650 of 680.
Skill increase:
+10% Endurance. Total: 70%
+5% Strength. Total: 60%

I was just a couple of centimetres away from completely closing the door. I strained all I could, heaving my whole body against it, but the beast that was pushing on the other side just wouldn't let me do it. Moreover, gradually, centimetre by centimetre the door began to open. At some point a mist-covered appendage slipped through the crack that formed. Inside the house the mist dissipated and I could see four sharp claws in the twilight. What is this, an overgrown wolverine? The claws dug into the door and left deep marks — exactly the same as those on the village gates. Was I suppose to think that this is the way the local youth got its kicks? It'll become a running joke if it gets around the village tomorrow — how the Shaman got scared by children's pranks. I was about to stop resisting, but then a message popped up:

Energy level: 30. Stop, you angry Shaman!

This was the automatic message I put in place back at the mine to stop myself biting the dust from the Energy loss. This was no joking matter. It's not like the local kids would have the strength to demolish my Energy in a matter of seconds. This is something else.

But what this something was I didn't have a chance to find out. A couple of seconds later a message flashed that my Energy had gone down to zero and I froze like a broken doll. Unlike in the mines, in the main gameworld Energy can be easily restored from zero, even without the aid of water. But until it is restored to at least ten points, the player freezes like a wax figure.

Another blow on the door threw me far back into the room and already mid-flight I saw some grey shadow speed after me. There was no mist around it, but in the darkness of the room I could not make out what it was. Only one thing was clear — the beast had two arms and two legs. Or four appendages, to sum it up. Why did I put out the lamp before leaving? That way I'd know what I was dealing with now. There was a flash of four sharp claws: a sharp pang of pain and the surrounding twilight became even darker. So, my house is not much of a castle, it would seem. Though it's not like it's really my house — I was getting ahead of myself.

There was a flash and it seemed to me that I almost immediately found myself at the entrance to the local cemetery. A very symbolic respawning point. A small temple stood a few meters away from me, shading me from the bright morning sun. Looks like that unidentified beast did get me in the end, and the compulsory twelve hours from the moment of death went by in a flash. Great.

I was about to head to the temple when I found myself staring angrily at a message that popped up:

Attention!

In connection with your death, your level of Experience has been reduced by 30%. Current Experience: 199; points remaining until next level 1201.

I checked my purse. That's right, it now contained only three thousand gold. The other half was lying in the summer house. I could only hope that no-one had come in and laid their hands on it. It should have been somewhere behind the bed and not really visible from the door.

But what was it that got me? Despite the fact that I had 680 Hit Points and 230 Physical defence, the beast sent me for a respawn with a single blow. I looked into the combat logs, hoping that this feature had become unlocked since my leaving the mine. Yes! Now we'll read what it was that swatted me. I switched on the filter for the damage sustained in the last thirty hours and saw several lines:

23:45:23 Damage taken. 28 (258 'Door hit' — 230 'Physical defence'). Hit Points remaining: 652

23:45:26 Damage taken. 28 (258 'Door hit' — 230 'Physical defence'). Hit Points remaining: 624

23:45:39 Damage taken. 28 (258 'Hit against the wall' — 230 'Physical defence'). Hit Points remaining: 596

23:45:41 Damage taken. 24762 (24998 'Unknown' — 230 'Physical defence'). Hit Points remaining: 0.

I looked at the messages dumbfounded. That was some swatting! Twenty five thousand damage can be inflicted by a mob that's no less than level 70. But where would an aggressive mob of such a level come from in Beatwick and why on earth did it decide to pay me a visit?

"Were you looking for something, my son?" a voice sounded nearby and made me turn around. A small, plump and pink-cheeked priest of some god was standing by the temple, thumbing through the prayer beads in his hands. A black robe covered him from head to foot, but failed to conceal the size of his enormous stomach. "Do you want to receive a blessing from Vlast? In that case you have to become his novice. Are you ready?"

So this was a temple of Vlast. The god of wine making. He was an analogue of Bacchus, Pan and other such gods from the real world. I went into the manual to read the main limitations imposed by serving this god and was surprised to see that there were none — any NPC or players could become this god's novice without any restrictions. This didn't concern just the novices, but you could even become a priest just a few months after becoming a novice. There were no additional costs or donations to be made. All you had to do is drink a glass of wine or homebrew every day and thus receive your divine blessing. Although if you failed to drink it, you'd incur a divine curse, not a pleasant thing, as a rule. This meant that you'd have to atone for your sins with two glasses of homebrew. All right, I was never that interested in Barliona's religions as a Hunter and as a Shaman had even less need of them. Of course, Vlast is a convenient god for levelling up the Faith stat, but there are just too many complications in this field. Not my thing. Now it was clear, however, where the priest got his large stomach — probably from saying all those daily prayers with his parishioners and anyone else who dropped by. With the devout aid of wine and homebrew, that is. I bet those guards I met by the gates yesterday were also his active novices.

"No, thank you. I respect Vlast, but I am not ready to become his novice. You have my thanks," I bowed to the priest, receiving a similar bow in response.

"As you wish. Vlast doesn't force anyone to serve him. Only someone with true insight could fathom the real depth of his teaching. Can I help you with anything else, my son?" the priest run the standard phrase by me.

"Yes. Holy father, can you tell me if there are any monsters in these parts that roam about at night and bring grief and destruction to the local people?" the incident with the respawn wouldn't let me be. I was dying to find out what dealt me all that damage.

The priest stopped fingering the prayer beads, looked around and then gestured me to follow him:

"Enter into the temple, my son. This isn't the place to talk of such things."

There was nothing interesting inside the temple. There was the altar with the depiction of a rather chubby Vlast, whose bleary-eyes gaze stared into empty space, and a couple of benches. That's it. The place was totally Spartan. The priest went behind the altar, took two cups from somewhere and handed me one of them.

"Vlasts' commandments do not permit one to start a conversation without wine passing one's lips first," the priest said in lofty tones. "I see that there's a reason that you asked me about the night monster," he began as soon as we had drunk a couple of draughts. It was ordinary wine and did not give any stat bonuses — just a 'slightly tipsy' debuff after drinking it. "I can see that this trouble has not passed you by. Yes, there is trouble in our land. People don't like talking about it and everyone's pretending that nothing's happened. You've seen the claw marks on the gates, yes? The Headman had to make up a story, saying that he was the one that scratched them on — just to calm the villagers down. But every seven days the claw marks appear again. It's just as well that the local kids got it into their heads that they are the ones getting up to this, so people stopped worrying. And the fact that every seventh night either a cow or a sheep disappears from the common herd — everyone blames the wolves for that. But no-one gives a thought about how wolves would get through closed gates. The whole village is surrounded by a solid stockade, which not even a mouse would squeeze through. Only the Headman and his sons know the truth, since they spend nights trying to catch the elusive beast. It's been evading them for two years now and they've only glimpsed the monster's red eyes a couple of times. From afar. Your help would be invaluable. Would you take this on? If you could at least find out what beast it is that roams Beatwick, you would receive an ample reward.

Quest available: 'Night terror of the village'

— SURVIVAL QUEST —

Description: Once every seven days a monster roams Beatwick, which brings trouble and destruction to the residents. Find out who is the night terror of the village. Quest type: Rare. Reward: +400 to Reputation with the Krong Province.

"I'll take it. I'll find out who is hiding under the guise of the beast," I accepted. Now it all became clear. The beast's properties could not be seen, because that was the nature of the quest. So it looks like I'll have to find out about it the normal way and not the one that only players could use. All right, I'll postpone this matter for a week, when it is time for the hunt once again. Our first meeting with the beast ended with its complete victory, but we'll see how things go from here.

"Thank you, Mahan! If you need help, you can ask for it straight away," the priest thanked me and I headed for the village. It was now time to collect my dropped cash and go wolf hunting. There was levelling up to be done.

END OF CHAPTER ONE

Want to be the first to know about our latest LitRPG, sci fi and fantasy titles from your favorite authors?

Subscribe to our **NEW RELEASES** newsletter:
http://eepurl.com/b7niIL

Thank you for reading *Survival Quest!*

If you like what you've read, check out other LitRPG books and series published by Magic Dome Books:

An *NPC's Path* LitRPG series by Pavel Kornev:
The Dead Rogue

Level Up series by Dan Sugralinov:
Re-Start

The Way of the Shaman LitRPG series by Vasily Mahanenko:
The Kartoss Gambit
The Secret of the Dark Forest
The Phantom Castle
The Karmadont Chess Set
Shaman's Revenge
Clans War

Dark Paladin LitRPG series by Vasily Mahanenko:
The Beginning
The Quest
Restart

Galactogon LitRPG series by Vasily Mahanenko:
Start the Game!

The Bard from Barliona LitRPG series by Eugenia Dmitrieva and Vasily Mahanenko:
The Renegades

The Neuro LitRPG series by Andrei Livadny:
The Crystal Sphere
The Curse of Rion Castle
The Reapers

The Expansion (The History of the Galaxy) series by A. Livadny:
Blind Punch
The Shadow of Earth

Point Apocalypse *(a near-future action thriller)*
by Alex Bobl

The Sublime Electricity series by Pavel Kornev
The Illustrious
The Heartless
The Fallen
The Dormant

You're in Game!
(LitRPG Stories from Bestselling Authors)

You're in Game-2!
(More LitRPG stories set in your favorite worlds)

The Game Master series by A. Bobl and A. Levitsky:
The Lag

The Naked Demon by Sherrie L.
(a paranormal romance)

More books and series are coming out soon!

In order to have new books of the series translated faster, we need your help and support! Please consider leaving a review or spread the word by recommending *Survival Quest* to your friends and posting the link on social media. The more people buy the book, the sooner we'll be able to make new translations available. Thank you!

Till next time!